PROXIES

PROXIES

LAURA J. MIXON

TOR®

A TOM DOHERTY ASSOCIATES BOOK
NEW YORK

PROXIES

Copyright © 1998 by Laura J. Mixon

This book is printed on acid-free paper.

Edited by Patrick Nielsen Hayden

A Tor Book
Published by Tom Doherty Associates, Inc.
175 Fifth Avenue
New York, NY 10010

Tor Books on the World Wide Web:
http://www.tor.com

Tor® is a registered trademark of Tom Doherty Associates, Inc.

Design by Lynn Newmark

Library of Congress Cataloging-in-Publication Data

Mixon, Laura J.
    Proxies / Laura J. Mixon.
      p. cm.
    "A Tom Doherty Associates book."
    ISBN 0-312-85467-6
    I. Title.
PS3557.08947P7   1998
813'.54—dc21   98-19417
                                       CIP

First Edition: September 1998

Printed in the United States of America

0 9 8 7 6 5 4 3 2 1

This one's for you, Stevie Chuck.

ACKNOWLEDGMENTS

To numerous folks who helped me make this book better than it might have been, I owe thanks.

A number of people, most of them current or former members of the Very Small Array, Author-Ized Personnel, and the Plot Busters—Steven Gould, Terry Boren, Melinda Snodgrass, Patricia Nagle, Chris Krohn, Sage Walker, Walter Jon Williams, Martha Soukup, Sally Gwylan, Rory Harper, Martha Wells, Kathy Ruedinger, and Tom Knowles—critiqued various incarnations of this book, helping me improve the text and iron out plot problems.

Dr. Richard Wetherald, a climate-change researcher, supplied me with fascinating materials on some possible effects of global warming, and Drs. William Gutsch, astrophysicist, and Mark Lupo, planetary physicist, helped me attain a degree of solar and mercurial verisimilitude.

Chris Crawford, physicist and computer programmer, and Steven Gould, computer programmer and writer, helped me get my orbital mechanics, orbital habitat design, and assorted computer details right. Lt. Col. James A. Gould (U.S. Army-Ret.) gave me some useful information about military operations.

Patrick and Teresa Nielsen Hayden and Gregory Feeley were especially helpful with some tricky formatting issues. (You'll see!)

Thanks, everyone.

Any errors and infelicities are, of course, entirely mine.

PR
PROXIES
XIES

PABLO

Bad News Strikes, and So Does Mother

Mother Taylor's summons startled Pablo out of a sound sleep. He-Krueger awoke and eye-clicked on the alarm chiming in his ears.

As the bells faded, Pablo-Krueger yawned in proxy—for what good it did—and rubbed his-Krueger's eyes. He was so tired. What time was it? Elsewhere, his flesh—a half-felt, ghostly entity—yawned, too, to better purpose, and stretched in its crèche, briefly breaking the seal of its respirator mask. Eddies of disturbed liquid lapped against its face, limbs, and torso. For a moment he smelled soap, till the respirator system carried it away. Meanwhile, he called up a time display with a hotspot blink.

6:50 in the morning, Austin time. Which meant it was 7:50, shay-Mother; rather early for a staff meeting. An emergency, perhaps. Fear filled him. And Buddy was gone again, he noted, from the emptiness that greeted him from that corner of his mind—or was perhaps just giving him the silent treatment.

What set him off this time? Pablo wondered. While he called up his linkware menu, he-Krueger sat up in bed in the darkened room; the bed's frame creaked under the machine body's movements.

It took a second or so to disconnect from Uncle Sam Krueger's proxy and switch over from the Austin facility to Shasta Station/Kaleidas, the orbital platform that housed his and Buddy's flesh. Reality fragmented and washed away as the linkware engaged, like grains of sand drawn out from underfoot, pulled to sea by a receding wave. A second later the transfer was complete, and he slipped down into his primary proxy at Kaleidas.

With an irrepressible, spreading smile, he flexed his mechanical hands and then ran them over the cotton-covered plastic of his chest and abdomen. This was no waldo, no robot, no mere extension of his consciousness. It was his body; it fit him like a favorite, well-worn shoe; it was *home.*

Pablo didn't spare a glance around as he shuffled hurriedly past all the flesh-holding crèches—each decorated with coins, icons, talismans, and evil-averting sigils—to the examining area in the back. The crèche chamber was a sacred place, and he didn't like to spend any more time here than he had to. He couldn't figure out why Mother was holding the meeting here instead of the main conference room. No doubt she had a reason.

Everyone was already there: Mother Taylor and the other three non-crèche-born members of the Plastic Menagerie—Aunt Jenna, Uncle Marsh, and Uncle Byron—and all twenty-six of his crèche-mates. Mother, in her own proxy body as always, was pacing beyond the examining gurney. Aunt Jenna was also in proxy. And Pablo and his crèche-mates, of course, all had their proxy bodies on; they had no choice. Unlike the adults, their flesh was confined to the crèche by a lifetime of disuse. And their immune systems were disabled; even if they had been physically able to leave, death from disease would soon follow.

In fact, the only two people there *in corpus* were Uncle Byron, who had yet to have his beanlink implanted, and Uncle Marsh, who'd always insisted he was too old for a beanlink and could barely tolerate a skinlink. Uncle Marsh liked telepresence in concept but didn't much care for the experience.

Nothing obvious gave her away, but Pablo knew Mother too well not to be able to read it—she was in that very dangerous place she got to sometimes. The place where she hurt people. She'd been there a lot, lately.

Tread lightly, Pablo, he thought, and wished desperately for Buddy's presence. However much Buddy hated Mother, at least he wasn't frightened of her anger. (He only jigged when she was *nice*.) Pablo didn't want to face her anger on his own.

"—gave our usual introductory presentation," Mother was saying. Then she spotted Pablo. "You're late. Please join us."

Pablo entered the examining area, shuffling in the light gravity to avoid launching himself over his crèche-mates' heads, and sat down next to Mara, who gave him a welcoming smile and pressed her leg against his. He put an arm around her shoulders and exchanged quick glances with Obediah, Joe, Mitchell, Roxanna, and his other crèche-mates—making contact, greeting them silently—as Mother continued her talk.

"As I was saying, Marsh and I proxied down to Washington late last week and gave a presentation to members of the new administration's transition team. The President himself didn't attend—which clued us in right away that we were in trouble, if we'd had any doubts!—but Thompson was there, with his dog Rasmussen. And of course, there were the usual attendees, Senator D'Auber and Secretary of Defense Morgan, plus General Utney and a couple of other political honchos." She broke off, a deep shadow forming under her perfect brow, and gazed at them all, the crèche-born kids. Her glance came last, and stayed longest, on Pablo.

"It didn't go well?" he asked.

"It couldn't have gone any worse. Thompson didn't ask a single question. And Rasmussen!" She snarled the name. "He humiliated us and cast aspersions at every opportunity. He had the nerve to call you crèche children *monstrosities!*"

Her voice by now was hoarse with rage. The crèche-born all looked at each other, wondering whether she was going to blow.

"Uncle Alan said that?" Joe asked, in a tone of surprise. "He's been really nice to me since he got here."

There were murmurs of agreement among the other crèche kids. Uncle Alan Rasmussen had been on-station for almost a week now. Pablo had been at their sister facility near Austin all that time, on his secret mission for Mother, so he hadn't met the man yet—though his crèche-mates had told Pablo and Buddy a little about him.

"Don't trust him," Aunt Jenna said sharply to Joe, standing up beside Mother. "Thompson has sent him here to collect information he can use to ax the project."

"Maybe we can play some fool-games with him, then," Mara said, and the corners of her mouth arched up. "Teach him a lesson."

The others muttered agreement. Mother frowned.

"No. He's smarter than you think. Don't get cocky. All of you—you're to just play dumb and stay out of his way. Let us adults handle him."

"And you older ones," Uncle Marsh added, "keep a very close eye on the younger ones. Run interference whenever necessary. He'll aim for the young ones," he added to Mother. "He'll figure they're more vulnerable."

"He won't know who's younger and who's not," Kali pointed out. They all wore adult proxies these days, ex-face. (In-face, they wore just about every kind of avatar imaginable.) "And we're not going to tell him."

"You're to stay away from him," Mother said in a tone that made them all cringe. "This isn't one of your face-games. If he figures out what's going on, that'll be the end of us. We've got enough troubles without trying to keep track of what lies you kids have been telling him."

Troubles? Again Pablo exchanged glances with Mara and Joe, who gave him shrugs.

"Why don't you fill them in, Jenna," Mother said, and sat down on a lab stool next to Uncle Marsh.

"We've just gotten some very bad news," Aunt Jenna said, in a bleak tone. "I just got the word from a NASA contact that they're going to move the *Courier* launch up by eighteen days—to this afternoon."

Pablo checked his orbital software, did a quick calculation, and started. "Shit! That's less than a week!"

The interstellar probe ship *Exodus* was the supershuttle *Courier*'s destination: currently docked at the antimatter production plant that shared an orbit with Mercury, *Exodus* would be ready to depart once *Courier* reached it with the last of the supplies and crew.

Mother looked grim. Amid the uproar of his crèche-mates' protests, Pablo searched her face, looking for something—some strength of will—to anchor himself to. "It's hopeless, then." It must be. Tell me I'm wrong.

"No." Mother stood as smoothly as a mantis crane unfolding itself, and her tone cut like titanium-filament razor. "I've spent years and millions of dollars planning to steal the *Exodus* and I'm not turning back now. Not this close. Byron." She turned to Uncle Byron. "A status report, please, on your progress with the omni transmitter."

"I'm doing the best I can, Patricia. But we're just not there yet." He sighed, heavily. "As I've told you numerous times, we really need Carli MacLeod. *She* was the creative genius on the omni project. And the very first thing Rasmussen did when he got here was to shit-can my latest recruitment request."

Mother stared at Uncle Byron till Pablo thought she was going to tear his throat out. He must have thought so, too, because he blanched and his hands went up reflexively.

Pablo surprised himself by asking—partly to distract—"What does Uncle Alan have against recruiting a new member of the Menagerie?"

It worked, at least briefly; Mother focused on Pablo, opening and closing her hands, clearly forcing herself back from the edge. She drew a long breath. "Thompson must guess that we're up to something—Rasmussen's just doing his bidding. They *especially* don't want Senator D'Auber's daughter on the project—makes it too high-profile, and too likely the Senator will bring pressure to bear on our behalf, at his daughter's behest."

She turned back to Uncle Byron, and her gaze hardened again. "Listen to me. We're almost out of time. We need that instantaneous link to *Exodus*, and we need it now. You're going to have to stop counting on having Carli MacLeod on your team and just do it."

With a sullen expression Uncle Byron said, "No, *you* listen. I'm tired of being bullied like this. I've been working my ass off, I've made progress, I'm doing the best I can. And what have I gotten in return? Nothing. You've been promising me you'd start me on the extended-life treatments for months, and I want to know when."

"God damn you, Byron—don't you *dare* try to blackmail me. We don't have time for this bullshit! I told you we'd start the treatments after we launched. And you promised me a breakthrough *months* ago! I'm beginning to think you're deliberately sabotaging the project . . ."

"Of course not! I said I'd do the best I could for you, and I've been trying. It's not my fault NASA moved the launch up."

"I'm sick to death of your excuses." Mother closed her eyes. "Just get out of here," she said, tautly. She opened her eyes and shook a fist. "Get *out* of here!"

Uncle Byron looked as if he wanted to say something, but, wisely, didn't. He left.

Mother stood there, looking after Uncle Byron. Then she exploded. With a roar she knocked pans and tools off the counter. Pablo and the others looked at each other in horrified disbelief. Mother attacked the bulkhead next, beating it so hard that paint chipped off it and tiny dimples appeared.

"Not the bulkhead!" Uncle Marsh shouted. "Christ, Patricia!"

This can't be happening, Pablo thought. Or maybe it was Buddy talking in the back of his mind; he wasn't sure.

After a hesitation Uncle Marsh leapt to restrain her. *In corpus* he was no match for Mother's proxy: he was quite old and thin. Fortunately, her proxy's reflexes—though horrifyingly strong—were slow. Uncle Marsh dodged her blows. Then he made a mistake and grabbed her wrist. She swept her arm outward, twisting her torso, and Uncle Marsh flew backward, smashing into the cabinets. Groaning, he crumpled.

Pablo and his crèche-mates sat there watching, stunned.

=Idiot! Don't just sit there—do something!=

Pablo stiffened. =Buddy?=

Resounding silence.

Pablo leapt forward and grabbed Mother from behind, with a vise grip around her arms and chest. She kicked and bucked. At that Aunt Jenna bounded over, too, and grabbed her around the legs.

"Let me go, you malignant fucks! *Let me go!*"

Tears filled Pablo's eyes, back in his crèche. Together he and Aunt Jenna pinned Mother to the floor. She shouted obscenities, twisted, bit at his face and neck, grabbed at his arms, and tore at the plastic skin. The physical pain was far less than the emotional.

"I'm sorry, Mother," he said, over and over, cringing under the assault but not loosening his grip. "I'm sorry. I'm sorry."

Meanwhile Uncle Marsh had gotten a drug from the cabinet. He bounded away down the rows of crèches, his strides dangerously out-of-control in the low gravity, till he came to hers. He did something Pablo couldn't see with her crèche's IV drip.

She grew more quiet. Finally Aunt Jenna released her and stood, brushing herself off.

Pablo sank to the ground, still hugging her. She huddled in his arms, and made a noise into his clavicle, like a cry. After a long, still time, she pulled back. To his surprise, her eyes were clear and calm.

"I'm all right. Let me go."

Baffled and distrustful, forearms and chest dotted with little streams and smears of red lubricant, Pablo stared at her. He looked at Uncle Marsh, who nodded. "She's all right now."

Pablo stood and backed away, watching her. His heart was pounding, back in its crèche. This wasn't the first time she'd gone berserk in his lifetime—especially lately—but it was the worst.

She rubbed her face and gave Uncle Marsh a rueful glance. "Looks like we need to adjust the hormone drip again."

Uncle Marsh looked sad. "You can't go on like this, Number One."

"It's not for much longer."

Uncle Marsh gestured at Pablo and the other crèche kids, who were watching, mute and wide-eyed. "You have to tell the kids sometime. Your behavior is out of control and terrifying them. It'll only get worse."

A deep dread settled over Pablo. "Tell us what?"

Mother ignored him. "I will, Number Two. I promise. Once we launch."

Uncle Marsh sat. His shoulders slumped and he rubbed at his face. " 'Once we launch.' " He shook his head. "It's a fantasy. We aren't going to make it."

"I'll come up with something. Give me a while to think." She stood, brisk again; it was as if the fit of rage had never happened. Mother turned to Aunt Jenna.

"Jenna, check all your projections. I want you to evaluate how we can accelerate our own schedule to map onto NASA's. Marsh will work closely with you on changes to the children's medical requirements."

Aunt Jenna took her cue from Mother, and pretended everything was fine. "Right away, Patricia. Come on, everyone."

She and Uncle Marsh herded Pablo's crèche-mates out.

As the rest left, Mother came to Pablo, hands outstretched. "It's all right, dear. It's just a hormonal imbalance Uncle Marsh is helping me with. I'll be fine."

Pablo nodded slowly, still troubled. *It'll only get worse.* He took her hands.

"What do you want me to do?"

"Sit tight, for now. Keep things under control in Austin. Report any relevant activity on Waldos, Inc.'s, Board of Directors. I've got to keep Rasmussen busy with other matters while we regroup."

"Maybe Uncle Sam could arrange some distractions for him through the Board . . ."

Mother gave him a warm smile and a brief hug. "I can always count on you, can't I?"

Yeah, he thought, sure. When I can keep Buddy under control. In his own way, he was as unpredictable as Mother.

A call came in from Obediah as they were talking. Pablo and Mother received it simultaneously.

"We're getting an emergency call from Austin security," Obediah reported, his voice strained. "There's just been another proxy theft down there."

Mother and Pablo looked at each other. He felt suddenly sick.

"The renegade again," she said. "Damn it. *Damn it!* This is the last thing we need!"

Pablo eyed her warily, but whatever Uncle Marsh had given her still seemed to be working.

"I'll get right on it," he said. "I-Krueger will brief you later today, when I know more."

Mother gave him a curt nod. "Go. Hurry."

He returned to his proxy stand and strapped it in, then called up his linkware, eye-clicked on the appropriate icon from the menu of choices that spread across his sight.

How many more disasters like this could they stand up to? he wondered. And, more plaintively, as the linkware carried him back to Austin, he wondered, =Buddy, where are you?=

THE RENEGADE

PIEBALD WOMAN STEPS LIVELY

With a spasm he awoke, and clutched the edges of the table with such desperate strength that his fingers dented metal. He didn't know why, but he felt sure he was dying. Someone was trying to kill him.

He cried out: a silent shriek of protest.

His body convulsed again, a puppet with tangled strings, and then vanished from awareness in a detonation of garish colors and disembodied limbs.

No—that was a dream. He was—where? A table. He had thought that the table was part of the dream, but it was real. A blurred face with an intent expression leaned over him. Whose? He should know that face. His mentor—his captor?

He lay paralyzed and helpless as hands moved, tracing arcs of light across his sight. A mouth emitted words that dripped down on him, slithered and wriggled around him. . . . The hands hooked wires to him and attached probes that made shrill noises wail in his ears and made his limbs and vision dance. Somewhere, drums were pounding. He fled the drums, into a wan void.

Retreat should have been a blessing. It wasn't. Oblivion was death. He screamed again, silent, writhing.

The voice, lights, and garbled sensations finally ebbed, and he lay quietly, leaden-limbed. Hisses, clicks, whirrings—all the soft whispers of machines—swelled to fill the silence.

Without will, his eyes came open and his body sat up. His hands disconnected the probes and pressed his skin back into place. A memory came—many memories, of experiences much like this.

So. He'd faced into a simile on the *v*-net, or booted up a simile crystal. That was all. Relief seized him. In the aftermath of adrenaline a wave of nausea rose, and died. He'd thought he was going mad.

While his hands were disconnecting the probes, he glanced at his naked body, at the high, round breasts and the broadened hips, the triangle of pubic hair with no male genitalia.

It shocked him. He—no, *she*—had faced into a gender blender. This could prove interesting.

But she also had this sense that the simile was skewed. Something was wrong—or missing—and she couldn't think of what.

Well. It'd come to her.

The skin of her simile body was mottled, cocoa and alabaster. The idea of being in a female body was arousing. Obedient, this body's nipples went hard, and an ache grew in her lower abdomen. Odd; faintly—somewhere—she could feel a penis growing hard as well. She wondered if she had picked a plain-action simile, or perhaps an intrigue. From the vague sense of foreboding, she guessed it was the latter.

Her body, apparently acting on a preprogrammed sequence, leaped down from the table and went toward one of the doors. Meanwhile she snatched information from the corners of her vision. In the dimness, naked bodies with their inner machinery half exposed lay on other tables beneath banks of flickering lights. Lab coats stained with dirt and oil hung by the door. Her hands snatched one up and slipped it onto her shoulders, then grabbed some plastic foot wraps from a cardboard box on the floor and pulled them onto her feet.

Come on, she thought. I want to do something. It didn't help, of course. The control wouldn't release to her until she had been guided to where she was supposed to be at game start.

These similes with long noninteractive stretches annoyed her. She couldn't imagine why she hadn't just reprogrammed the beginning before facing in.

Well, she just hadn't, that was all. She'd simply have to ride it out. A programmed look to the left, to the right: the corridor was empty. She let herself relax into the movements, as though they were her own. Her body glided through the halls, made a series of turns, dodged into empty rooms when other people neared. Finally the body came to a door, opened it, and stepped outside. It carried her at a run across the concrete.

Someone was watching her. She could feel someone's attention on her. Was someone floating her? Or was it part of the simile?

Her feet splashed into the mud on the far side, and then the body halted and the control ceased. For the moment, at least, she had a chance to catch her breath and look around.

The sky was overcast, dark gray and purple. Rain, little more than a warm drizzle, beaded on her long forearms and face. A stench of rotting vegetation overwhelmed her. With a mental turn, she damped her olfactory sense.

Then her head swiveled and glanced over her body's shoulder. The buildings at her back huddled together, dim rectangles in the gloom. Spotlights mounted on their upper corners cast light onto the acres of concrete that surrounded the complex.

Some sounds she couldn't identify registered on her awareness as she stood there: rustlings, and squeaks that twisted around on themselves like the cry of poorly lubricated bearings. She waited for the programming to kick in again, but her body remained still.

They had finally given her control of the scenario, then. Good. She increased the magnification of her hearing and sight and began to pivot, targeting the source of the noise. Footsteps in a patio of the building complex now echoed above a moaning chorus of machines. After a few seconds she could also see movement through the windows of the closest building. But the strange sounds came from somewhere else. She turned slowly in place, cocking her head.

A short distance away, a chain-link fence entangled in vines and leaves held back wild plant growth. The sounds issued from there. She focused her vision on the areas of movement in the plant growth, magnified, and augmented with infrared. There—and there—blotches appeared, the heat signatures of small animals moving about in the bushes. One took flight in a breath of feathers, striking blows to the air.

Birds. She relaxed and smiled, relieved. Her sight and hearing returned automatically to normal magnification and range, and she began slogging through the mud.

Something roared; she spotted a shack at the fence, next to an opening gate. A huge land vehicle was passing through the gate. The vehicle paused and the driver exchanged some words with the one leaning out of the shack's window. Their words were gibberish.

Strange. This must be a foreign-language simile. Maybe that explained the sense of wrongness she had felt earlier. But no, that was something else, and she knew suddenly what it was.

There should be others with her. Why was she alone? Where were the others?

She'd been betrayed. She remembered the face she'd glimpsed when she'd first faced in. He had betrayed her. She froze in her steps, terrified. I can't do this alone!

The land vehicle began to move again. Its giant treads threw mud high into the air as it bucked and strained. Then it began to crawl forward. The driver waved to her.

Just a simile. All she had to do was stay calm and she'd be OK; she'd be returned home, eventually, to the others, to reality.

I can do this, she thought. I am strong. She repeated those words until she believed them.

This isn't just a game, a voice inside her head said. *You have been chosen to accomplish a mission. Lives are at stake and you are the only one who can help.*

She made her way toward the gate across the ruts and gouges left by the vehicle. A uniformed man carrying a rifle came out of the shack. He stopped and held up a hand, but she ignored him and walked by.

The man spoke sharply and grabbed her arm. She shoved him away and continued walking. He fired his weapon. She leapt, striking the man full in the chest, as a bullet whizzed past. Something exploded behind her. Wood burning and something else—something with an acidic tang—stung her nose. Good programming, she thought, surprised. Nice detail.

The man had stumbled back to his feet. He aimed the rifle again. She spun inside his arm, drove her right palm into his nose, and felt bones and cartilage crack. He flew back in an arc and landed with a splash in the mud.

She bent over him. His eyes were staring and red lubricant ran from his crushed nose, mixing with water. She sharpened her vision and hearing; his body had stopped functioning.

At that instant she felt the other body—the body within her body—again. She froze, confused. Even as she stood looking at the corpse, she could feel her other self. Buoyant limbs—the measured rise and fall of a thorax—needles and tubes punctured the skin of her chest, belly, and arms. She swallowed, and a saline trickle worked its way down her esophagus.

She was two places at once. Someone, somewhere, was playing drums. Thump-THUMP! Thump-thump-thump.

She should know a good many things she did not. She didn't know what the other body was, nor who she was. She couldn't remember her name or anything about her past.

She had nothing to hang on to—she was no one.

Her vision blurred, a band squeezed her chest; she staggered and went to her knees in the mud. Somewhere she was twitching and thrashing, screaming, beating fists against slick cool surfaces. The drumbeats grew louder.

A name came to her then, as though someone had put it there. Dane Elisa Cae. I'm Dane Elisa Cae.

She grasped at the name and, clutching it, forced her breathing to slow. The panic faded, as did the sense of the other body.

She rocked back onto her haunches and looked around, shakily. The vehicle had passed behind the buildings. No one else was in sight. Only now did the words the driver had spoken with the man in the shack come to her: It had been an exchange of greetings. It *had* been English they were speaking.

Something was wrong with her interface, then. It wasn't transmitting speech properly. Well, difficulty understanding what people said could complicate things, but there was no backing out now. She'd have to compensate as best she could.

Dane Elisa Cae launched herself onto her wonderfully long, powerful legs and ran away from the complex along the ruts in the mud, and knew they wouldn't catch her. She would return to the others, soon. She would go home. It burned beneath memory like an ache of desire. *Home.* But first she must find something. Someone.

DANIEL

Big Trouble in Little Austin

A muffled boom rattled the glassware. Daniel sat up straight. "What was that?"

Teru, across the workbench, shook her head, not looking up from her sensor field.

"Didn't you hear it?" he asked. "Sounded like gunfire."

"Scram jet boom, I imagine."

"This early? The commercial flights don't start till six-thirty."

Teru, frowning with concentration at her data, didn't respond.

Daniel felt a spike of annoyance at her lack of response. He used his screwdriver to dig around in the test unit's eye sockets, set into a disembodied proxy head whose skin had been peeled away and its subcutaneous coolant lines pinned back to reveal the inner workings of the face's motors. After tightening the ligament lines and tinkering with the eyeball controller servos, he reconnected the eyeballs to their leads and popped them back into their orbits. Then he dropped back wearily onto his stool and called up his data displays with a double-glance at an icon, from the virtual menu at the top of his vision.

Everything checked out. He canceled the readout with another double-glance.

"Whenever you're ready," he said.

"Half a mo. Almost there." Teru's dark fingers were dancing in the sensor field's aurora as she sought to comb out tangles in the program module they were debugging. *Half a mo.* He had always loved her British accent and turns-of-phrase. It was one of the first things that had attracted him to her, several months ago. He eyed the nape of her neck rather wistfully. Her proxy unit was being serviced and she was present *in corpus* for a change. A nice change.

"Try that," she said, sitting back to eye the readouts that spiraled down through her display tank.

Daniel double-glanced at another of his icons, activating the program again. Beyond the heads-up display, the proxy's eyes first rolled around, then looked left, right, focused on an object across the lab, then crossed. They did this movement twice slowly, twice at a moderate pace, and twice very quickly.

Daniel studied his own readouts. "Damn it." He tossed his screwdriver onto the workbench counter. Washers, O-rings, and tiny screws skittered and bounced. "Still blurring on the roll-to-left motion at the faster two speeds." He rubbed his neck and stretched with a groan. "Teru, I've got to take a break. I'm going to hit the cafeteria for a caffeine run."

They were on a deadline and had been at it since 3:30 A.M. Not that he minded; alpha-testing software was about the only time he got to spend with Teru anymore. But the tedium of the task was putting him to sleep. He needed some kafe or something.

Teru glanced down and to the right, viewing a virtual readout of her own. "Five-twenty. All right." She pulled off her linkware beanie and rubbed at her fuzz-covered scalp, around the beanjack at her crown. "Bring me a cup of tea with cream, will you? Or some reasonable facsimile."

As she spoke, James Scott burst in through the doors, panic twisting his face. "We've got trouble. Big trouble."

Teru and Daniel exchanged a glance. One of the newest members of the project, James Scott got rattled rather easily.

"Calm down," Teru said. "What's wrong?"

"One of the proxy units in Rework is missing," James Scott said. "It disappeared while I was delivering some parts to the Tooling department."

Daniel and Teru looked at each other again, this time in alarm. Daniel remembered the boom.

"Another renegade," he said. "Shit."

"You were right, James," Teru said. "That's big trouble."

Security had been breached yet again, the life of some innocent somewhere was in danger—and the whole stinking mess was going to fall in Daniel's lap, because he'd developed the tracking system after the last time, and because he'd had the ill luck to hear about it first this time.

"Has Krueger been alerted?" he demanded. James Scott shook his head, eyes wide and wild. "Did you alert Security?" Another shake of the head. Alarms started whooping outside.

"They're alerted," Teru said, dryly.

"Come on, then," Daniel said, and took James Scott's arm, propelling him toward the door. "We'd better brief Krueger."

CARLI

DON'T LOOK BACK (YOU NEVER KNOW WHAT MIGHT BE LURKING THERE)

Carli had one final trip to make back to her old office at the University of New Mexico, to pack up the last of her belongings. She went in very early, before sunrise. She'd made her good-byes to everyone at the party the other night; there was no point in doing it all over again.

As she dashed up the wide stone steps of Ferris Engineering Center, the doors opened before her, blasting her with conditioned air. The U-Haul robot trundled after her on its rubberized treads, straining up the steps. While waiting for it to reach her, Carli unhooded and took off her gloves, then unzipped her paisley cool suit partway and turned up the thermostat set at her neck. She hadn't removed the suit since entering the UNM environment canopy.

At her office she paused, and ran fingers across the coarse grooves of the nameplate on the door. Black letters etched in buffed bronze said, "Carli MacLeod, Assistant Professor."

Several months ago, when she had first officially separated from Jere, she'd ordered new notepad stationery: "From the desk of Carli D'Auber." But she still sometimes thought of herself as Carli MacLeod, and often had to correct herself in midsignature. The maintenance staff had never gotten around to processing her order to replace the door sign, and she hadn't pushed it. Maybe, despite everything, she still had mixed feelings, on some level below consciousness.

But she doubted it.

Miguel Ortega, the dean, came up while she was unlocking the door. "Wow, you're in early."

"Hi." She motioned for him to step inside. He and then the U-Haul, humming, followed her into her office.

Miguel's creased face featured a prominent nose and ears, and his eyes were dark, with a lingering melancholy in them, like those of a sad hound. His hair was the color of iron. A *natureil*, he wore a floor-length, sand-colored skirt of gauze weave. Drapes of white gauze cotton with full sleeves billowed out around his barrel-like upper torso. His linkware—stereo specs, earphones, lamé-mesh gloves—hung from his belt. His kelly unit, resembling an antique pocket watch, dangled from a chain at his neck.

"I'm glad I caught you before you left," he said.

Carli gave him a smile. "I'd hoped I was going to get away clean."

"Not a chance. I've had my spies on the lookout."

He perched on the edge of her desk, dangling a leg and swinging his kelly on its chain.

Carli entered the PIN the cashier at U-Haul had given her on the robot's control panel and as the compartment opened, she began to empty her desk drawers and shelves of what remained. She packed the last of her publications, papers, and data lozenges and crystals in the bottom of the U-Haul robot box's compartment, and stuffed handfuls of gelpaper nuggets around them. Then she removed her certificates and jellies from the wall and began to pack them, along with her geodes and other knickknacks, in around the data and magazines.

So much stuff to take away, and so few real memories. She had had one of the most promising careers a person could hope for. Now, nearing forty, all she had—professionally and personally—were ashes and broken dreams.

"Have you found an office yet?" Miguel asked.

"Yeah," she said. "Downtown, in the Galería area. It's a real bargain, and the last occupant was a small electronics research company, so there's already a lab. I've already transmitted the street address to your in-box."

"Good." After a pause he said, "I hope you've considered the consequences of what you're doing. It's not that easy to start your own company and you haven't got much experience that way."

"I've got the money to do it. I got a sizable divorce settlement that's going to keep me afloat awhile. And I've got some good, marketable ideas that some people are interested in. There are all my contacts from my work here and my NASA days. And even one or two of my former OMNEX contacts are still talking to me. Trust me—I'll manage."

He sighed. "OK. I admit that there's a certain measure of selfishness in my concern; I don't want you to go. But it's not only that. It's a mistake to make too many changes in your life when you get divorced."

Carli eyed the dean. He returned her gaze without flinching.

"I'm speaking from experience," he said.

She frowned and ran a hand through her hair.

"Miguel, it's just . . . Look, I've spent too many years hiding in this little office, teaching the same old undergraduate classes and dabbling at my research. I've got to make a change."

"Says who?"

"Says me. I'm never going to finish my doctorate because I don't want one. Academia isn't for me. I want to freelance again. I did some good work in communications technology once—"

"That's an understatement."

"—and I'm tired of letting OMNEX's gag order cow me. There are plenty of areas in communications that I can explore, technologies that have nothing to do with the omni transmitter."

His expression was sour. "You were robbed. OMNEX screwed you to the wall and it isn't right."

"Yeah, well," she said, with a shrug, and looked out the window. Then she turned back to Miguel. "Please understand. You've been wonderful. I'm grateful for all the university has done for me. But I need a change. It's not just the divorce." She struggled for words, and then shrugged. "I just can't stay here anymore."

"Well." He coughed. "You have to do what you have to do, I suppose. We're sure sorry to see you go, Carli." His kelly chirped at him; he glanced at it and stood. "I have a call. Be sure to drop by. Often."

"I will."

"You'd better."

She threw her arms around him, surprising them both, and pressed her cheek against his chest. Tears gathered in her eyes, but he had already turned away.

A handful of undergrads in dreadlocks and hair sculptures, in loin wraps, body paint, or vests and loose trousers, had gathered outside her office by the time she finished packing. She stepped into the hall—tailed, with its motor humming, by her U-Haul robot—and pulled the door to behind her. The students surrounded her, all talking at once.

"Dean Ortega said this was your last day. . . ."

"Who's going to give the final in Optics Two-twenty-three, then?"

"What are you going to do now?"

She heard movement behind her, and turned. The student who stood there was a young man she had never seen before. He moved back, lowering his hand as if he had just tried to touch her.

Something about how he looked or moved was unnerving. A

teenager, he was tall and had a slim build. He had eyes languorous and black, rimmed with long, dark lashes. His lips formed a cupid's bow, with a sardonic twist to them, his dark brown hair had a gold gloss to it, and his skin was the color and texture of fine Chinese porcelain. He wore a baggy, sleeveless top of khaki green and a loin wrap the color of charcoal, and though he was wiry, the musculature in his arms, chest, and thighs was exceptionally well-defined. She guessed he must be a muscle dancer; she wouldn't be surprised if Paint knew him.

He slouched against the wall with his legs crossed at the ankle and his fingers tucked into his sash, in a position that ought to make him appear relaxed. But he didn't. He seemed stiff—tense—and he was staring at her without blinking in a manner that seemed either hostile or blatantly sexual. Then he spun and ducked around the corner out of sight.

She frowned. Very odd. But frankly, mentally disturbed students were no longer her concern. After spending a few minutes talking with the remaining students, she headed for the main entrance. Her kelly pendant tinkled as she was crossing the main foyer. Incoming call. That brought a nervous frown; she had turned on her screening routine so that all but emergency voice calls would be deposited in her inbox automatically, in case Jere tried to reach her again.

Carli opened the locket, accepted the call, switched her input to *virtu* mode, and slipped on her specs and netglove. She touched the virtual phone icon and a projection of her nephew Paint resolved into focus before her. To her relief he seemed anything but distressed: he grinned down at her from his two meters of lean height—bare-chested, muscular, wearing baggy harem-style pants. Loose curls of honey-red hair tumbled around his face and down his back. Unfocused figures moved behind him.

"Have you been cracking my phone line, you animal? Or is this a real emergency?"

He shrugged. "Auntie, you'f to come by, pim-side. I've hooked a big-jelly and we're partying up the NASA star probe launch, shay-new."

A sour taste tinged the back of her tongue. "Damn, that's right— they moved the launch date up." She was mildly surprised that she had forgotten; she'd heard it on the news only an hour before. "What time is the launch?"

"Four-forty."

She grimaced. "Thanks for inviting me, but I can't make it today. I'm busy moving into my new office."

" 'Not today'? From Carli the spacewoman? How can you say that? No's out. We'll help you move later. Where are you?"

"Just outside Ferris."

"Schick. The door'll be open."

She sighed. "All right, all right. I'll be there this afternoon, after I finish at the office." But he'd already disconnected. Well, he'd just have to wait.

Her kelly reported the time as 9:12 A.M. and the temperature as 38.4 degrees Celsius under the canopy; warm but not unbearable. She tucked her hair into the hood of her suit but left the half-mask that covered the lower portion of her face unstrapped. Then she dialed up a new pattern to replace the cool, glowing paisley, and the skin of the suit rippled, settling into soft, shifting geometries in a wash of rainbows. She turned her thermostat down and cool eddies spiraled downward about her torso and limbs.

About then she realized she had heard the door open a second time while adjusting her cool suit. Whoever had exited should have passed her by now. She turned. No one was there.

She walked back and looked around. Perhaps whoever it was had gone down the walkway toward the plaza—but they would have had to sprint *really fast* to be out of sight before she'd turned around. And she would have heard them running. Or they could have jumped over the wall to the ground level. But that was a full story below. She must have been mistaken.

With a little frown, she ran down the steps and started walking toward the Central Expressway lock. Her moving box bumped down the steps after her.

Student density was light at this hour. Only a few teenagers strolled across the plaza in front of the University of New Mexico's College of Physical Sciences. One young man with polymer-treated dreadlocks, heavy makeup, and a loin wrap of watercolor-green, -orange, and -pink plaid lounged on a bench, eating Googles from a waxed paper pouch. A flaxen-furred mongrel begged at his feet.

Several stories overhead, the photo-sensitive fabric of the canopy rippled like magenta and orange syrup. It cast racing shadows across the pavement and along the walls of the university's adobe buildings.

Yale Park was at the inner border of the environment canopy. The city noises carried, only a little diminished, through the canopy fabric, and vibrations from the passing subtrains made the soles of her feet quake. Traffic and people moved past outside the canopy: garnet-streaked machines and figures, turned into wraiths and outlandish creatures by the quivering of the canopy fabric.

As Carli walked through the park, a series of different smells wafted past her nose: ozone, cut grass, barbecued beef, fried potatoes, and, faintly, sewage. The young sprawled on the park's grass and piled on the picnic tables, some envie-suited types but mostly *natureils*, dressed scantily and/or body-stained in bright colors. They laughed, hugged, and shoved each other, talking, and ate fast food from paper wrappers, bought just outside the canopy across Central. A miniature gardening robot wandered among the tables, gathering debris. A spider, a multipurpose waldo, was pulling letters from the mailboxes outside the post office on the west side of the little park and dropping them into its underbelly pouch.

The inner door of the lock opened for Carli as she and her robot passed through, then the outer door. A gust of cool air propelled her onto the street.

Noise and humid heat blasted her; she drew a breath, and the air seared her throat. The heat begun to turn her cool suit into a sweat box. She pulled her half-mask across her face and velled it as she dialed up a higher setting on the specs' polarization, and cranked the thermostat setting on her cool suit way down. The glare darkened to shady clarity, and more cool tendrils spread downward around her body. People jostled past her.

Carli squinted through the haze at the storefronts and the bridged culverts above the sunken railway system. Suited pedestrians and swatched *natureils* moved along the bridges and sidewalks. She tapped a hot-key on her kelly as she crossed the bridge over the street. An option menu bar appeared at the top of her vision.

She donned her mesh glove and chose "Net Link" and then "Download Mail Buffer" from her menu selections. Local advertisers had gotten more clever ideas on how to get past her buffer filters again; along with the usual newsbytes and public announcements, the mailbox was brimming with spam.

(T) TIME @ TEMP @ HUMIDITY :: 16:22:33 @ 36C @ 62.2% (T)

(P)PSA: 20 HEAT STROKE DEATHS OVERNIGHT, 82 ADDNAL CASES OF SEVERE HEAT STROKE, 14 DEATHS 6 INJURIES DUE TO REFUGEE ACTIVITY

**WEST OF CITY. WARM FRONT PREDICTED TO
REMAIN FOR AT LEAST ANOTHER DAY DUE TO
STABLE LOW PRESSURE FRONT OVER ROCKIES.
HIGH EXPECTED NEAR 44C—UNSUITED
INDIVIDUALS ARE ADVISED TO REMAIN INDOORS
10A-4P. (P)**

And just last night they'd been predicting a cool front to move in.
Well, the heat wave had to break sometime.

(A) ** It's almost Christmas! Let him know how much
you care. Buy him that special gift from Alman's,
Ltd. Winronado-Plex Sublevel 4 **** (A)**

**(P) (PSA!) CURFEW—2300-0600 NE HEIGHTS, N
VALLEY. REFUGEE ACTIVITY N & E OF CITY
PERIMTR. NE HEIGHTS RESDNTS BETWEEN
MONTGOMERY&JUAN TABO/WYOMING &I-395
TRAMWAY LOOP !!! STAY INSIDE TONIGHT !!!
(PSA!)**

**(A) ****Beanhead Inc Announces Its Autumn Closeout
Sale! Software and Game Specials—While They Last!
Maximum Force Cops-$2854.99; Posse III-$2799;
TimeWalker 2.0-$1499 New/$999 Upgd. (A)**

A new version of TimeWalker was out? And just in time for the
Courier launch. The timing had to be deliberate.

She toyed with the idea of upgrading her software and then, with
a frown, threw the advertisement away. *Courier* was nothing but an
unwelcome reminder of a life she'd long since left behind. She wished
now she hadn't accepted Paint's invitation to watch the launch.

By this time she'd reached the subway station. She headed down
into the darkness.

DANIEL

HONEST, IT'LL BE DIFFERENT THIS TIME

Daniel would never have been able to afford a trip outside the gravity well, even in proxy. Shipping a human body and associated luggage up the gravity curve was hideously expensive: the tickets would take a year's-pay-sized bite out of Daniel's salary; beanlinking up with a waldo, merely a month's pay. So this biz-expensed beanlink visit to one of the world's largest habitats, Shasta Station—accompanying his boss, Krueger, to brief the Kaleidas project's honchos on the escape of the renegade—was almost worth the price of admission. Almost.

After a brief jello-net exchange with Alamo's rental clearinghouse syntellect, he and Krueger beanlinked into a couple of tourist waldos and rolled out of their storage lockers onto Shasta's main concourse. It was a long, curved atrium, with traffic lanes running down the middle. The fluorescent jello banner that stretched from one side to the other, suspended in front of the second-floor tier, blinked and scrolled cheerily at them.

Shasta Station Welcomes You!
Local Time (U.S. EST) = 11:05 AM.
Coupons and Tourist Info Available at the
Visitor Courtesy Terminals Located Throughout
the Concourse.
WELCOME SHRINERS!!

"They spare no expense," Daniel remarked on a private frequency, as he ran a check on his waldo's systems.

It was an economy model, an eighteen-inch-tall canister in a somber, two-tone green with only the bare-bones equipment: a camera (visible light only) with headlight; a low-quality sound system; and two three-fingered arms. No tactile sense, he noted, mildly annoyed, no binocular vision, nor interchangeable "hands"—though it did have a roomy compartment in its belly, presumably for the storage of purchases.

"Let's get a move on." Krueger-waldo—identical to Daniel's except for the color: a jolly cherry red with gold trim—rolled forward onto the main walkway. Daniel signaled his waldo to follow, and after the characteristic, irritating pause, Daniel-waldo bumped over the curb and into the traffic lanes. Way out into the middle of the lane, into oncoming (albeit slow-moving) traffic.

Embarrassed, he-waldo corrected course quickly, veering back into his own lane. Due to signal-response lag it took Daniel-waldo a few tries to get headed in the right direction and avoid clipping the vendor stands in the meantime. The people, robots, and waldos in the area seemed to hardly notice. No doubt they were used to tourists tooling clumsily around, breaking any number of traffic laws.

Signal-response lag went with the territory, but it was a real pain in the ass. Even a pilot as experienced as Daniel occasionally overshot turns, or undershot them in a vain attempt to outwit the lag. In fact, he was surprised at how well Krueger, who was not as experienced a pilot as he, was managing his own waldo.

Grumble, grouse, he thought. Krueger's right, Sornsen; get a grip. He-waldo hurried, servos humming, switching lanes between tourists and Shastans, human and mechanical, to catch up with Krueger-waldo. Meanwhile he craned his camera 360 degrees, looking around.

Without binocular vision he might as well have been viewing it on twodeo, but it was exciting anyhow. They were in the town green, an open area with three levels of balconies overlooking it. The concourse was crowded, by Earth standards, even with half the people present as wastecan-sized waldos. But Daniel knew enough about orbital economics to realize that the green was lavishly spacious, by orbital standards. In space every cubic inch came with a hideously expensive price tag. But he knew that even if it weren't for the locals' needs, the tourism the habitat depended on must make this green economically not only feasible, but necessary. I'll bet the residential areas are about as roomy as a rabbit warren, he thought.

They passed a blur of shopfronts and tiny, fountained plazas with benches, on which people sat talking or reading books, and trees in little cages. Nearby, four glass-front elevators crept up and down a set of columns, next to an escalator. Sheets of luminescence—jello-sheaves—hung down, flickering like an artificial aurora borealis. They apparently also served as sound barriers, so the crowded plaza wasn't as noisy as it might have been. Beyond the elevators he spotted a small carnival with a merry-go-round and a loop-the-loop water-sled-coaster.

Farther down the concourse, more brightly lit, shifting jello-signs announced the presence of casinos, dance halls, and hotels.

Daniel double-glanced at the Alamo icon in front of his vision, and a set of files appeared. The first was a thumbnail description of the habitat, and the others were maps and a jello of the station. He called up the thumbnail and the jello and displayed them, translucent mode, in the upper left and right corners of his vision, respectively, scanning them as he navigated the concourse.

SHASTA STATION

POPULATION—5,102
ELEVATION—18,904 miles (100 million feet) above sea level
SIZE—18.3 million cubic meters
ROTATIONAL SPEED—1.01 RPM
ROTATIONAL ACCELERATION—39–84% of gravity
ORBITAL PERIOD—14 hours, 37 minutes
PRIMARY IMPORTS—water, lunar and asteroidal ores, silicon, specialty organics, oxygen, and nitrogen
PRIMARY EXPORTS—pharmaceuticals, optronics, highly refined iron, copper, titanium, and iridium

---

Apparent gravity here was between thirty-nine and eighty-four percent of Earth's? That surprised Daniel. He didn't feel all that light. His waldo's gyros must be very crude. Daniel wondered whether Kaleidas's imports were included in those totals. He seriously doubted it. Their exports—proxy parts, miniature antimatter batteries, and highly experimental linkware for the proxies the Austin plant assembled—certainly weren't.

Daniel and Krueger had waldoed into the public habitat. Daniel wondered why the Kaleidas people insisted that Krueger and Daniel rent cheap commercial waldos for this briefing, instead of providing them with the much more sophisticated and comfortable proxy machinery they must have had on hand in the secured habitat; he suspected it was some sort of power play, or simple vindictiveness.

Shasta Station was a big, spinning barbell almost a third of a mile long, with the public and classified habitats separated by a long shaft. To get to Kaleidas they would have to travel the length of the shaft, "up" to zero gravity and back "down" the other side of the barbell. Following their jello maps and verifying with signs posted on pillars, they made their way out of the main concourse, onto some tracks set into a series of corridors, and up a set of waldo lift-tubes. Shortly they reached the antechamber to the interhabitat elevators. In addition to the commercial and residential traffic, industrial-sized waldos moved cargo beyond the traffic-control fences and below the catwalks. Cheerful signs welcomed tourists. Lighted arrows and signs directed people down different hallways. As they entered the space, chimes sounded and lights flashed around the two-story perimeter of a set of doors. A syntellect voice announced the arrival of a lift. Daniel- and Krueger-waldos got in line to board, along with a group of other people and waldos.

The elevator was massive—not only was it at least two stories high; it was wide and deep enough to fit a good-sized military collocar. The elevator syntellect required that all passengers enter a destination and an approval code before boarding; Daniel and Krueger entered the codes Kaleidas had earlier transmitted to them.

The "codes approved" light came on and they were admitted into the elevator by a smiling human attendant. Daniel followed Krueger-waldo onto the mounting tracks, which ran all the way along the floor, walls, and ceiling. Several people shuffled into the lift with them.

Then the doors shut and, after soft chimes rang an alert, a syntellect voice said, "All human passengers, please vell yourselves to the wall or take hold of the grips provided. Waldo passengers, please direct your waldos onto the tracks. Gravity will increase rapidly and then diminish as we proceed."

And they proceeded. The elevator shot up. Then the pressure relented and, as the elevator's acceleration slowed, the human passengers' hair began to float. Those using handholds lifted off from the floor.

The elevator braked, nearing the nulgy node, and those using handholds swung toward the ceiling. Daniel-waldo, even with his unit's rudimentary gyros, had a sense of being upside down. The sense of gravitational pressure went away entirely as the elevator stopped and the door opened. The half dozen humans swam out into a big spherical bay—some gracefully propelling themselves, others laboriously clawing their way along the handholds. The other waldo passenger rolled out along the track.

Then the door closed again. Daniel-waldo and Krueger-waldo were alone in the car. A syntellect voice said, "Samson Endicott Krueger and Daniel Raleigh Sornsen, your access codes have been verified and your beanlink signals traced and confirmed. Access to secured habitat has been cleared. Stand by."

Gears churned and motors hummed. The sense of being pulled toward the floor returned, as the elevator dropped toward the secured habitat. Then, gradually, a competing pull toward the elevator ceiling took over and increased. Yes, the ceiling was definitely becoming the floor. Daniel noted that the elevator's comm consoles and tracks and so forth had all been designed so that the elevator was as functional upside down as it was right side up. His waldo's gyros weren't sensitive enough for Daniel to tell how strong the pull was at the point where the elevator stopped.

"Get a move on, Sornsen," Krueger-waldo ordered, as the doors opened.

Daniel led the way across the ceiling and down the wall, onto what was now the floor, and out of the elevator. Krueger-waldo rolled out beside him. Two men—Marines, in dress uniform—stood on either side of the elevator. One of them stepped smartly forward; the other remained at attention, seemingly oblivious.

"Dr. Krueger? Mr. Sornsen?"

Krueger-waldo answered for both of them, after the signal-lag pause. "That's right."

"Follow me, please."

Krueger-waldo and Daniel-waldo rolled along behind the Marine, through bare halls lined with doors. There wasn't much to see. The corridors were claustrophobically close; handholds and Velcro lined the walls; steel grating and waldo tracks lined the floor and ceiling along the sides.

The Marine led them to a door at the end of a corridor, keyed in a code, and, as the door opened, left them there. Krueger rolled on in. Daniel followed.

At a large table sat two people, both white, separated by a couple of chairs: a man in his fifties, perhaps, grey-haired and bulky; and a young, drop-dead-gorgeous woman with blue-black hair that went down past her knees, twisted into an elaborate webbing of braids that draped over her shoulders, bodice, and back like gleaming black lace. The man was dressed in a conservatively cut, blue pin-striped sheath suit; the woman wore a candy-red micromini dress that displayed her large breasts to good advantage, and likewise her incredibly shapely, long legs. The woman was a proxy; the man was *in corpus.*

She leaned her elbows on the table and cradled her chin in her hand, regarding them, as the older man stood. He looked from Krueger-waldo to Daniel-waldo and back, eyebrows raised. The conversation that ensued was filled with pauses caused by signal-response lag.

"Dr. Krueger?"

Pause. Krueger-waldo rolled up to the table; Daniel-waldo followed suit. "That's correct. And this is my associate, Daniel Sornsen. You"—gesturing with his three-fingered claw at the man—"must be Alan Rasmussen of the Department of Environmental Protection. And Dr. Patricia Taylor"—gesturing at the woman for Daniel's benefit. "Good to see you again, Patricia," Krueger-waldo said.

Daniel stared. *That* was Patricia Taylor? *The* Patricia Taylor?

Rasmussen slammed his fist onto the table. Since his words came hard on the heels of Krueger-waldo's, he must have started talking shortly after Krueger-waldo had started to broadcast. "You idiots in Austin let a classified, twenty-five-million-dollar piece of equipment, powered by highly dangerous antimatter batteries, just get up and walk away—not once, but twice! Are you mere incompetents, or is this sabotage?"

Krueger let the already lengthy pause lengthen even more, obviously considering his words.

"We've taken additional precautions since the last theft, in case the renegade got past our increased security. We've been installing homing devices in all our proxies, right, Sornsen?" he-waldo asked, turning to Daniel-waldo, who nodded his camera platform.

"That's correct."

"This one has such a device in its neck," Krueger-waldo continued, "and we're tracking it down now. Sornsen, please elaborate."

Daniel accessed his readouts, studied them. "It's heading northwest across the mudflats toward Amarillo," he-waldo said. "Teams were dispatched as soon as we discovered the proxy missing. We will have recovered the proxy within the hour."

Krueger-waldo's camera platform swiveled from Daniel-waldo to Taylor, and then pivoted back to Rasmussen. "We believe it may be seeking out Kaleidas candidates again; there are three within a couple days' run of the renegade, so we put them under surveillance this morning just for good measure."

Rasmussen said, "Then don't capture the renegade right away. Follow it. Find out who its intended victim is. I want some answers from you people." Krueger-waldo spoke, but Rasmussen talked over him.

"I'm aware of the risks. But we can't afford to let the saboteur escape this time. This breach in security is unacceptable."

Daniel-waldo, wondering why he was sticking his neck out, interjected, "I don't understand."

Daniel-waldo had spoken during a pause in Rasmussen's tirade, but due to signal lag, it came out in the midst of further rantings. Rasmussen broke off.

"What?" he snapped. Daniel-waldo cleared his throat. It came out sounding like signal noise.

"I don't understand what good it'll do to attempt to capture the proxy, sir. In the first place, as you yourself pointed out, it's dangerous to have a classified piece of equipment out wandering around among civilians. Unless X-rayed or cut open, our proxies are almost indistinguishable from human bodies, but if an accident were to happen, the news would be all over the nets in no time, and we'd all be in serious trouble. And to no useful end, since the renegade pilot will merely disengage from the interface when we overpower the proxy, like last time. We'll be right back where we were last time this happened—and by delaying that capture, we'll be risking the life of a potential candidate besides."

A pause. Rasmussen gave him-waldo a hostile look, and Daniel had an intuitive flash: Rasmussen *wanted* the proxy to be discovered by civilians. He was trying to sabotage the project. Daniel glanced at Taylor, whose expression was impassive. Did she know what Rasmussen was up to? She wasn't participating in the meeting; why was she even here? Probably as a courtesy, because of her stature.

"You people should certainly have the resources to protect the lives of innocents from one of your own proxy units," Rasmussen was saying. "The American public has paid through the nose for this technology."

Pause. "That's not the point, with all due respect, sir. As I said, the renegade pilot isn't going to stick around anyway once he, or she, realizes we've captured the proxy."

Rasmussen gave him-waldo a mild smile. "Your people have made progress with your Odhiambo psych-profile tests, have they not? The pilot needn't even know the proxy has been captured. You can present the renegade with a series of guided simulations that will reveal who the pilot is. Am I correct?"

Pause. Daniel avoided glancing at Krueger-waldo. Rasmussen, still smiling, waited, looking again at Krueger-waldo, who returned his regard.

"Your plan neglects an important consideration," Krueger-waldo said. "We can't stop the renegade unless we use our own proxies. And the more proxy bodies we have out there in public, running around, the greater risk we run of exposure. Which will not suit the ends of either the DOEP or the congressional oversight committee. Are you going to tell them it was your idea we send our own people out there in proxy?"

"I'll take full responsibility. Just do it. I want to know who is behind this."

Pause. Daniel could almost smell the burning synapses from Krueger fuming. "I'll get back to you on that."

"Do that," Rasmussen replied. "If you have any problems with it, call Secretary Thompson. Or better yet, perhaps Waldos, Inc.'s, Chairman Morrison will be following up with *you*."

"Yeah." Krueger-waldo sounded thoroughly disgusted. "Fine."

A STROLL DOWN MEMORY LANE

At her new office, Carli got her *virtu* and jelly operating systems set up on her comunit, and then spent some time opening boxes and filing research materials. In one of her older boxes, which had been sealed for years while she was at UNM, was an old brown folder with the words "M^AC^LEOD" written on it.

MacLeod. The MacLeod. That's what they'd called the technology back then.

Carli carried it over to her desk, sat down, and brushed the dust off it. Even just touching it summoned up old shades; her fingers tingled and her stomach started to churn.

Don't do this, Carli, she thought. Let it rest. Put it back on the shelf. Better yet, toss it in the incinerator. With a grimace, she opened the notebook. Data crystals lined the interior pockets, and several sheaves of paper with handwritten notes on them were folded and tucked carefully into the center crease like sleeping children.

A memory surfaced—compact like a neatly programmed bit of code, so fresh and tart and crisp, like the bite of an apple, that it stung her nose and made her eyes water.

She'd been in a restaurant with Jere; they'd left a party early to have their own private time, celebrating the opening of the first plant to make the MacLeod, her instantaneous-transmission technology. It was only a few years after they'd married—about the time Paint had gone underground to dodge the draft; a couple of years before Jere had secretly turned Paint's name and whereabouts over to the authorities.

"It's not perfect," she'd protested, smiling, her cheeks heating up under the glow of his pride. That grin of his. And his eyes had been shining on her like footlights. "It's not an ideal technology on Earth itself, you know."

"But why? At the party, Byron Kowalski was talking as if this was going to transform communications all over the planet."

Carli shrugged. "It has a lot of implications that could have an effect on communications here on Earth. But it's going to have a much bigger impact in space."

"But Byron said—"

"I know what he said, but it's too power-hungry to be stationed Earth-side. Even a huge conventional power plant dedicated solely to the MacLeod wouldn't work. To make it economically feasible we have to use antimatter reactors to power the particle accelerator. Too dangerous. There's a good reason antimatter is illegal, planet-side."

"Jon Darlington told me OMNEX plans to build a space-based matrix of MacLeod communications nodes that will link the entire inner system."

Carli shook her head with a laugh. Darlington, a VP at OMNEX, had big ideas, maybe bigger than even OMNEX could handle. "It'll take decades and hundreds of billions of dollars to complete. I don't know if it'll ever happen."

He touched her face again, drawing a smile from her. "Think big, my dear."

"It would be nice, wouldn't it?"

His mouth twisted. " 'Nice.' Heh. We could do whatever we wanted, have whatever we dreamed of, with the royalties."

"Mmmm . . ." She swirled her drink around in her glass, playing with the roseate rays of light it cast onto the table. "Its real potential is much greater, if we could just figure out a way to improve the sensitivity. The theorists tell me that the sensor's actual efficiency is only forty percent of the theoretical limit. It's odd. Byron and I have been toying around with some possibilities—"

She broke off when he laughed and grabbed her hand, giving it a gentle shake. "Hey, come back here. This is our time. Make your next breakthrough later."

He'd proposed a toast and they had held hands across the table and chatted about the future. Talked about maybe taking some time to start a family, before too long . . .

That night they'd made long, sweet love and she'd stared into the dark for a while, after Jere was asleep, thinking about the MacLeod and her future. It had all seemed to lie before her, a path made of golden cobblestone and dancing rainbows. Substantial improvements to the MacLeod's design were forming in her mind; she could almost taste those extra kilobytes per second of bandwidth, those extra light-seconds of range, hovering tantalizingly, just beyond her reach. With a few months' work and her team behind her, she could make dramatic improvements.

Two weeks later OMNEX had sued for ownership of the MacLeod and, after an ugly battle that stretched on for years, had won.

If she tried to build on her work, it'd simply go to line some wealthy executives' and investors' pockets. To even *try* to work on it, hoping to someday be able to outwit OMNEX's stable of prizewinning attorneys, she would need financial backing, which no sensible funding agency or investor would provide. Nobody would take on OMNEX.

The omni, they called it now. It was transforming interplanetary communications and making all sorts of breakthroughs in space exploration possible. It was her baby, and nobody even knew.

The MacLeod. She ran her fingers over the label. It was ironic; even if they *hadn't* changed it to "omni," it wouldn't have her name now. It would have Jere's.

She'd taken his name with no second thoughts. She had wanted that sense of deep union that sharing a name would give them, and he hadn't wanted to share hers; he'd been afraid it would hurt his political career. So in what had seemed at the time a bold flouting of tradition, she had abandoned her own. She hadn't thought it would matter. Merely one in a long line of mistakes she'd made in that marriage.

Still, the old irritation, the sense of incompletion, gnawed at her, an ache deep in her bones, as she eyed the notebook. There's no reason for that 40 percent limit, she thought. With a sigh, she snapped the notebook shut.

She crossed the room and shoved the notebook decisively onto the shelf, between a couple of other old data notebooks. Then, with a yelp, she glanced at the readout on her kelly pendant. It was after four o'clock; she was going to be late for the launch at Paint's.

DANIEL

THE DR. TAYLOR AND HER CRACK CADRE OF CRÈCHE-KID PROXY-JOCKS

After the meeting, Dr. Taylor offered to escort Daniel- and Krueger-waldos back to the elevator. Once they were in the hall, after the door closed on Rasmussen, Daniel-waldo said, "A man of some charm."

She shook her head in warning, drew a circle on her throat, meaning *switch to radio*, and sketched with her hand in Technislan an encryption code. Daniel-waldo and Krueger-waldo exchanged glances.

"You must have some idea," she broadcast, once they'd switched over and keyed in the code. "Whom is the saboteur after?"

Pause. A moment of regard.

"Go ahead, Sornsen," Krueger-waldo said. "Fill Dr. Taylor in."

"My hunch," Daniel-waldo told her, "is that it intends to head toward Albuquerque or Santa Fe, once it gets past the mudflats. There's a potential Kaleidas recruit in Albuquerque and another in Santa Fe, from the rosters your people gave us after last time. The renegade seems to be familiar with the terrain, and I'm almost certain it's after one of those two."

Taylor nodded as if Daniel had confirmed her suspicion, and sketched another encryption code in the air. Daniel was skeptical and disturbed. What was she so paranoid about? He-waldo and Krueger-waldo changed their encryptions, and she leaned toward them.

"Listen. I know whom the renegade pilot is after. Carli MacLeod, in Albuquerque. MacLeod is crucial to my work. The renegade is trying to stop me, I'm sure of it. And if it kills her, it will have succeeded." She paused. Neither Krueger nor Daniel responded. "Do you understand what I'm saying? I'm existing on borrowed time. I need MacLeod."

"We've had her under surveillance since this morning," Krueger-waldo said after a long hesitation. "We haven't given the renegade a chance to get anywhere near her. But Rasmussen—we can't afford to alienate him. If the DOEP gets onto our backs, we'll have more trouble than we can handle."

Taylor flicked a hand. "Make an effort to capture the proxy; I don't care about that. But MacLeod mustn't die. Whatever the cost, she must not die. I need her. And fast."

She exchanged an intent look with Krueger-waldo, who, after a long pause, grunted acquiescence.

"We can support you on that," he-waldo said. "But we can't afford to sacrifice our projects simply for the sake of your recruitment efforts. If Rasmussen even *suspected* we were going behind his back, it might lead to a DOEP investigation, and that would reveal too many things about our research that we'd prefer to keep under wraps for a while. At least until the political winds change."

He-waldo referred, of course, to President Thaxton's pulpit-pounding campaign speeches about the "flagrant waste of taxes" and "pie-in-the-sky fancy-ass research projects" this fall.

They had nothing to worry about for a couple of months; the political grapevine had it that he was still gathering moderates' support for his upcoming battle to ax the various high-tech government-industry cooperatives that had formed over the past two decades. And the head of the Department of Environmental Protection, Secretary-elect Thompson, was Thaxton's personal appointee.

It wouldn't be that easy for the DOEP to cut off Project Kaleido-Scope's funding. While the Department of Environmental Protection might see Austin's and Kaleidas's work as only marginally valuable anymore, in terms of their own agenda of funding environmentally adaptive technologies, the commercial spin-offs from their work had been so profitable over the past decade or so that the DOEP wouldn't have much political support in Congress for cutting their funds, nor would their industrial partner, Waldos, Inc., readily let go of an important source of new income streams. And when all else failed, their ace in the hole, Senator D'Auber, had always been a valuable ally, keeping them out from under the ax when other research projects were cut from the federal budget.

But though Thaxton and D'Auber both belonged to the Fiscal Democrats party, they were at odds in all nonfiscal major issues, and Thaxton had publicly supported D'Auber's opponent in the last election. The Populists were now in a majority in Congress, so D'Auber was in a politically weak position right now; thus with Thaxton behind them, the DOEP could do an end run around D'Auber. On top of which, Thaxton wasn't above using political strong-arming to get Waldos, Inc. to sell back to the government its share of its two secret co-op ventures, Austin and Kaleidas. So the managing subsidiary's Board of Directors had some worried members on it these days.

And Daniel bet that this put the pressure on Krueger, who sat on the Board and occasionally played *v*-golf with the chairman and the president, more than on his remote, reclusive peer, Taylor.

"Well," she said mildly, "perhaps Thaxton will be more reasonable than we're giving him credit for."

"Not bloody likely. Too bad he had to be told about Kaleido-Scope."

"Yeah. But necessary." She leaned toward him-waldo. "Now, about MacLeod. Look, you don't have to worry about the Board; I've given them plenty of high-yield reasons to like me over the years. If they can find a way to give me what I want without a direct confrontation with the DOEP or the subcommittee, they'll do it. All I need is for you people to keep her alive and get her to Austin."

"We'll make sure she stays alive, Patricia," Krueger-waldo replied after a moment. "We would have, anyhow. And I'll see what we can do about recruiting her for you. I simply can't make you any promises that we'll succeed."

"I suppose that'll have to do," Taylor said. "Thanks, Sam."

They had reached the elevator bank with the Marines on guard; Taylor left them there with a brief good-bye. After they'd boarded and started back to the public sector, Daniel switched over to a direct link and transmitted, "Taylor's more than seventy years old, isn't she?"

"Yep. Quite a bit more."

"How does she get away with such an outrageous proxy?"

Daniel was unsure how to interpret the long pause that followed his question. It couldn't be signal lag, since their signals were now being transmitted directly back and forth from their own crèches, right next to each other, back in Austin. Finally he said, "Her contributions outweigh her eccentricities, I suppose."

Daniel refrained from responding. Eccentricities? Rumor had it she was a raving lunatic. And the sex-goddess proxy she wore sure didn't suggest that she had much self-restraint.

But then, a lot of the people he knew on the project got strange after a while, in one way or another.

The elevator started up the central shaft.

"I hoped we'd get a look at their operations," Daniel said. "Their team of child pilots is supposed to be really hot. Do you know anything about them?"

Krueger made a grunting noise. After a minute he said, "A little. I've had a couple of tours."

"What are they like?"

"They run a slick operation, all right. Those kids can handle any waldo there is, doing just about any task. And they also cruise the nets in *virtu*-engines much more sophisticated than currently available technology. Bizarre stuff. I've seen jellos of them cleaning up nuclear waste, patching a hole in a tumbling ship, piloting diagnostic micro-waldos into a man's liver, tracking a packet of stolen data across the *v*-net. All kinds of stuff."

"How many are there?"

"Same as Austin . . . maybe a few more. Two dozen or so? I don't know."

Daniel paused. "It can't be good for them to spend so much time in proxy, though. You know? It must give them a pretty messed-up view of reality, living in machine-face and *virtu*-face all the time."

"You don't know what you're talking about." Krueger's tone was sharp. "Imagine the resources at their fingertips. All humanity's knowledge, a vast array of experiences and interactions, throughout the nets, across the world, in space! No offense, Sornsen; you're one of my best pilots. But no adult-trained proxy pilot can imagine what they experience, what they're capable of."

A shudder ran through Daniel's body, in his crèche back in Austin. "Yeah, I'm sure they're amazing. But it's still jade."

COURIER RIDES FLAME

Carli left the downtown canopy's lock. The late afternoon sky was swathed in gauze, and the sun, amber and swollen, hung in the western sky above the Three Sisters, the extinct volcanoes on the lava flows of the West Mesa. A cluster of sun dogs mocked the sun. Another miserable November day was about to end. And unless serendipity—and a remotely possible thunderstorm—intervened, it promised to be a miserably hot night.

Carli strapped her half-mask to her face, and coolness spread over her cheeks and neck. She sighed with relief at its touch and started for the train station, slipping on her netspecs and glove.

**(PSA!) POWER BLACKOUT SW QUADRANT 2330
11/18 to 0600 11/19.
ICE AVAIL TO SENR CITZNS & ILL. APPLY < 2300 @
LA GALERIA/WINRONADO SUPERPLEX/RIO
GRANDE HI SCHL (PSA!)**

(C) ** SAVE NOW AT SAV*MOR! SPECIALS: FISH $52.99/KG::
TOP-QUALITY RECON BEEF $46.50/KG :: MILK-MATE
$10.00/L! DEALS LIKE THIS WON'T LAST! OPEN 7 DAYS,
24 HOURS! BUY NOW AT SAV*MOR! **** (A)**

**(C) © correspondence recvd 4 hrs 3 min 22 sec ago ::
4445-78101 [savmor mgr] -> 3910-10003
[carli.dauber]
the milk, tomatoes, potatoes, onions, and carrots
you requested yesterday are in. pls don't delay in
waldoing over to examine them as the demand is
high for these items and i can't hold them up. we
also got an unexpected carton of voulou olives
packed in oil, if you're interested.
—jim smucker©(C)**

She dashed down the steps to the subway, hearing a train coming. With a flick of her fingers she relegated all but the weather report and the public service announcement to the little garbage can that floated in the lower right quadrant of her vision. As she boarded the uptown train and grabbed at a handhold that dangled from the ceiling, she called up her linkware and waldoed over to the grocery's *virtu*-foyer.

WELCOME, VIRTUAL SHOPPERS! SAVE MORE AT SAV*MOR!

Carli perused the list of specials. An iconic shopping cart appeared before her, and she filled the cart with numerous items by going to the assorted pages, grabbing food icons, and dropping them into the cart. Then she selected "INSPECT PRODUCE" and downloaded into a waldo mounted on a rail in the produce section.

Steering the little, one-armed machine over the fruits and veggies, she reached down occasionally with her gloved hand to give the produce a squeeze. Without her more sophisticated *virtu*-hood and -gauntlets, and her stinklink processor, which were at home, it was hard to be sure she was getting the best produce, but she wanted to get the shopping out of the way. She decided to take her chances.

After tagging the best-looking and -feeling tomatoes, potatoes, onions, and carrots, at the last minute she chose a handful of Golden Delicious apples, too, because they looked especially good. A delivery waldo began collecting and bundling her choices as she withdrew. Because she was feeling decadent, she also selected some Voulou olives from the store's deli section.

By the time she'd paid the bill and arranged a delivery time, her train had reached the university stop. She debarked, exited the station, and started up the steps. Phase Two rush hour was in full swing; the crowds were a good deal heavier than they had been when she'd left that morning.

She sent a brief note to a colleague in Ecuador, and glanced through her news-clippings file. Then she logged off. By this time she had reached street level and navigated the worst of the crowds. Carli shoved her way onto the culvert bridge and down the other side, across the sidewalks and onto Buena Vista. The crowds lessened as she headed southward into the student ghetto. Paint lived with Fox in a little three-room place behind someone's house, on the far side of Lead.

Carli had this lingering sense, again, that someone was watching her. When she reached the house she looked back along the street toward campus. Diseased elms spread a splotchy green over the street. Students, *natureils*, and suited pedestrians were on the street, but no one was even going in the same direction as Carli.

Relax, D'Auber, she thought. Paranoia doesn't suit you.

She went around the side of the house, past a bony old Doberman that lay in the shade by its doghouse inside a fence, jowls on paws, eyeing her amid snarls and snaps at the flies that tormented its ears and sipped water from its eyes.

Paint and Fox's little stucco unit, a small house in the landlord's backyard, was painted an unfortunate shade of grey. Peeling turquoise blue trimmed the windows and door. The wood of the front door had weathered to the point that it had become almost as grey as the house paint, though flecks of turquoise remained. The screen door was permanently propped open. A beat-up old couch and a megapot with a dying cactus took up most of the porch. The front window was mirrored, but the glass was old, and the silvering had worn away in patches. Carli could make out shadowy movement inside.

It looked like a lot of people in there, in close quarters. Their voices carried faintly through the window and walls. It sounded like a big party, not a few friends getting together to watch the launch.

"Damn," Carli muttered. Her heart rate climbed to an alarming rate and her palms were sweaty—and it wasn't from overexertion or heat.

If she was going to watch this stupid launch, it should be in private, or with at most a couple of close friends.

She stepped up to the porch, tapped on the door. Copper baffles hung from the roof, shaded by tarps and attached to the HVAC unit that perched on the sill of the bedroom window. Makeshift heat fins, Paint's own invention. The waves of heat rising from them warmed her exposed skin, the left cheek and hand, at ten paces.

Paint ushered her in and shut the door quickly. He smiled, slapped her on the back, and said something she couldn't make out over the babble, probably some kind of greeting. She nodded with a smile, sliding her specs and mesh glove off and tucking them into the pouch at her belt.

Paint gestured for her to sit down somewhere, and then dodged obstacles to the kitchen. Carli was on her own. In a manner of speaking.

Paint's glastic love seat with cheap airgel cushions, a rocking chair, two folding chairs, three mobiles, and a bookcase, along with a good dozen or more people and an awful lot of noise, filled all the space in the living room. In spite of the air conditioner and ceiling fans, the air was warm and close and smelled like a locker room. Carli looked around at all the round, made-up children's faces and tinted polymer hairstyles, the knees and hands and firm breasts and trim bellies, and felt ancient at thirty-eight.

The rental jellovision was a seven-footer with a silver plaque on its base that said "Property of U-Rent-M" and a bar code, which mostly blocked the hall to the bathroom and bedroom. How Paint could afford it, much less get it through the front door, was anyone's guess. Though if anyone could figure a way to get a two-hundred-pound, seven-foot-by-four-foot-by-eighteen-inch glass tube through a three-foot-wide door without breaking either, it was Paint.

The jelly was already on, displaying a split tube. In the lower half, two J-net anchors were talking; the sound was turned up loud enough that if she concentrated, she could make out most of what they said.

The top half of the jelly showed the launch pad. The DC-7y supershuttle, *Courier*, stood poised for flight, chemical rockets built into its back. Trails of steam leaked from various vents. Tiny humans and ground vehicles crawled around on the expanse of concrete beneath *Courier*.

Carli, unzipping her cool suit with her free hand, paused in midzip to study the shot. She swallowed a knot that had formed in her throat. God, it was beautiful, that shuttle.

Fox came out of the kitchen. He was a Chicano, dark-skinned and dark-haired, compact and well built like all muscle dancers, and he had a hawk nose and brown eyes. He gave Carli a hug.

"Did we get the contract?"

"I don't know. I left a message with Jan to call yesterday. We'll hear soon enough, I expect. We'll need at least a couple of weeks to get organized, anyhow. But it'd be nice to know. He practically drooled on the floor when I talked to him last week."

As she talked, he helped her finish removing her cool suit. Carli struggled out of it, then disconnected the tubes from the cool pack. A faint whiff of ammonia stung her nostrils. Fox hung the suit and pack with the others on a hook by the door.

A blond woman with a gorgeous smile handed Carli a Chinese paper fan, and Carli immediately put it to use; her white stretch cotton halter and shorts had already dampened with sweat. Fox slapped the leg of a young man sitting on the love seat.

"Hey, *chingada*, move your ass and let Carli sit down!"

The young man stood and offered Carli his seat with a sweep of his arm.

Carli felt her skin heat up but decided to accept the offer, since there was no room anywhere but the floor and she wasn't on ass-to-elbow terms with anyone here.

She sat next to a kid maybe ten or eleven, who looked like a younger version of the one who'd given her his seat. He grinned at her, a gap-toothed smile. In his lap he had a mock-up of *Exodus*, the interstellar probe ship that was *Courier*'s destination.

The kid opened the plastic panels to show her the innards of the mock-up. Holographic figurines in flight suits walked in the halls, and lights blinked on the tiny machines.

On her other side, a college-aged young woman in a crimson, strapless stretch sheath, with waxed curls in front of her eyes and her face painted all over like a fish, balanced on the arm of the love seat with an artist's pad on her knees and pieces of charcoal in her lap and hand. Her fingers were smudged and the fingernails filthy.

Carli craned to see the drawing. The woman was working on a sketch of the shuttle as a half-finished phoenix, beak outstretched, rising from the flames and smoke.

Carli grinned. "It's good!"

The girl's face lit up. When she smiled, she looked no older than fifteen or sixteen. "Thanks."

"All right, everyone—shut up, shut up!" Paint beat on a pan with a serving spoon, and the noise died down. Faces turned to him. "I want to hear what they're saying."

He sat down on the rug in a tumble of arms and legs with Fox. Carli looked at the screen. The J-net station was spotlighting some of the colonists, giving thumbnail sketches of their life histories.

"I'd go in a minute," one boy said.

"Not me!"

"I would. It'd be utter schickitude."

"Me, too."

"Heights jade me total. Brrr."

"Carli was in the training program for a while," Paint said, and everyone looked at Carli.

"Wow, jink!"

"What was it like?"

Carli shot Paint a dirty look. "It was a long time ago," she said.

"Have you ever been in space?" the girl sketching the shuttle asked.

"I had a thirty-six-month stint on an orbital platform, back in my twenties, doing communications work. I was an alternate for the interstellar program for a while, but . . ." she shrugged.

"How come you're not in the program anymore?"

"Do you know any of the astronauts leaving today?"

"A few of them," she conceded. She gave Paint another look. He shrugged apologetically and banged on his pot again.

"She can answer questions later. I want to watch the broadcast."

The anchor was discussing with a mission spokeswoman of the shuttle's planned trajectory and linkup with *Exodus*, now docked at Icarus, the antimatter production facility that shared an orbit with Mercury.

"The supershuttle is being used to transport the last of the crew and supplies," the spokeswoman said, "to *Exodus*, which is currently docked at Icarus Station. Most of the crew is already aboard the vessel."

"When will *Exodus* depart?" the anchor asked.

"In about six days. They'll be receiving a waldo sling-packet, a cargo pod, scheduled to leave the moon base Einstein Station the day after tomorrow, and a few days later *Courier* will arrive with the last of the personnel, equipment, and supplies. Once *Courier* arrives at Icarus, *Exodus* leaves the solar ecliptic, and its interstellar journey begins."

"How long will the journey take?" the anchor asked.

"About one hundred and fifteen years, by our clocks. For the probe astronauts, about eight years less, due to relativistic effects."

"I understand there are enough provisions for new generations to be born on the way to Ursa Major and back."

"That's correct."

"Dr. Smith-Williams, there are some who worry that the probe astronauts will fail to bear a new generation, or the next one will . . . and that *Exodus* will end up as an interstellar ghost ship. Or that the succeeding generations won't be motivated or properly trained to fulfill the probe's mission."

"That's highly unlikely. Careful measures have been taken."

"Such as . . . ?"

She cleared her throat. "You've raised several issues. First, the possibility they'll die off. According to current theory, forty is the minimum number of humans that can effectively perpetuate the species.

With modern technology, that number is certainly high. In fact, frozen sperm and ova are aboard ship for use by women who desire to give birth but can't, or who don't have or don't desire a male mate. There are twenty percent more women of childbearing age than there are men, to increase the number of fertile combinations."

"Lucky fellows."

The NASA spokeswoman gave him a strained smile. "Births will be carefully controlled, to keep the ship's microcosm in balance. The astronauts are prepared for all this. Second, regarding the descendants' education. The children of *Exodus* will be brought up with a rigorous education that will prepare them for their roles."

"Are the astronauts prepared to spend the rest of their lives around each other, in such cramped quarters?"

"They're quite prepared. They've spent years in training for this. Of course, the ship is actually both massive *and* large in volume, though only the interiormost portions will be habitable at relativistic speeds, due to radiation from the impact of space dust on the hull. However, since they'll have full and instantaneous access to the nets, the astronauts and their descendants will be able to remain a part of the Earth community, and even waldo back here for meetings with families and friends. So it won't be all that crowded or isolated for them."

"Instantaneous access?" The anchor seemed surprised. "How can that be, at such a great distance? I thought signal lag would preclude it."

"Omni technology works in the presence of large masses," the spokeswoman said. "As the *Exodus* approaches relativistic speeds, its mass will increase. The ship will accelerate at approximately one gee until it attains a velocity of forty percent of the speed of light, and at approximately eighteen percent of light speed, about fifteen months into their journey, the ship's mass will become great enough for the astronauts to use the ship's omni to communicate with Earth."

They went on to discuss a couple of other issues. Though the spokeswoman hadn't mentioned it, Carli remembered from her NASA days that, even if the crew's descendants *had* died off by the time the ship neared 47 Ursae Majoris, the ship could be programmed to automatically deploy its omni transmitter and do a long-distance, waldo-based exploration of 47 Uma's possibly habitable fourth planet. If Earth's civilization still existed by then, she amended gloomily.

"Coming up next," the anchor said, turning to the camera, "the liftoff. But first these messages . . ."

Paint turned the sound down, and several people jumped up and squeezed around the jellovision in a race for the bathroom. After a silent eyeblast of ten-second spots that lasted long enough for half the occupants of the living room to make a trip to the bathroom—**BUY-BUY-RENT-BUY-DONATE-LEASE-BUY**—Cape Canaveral effervesced in the tube again.

The trails of steam under *Courier*'s belly were bigger now. The display suspended midtube showed it was T minus fifty-three seconds and counting.

Paint didn't have to tell everyone to be quiet now. The J-net anchors shut up, too, and the voices of NASA flight controllers and the shuttle pilots came on. Computer checks clear. All systems go. T minus thirty seconds and counting. Backup coolant systems check. And so on.

Then it was T minus two seconds, T minus one, and Carli didn't hear the voices anymore; she caught her breath and held it—and the shuttle trembled, rose on a column of glowing steam into the blue Florida sky until it became a speck. The speck shrank even smaller, and then the jello image switched to a cube of 2D images; the speck that was *Courier* jumped about as telescopic cameras tracked it. Safely away.

Carli brushed away tears and stood.

"You jigging?" Paint seemed surprised.

"Yeah. Thanks for inviting me over. Fox, I'll see you at the office tomorrow. We can finish unpacking and get things organized in the morning."

"Come by The Bomb tonight," Fox said. "Paint's got a show."

"Hmmm. Maybe. Don't count on me."

Carli decided to grab a bite to eat at a downtown sidewalk café, instead of going straight home. Home would be too empty; stillness and solitude made it far too likely that she'd start to brood about Jere or the launch. Or her brother Dennis, or OMNEX, or some other damn thing.

And maybe she would head out to Rio Rancho and watch Paint dance at The Protein Bomb after all. Today was a landmark: it was her first official day as a freelancer again. She deserved a celebration.

She ran down the wrought-iron steps to the expressway station, logging back into the net.

(C) (A) ** Robo-Fantasies—Share a nite with the
Wo/Man of your dreams! Wet—Wild—Fully Lifelike!
Will do anything and everything! We mean
EVERYTHING. All but human, and completely in
your control. They're Hot! Hot! Hot! Call now, while
supplies last. Dial 888-Robo-Sex. ******

**(C) (T) TIME @ TEMP @ HUMIDITY :: 14:56:37 @ 50C @
69.8% (T)**

($) Your October GridLink bill is as follows:

* *** $ 961   –Bulletin board and conferences**
* *** $ 8,225 –electronic mail**
* *** $ 13,006 –news clipping service**
* *** $ 1,044 –entertainment similes**
* *** $ 100   –waldo rental**
* *** $ 200   –base fee**

** $ 23,536 –Monthly Total

**For your convenience, your monthly bill has been paid
out of your First Federal account, #216-01-88130.
Please e-mail our billing information sysop, acct-mgr Delia
[Delia@CustService.GridLink], with questions. Have
a nice day, and thank you for using GridLink! ($)**

An item appeared in the queue as she was deleting the other messages, and the sender's name made the hair on her arms and the nape
of her neck tingle.

A note from Sid. Jeez. How long had it been since she had actually responded to Carli's e-mail? Carli had no idea whether Sid was still
on the Ursa Major mission's launch team. Though she couldn't be—
if she were, given the time the message was posted, she would have had
to send the note *postlaunch*.

With a touch of her netgloved hand Carli called up the note. The
text scrolled down her vision, obscuring the other people on the train
platform.

**(C) (C) correspondence sent 0 hrs 0 min 18 sec ago ::
4113-66401 [cynthia.jimenez] -> 3910-10003
[carli.dauber]**

Hey, babe! Can you believe I'm actually writing
this from space? We just blasted off. Did you watch
the launch?
Never thought the day would come. Especially not
__eighteen days early__. Still don't know how the
brass pulled that one off. They were afraid the
looming deadlock over the federal budget would
shut us down till Thaxton gets into office next
January. And that'd be death to the project for sure.
So we're on our way! Damn, but I wish you were
here.
Anyway, right now I'm sitting next to a portal and
watching the Earth turn from a long, slow, blue-
white-and-brown curve, tighter and tighter till it's
almost a globe now. The gees are a bit much of a
muchness; it's even a strain to type at the moment.
At this rate, Cap'n Crunch says it'll take us about six
days to reach Icarus Station.
Sorry it took me so long to get back to you.
These last few months of training were BRUTAL.
But I knew I had to get a message to you as soon
after liftoff as possible; we'll be out of range of the
nets in about an hour or so, and then all net
communications will be strictly official, through
NASA channels.
If you get this in the next little while, write back
and give me a send-off. Otherwise, well, maybe we
can get back in touch in a couple years, when the
ship reaches a high enough velocity for us to use
the omni, or should I say, the MacLeod?
I'm supposed to pass along regards from the
rest of the crew. The captain, Greg, and Lorraine in
particular send their love and best wishes. Keep us
in your thoughts.
Your dearest chum,
Sid

Smiling, brushing away more tears, Carli sat down on a bench inside
the train terminal to type up a reply.

**Dear, dear Sid,
I never expected to hear from you again. Thank you
for thinking of me at such a time.**

Carli paused there for a long time, staring at the words that dangled before her eyes, not knowing what else to say. Then she heard the 5:37 Downtown Express coming.

"Shit." Quickly she put her right hand, the netgloved one, back to the virtual keyboard.

**My thoughts will be with you during your long voyage. I
envy you. Regards to the rest of the crew. Do get back in
touch when circumstances permit.
love—Carli**

The train docked with the curb. Carli sent the letter off, took off her specs and netglove, and shoved her way on board. The train's interior was dim, more humid but perhaps a little cooler, packed with commuters on their way home.

Carli managed to squeeze into a seat between a fat man and someone's purse, just as the train lurched into motion. She slouched and let unfocused thoughts scroll past, about supershuttles and interstellar missions, about war and marriage and her long-dead brother Dennis.

Then, slowly, she stiffened, staring. That feeling of being watched was growing on her again . . . and as several of the passengers around her swayed, she caught a glimpse of unblinking black eyes staring at her.

PABLO

WORRIERS

Pablo was getting worried about Buddy; it was late in the afternoon and Buddy had been missing since yesterday morning. All Pablo's mental calls and linkware attempts to locate him were utter failures.

It was infuriating. He didn't have time for this hide-and-seek bullshit; he was buried beneath a mountain of unfinished tasks and needed Buddy's help.

Pablo wasn't the only one stewing over events in progress. Mother called Pablo on a private jelly channel just before dinnertime, and reached him in his-Krueger's office.

"You did an excellent job as Krueger in the meeting with Rasmussen and Sornsen."

Pablo felt his flesh warm with pleasure. "Thanks, Mother."

"Now, I'm worried about this renegade business. It could mess up our plans. What have you been able to find out?"

Pablo shook his head. "Not a lot. It's like the last time. No trace of break-in. It's got to be an inside job."

"Mmmm."

"I've already run checks on all current Austin personnel and I'm doing another run on everyone involved in the project over the past seven years. Anyone with sophisticated enough beanlinkware to interface with the current proxy model. So far I haven't come up with anything."

"Where is the renegade now?"

"Still heading west. Near the Texas–New Mexico border." He hesitated. "Do you really think it's after Carli MacLeod?"

Mother shook her head. "That was for Sornsen's benefit. The renegade definitely has it in for us, but I think he, or she, is targeting people at random using one of our recruitment rosters. I wouldn't even be surprised if Rasmussen is behind this stunt in some way—" Her eyes suddenly slitted. "Yes. Yes . . . remember how he didn't want us to catch the renegade? . . . He has a lot to gain. . . ." She sighed. "I've got to do something to neutralize that bastard. In my copious spare time." Then she shook her head, frowning. "Anyhow, the big risk for us is that the renegade will do something stupid and end up on the news."

"Would that really be a bad thing?" Pablo asked.

"What do you mean?"

"I mean," Pablo said slowly, "I think the renegade situation might actually be helping us. It's drawing everyone's attention away from us at a critical time. And even if the renegade *is* found by local authorities and there's news coverage, there'll be confusion over what's going on. We'll still have time to get away."

Mother looked surprised, then thoughtful. "Hmmm. I hadn't considered that. Maybe you're right."

"But I'll keep looking."

She frowned. "On second thought, perhaps that's not such a good idea. I think you're right and we *don't* want to solve the problem too soon. Take your focus off finding the renegade, and look for ways to use the situation to recruit Carli MacLeod, instead. And of course, keep an ear on what the Board is up to, also, if you can."

"I'll try."

"Later, then."

"*Te amo*, Mother."

THOSE LOW-DOWN, DIRTY BIFURCATION BLUES

As Pablo was ending the call with Mother, Buddy presented himself.

=Where the hell have you been? Everything's going wrong. The launch has been moved up. . . .=

=Don't start. Please. I need your help. I've got to take care of several of Uncle Sam's administrative functions. Could you take over the beanlink traces?=

=Maybe I'd better do the meetings. I've done Uncle Sam more than you have.=

The upcoming meetings—a biweekly staff meeting, a private reprimand of one of Uncle Sam's managers for her team's poor performance, and then logging onto the net for a *virtu*-meeting of Waldos, Inc.'s, Board to brief them on the renegade—promised to be not only

Buddy lowered his shields.

=I know. I peeked in over your shoulder.= Amusement. =So the old witch is worried, eh?=

=Sure. Or I could handle the administrative stuff, if you prefer, and you could do the searches.=

A mental shrug. =Your choice.=

He beanlinked over to the computational lab, and called up and queried the secured search routine Pablo had started.

In Pablo's absence it had made some assumptions that probably weren't ideal. He settled

tedious, but terrifying as well. If he
didn't play it just right, he could ruin
everything.

I must be out of my mind, he thought,
to choose to do this when I have an easy
out.

On the other hand—and he shielded
the thought from Buddy—he knew he
couldn't trust Buddy to play it straight.

down to make corrections
and finish the searches.

He overheard Pablo's
thought. Too true, he
mused privately. But hey,
my heart is pure.

DANIEL

SURVEILLANCE SUCKS . . . AND NOT IN A GOOD WAY

Daniel pulled the heavy door open. The smells and noise that issued on a current of moist, icy air from inside The Protein Bomb made him reel. He entered, and stood with a hand on the doorjamb while he muted his olfactory and aural inputs, and dropped his tactile temperature sense to human-normal.

Carli MacLeod had lost him on Coors and 4th. Several whips had come out of an alley before him and he'd had to wait in the shadows until they had passed. This establishment was the only place open that she could have reached so quickly, though, and her tracking signal was definitely stronger now; she had to be in here.

Then he spotted her making her way through the crowds toward the back of the dance floor. She stopped to talk to a pair of young men who were laughing, enjoining her to dance.

Daniel had replaced Teru at the pilot interface several hours earlier, on his return from Shasta Station. Teru had managed to tag MacLeod's cool suit that afternoon. Daniel had been following MacLeod's signal through the wet streets of the West Mesa commercial district since she had left that apartment in the university district.

She had eaten at a café and then headed out to Rio Rancho. With the onset of twilight a fog had settled over the city, and had turned to a drizzly rain. Meanwhile Daniel had sneaked dutifully along behind MacLeod, concluding early on that little in this world was more boring than keeping someone under surveillance.

He spotted only one public exit from this place. Unless she was a friend of the management, Daniel wouldn't have to worry so much about losing her for a while. He turned off the pinstripes and unzipped his cool suit, peeling it down to the waist. Then he wiped at the rainwater on his face.

The air was hot and steamy. Naked people, both painted and unpainted, and mostly naked people with patches of color and lights strung over their loins and torsos crowded the dance floor, writhing to loud body music. A maelstrom greeted him: raised voices, laughter, music that rippled and pounded and stalked you like a live thing, sweat and incense, a confusion of moving images, piñon woodsmoke from open braziers around the room's periphery. Those caught Daniel's eye; legally a little risky, open burning like that.

Like high-voltage fireflies, or camera flashes, tiny, holographic images shadowed and illuminated the mist-filled room in needles of brilliance, a galaxy of pinpoints that exploded among the dancers: lighting a breast in one place, a thigh in another, a grimacing mouth somewhere else. These were underlain by slow pulses of color from the walls, ceiling, and floor.

Two groups of people, one entering and one leaving, collided with each other and jostled him aside. He strained to see past them; MacLeod had disappeared. But he spotted a raised platform across the dance floor that would make a better vantage point.

A young woman stood before him. Her body was almost that of a child: tiny breasts, thin hips and legs, a small triangle of blond pubic hair. He focused on her face; her lips were moving. Daniel shouted, "What?"

". . . check your clothes?"

"Oh. Right."

Daniel pulled his cool suit off, then his boots. Then he fumbled with the stays of his cotton shirt. The girl-woman smiled and helped him undress. The clothing should have been soaked with sweat; he hoped she didn't notice.

She pressed microcrystal studs into the collar of his shirt and the waist of his drawstring pants, and pressed a third one to his wrist. After a hesitation, he took his briefs off. She flashed him another smile and pointed to the shelves of clear acrylic by the door.

"Shoes over there," she shouted.

He stared at the black boots he held and then looked up to see her disappear, dancing, into the throng with his clothes slung over her arm, the wiry muscles in her calves, buttocks, and arms moving, swelling, and contracting to the music.

Muscle dancer, he thought. He was thankful that his erection remained back at Austin where it belonged.

He squeezed his boots onto the shelf amid the thousands of other shoes, and then he walked down the ramp onto the dance floor. MacLeod was still nowhere to be seen. Sweaty bodies jarred Daniel as he worked his way to the back, where the elevated platform of tables was.

When he finally made it off the dance floor through a blast of wind at the base of the steps, he leaned briefly against the railing. The wall of wind cut off some of the sound from the floor; the music was loud here but not deafening. He adjusted his hearing anyway, dampened the lower frequencies and augmented the upper. The voices of those at the tables became clearer to him. He looked around at the people who sat at the tables, and started—MacLeod sat alone at a nearby table and she was looking him over.

A pickup was not at all what he had had in mind. But there were no empty tables he could slip over to. Well, he thought ruefully, it would be an extremely effective way to keep her in sight.

Daniel returned her gaze in what he hoped was a convincing fashion and, after a pause, walked over. He gestured at the empty chair across from her.

"May I?"

"By all means." She extended a braceleted arm in invitation.

Daniel sat down and looked her over. She was maybe a couple inches shorter than his real body. She wore no makeup. Her figure was a woman's figure—not girlish. Her breasts were full but not too large. Her nipples were a dark pink, and they were erect. The sight gave him another erection, back in his crèche in Austin. Her hair was a blond so pale it was almost silver, unwaxed, in a simple bob just above her shoulders.

But it was her face that was most unusual. It was the sort of face you could watch for hours and never grow bored with. This was not simply because of her features themselves, which were vaguely Scandinavian, Daniel thought, with her square jaw and freckles. It was because her face was such a clear mirror of her feelings.

She had eyes of a quite amazing grey. He would never have thought grey eyes could be such an attractive color. They were large and wide-set, and at the moment they were filled with curiosity—as well as some other emotion Daniel couldn't name. Crow's-feet spread out from the corners of her eyes, and a smile hovered at the corners of her lips—but beneath all this, Daniel saw a shadow when he looked at her, the same shadow he remembered on his mother's face for years after his brother had died.

Her kelly, fashioned into a locket pendant, dangled between her breasts; her arms, chest, and face were blanketed in pale brown freckles that made her appear younger than her thirty-eight years. Her netspecs, an expensive model, with built-in earphones, hung around her neck. A mesh glove—again, an expensive model—lay next to her drink.

OK, Sornsen, he thought, you've got a crush. Get a grip. You have a job to do.

"Carli," she said, touching her sternum with her fingertips. She had short, undecorated nails.

"Daniel. Do you—"

"Come here often?" Her face creased in a grin, forgiving the cliché. "Occasionally. And you?"

"Every once in a while," he replied. He stared out at the dancers, most of whom were abominable. Then he looked back at her. "Actually, no. This is only my third time in one of these bars, and my first time sober."

Her eyebrows went up, then her face went still. He wondered if he had said something wrong.

"I see," she said. She pursed her lips, lowered her gaze briefly to her drink, and then looked at him again, eyebrows still elevated. "You have the build of a muscle dancer."

"I'm an athlete. Not a dancer. I haven't got the grace for it." The lie came easily, which Daniel wasn't sure he liked. But it disarmed her; she nodded slightly, as if something had been confirmed. Her mouth twisted into a wry little smile.

"You do appear a little ill at ease."

Daniel suppressed a wince, and then a nervous smile. "Supremely," he said.

She leaned back and put her arm over the back of her chair. "It grows on you," she assured him, and then looked out at the dance floor, seeming preoccupied. Sure, he thought. It grows on you. Like the Mold.

A waiter came by. Daniel ordered a Phase-out and a bowl of olives. He sat back.

"What are you thinking about?" he asked.

Her gaze leveled on him.

"I must say you're not at all what I expected."

He half-smiled in return. "What do you mean?"

"I mean that I was uncertain whether you would follow me in here. When you did, I expected that you might introduce yourself. But since you sat down, you're not behaving in accordance with my expectations at all."

She paused, but Daniel only looked at her. His smile had frozen in place.

She went on, "Of course, my first thought when I noticed you at the university was that you were obsessive, maybe even psychotic. But all your mannerisms are so polite—you've been keeping your gaze so carefully on my face. If you were a psycho, there would be something, well, *wrong* about you. Something off.

"You do," she said thoughtfully, "have a very strange look about you, you know. But I've figured out what it is. You don't blink enough. I've been wondering if you have artificial eyes." When Daniel said nothing, she continued, "But I don't really think you're an ax murderer or anything like that.

"The second possibility is that you're with the government. But if you were a government agent, you would be older, and glibber, somehow. You'd have more gloss to your approach. So what are you? Why have you been following me all evening? I've been trying to work it out."

Briefly Daniel felt annoyed at Teru—though in fairness there had been no time for a debriefing—for being seen by MacLeod in Daniel's proxy and not telling him. Then an image of Krueger formed in his mind. He's going to be really unhappy about this, Daniel thought.

I'm a proxy-jock, though—what do they expect? and he mentally discarded his orders. He leaned forward.

"You're right. I have been following you. I can't tell you why, not here. But I mean you no harm."

She returned his gaze for a moment without speaking. "How reassuring," she said finally.

The waiter brought Daniel's drink and the olives, and then pressed a lighted rod to the stud at Daniel's wrist. MacLeod turned down another drink. Her gaze was again on the crowded dance floor.

Daniel took a gulp of the sour green liquor and followed with an olive.

Tell her about Kaleidas? And if she wasn't the one the renegade was after (unlikely at this point, but still a possibility), if she wasn't selected for recruitment or didn't want to be recruited? . . . He had better think of a convincing lie. One that a smart, skeptical daughter of a senator would believe.

The music collapsed into silence in the way that only body music could. The lights died down and the dancers began to leave the floor. Soon only one was left: one of the two young men with whom MacLeod had been speaking.

He stood alone on the darkened floor. The floor and wall lights were dim. He bowed his head as though he were lost in thought, and the light turned his long red hair to liquid copper. The hair stood out from his head in a hundred stiff, fingerlike plaits and then fell over his shoulders and down his back. Hair that long worn unwaxed was unfashionable, but on him it demanded acceptance. Daniel could not see his face, only shadows.

His body was excellently muscled; Daniel could almost count the tendons. He stood so still that Daniel thought for a moment he must be a proxy. Human bodies did not come so perfect in proportion and shape. He wore a codpiece of ivory-colored satin, on a thong. Copper wires with white jewels dangling from them coiled around each forearm.

There was no sound. No one moved or breathed. Then the lights exploded into sudden brilliance with the man at its focus, and he moved. His head went up—he was staring right at Daniel. The tendons in his neck stood out. An arm shot out, the hand balled in a fist that trembled as if it clung to life. And then he melted to the floor. And burst into motion with the music.

The man did things with his body that Daniel would have thought impossible. Knots of muscle ran along his arms, back, abdomen; down his thighs and up again. He moved with sinuous seduction, with jarring stops; he flowed, coiled, froze in impossible shapes for a heart-rending beat, burst into motion again. Sweat dripped from him, was hurled from his hair. Every movement shouted passion, terror, rage. His body was an unvoiced scream.

The music stopped, sharp and discordant, as the lights slammed off. An afterimage of the dancer lingered: legs apart, arms out, their fists clenched, and head up, lips pulled back from his teeth in a rictus. Murmurs started in the darkness.

When the music and color pulses began again, the dancer was gone.

Daniel looked back at MacLeod. Her eyebrows were up, but she didn't speak, and neither did Daniel. They sipped at their drinks.

After a few minutes the dancer appeared from a back door and walked over to them. He pulled up a chair and sat on it backwards, arms over the chair back and knees protruding to the sides. He smiled at Daniel. His eyes were traced by eyeliner, his lips reddened with some rouge. Light makeup for a professional muscle dancer, but he needed little. He had removed his bracelets and put on a short robe of ivory satin that matched his codpiece. He wiped the sweat from his face, neck, and chest with a towel, and looked at MacLeod.

"What'd ya think, Carli?"

She gave him a fond, amused look. "Outstanding, as usual. Daniel, this is Paint. Paint, Daniel."

The dancer's gaze went to Daniel, and stayed there. "Got plans f'later?"

Daniel crossed his legs, uncomfortable. "Yes."

The dancer shrugged again. "Shame. You sure pick pretties, Carli." He stood. "Back on the floor." As he passed Daniel, he ran a finger along Daniel's shoulder. " 'F ya change your mind," he said.

There was amusement in MacLeod's eyes when Daniel looked back at her.

"Is your name really Daniel?" she asked.

"It is."

"Daniel, or Dan?"

"Daniel. I hate nicknames."

She laughed. Her laughter was as light as her eyes. "You *are* young. Well, come, Daniel. We'll go someplace where you're more comfortable, and you can tell me why you're following me."

When they got out onto the street the rain had stopped. The storm had cooled the air. The clouds glowed amber and salmon; the buildings were dark monoliths against them. The mercury streetlights were hazed by fog. Water running down the sheer walls and through the gutters gurgled beneath a distant shouting.

Whips were on the prowl, Daniel realized, and wished he were back at Austin. Whips had killed his brother when he was a child. And the proxy body he wore made him feel more vulnerable, not less. He was still paying for it with service. He could defeat five, or six, but they traveled in packs of a dozen or more. If he damaged or totaled the proxy, he could end up indentured for the rest of his life.

MacLeod seemed unconcerned. She took a deep breath. "It's cooled down quite a bit, don't you think?"

"Sure has." Then he looked down and cursed. The boots on his feet were brown, not black.

"I'd better go back," he said. "I picked up someone else's boots."

"Nonsense. It's expected. You've changed your shoes, Daniel."

"Is that where the saying comes from?"

"If it isn't, it should be."

They walked along the street. A government collovehicle hummed past, a few bikes and a ricky, but hardly anyone was out, even though it was a good hour or more till curfew. The shouting had ceased.

"Where do you want to go?" MacLeod asked him.

"Anywhere but a body bar, if that's all right."

"Sure."

"I've seen other dancers, but never anyone like him," Daniel said. "It was incredible. Disturbing."

"He's angry," she said.

"He doesn't want to go down without a fight, but there's nothing to fight against. I remember the feeling."

She gave him a sharp look. "*On the Brink,* eh? But you no longer feel like fighting?"

Daniel paused. "I read the book. I believed it for a while." He hesitated, then decided to be direct.

"I still do. And as a matter of fact, I am fighting now. Not just raging, not blowing my energy off uselessly into the cosmos. There are ways to make a difference."

They crossed a bridge over the drain and the train tunnel. A train rumbled by and the bridge trembled beneath their feet. She was looking at him sidelong. "And what way is that?"

"I looked hard until I found some people who are going to change things, who are taking action to help save the planet."

MacLeod was looking at him through narrowed eyes. "Ah. Suddenly I understand. A fanatic. Someone With An Answer."

Daniel shrugged, hackles rising at her sharp tone. "As it happens, I do have an answer."

"And what is that?"

He gazed at her without replying. They had stopped walking.

"I see—Someone With A *Secret* Answer," she said. "Devoted to a clandestine cause that will save the world. What group do you belong to? Priority Earth? SYN?"

"You haven't heard of my group. We really *are* secret. Your father has, maybe, heard of us once in his career."

"Is that a fact? Well, allow me to be blunt. There is serious work being done right now, and extremist groups like yours only make a mockery of those efforts. I have nothing but contempt for people like you."

Daniel's hands went up. "Look, this is going off on a tangent. You

misunderstand me. I'm not a terrorist and I'm not trying to win you
to any cause. Your life is in danger."

She glanced at him, archly. "My, how dramatic. From whom? You?
Or perhaps another terrorist group?"

He gripped her arm. "Whether you believe it or not," he repeated,
"your life is in danger. And like it or not, we're going to protect you."

"Take your hand off my arm." Her voice was low and dangerous.
He released her.

"I'm not interested in your cause," she said, "and I don't believe
your threats. And if I see you following me again, I have some friends
with connections who will be delighted to make life very difficult for
you. Do you follow?"

Daniel looked down, briefly, pinching the bridge of his nose and
trying to decide how much to say. When he looked up again, he was
staring into a pulse gun she had leveled at him. He'd better make this
good.

"You don't have to believe me now," he said. "Just listen. There
will be a woman. Or something that looks like a woman. It will be tall
and have an unusual complexion. It's so strong and can move so fast
you won't be able to fight or run or even yell for help. It's killed once
already and we think it's after you.

"So if you see it, run like hell and pray it hasn't seen you. Got it?"

She was holding the gun two-handed now, mere inches from his
face. "I didn't want to get nasty, Daniel," she said, "but you're forcing me to. So I'm going to count to three. If you're within my sights
at that time I'll blow your brains all over the street. One."

"Ask your father about KaleidoScope," Daniel said.

"Two." Her hands were steady.

"You'll hear from me again—if you're lucky."

Daniel exploded into a flat run, and made it halfway to Coors Road
in seconds. She never made it to three, he thought with satisfaction.
His heart rate, back in Austin, crept back down from stampede mode.

He looked back, amplifying his infrared. Tendrils of light, the heat
plume from her cool suit, curled upward like glowing smoke through
the fog. The plume stayed in the same spot for a moment, then receded.

At a safe distance, he followed her down into the subway. He rode
in a separate car in the train on the way to her home, and once she had
gone inside her apartment building, found a step to sit on across the
street. A stripboard suspended over the culvert blinked commercials

and public service announcements at him, casting a blue glow across the empty street.

Daniel heard slow footsteps splashing through the rain gutters, and sprang to his feet, focusing on the sound. A dark figure wearing tattered layers climbed over a fence from inside the culvert and shuffled up the street. He zoomed and scanned on the figure.

The infrared pattern was clearly human. Not the renegade, then. His amplified hearing caught snatches of conversation from the rain tunnels. Peteys. He released the breath he'd been holding and sat back down. He activated a strong, scrambled signal on an Austin frequency.

"This is Sornsen," he subvoked. "Anyone monitoring?"

"Go ahead; we're receiving." Reception was poor. The fog was interfering. From the voice, it was Krueger himself.

"I made contact with MacLeod. She spotted me following her, so I had to tell her a little."

There was a silence. "I hope you were circumspect, Sornsen."

"I was. She's touchy, boss. And smart. There'll be problems. I told her nothing about us, just told her to ask her dad about KaleidoScope. We'll have to let something leak to him."

Krueger was silent for another second. "We don't have to let anything leak. Her father knows about us."

"Oh. Is that a problem?"

"No. I don't know. I hope not. I'll take care of it." Pause. "It better have been necessary."

"It was. She got hostile. I'll keep a very circumspect eye on her and wait. Unless the renegade makes a try, in which case—"

"You'll disarm both and bring them here whether they will or no."

Daniel hoped he was hearing irony in Krueger's voice. "Right," he said. He paused. "Listen, there's one other thing. She met with a muscle dancer named Paint, who dances at a local club—The Protein Bomb—possibly on a regular basis. The file on her didn't say anything about her having links with the underculture, and I don't remember a boyfriend or anyone else like him in her file. Do you think it's important?"

"Might be." There was a moment of white noise. "We'll check on it at this end. Also, we've lost the renegade's signal. . . . Don't panic; it's probably just the fog and all the sunspot activity. We'll keep trying to track the renegade down. We know that it's currently somewhere north or east of the Sandias," Krueger added, "so keep your eyes open."

"Right."

"And be careful."

Daniel snorted and didn't reply. He deactivated his throat transceiver and moved into the shadow of the doorway across from MacLeod's apartment building.

GEE, MA, I WANNA GO HOME

A call came in on Uncle Sam's kelly. Pablo assumed prime. With a double-twitch of his closed eyes, he called up his proxy control system, shut down the simile he and Buddy were playing with Mara and Obediah, and faced into Uncle Sam's proxy.

A call came in, interrupting the simile they were running. As usual, Pablo assumed prime and faced them into Uncle Sam's proxy.

All was still. The lights were dim; moonlight spilled in through the glass wall, illuminating the sharp angles, statuary, pots, and other surfaces of Samson Krueger's office. Outside, in the shadowy bushes, rodent eyes gleamed.

It was dark. The room was filled with soft sounds: the cool air coming from the HVAC vents at the bed's foot, the tapping of footsteps in the corridor outside.

The transmission was from Uncle Daniel.

The transmission was from Uncle Daniel. He listened.

"Go ahead," he-Krueger said, sitting up in bed, in Uncle Sam's voice, "we're receiving."

His Krueger syntellect was loaded and standing by; swiftly as he spoke he called up the chat analyzer.

"I made contact with MacLeod," Uncle Daniel said. "She spotted me following her, so I had to tell her a little."

The horizontal bars in the "Krueger's Mood" window indicated that Uncle Sam was likely to be irritable—being awakened from sleep after a series of minor to moderate administrative hassles that day, on top of the escape of the renegade, would lead him to be even more out-of-sorts than usual—though the syntellect also noted that Uncle Sam tended to be a bit more tolerant of Uncle Daniel than of most others under his authority.

Three modes were lit up in the "Suggested Responses" windowpane.

DOMINATE [DIRECT MODE]: "God damn it! You should know better than to disclose classified information!" [probability 35%]

Buddy considered the suggested responses.

DOMINATE [INDIRECT MODE]: "Congratulations, Sornsen; you've just put eighteen years and hundreds of billions of dollars of covert research at risk." [probability 39%]

BUILD/CONSOLIDATE RAPPORT [DIRECT]: "I hope you were circumspect." [probability 26%]

None was overwhelmingly the preferred response. He hesitated.

=Buddy?=

=Uncle Daniel is quite loyal toward Uncle Sam. We could be challenged as an impostor at any time. We need allies. It seems to me that antagonizing him when he doesn't threaten us serves no useful purpose.=

Buddy was right.

"I hope you were circumspect, Sornsen," Pablo said.

"I was. She's touchy, boss. And smart. There'll be problems. I told her nothing about us, just told her to ask her dad about KaleidoScope. We'll have to let something leak to him."

Shock. Uncle Chauncy D'Auber was not only intimately aware of the goings-on, he had power over Mother. She wouldn't like this development one bit.

=Big trouble. Mother will have to be informed immediately.=

Shock. Mother wouldn't like this news; Uncle Chauncy was a powerful man, and he frightened her.

He concealed from Pablo a sense that—he didn't yet know how, but—this could serve his purposes.

=I'll twin up and brief her.=

Pablo shielded the thought that sprang into his head: Great. *He* gets to go home and *I'm* stuck here playing "Spot the Impostor" with Krueger's staff.

Buddy shielded his own awareness of Pablo's resentment, and his relief that it would be him briefing her rather than Pablo. Pablo had no self-preservation instincts when it came to Mother.

=All right; go.=

He released the face controls to Buddy.

He took hold of the face and—

Pablo memorized the chat analyzer's recommended response, and once the proxy interface control was returned to him, said, "We don't have to let anything leak. Her father knows about us."

"Oh. Is that a problem?" Uncle Daniel asked.

—took over prime from Pablo long enough to activate twin mode and face into his proxy control system. Then he released the Krueger proxy to Pablo and returned to their own, principal proxy back home, in Kaleidas.

With a sigh of sheer happiness, he slipped his body on. He'd been too long away.

Is what a problem? Pablo wondered; the inputs coming from Buddy were distracting him.

=Shield, please.=

=Right.=

"No. I don't know," he-Krueger stammered. He erected his own barrier between him and Buddy, and scrambled to recall the chat analyzer, which Buddy had put away a few seconds earlier. "I hope not."

He found his place, ditched the careful strategizing, and chose the most likely response. "I'll take care of it. It better have been necessary."

"It was. She got hostile. I'll keep a very circumspect eye on her and wait. Unless the renegade makes a try, in which case—"

"You'll disarm both," Pablo-Krueger extemporized, "and bring them here whether they will or no."

He didn't need the chat analyzer to tell him how fiercely Mother wanted Carli MacLeod.

Daniel was talking. "Listen, there's one other

He pushed off, and his body tore loose from its Velcroed position on the wall by his crèche.

=Sorry. Shield me back.=

He raised a barrier between himself and Pablo and, avoiding with a shudder a glance at the cocoon that held his and Pablo's host body, propelled himself toward the exit.

He could tell he had been Earth-side too long—his first stride sent him soaring through the air in the low-gee chamber. After that he remembered to shuffle.

The door was a round-cornered rectangle against the far wall, twenty meters away. Before it lay racks of machinery and crèches. Flesh-tender robots crawled along tracks set amid the banks of icon-decorated crèches; he ritually touched his fingers to his lips as he passed them; the machinery whispered greetings.

In the exam area at the back, beyond the banks of crèches, Uncle Marsh was bent over an open crèche. The physician's casual attitude toward the contents of the crèches never ceased to amaze him. Keeping his distance, Buddy called out a greeting.

Uncle Marsh looked around. "Pablo! You're back!"

"Only briefly." Buddy gestured at the open crèche. "Nothing serious, I hope?"

"Not at all. Luis has a clogged colostomy tube, is all."

thing. She met with a muscle dancer named Paint,
who dances at a local
club—The Protein Bomb—
possibly on a regular
basis. The file on her didn't
say anything about her
having links with the un-
derculture, and I don't remember a boyfriend or
anyone else like him in her
file. Do you think it's
important?"

He called up a key-
board and made a note in
his to-do pad.

"Might be. We'll check
on it at this end. Also," he-
Krueger added (glancing
at the to-do list reminded
him of something he
should let Uncle Daniel
know), "we've lost the
renegade's signal."

The chat analyzer sug-
gested following up with
a reassurance. "Don't
panic; it's probably just
the fog and all the sunspot
activity. We know that it's
currently somewhere
north or east of the San-
dias, so keep your eyes
open."

"Right."

"And be careful."

Severing the connection,
Pablo settled back onto the
bed and reactivated the
simile. Without Buddy or his

Near the entrance, at the altar, two
other crèche children were depositing
gifts of coin, toys, and food at Mother's
crèche. With expressions of delight and
surprise, they greeted Buddy by hand signal; he returned the signal.

"Where is Mother?"

"In her chambers," Mara replied.

"Will you be here long?" asked Joe.
"Join us at face-play later."

"Can't—sorry."

She answered his knock, wearing a robe
and a frown.

"Mother."

"Pablo! What are you doing here?
What's wrong?"

Then, glancing both ways down the
corridor, she opened the door and gestured him in.

She sat down at her desk. Her computer's sensor field churned out data,
emitting a lattice of symbols and numbers that tumbled down, forming a heli-
cal cone. Buddy stood in the small open
space between her desk and her sheet-
snarled bed, arms at his sides, focusing
on remaining calm.

"Why are you here? Have you been discovered?"

"No. All is well."

"Then why aren't you back in Austin?"
She slammed a fist onto her desktop.
"Idiot! Someone might detect Krueger's
disappearance!"

He shook his head, held up his hands.
"It's all right. I'm twinning. I-Krueger am
currently receiving a report from Uncle
Daniel Sorensen. I came to give
you some important news."

"Twinning?" Her expression changed.

crèche-mates, it was paltry distraction.

"Really? I couldn't tell. You've mastered the skill far better than I could ever have hoped. But—it's risky, Pablo. Why didn't you radio me instead?"

Buddy hesitated. "I needed to come home. To see the others." He studied her expression. "You're angry."

Mother lowered her head briefly, shook it. "No, I'm not. Come here."

Buddy eyed her outstretched arms, and revulsion and terror surged through him. He dropped his shields.

=Pablo! Pablo—*I need you!*=

Buddy's distress intruded on his awareness. He deactivated the simile and returned to Uncle Sam's proxy, reaching out mentally.

No response.

Suppressing a shudder and a wave of nausea, he went to Mother.

Relief came, as he sensed Pablo's awareness.

Leaving Krueger's proxy on auto-pilot, he went with Buddy to Mother, and—

She took Buddy into her lap, as Pablo joined him. Buddy inched back from the face.

—laid his cheek against her chest. With a happy sigh, he thrust a plastic thumb into his mouth.

Mother, he thought. *Te amo.*

To Buddy's disgust, Pablo stuck a plastic thumb into their mouth. It's her fault he's like this, he thought. Bitch. I hate you.

=*Buddy!*=

Why did he have to be so damned antagonistic? Why couldn't he just,for once, try to get along?

He shouldn't have called Pablo. This was only making things worse. Pablo, you naive little idiot.

=Leave this to me.=

Slammed back into Uncle Sam's body, Pablo drew his-Krueger's knees up and

So saying, he shoved Pablo out of their proxy and threw his shields up, hard.

leaned against the pillows—out of breath, mouth dry. He could feel his face burning, back in its crèche, and a lump of grief tried to work its way up his throat.

=Damn you, Buddy. You'll ruin everything.=

BUDDY

HE'S NO MAMA'S BOY

Mother stroked his head. Buddy pulled the thumb out of his mouth, suppressing another shudder.

"You must hurry," she said. "They could come across Krueger any day. We are at grave risk every moment you are down there."

"I understand. I'm doing my best."

"What is your news?"

She *really* is not going to like this. "Uncle Daniel has revealed to Carli MacLeod that her father is involved with KaleidoScope."

He felt her stiffen; he wished he could see her face, but he didn't dare move for fear of setting her off.

"I must think about this," she said, slowly. "This is potentially explosive. Damn. Damn. This will call for some swift damage control." She nudged him off her lap. "Go back to Austin now and await my instructions."

Buddy didn't move.

"What are you waiting for?" she snapped.

He didn't give a shit about her, but he cared for Pablo, and spoke up on his behalf. "It's hard, Mother. We're lonely. We fear discovery."

She gave him a sharp, odd look. " 'We'?"

He went cold. "I."

She slouched in her chair with a sigh. "I know this must be difficult for you. But you can't bail out now. If you leave, they'll find out about Krueger."

"I'm tired of this game, Mother. Let us come home."

She took his face in her hands. "Pablo. Listen to me. We can't turn back now. You can't imagine what's at risk."

Anger, briefly, overcame common sense. "I don't care anymore."

With a snarl, she jerked her hand back as if to slap him. He managed not to flinch. She stared, and he wondered if she was going to lose it completely. Come on, bitch, he thought. I'm not afraid of you. Come on.

She must have read something of his feelings in his proxy's face, because after a moment she lowered her hand.

"You'd better care," she said. "If we don't succeed with *Exodus*, they'll arrange an 'accident' for you children." Buddy started to speak; she interrupted. "I've been in this business for a long time now; I know what they're like. It's a dirty, dirty business. They'll do anything to save their asses.

"You *have* to trust me and do as I say. You're the oldest and smartest; you're the only one I can trust with this. Think of your crèche-mates."

He said nothing. He *was* thinking of his crèche-mates—of Pablo, the poor fool, and the rest of the children who trusted this woman, despite her manifold cruelties.

But what if she was right?

No. Like everything else, it was manipulation. Manipulation and paranoia.

The tension between them ebbed as the annoyance on her face transformed to thoughtfulness.

"I have the solution." She paused. "It won't be easy. I don't know if you can do it."

He straightened, indignant. "I can do it."

More manipulation, he knew it, but even so he wasn't immune.

"Very well, then. Forget our original plan. Order Sornsen to bring Carli MacLeod in, immediately. Ship her here to Kaleidas—tell her whatever you have to, to get her to agree, and drop your efforts to influence the Board of Directors. Once we have MacLeod we won't need an in with the Board; we can cease this charade once and for all."

This acceleration would screw up *his* plan.

"What about our window? They'll still have time to stop us, if they find out too soon."

"Once we have MacLeod, it won't matter."

He looked at her without speaking.

"Well," she said. "You want to come home; this is the only way."

"All right. I'll do it."

He had to agree; he had no choice. But he didn't have to act on it, or tell Pablo.

And he didn't have to go back to Austin right away, either, come to think of it—the kids swapped bodies all the time without the adults' knowledge. They'd even made a game of switching out and fooling the ID software during some of Aunt Jenna's proxy and psych tests, just to see if they could, and they'd never been caught yet. It was hilarious to stand there while the grown-ups were talking to their bodies, thinking they were talking to one child when they were actually talking to a different one . . . and not understanding all the children's giggles and significant looks.

Yeah, he could borrow one of the other kids' spare proxies, and hang around for a while, be with his crèche-mates, right under her ugly nose, without her knowing. Think you know everything, don't you, old hag? he thought, as he left her quarters. Well, you don't. Not by a long shot.

Hang around for a while. Yes, he liked that idea. Who needed Pablo, anyhow?

CARLI

Entropy and Pain

The box of groceries sat outside her apt door. As she keyed in her unlock code, the jellophone started chiming inside the room. Carli pushed the door open and pushed the groceries inside with her foot. She slammed the door behind her as the bar of light globes suspended over the couch came on, threw her cool suit over the arm of the squish-chair, and caught the phone on the fourth chime.

The jellowall began to glow; a milky image of Tania—an ex-girlfriend of Paint's—coalesced beyond the glass surface. The cat rubbed against Carli's legs and yowled.

Tania was crying, and looked as though she had been for some time. Her voice had a tremor. "'N I come stay with you tonight, Carli?"

Carli sat down in the desk chair, picked up Argyle and stroked him. Argyle pushed against her hand, began to lick her knuckles with his coarse tongue. Carli tried to meet Tania's skittish gaze.

"Tania, what's wrong? Damn you, Argyle, don't bite!" She dropped the cat on the floor, stuck her knuckle into her mouth, tasted salt. And she studied Paint's old girlfriend.

Tania's face paint was smeared all down her face and neck, revealing rows of half-healed burns and cuts. Her eyes were raw and frightening. She hugged herself; her arms and legs were visibly trembling. Carli had seen her this bad only once: three weeks after Paint had been sent to prison. Argyle jumped back up in Carli's lap, kneaded the flesh of her thighs, and began to purr. Tania was talking.

"It wasn't supposed to be . . . 'T's usually jink; something went wrong this time. . . . I'n't know what to do or where to go. He's hurting me, *really* hurting. . . ."

"Just a minute, Tania. Lights down."

The bar of light over the couch went dark. Carrying Argyle, Carli went over to the window, depolarized the glass, and looked out. The knots and coils of whitewashed copper cooling pipes partly obscured her view of the street, ten stories below, but the fog outside the glass was so thick now that she would not have been able to see anyhow. The world outside was drowned in eerie, luminescent soup.

She was sure he was down there.

Carli considered. He had not struck her as all that dangerous, until she had seen him sprint. Anyone with that kind of mass-acceleration ratio was not to be underestimated, no matter how pretty he was, nor how sincere he appeared.

She glanced back again at Tania, who was wiping her nose on a rag. Carli could make out bruises on her wrists, and welts on her shoulders.

Carli made a decision. That Daniel person might be a bit of a loon, but she was reasonably sure he was not homicidal. And Tania would have more protection here than she would alone, or in some sadistic maniac's apartment.

She moved back to the phone. "You can stay here. Can you make it OK?"

Tania sniffed and wiped, nodded. "I have a can of snitch. And I'm not too far. Thanks, Carli. Thank you. I didn't know who else to nack on. I didn't know what to do. . . ."

"Just come on over. You can share the couch with Argyle." Carli hesitated for a moment. "Come the hidey way, all right?"

Tania and Paint had always used the hidey way to get to Carli back when Paint was being sought by the law. The suggestion was an awkward reminder. Carli added quickly, "It'll be safer that way. No one'll know you're here."

Tania nodded. "You're schick, Carli." Her eyes were dripping water again, but her expression had already started to alter. She was beginning to look casual/hard. Her street face.

"Be careful about the curfew. And especially the whips."

A smile, almost a smirk, came onto Tania's face. It was a bit garish and haggard, but Carli was relieved to see it. A sobbing, stumbling Tania on the streets might as well have been wearing a big, bright neon *mug-me* sign.

"No big jig," Tania said. "See ya."

Carli broke the connection and sat down.

Kaleidoscope. *Ask your father about Kaleidoscope,* he had said. She couldn't imagine why he had thought her dad would know—or care—about his cause. Or perhaps he had thought just mentioning her dad would win her over. Like name-dropping her own father would somehow persuade her he was for real. Either he was incredibly naive, or he thought she was.

Fanatics were the last thing she needed in her life right now. No matter how nice-seeming or how articulate they were.

She gave Argyle a nudge. He landed heavily on the floor and moved at a stately pace to the couch, tail high. Carli pulled the pulse gun out of her pouch, checked the battery charge. Dead. She put the jellophone recorder on playback and went to find the charger. Stupid to carry a dead weapon anyhow. It was asking for trouble.

Her agent, Jan Wilson, appeared beyond the jellowall and, pacing, spoke to her while she was emptying her desk drawer onto the littered desktop.

"So how come you turned your kelly receiver off, D'Auber? 'Way, the *good* news is, the last of the paperwork has been processed. The rest of the divorce-settlement money is now in your acct. You've got enough to live high for a solid year, 'f you don't blow it all in Vegas. The *bad* news is, FFS Corp turned down your proposal. Fraser wants more details before he'll commit himself."

Carli turned around; behind the wall, Jan was examining her platinum-sheathed fingernails, legs crossed.

"That jerk!" Carli exploded. "He promised me—"

Jan Wilson's voice was talking over hers. ". . . real jig 'f y'ask me. He says they're being careful because their most recent joint venture with Yashiva Cooperative is eating up all their capital, but I think he's scared of OMNEX and the gag order. You're a high-risk investment, twitchie. Now, I know what you're going to say, but imho, it would be shitso to give them more information about your proposal than you already have. They're on your heels, twitchie, and they want the jig, if you know what I mean."

Carli leaned across the desk and hit the [FFWD>>] button. Wilson was a good financial agent, but her pseudo-jinkdom was annoying. Jan twitched, talked, and paced in fast motion. Carli leaned back, drawing a mental image of Peregrin Fraser, head of research for the Canadian firm FFS Corp, his tubby little body skewered on a spit, baking slowly over a butane fire.

The image was momentarily satisfying, but she shrugged off the anger. There were other sources of funding, and she had enough to live on for a good, long while.

Her ex-husband, Jeremiah, coalesced beyond the wall. He was looking at something in his lap, a photo perhaps; then he looked up, wearing a pained smile. There were dark circles under his eyes, and vertical lines between his brows. "Hi, Carli. Checking in again. Give me a call."

"Don't count on it," she said, and hit the fast-forward again. The wall flickered and her mother came on, sitting at her antique rosewood rolltop desk.

"Doll, can you come to Santa Fe for dinner tomorrow? Dad will be back in town, so we're having Jo, Michael, and the Rodrigueses over. . . . You remember Rhona, don't you? I think you went to St. John's with her niece." After a pause, she added, "Jeremiah is coming, too. Papa thinks he can help you with some useful contacts in the defense industry. . . ."

What defense? Carli thought, and fast-forwarded again.

No other messages.

So now Dad was trying to fix things between her and Jere. God damn it, she thought. She curled up on the couch, picked up Argyle, and buried her face in his fur, stroked his ears. He hooked his sharp claws into her shoulder and purred.

Her mind wandered again to Daniel. *Ask your father about Kaleidoscope.*

She hadn't spoken to her father or her mother—not about anything more important than shopping on the nets—in years.

I stopped raging and found some people who had some answers.

But the truth was, there were no answers. The world was stewing in its own pollution. The Earth was on the brink of becoming uninhabitable. And even if all the fixes worked—the orbital power stations, the stratospheric bacteria, the massive cloud seedings—it was too late to go back, too late for the more than a billion humans who had died or the billions more who were dying. Too late for tens of thousands of animal and plant species already extinct.

China, India, South and Central America, Africa—the death toll, human and nonhuman alike, was unspeakable. The U.S. was buying much of its food from Common Europe, Russia, and Canada, exporting its orbital and lunar technology, eking out barely enough raw resources from the moon to stave off economic collapse while fending off a rising tide of refugees it couldn't possibly incorporate. The world economy and the ecosphere were entwined in a death lock, a plummeting spiral. The interstellar probe was no panacea; it was a hallucination someone had had staring into the smoke of an opium pipe.

Nobody has any answers. The planet is dying and we're stuck with it. Damn Newton and his inertia, and while you're at it, damn thermo-dynamics. God damn entropy straight to hell.

She cleared the mess off of her desk, then went into the kitch-enette and poured herself a glass of Deluge. She sprinkled the last of her cinnamon into it, went into the living room, and sat down in the dark to watch the cascades of blinking neon, sodium, and xenon out-side, to brood and await Tania.

CELLOPHANE THOUGHTS

Dane Elisa Cae had discovered during her long run across the mudflats that day that she had access to memories, after all. But they were few, and fragile and transparent if she probed too hard: cellophane to her mind's touch.

She had been born in Coral Gables, in a small wooden house shrouded in white, peeling paint and cast iron; her only clear memory was of how her parents and sister and brothers had died when she was a teenager, in a mud tsunami that had wiped out half the city when a killer hurricane had hit.

She had been at school that evening, rehearsing for a performance of *A Streetcar Named Desire*. She remembered how she had longed for the role of Stella, but because of her freakish complexion she had been relegated to costumes. It had been raining for months, but the weather had always been wet in southern Florida.

She remembered looking up from her stitching at the other cos-tumers when the rumbling had started. She had thought it was an earthquake.

Other memories—vague ones—surfaced and receded: faces that had no names, disjointed wanderings, a rhythmic pounding, like drums, and a tiny voice. But the memories were either buried too deep for her to keep her thoughts on or they were unreal; she was uncertain which. They floated like debris through the chambers of her mind, blobs of memory unconnected by any bond of continuity.

She had run all day and most of the night. Now she was curled in the rusting hulk of an old land vehicle. The smells of rust and rotting cloth filled her nostrils, and she loathed the stench with an intensity that surprised her.

She shifted among the rags and flaking, moldy foam and rusted steel springs of her bed. The light grey blanket of the sky had long since faded to blackness. She had run very far and fast, and did not have an inkling where she was.

Her memories of the place with the buildings and the man at the gate had grown confused and false-seeming, almost as if she had dreamed them. Her only clear memories were that face she'd seen on awakening, that she should have known, and running down the road later with the rising sun heating her back.

But the certainty had grown in her over the day that this was no dream, no programmed simulation or mental game, as she'd first thought. She was here for a purpose, and she was guided.

Her destination had no taste in her mind; she moved solely on faith. Whatever directed her was invisible—completely intangible unless she strayed. And even then the correct course was the merest shining touch that brushed against her mind, or a quiet voice whispering secret commands. But she knew. She'd been chosen.

Dane sifted through her emotions, scrutinizing them. She was restless—and a little frightened. This told her she must be close. She strengthened the light receptivity of her eyes and looked out through the spikes of broken glass and twisted metal.

The clouds captured the orange glow of a city, beyond the black teeth of high mountain peaks. Between Dane and the mountains lay a wide bog that smelled of mold and rotting matter.

Or perhaps the ocean reached this far now. Dane Elisa Cae's last memories put her in Louisiana, so perhaps she was still near the coast. But New Orleans and Houston were long gone; she knew that much. Large sections of the South and East had long since drowned in shallow swamps of muddy, saline liquor: the new Atlantises.

Tomorrow she would find a road or bridge that crossed the bog. Or she would cross on foot. She would climb the foothills at the mountains' base and be in the city by midday. Satisfied, Dane Elisa Cae closed her eyes.

As her thoughts began to drift, the guidance spread through her like a dye through clear liquid. Of their own will, her fingers reached up and touched the back of her neck. Something was wrong there. She scowled and scratched at her neck till the skin peeled away and she dug out a tiny lump of metal trailing hairlike wires.

She sharpened her eyes to look at it, unsure whether she was more disturbed because it was there, or because she wasn't surprised it was there. Then she crushed it between her fingernails like an insect. She shifted again and pillowed her head on an arm.

As Dane fell asleep she found herself longing for arms about her, for comforting whispers, for living dreams and a black sky that blazed cold and fierce with stars.

DANIEL

WHIPS ON THE PROWL

Whips were nasty fighters. Daniel had had his own run-ins with them, during those years he'd spent in petey camps, before they'd gotten permanent-resident status. And supposedly things were even worse now—if that was possible. He'd seen a number of newscasts and documentaries in recent years that had made his skin crawl, so they were on his mind as he sat watching the front door of Carli's apartment building.

Occasionally as the hours passed he heard the distant, keening barks of whips hunting through the wet canyon streets, and police sirens. The cops would be hunting whips, or perhaps tracking illegal petes, not him. But the sound brought up old, unpleasant memories, and the hairs on his nape and forearms prickled. It was his own body's symptoms he sensed, not those of the proxy, and the flickers of double awareness left him vaguely nauseated and disoriented.

Then the shouting started less than a city block away, and drew quite rapidly louder. It was very near.

"*Fuck.*" He came to his feet, pressed himself against the black, shining bricks of the portico wall. His head went back. There was a sharp pain in his chest, back in the crèche, a constriction that he recognized as fear.

They were close, and drawing nearer. If they found him, they couldn't kill him—but they could hurt him, before he would disengage from his proxy, real bad. Nasty things sometimes happened to the minds of people who were severely injured in proxy.

Daniel licked his lips and activated systems displays. Needles jittered across his vision. He shut down all cosmetic systems—breathing, pulse, all smooth and semismooth muscle simulations—and shut down his antimatter cooling system to cool skin temperature to ambient, on the off chance they had IR shades.

Shutting off the coolant system that carried excess heat from the antimatter reactor to his proxy skin's surface, without shutting down the reactor itself, was risky. If internal temperatures were to rise above the boiling point of water, the cooling system would fail and heat generation would rocket upward. First his skin would melt, then his titanium and metaceramic frame would start to glow . . . and a few seconds later the antimatter storage bottle in his abdomen would fail and he'd leave a mile-wide crater in the ground.

Of course, that'd never happen—there were all kinds of fail-safes. If internal temperatures reached 200 degrees Fahrenheit, the reactor would simply shut down and the proxy would vent steam through its ears, nose, mouth, and anus (which gave a whole new meaning to the term "blowing his cover"). Still, it was hard to suppress his nervousness as he watched the temperature needle on the inner edge of his left eye creep upward . . . one hundred ten, one twelve . . .

The stance he had frozen himself in was very similar to the pose the dancer Paint had adopted at the end of his dance. Paint would appreciate the homage, he felt sure. The sincerest form of flattery.

One fifteen, the temperature needle read. One seventeen.

As motionless as Paint had stood earlier that night, though, Daniel was more so by far. His body was a far simpler, more powerful, and more obedient machine than any human body could claim to be. No ghost movement, no hissed intake of breath or scent of sweat and fear, would taint the whips' awareness as they passed him.

He would be as invisible, as unimportant, as a statue or a piece of abandoned machinery. Which, but for a trickle of current and the barest trace of a radio signal, he was.

One twenty. One twenty-three.

This might be some sort of blind behind which the renegade hoped to get Carli. But it wouldn't fit with Teru's analysis of the renegade's behavior from this incident and the former, quickly aborted one; whoever it was tended to show little creativity in its attempts at murder—merely a detachment so complete that, however cold-blooded it was, it seemed almost an innocent.

One twenty-eight. One thirty-two.

Beneath the eerie calls of the whips, Daniel heard the slap of footsteps in the water, a hiss of breath—the victim's. His own breath back in Austin quickened.

One thirty-five.

He had promised Krueger. Low profile. No heroics. He couldn't fight a pack of whips alone.

He would remain in the shadows and let them pass.

One forty-eight. He was doing fine; they'd be past well before the coolant safety systems triggered.

"Kai-ah-ah-ah-kaieee!"

At the scream, his own spine stiffened in its crèche. That cry carried the scent of blood. They had spotted their victim. Right next to his hiding place.

Shit. No room for heroics.

One fifty-seven.

The victim stumbled almost at his feet, where streetlight and shadow met. She looked up at him; her stare held a plea. She was an older woman, tawny leather skin, hair in a loose black knot—a style pathetically out-of-date—torn, sleeveless dress of cotton stripes, dyed burlap bag twisted with rope slung on her shoulder. A petey, or she might as well be.

One sixty-four.

Panting, she looked back and terror widened her gaze—she clawed her way to her feet, and was gone.

The whips passed him, galloping and howling, two breaths later. Their long hair hung in ropes, tied by bits of plastic—yellow, red, green, blue, orange; their skinny chests were bare, smeared with body paint, their bodies emaciated and pale as mushrooms. They were children.

Daniel glimpsed a face or two as they cavorted past—strips of plastic and tattered cloth fluttered about their loins; bony knees and elbows flailing; wild, gaunt faces; teeth filed to razor's edge. None of them was older than Daniel had been when he was recruited by KaleidoScope. They were more revolting, and pitiable, than terrifying.

The whips in their hands, though, which they cracked as they capered and howled, those were ugly. Fashioned of plastic, leather, bits of metal and glass, those would peel the skin from a person's body like wet tissue.

One seventy-two. They were passing now. Stay still, Sornsen. Stay still.

There were perhaps fifteen children. They loped easily, in groups of three or four, running without effort: toying with their prey. There had been death in that woman's eyes, and these children made a game of it, drank it, mainlined it.

One seventy-four . . . one eighty.

He'd seen the same look in the eyes of the whips who'd killed his seven-year-old brother, so very very long ago, when he'd stood up to them and refused to do what they said. Daniel had been three. While he hid under a pile of rags, watching, they had gang-raped Morris and then cut his throat.

Daniel had forgotten. No—not forgotten; simply refused to remember.

So much blood. It had gone everywhere. He recalled his mother's screams, when they'd told her.

One eighty-six. His proxy had plenty of coolth left. But he didn't. Rage went off in him like a psychic antimatter blast; he slammed cooling and power systems on. Power flooded his limbs and he shot out of his hiding place after the whips. The two who lagged farthest behind died instantly, their necks in his hands. It was easy. Their spines were as fragile as sand dollars: *crack,* and they went limp.

He dropped them. A group of four ahead—the one Daniel was closing on turned, laughing, to call back. He saw, instead of his comrades, Daniel—his laughter turned to a scream, and he was squeaking as he went down, throat crushed. Daniel did not remember striking him, only the surprised look on his smudged, child's face and the bony white hands at his throat as he collapsed—

The scream warned the rest. They turned away from their prey to do battle. Their whips recoiled, uncoiled, serpentine, as they surrounded him. Silently—these children were accustomed to fighting.

The whips did no harm to Daniel—his pain receptors couldn't be totally deactivated, but rage had deadened his awareness of pain. And his synthetic skin wasn't so easily torn as the real stuff.

It was over quickly. Daniel spotted their leader—walked into, through, a sheet of metal edges and glass, and enveloped the neck of a boy. Thumbs under the chin, a quick, twisting shove—the boy's eyes glazed; his mouth went slack. Daniel dropped him, stared down at him.

When he looked up, the others were disappearing into alleys, arms supporting each other, glancing back at him—silent like ghosts.

The woman, the intended victim, clung to a lamppost a short distance away, heaving great breaths. At Daniel's glance, she, too, slipped away. In that instant before she left, though, there had been a look of horror on her face.

There was blood on his hands, real blood that mingled with the crimson siloxane hydraulic fluid leaking from the gouges in his hands. Only a little real blood; the hot condensate that dripped from the cooling fins overhead was washing it away.

The four corpses and he were the only things in the street that didn't belong there. The street-cleaner waldos would find the bodies before morning, Daniel thought, and summon the cops. He slipped back into the shadows. Some part of his mind was whispering, *God, they're dead, my God, I killed them.* . . . Daniel sank against the wall of the building and pressed a cheek to the cool stone.

This hadn't been in the job description.

"Austin."

The word, as he subvoked it, lashed back into his ears like a schizophrenic whisper.

"Austin."

His forearms dribbled silky red liquid from a dozen razor-clean stripes. His face had taken the worst of the whipping; he must look dreadful. He had to get out of here—the waldos might come by any time.

Daniel shoved himself away from the wall. Trembles spread up his arms into his chest. He wondered if he had contracted epilepsy. His teeth were chattering.

Impossible. Proxies did not mirror adrenal function so closely. Self took no damage; this isn't real blood dripping into my eyes.

"Austin, this is Sornsen; is anyone monitoring? . . . *Austin!*"

He stumbled down the street, shouting over a broad range of frequencies, weaving like a drunkard in his haste to escape. *God damn you, Austin, fucking incompetent shitheads, answer, you assholes, answer, ANSWER.*

Someone finally heard him call, and they gave him directions to a pickup point near a pay phone at Central and Wyoming. He sank to the ground, stared at the marching tiles of the banner over the street, forgot where he was. He heard someone calling him, over and over, but he couldn't hear the words, and it didn't seem to matter much.

His eyes were running with tears, somewhere far away; a lump of nausea sat in the pit of his stomach. Morris had stayed behind to protect Daniel, instead of running.

He'd thought he'd put that memory to rest, long ago. It wasn't his fault; he knew it wasn't his fault.

Then his body jerked upright like a puppet. Someone—it had to be Teru—was monkeybacking him. She was taking over the proxy-pilot interface.

Panic seized him. He struggled against her, and his proxy's linkware reeled, a prisoner of conflicting commands—

No, not death, you'll be home soon, don't fight me, she was saying, and he realized he was screaming across the electromagnetic spectrum, all sorts of insanity, splashing and dancing like a madman in the gutters, across the sidewalk and into the street.

Then his linkware control of his proxy was gone. He listened and watched and felt the motions as his body straightened, rearranged its clothing. The walk wasn't even his.

She, Teru, ushered his body into an empty collocar that waited at the curb. Daniel didn't recall the car arriving. Dawn had come during his so brief struggle with Teru—too soon.

Time had escaped him; he had lost control.

Panic rose again, a scream in his throat, stopped at the cool black glaze of the interface. The proxy's mouth didn't even twitch as it settled back into the low passenger's seat.

As the vehicle rose on a column of pneumatic pressure, the dash lights and black cushions of the car, the sticky heat against his legs and back, the smell of warm plastic and mold and the hiss of pneumatics, tunneled away. Somewhere, narcotics slipped into his veins, spread through his muscles like mint ice. He slept.

KNOW YOUR ENEMY

By dawn the temperature had dropped. Dane awoke with a sense that she was shivering. She shook out her limbs, which were as stiff as if she had slept in an ice bath. She willed herself warmer, and when she was more comfortable she climbed out of the junked car and looked around.

She could see her surroundings more clearly now. Heaps and mounds of refuse, bits of plastic, wood, and rusting machines lay all about—remnants of an earlier time, a disposable civilization. Miner waldos, great grey and blue machines with long necks and boxlike, grabbing mouths, crept along, scooping up and dropping debris into their hoppers, where dozens of tiny waldo hands sorted them into different compartments. Other machines with pipes extending into the ground seesawed in place, next to big green tanks. Dane was unsure of the seesaw machines' purpose. Beyond them in the distance was a plant of some kind: tall, silver, cylindrical towers and stretches of pipe reflected sunlight.

The sun hung a fingerbreadth above the eastern hills. Overhead, the sky was dark and empty; a froth of white above the western tablelands was the only evidence of clouds. Far to the southwest lay the city. She looked toward it, and shivered again. She had dreamt of the city—vague, troubling dreams—dreams of death, underscored by drum beats. They dampened her desire to pursue whatever destiny awaited her.

Dane rose and picked her way through the detritus, giving the waldos a wide berth. Once she had reached the algae-filled pools that marked the northern edge of the bog beyond the mounds of trash, she began a swift-strided walk along its perimeter.

Just before dawn she had seen lights far away to the west, moving toward the sky glow that was the city. A road. She wouldn't have to cross the bog.

She didn't want to stay on roads. She didn't know whom she was hiding from, but she knew that she had enemies, people who sought her even now. Traveling on roads meant a greater risk of discovery. But crossing the bog would be much more difficult and time-consuming, and time was a critical factor.

The terrain was hilly and rough, cut through by muddy streams; the air stank of compost. She forced her way through branches and undergrowth. The soil on which she trod was spongy, rich with rotting vegetation and overgrown with gourd and grape vines, with wild, thorny bushes covered in red and yellow berries, and prickly pear cacti as tall as oaks, with enormous scarlet flowers on them.

Wasps and bees hovered over the desert flowers; ants and beetles crawled across the ground. She also startled several birds from their ground nests and spotted a few lizards, but saw little else in the way of animal life.

She found the walk pleasing, not at all tiring. Still, it took her some time to reach the road.

Finally she scrambled down a hill, waded through a warm-water stream filled with mucousy scum and the white bellies of dead and dying fish, blanketed in flies. Then she bounded over a fence of barbed wire, and landed on asphalt.

Heat waves rose from the tarmac and pungent tar bled from its surface. The road curved out of sight to the north, and topped a hill about a quarter of a mile to the southwest. She neither saw nor heard any vehicles. Across the road was an adobe house within a barricade of broken glass and barbed wire. Large dogs lay in the shade beneath the porch; Dane saw the green glitter of their eyes.

A young, dark-skinned, black-haired woman in a short dress with spaghetti straps came out the front door. She carried a long stick in the crook of her arm. Dane zoomed on the stick and realized it was a rifle. The woman shooed away the puppies that tumbled out of the house behind her. The rest of the dogs raced back and forth on their side of the barbed wire, leaping and howling at Dane, driving themselves into a frenzy. Even though they couldn't reach her, Dane backed away several steps. The woman squinted at Dane Elisa Cae, and shielded her eyes against the sun.

Dane Elisa Cae stared back at her for a moment. Then, still watching the woman, she started at a slow pace along the road. She wondered whether this woman was an enemy, and if so, whether she should kill her.

Dane hesitated at the gravel driveway that went to the house, and then decided to keep walking up the road. At the top of the hill she glanced back. The woman was crossing the yard, her back to Dane, and the dogs were tumbling and leaping about her. She appeared to have forgotten Dane Elisa Cae.

Gradually more houses appeared along the road, many of them like the first one Dane had encountered: heavily barricaded, with packs of large dogs roaming the yards. One yard held three enormous, grunting pigs, sprawled in the mud under an awning next to a human-sized block of ice.

Beside another home set far away from the road, the pasture contained a pond so rancid Dane could smell it clear from the road. A rusty windmill stood over a trough and a mostly trampled bale of hay, around which were gathered several listless, bony cattle. An equally emaciated horse, a grey dappled with black, was rolling in a pile of manure. As Dane watched, the horse lurched to its feet and lifted its head to sniff the air in Dane's direction.

Most of the houses she saw were burned out and looted, with shattered windows and doors half off their hinges. Some were boarded up—clearly abandoned. Then the rolls of barbed wire that isolated the road from the countryside veered off into the low hills to the east and west.

A wooden sign at the wire had writing in black letters. She stared at it, but couldn't read it until she concentrated, hard. "Sandia Indian Reservation." In handwritten letters beneath it was: "PUEBLO INDIAN LAND! KEEP OUT! TRESPASSERS WILL BE SHOT!!"

Someone had sprayed red and purple symbols all over the original words, partially obscuring them. Dane couldn't read the red and purple lettering, no matter how hard she tried.

On this side of the barbed wire, small clusters of shacks spotted the hillsides. A network of footpaths wound among them. People came down the road, approaching her, and turned onto the footpaths, pulling two-wheeled handcarts filled with things, or riding bicycles or unicycles, or on foot. Dane slowed her pace.

At first there were only a few people, but after a while she found herself amid a group of over a dozen. She circled and craned her neck at them as they passed her. Anyone might be her enemy. How could she know? Dane couldn't keep her gaze on all of them at once.

The others were inclined to ignore her, though she caught two or three of them staring at her surreptitiously.

She topped a hill and saw where the people were coming from. Spread out across a small valley on both sides of the road was a crowd of several hundred people at least. Many were packing up to leave, or already leaving; a number still lingered, though. Some sat behind blankets and tables that had . . . things on them. Beans, rice, corn, a scattering of small, greenish tomatoes, sickly apples with wormholes in them, and oranges. Also gadgets and hand tools, and shoes and clothing. Baskets and thatched grass rugs, beadwork, small bottles with perhaps perfume or perhaps medicines, vials and philters of powder or oil. Live animals were penned or tied to stakes—dogs, goats, chickens, other fowl Dane did not recognize. Books, mostly old and worn, some with torn covers or broken spines. Magazines. People picked up the things on the blankets, or walked around them to examine them, and argued with the seated people over them. Here and there sat the old, and occasionally younger people as well, in the shade, fanning themselves languorously.

One woman had a table piled high with loaves of brown bread. An overpowering, sweetish smell made Dane choke as the woman scooped loaves from the depths of an adobe oven with a long, spatulate stick. Dane paused to watch. The aproned old woman flashed her a smile, spread the bread on the table.

She said something and held out a loaf, mopping at the water that collected on her face and dripped off her chin with a towel. Dane touched her own face, which was dry. Why was there water on the woman's face?

Sweat. It was sweat. She'd heard of it somewhere.

The woman smiled at Dane again, and at that, grief collected in Dane's throat. She had that curious, detached feeling. Distantly, she remembered a woman's smile—a smile that had meant everything to her. Then someone bumped Dane's shoulder, and she moved on.

One table held some items Dane was familiar with. She saw three hand drills; some carpentry tools, both electric and nonelectric; an electric refrigerator; a hand transceiver; an ancient jellovision set. The man at the table had just started to pack up his things. He was draped with a cowled cape of finely woven, blue-dyed cotton, gathered at the waist. His face was freckled, reddened and peeling.

When he noticed her attention, the man leaned on his palms and winked at her. Dane shoved her way into the crowd and hastened back down the road. She didn't slow until she had put some good distance behind her.

At the far edge of the tables and blankets, some children scrambled around the base of a tree, shouting and laughing and swinging on a rope. Curious, Dane turned aside from her path to approach them.

A number of people gathered as she approached, watching her and talking among themselves. A stocky man with large arms, wearing a sheet of cotton draped across the upper half of his body and jeans underneath, came up and said something in a threatening voice.

This was an enemy. Was he not? But doubt lingered. She concentrated on what he had said. Again, it was English, and again she had an inexplicably hard time understanding.

"Who are you? What do you want here?"

She was Dane Elisa Cae. But she didn't know what she wanted, and she didn't know a proper way to reply.

Dane decided to take a big risk. Instead of attacking him she merely turned and began walking again. The group watching her dispersed as soon as she left the vicinity of the tree.

She felt pleased at the outcome. The proper choice seemed to be to wait until she had more information about people's intentions toward her, as she had with this man and the woman in the house on the road. That would be how she could identify her enemies.

From the top of the next hill she could see the city, her destination, and the intervening ghetto of the villagers. Shacks and houses made of plywood, corrugated tin, mud, and sticks, even sheaves of plastic and cloth, blanketed the hills and valleys that lay between her and the city. Thousands of people must live here. The huts were crammed together haphazardly, and a spray of electrical wires led into a few of them from the massive power lines hundreds of feet overhead. Behind some of the huts, beneath tarps supported by sticks, small plots held rows of struggling plants: corn, tomatoes, beans. They, like the houses on the road, were protected by barbed wire.

She polarized her vision against the glare of the midmorning sun and looked across the foothills toward the city. The shantytown was in the foothills, rimming the northeast edge of the mountains. To her west, a muddy river wound southward. Spread throughout the river valley lay a vast city, blanketed by a thin, greyish haze. The city spilled up onto the lava flows beyond the river and disappeared over the western horizon, past a string of volcanoes. To her southeast, bordering the city on the east, worn granite cliffs rose a full mile into the sky.

Between the mud village and the city, an expanse of ground blackened by fire blocked her passage. On the near side of the scorched ground were evenly spaced poles, and on the far side was a deep trench. A dozen or so feet beyond that was a very high wall. This barren zone followed the rise and fall of the hills, then dipped down across the valley as far westward as she could see, and disappeared to the east up the mountain slope.

As she studied it, two groups of young men bounced past inside the scorched area in ethanol-powered Jeeps. She zoomed on them, but the exercise earned her no new information.

The road she stood on dipped and crossed over a major eight-lane highway that passed through the barrier into the city, about a mile to her west. Dane zoomed in and focused on a car speeding south on the highway. The car slowed as it neared a pole that barred the road and a small building at the barbed wire. A round, blue and white sign that said "AT&T Public Jellophone" glowed above a phone booth mounted on the guard-shack wall. Two men with rifles spoke to the car's driver, then waved the car through the opening pole gate.

Better to go overland, she decided, across the stretch of burned earth, leap the trench, and climb the wall. Just in case the men in the shack were enemies like the first guard she'd encountered had been. She had the feeling she should also be careful to avoid the young men in Jeeps.

Dane left the road and made her way through the vines, cacti, and bushes toward the barren area.

The trench was perhaps ten feet deep and twenty feet wide. When she came to the hill above it, she considered for a moment. It was quite a jump, and she wasn't at all sure she could make it.

There was only one way to find out. She started down the hill, pumping legs and arms hard, building speed rapidly till her surroundings were a blur, past the poles, and then dove over the trench, soaring over it in a parabolic arc. On the far side she tucked into a somersault and struck the ground rolling. Then she stood, feeling pleased.

But something was suddenly wrong. The sense of displacement, of twoness, returned. A band tightened across her chest. Her heart was racing. She felt her lungs pull in great gulps of air, she felt herself thrashing wildly, though she could look down and see her arms still as dead things at her sides. Her knees buckled and her vision blurred.

Then, like a faucet shut off, the feeling vanished. She blinked, looked around, brushed herself off. Her hands were trembling. That pounding—the dull beat, beat, beat—came back to her, and the voice that kept time with the beating, a faraway voice. She heard it again, in the back of her mind.

Fantasies, she thought. Not real. Pressing palms against her ears to shut out the drums, she forced her feet to start moving again.

A rumble—a real sound, not a phantom one—registered on her hearing. She lifted her head, changed the magnification of her sight.

There. A Jeep was coming from the west, followed by an electric all-terrain vehicle. They would reach her before she could get to the wall, even at her fastest run.

Perhaps they were not enemies. Wait and collect more information, she decided.

They wore hooded Teklar suits with backpacks, and dark specs. Heat waves stained the air above their heads. They gestured at her and each other; she couldn't process their shouting quickly enough to understand it. Their faces were snarling—and as the vehicles sped past they leapt on her, eighteen or more of them. She learned from them how to tell an enemy.

Dane Elisa Cae spun among them like a dervish, lashing out at the bodies behind the clubs and chains, smashing bones. She downed several of them before, with sheer numbers, they pinned her to the ground. They beat her with clubs and chains, their fierce, grinning faces and shouts and jeers hovering behind, with a rhythm that summoned the pounding and the tiny voice in her mind, until the horror of the violence and the repeated shocks of their blows caused her to slide away from consciousness.

WATCHWORKS AND LIZARD TAILS

Carli crawled out of bed when her alarm went off at 7:30 A.M., sat on its edge, and tried to rub the bleariness out of her eyes. It had been a long night.

Tania had come. She had brought along some sprite, and had offered to share a gram of the chocolate-colored fungus with Carli, who had declined politely. Carli had tried the hallucinogenic saprophyte once, as a teenager, and hadn't liked it.

They had talked for a little while after that, and staring at what Tania had become had been nightmarish enough without hallucinogens. Then, fully loaded, Tania had borrowed Carli's netware and passwords, and faced into the nets. Carli had gone to bed. She should have told Tania no, she couldn't borrow her linkware, but she hadn't had the heart to.

Carli went into the bathroom. Bright, tiny, orange and blue flowers of fungus had already begun to sprout where the shower tiles met the drain and around the lower edge of the medicine cabinet. Time to spray again, she thought absently.

Then she noticed a sour, nauseating smell. She looked down and grimaced; Tania had been sick in the sink sometime during the night. Carli turned the tap on, full force. Screw the water ration, she thought, and left the bathroom with the water still running. She pulled on a robe and dragged a plastic-bristled brush through her hair.

Dreams flickered, ghost-fire, on the periphery of her memory. The last, most vivid and shortest of the dreams: a doll of ash and mahogany. Carli had held it in her hand. She vaguely remembered having fitted the blocks of light and dark wood together, carefully inserted the rows of razor teeth. The doll's mouth was jewel red, its eyes gold. It knew her and she was afraid of it. And pitied it.

It had smiled at her when she had slid the last piece into place. Then it had sunk its diamond teeth into her thumb. With a curse she had smashed the doll against the floor. Its innards were the workings of a fine Swiss watch that bled crimson oil.

She had had another dream she didn't remember so clearly, a dream of dismembered hands.

She went back into the bathroom and scrubbed the sink several times over with antiseptics and towels. Once she was satisfied it was clean, she took the sopping, foul-smelling towels and dropped them in the hamper, then scrubbed her hands clean. She brushed her teeth and took a draft of cool water into her cupped hands.

When Carli laid her hands on the rim of the sink, the sight of them and the dream image conjured a sudden memory of Dennis: his veined hands, blue from blood leaked into the tissue, trembling and twitching like lizard tails on the dark yellow coverlet in the vet hospital. The hands had been the only things that had stayed the same while the gene bomb was busy remaking the rest of him into something nonhuman.

She went into the living room. Tania lay nestled in the squish-chair with her face half buried in it, an arm hanging over the side, Argyle curled between her legs. Carli couldn't believe she could sleep like that; Argyle must weigh close to ten kilos.

Carli picked Argyle up and dropped him on the floor, and sat down on the chair's rim to look at Tania. One thin hand pillowed the girl's head. Her eyes, lids bluish and transparent as a newborn's, were open and unfocused; she sprite-dreamed. The nethood lay half off, next to her head. Carli picked it up carefully, pulling the lead free from beneath Tania's head, and put it on its mount on her desk. Tania still wore the gloves; she'd have to get them back later.

Tania's skin was raw-patched paste that lay gingerly across the bones and tendons of her face, neck, shoulders, arms. She was covered with tiny scars and open sores; her hair was straw. Behind her ear, a fingernail-sized patch of spider-black fur grew. The Mold.

Carli's eyes narrowed. She touched Tania's cheek, and a sharp breath slid through her teeth. Then she pulled the blanket up over the girl's shoulder, stood and went into the kitchen.

Six years ago, when Carli had met her, Tania was seventeen—a strapping blonde with a long stride, her hair and complexion as soft and fine as an infant's, a quick smile, and an air of innocence that suffused her like a nimbus.

Carli wondered whether Paint had seen her since his release from prison, wondered whether it would affect him if he had. He had called her Tender. She had been flattered, but Carli had seen the flatness in his eyes and recognized the nickname as an accusation. And a prophecy.

Tania was broken. She had shattered against the world like a china doll.

Argyle paced and complained stridently among the stacks of dirty dishes while Carli swiped at the column of ants that crawled up the wall, smashing most and sending the rest scurrying. Then she shook whitish powder into a bowl of water and whipped the mixture into a froth of pseudo-food. She stirred powdered eggs into an electric skillet, started the coffee, and shushed the cat—with limited success.

Tania stumbled into the kitchen wearing one of Carli's old terry cloth robes—the taupe one that Paint had usually worn—and faded slippers of pink nylon fur. She scratched her head and looked like a doddering old lady.

" 'Ts'jink, Carli," she said, and picked up Argyle. "I'm up."

She buried her face in the cat's neck and carried him into the other room, murmuring incoherently to him. Carli followed in a couple of minutes with a tray of eggs, buttered toast, and coffee. Tania had turned the jelly on; she had adjusted the sound level, annoyingly, not quite high enough to understand but just loud enough to be distracting. Carli turned the sound down and sat.

"Just like old times," Tania said. She pressed her lips against the white fur of Argyle's belly. "You still love me, don't you, Gyle?"

This was too much for Argyle. With a grunt of displeasure he squirmed free, jumped heavily off the couch, and squeezed underneath it. Carli handed a mug to Tania and then leaned back.

" 'S really schick, Carli," Tania said. "Shards jaded me total; 'n't know what I'd'a done . . ." She caught a whiff of the steam rising from her own mug, and her eyebrows went up.

"Real coffee? Oh. Your dad."

Carli merely stretched her lips across her teeth in an attempt at a smile.

Tania tried a sip of coffee. Her expression grew thoughtful. Carli got the impression she thought the stuff was overrated. Carli handed her a plate of pseudo-eggs piled on toast. Tania pushed her food around the plate and then abandoned it without taking a bite. In the meantime a flood of words spilled out, nonsense mostly, punctuated by giggles and nervous tosses of the head. Her voice held an unspoken plea.

Carli couldn't bring herself to answer that plea. She merely nursed her own brew, picked at her breakfast, and muttered an occasional polite noise.

Finally Tania set her fork down, took a deep breath, and gave Carli a nervous smile. "Ya seen Paint lately?"

Carli looked up at Tania. She nodded, considering her words. She knew that Paint knew that Tania still asked around about him; it made him angry, but Carli suspected it also flattered him. She leaned back and tucked a leg under herself, gulped down the last of her tepid coffee.

"He's gone semipro," she replied. "Has a regular show at The Bomb. He still does computer consulting on the side, to pay the bills. When he has to."

Tania's voice was so thin as to be almost inaudible, but her gaze was like a searchlight on Carli's face. Her tongue flicked across her lips. The gesture was nervous, intense.

"He jink?"

Carli nodded. Her face felt frozen in place. Let him go, Tania.

"He's doing real well." She stood. "Can I get you some more coffee?"

Tania lowered her own gaze. Two tears, crystal-like, appeared on her cheeks. She swiped at them, sniffed. "Thanks, no."

Carli went into the kitchen, threw the scraps into the reprocessor, and started cleaning up, crushing some more bugs that scurried underfoot in the meanwhile.

"Tania, could you spray the bathroom for me?" she called. It took real control to keep from snarling, which surprised and upset her. Through the arch she could see Tania's bent head. Tania was still weeping.

"Sure."

With a deep, languishing breath, Tania wiped her eyes, stood, and went into the back room. Carli sighed and pushed her hair off her forehead with the back of a wet hand. In the corner above the sink, another colony of decay had begun to bloom in red and purple. She stared at it briefly, the sour taste of irrational rage in her mouth.

"Shit."

She hurled her sponge into the oily dishwater, splashing the counter. She was sick of the mold. She had just sprayed the other day. Everything was rotting.

She walked carefully into the living room, sat down on the couch. Her eyes were dry; she hadn't cried since before her divorce. But her hands, on her thighs, were trembling again. Like severed lizard tails.

She realized gradually that she was staring at a scene on the jelly of the street outside her apartment, and, surprised, turned the sound back up to hear the story. Some old woman from the city's outskirts had been attacked on the street, and then rescued by a vigilante.

Coming up, the announcer said, the weather, an update on the impending *Exodus-Courier* rendezvous, and coverage of the grain wars in Central Common Europe, and the malaria and schistosomiasis pandemics spreading up the New England coast. But first, this word from our sponsors.

Carli shut off the jelly and went to change for work.

HE'S STILL OF TWO MINDS ABOUT IT ALL

On transfer back to Kaleidas he headed straight for the out-view lounge. It was deserted. Non-crèche-born workers tended to avoid the place, and the other crèche children would certainly be taking a brief respite from their implementation tasks, playing face-games while the team leaders were occupied. The other team leaders would already be gathering for Mother's briefing in the main crèche chamber.

He sensed Buddy's objections. But he still had ten minutes before the meeting, and there'd be little enough time to visit the lounge later.

=Why don't you go check out a proxy, then, and visit the others yourself, while I'm in the meeting?=

Pablo was reluctant to see Mother. It was odd; that was usually Buddy's role. Maybe it was all these mood swings. Mara had sent him a private message that Mother was more edgy than ever. Several of the younger children were in semipermanent hiding these days, with the older kids twinning to cover for them on tests and in meetings.

A twinge of jealousy made him scowl. = You leave Mara alone.=

Buddy tagged along with Pablo. It beat hanging out, blind and deaf, in the back of Pablo's mind . . . but only just.

Why is he wasting our time in here, Buddy thought irritably, when we could be with the others?

There was little enough time for *that*, either.

=Right—and alert Mother to the fact that there are two of us.=

It had been Mara's idea to shield the younger ones from Mother's rage. Ahh, Mara!

He frowned, surprised and annoyed. =We're supposed to be in this together.=

Ignoring Buddy, he looked around. The lounge's floor was made of superhard, transparent metaglass. Radiation levels were rather high here; corporeal personnel weren't allowed to remain for more than fifteen minutes, once a day.

The ceiling lights shone dim gold. Pablo walked across to the back—the balls and heels of his boots clicking on nothingness, ka-TICK, ka-TICK, a carpet of stars and a crescent moon far, far beneath his feet—and sat down in one of the chairs mounted on the walls.

Belts snaked out to contain his arms and legs, and at his command the chair rotated to face straight down. Hanging there, he stared down at the Earth's great, dark curve, its edge limned with white brilliance from refracted sunlight. The hemisphere tumbled past underfoot in a lazy circle that would carry it out of view in a moment or two.

He glanced around the rim of the room. It would take a lot of explosive to dislodge the metaglass flooring, when the time came. Enough that it might rupture the bulkheads and kill them all. He sure hoped Joe knew what he was doing.

Buddy shielded his thoughts while Pablo's mind wandered.

Today's meeting should at least give him an idea of how much time he had left.

He would be glad when this was over, one way or the other; he was tired of having to guard his thoughts around Pablo; the constant dread of discovery preyed on him.

He heard a sound, and took over the interface long enough to sharpen his Pablo's hearing. A faint pounding and the buzz of power saws carried through the thick bulkhead above. Surely they're nearly done setting the rocket engine in place by now, he thought.

The lounge was located at the very bottom and center of the habitat. Centripetal force was strong here, the strongest of anywhere on Shasta Station/Kaleidas. Usually its powerful pull made him feel sleepy and serene. But after a month of Earth's greater gravity, it had little effect. A pang of homesickness struck him at the realization.

Buddy shared the feeling.

The five crèche children who headed the Plastic Menagerie's other implementation teams sprawled on the floor across each other's laps, in the open space at the back of the crèche chamber, the flesh examination area. Mother sat on the counter at the very back, beside the sink, her feet on a lab stool. Uncle Byron stood beside her, and Aunt Jenna stood at a comunit with a large projection jello. Uncle Marsh sat near the back, behind the team leaders.

Mother had a pointer, which she was tapping against the counter. She glanced pointedly at Pablo when he entered the room.

The others whispered and signed excitedly as he passed. Mara touched his hand. Pablo gave her a smile.

Buddy pitched in on the smile.

"Late again," Mother said. "So glad you could join us." Pablo suppressed a wince, and sat down with the others.

Screw you, old woman.

=Buddy, don't.=

=Relax. I wasn't talking to you.=

Pablo gave Buddy the finger, mentally, and threw his shields up. Buddy's presence evaporated.

Oh, it's like that now, is

That was why he'd been reluctant, he realized. He hated being caught between Mother and Buddy. The last thing he needed right now was harassment inside his own head. Buddy blamed everything on Mother.

She dropped lightly to the floor and balanced on a toe. "We'll have to make this fast; Rasmussen has beanlinked down to Earth to attend a meeting with his superiors, but we can't be sure how long that meeting will last.

"As you all know, with *Courier* launching three weeks early, all our careful planning has been junked. In a word, children, we are in deep shit. The only thing that will save us now is if we are really really smart, and really really lucky.

"So every team had better be well ahead of its target goals." Her glance strayed to Uncle Byron, who, judging from his posture and intent expression, was getting a report from one of his team members. Everyone else looked at each other, anxious expressions on their faces.

"Ursa, report."

Ursa bounded out of the puppy-tangle and came to the front. Her proxy was an adult body, as all their proxies were, but Ursa was one of the younger ones: a Second Waver, a shy nine-year-old girl with a sharp mind. She held a kelly shaped like a flatscreen, and held a stylus. She read from her screen with a breathless quickness, not looking up.

"We are almost finished disassembling and loading the last six spare crèche support systems. After our last set of adjustments, the substitute cargo pod's mass and dimensions are essentially identical to the original."

it? Buddy thought, and put up his own shields again.

Pablo's defenses were permeable enough that Buddy could see and hear the goings-on, albeit through a distorted haze.

"Good work," Mother said.

Ursa looked up with a pleased smile, and clutched her kelly to her chest.

"NASA's lunar security," she went on, "continues to be fairly lax, and thus far we have encountered no signs of suspicion. We anticipate no difficulty in removing their cargo pod and substituting ours. The switch is planned for oh eight hundred and four hours tomorrow, two hours and forty minutes prior to cargo pod launch."

"Very good." Mother gestured for her to sit down. "Joe, report."

Joe was First Wave, fifteen, almost Pablo's age. "We have finished converting the maintenance waldos. Preliminary testing of the plasma jet is completed. All is in order. Testing will continue on all circuitry and programming." He hesitated. "We are still awaiting the last shipment of cesium, which is needed for launch." His glance flicked to Mara.

Mother lifted her eyebrows at Mara, who stared back with wide eyes through a film of blond bangs.

"Well?"

Mara's shoulders hunched. She lowered her gaze. "We are trying, Mother. Kai-Toy's security is tight since the last shipment was discovered missing, and the uncle who was accepting bribes to give us supplies was caught and fired. The others are afraid they'll be caught, too."

Mother turned to Joe. "Once you've got the cesium rods, how long will it take you to load them into the feed tanks and melt them?"

"Not long. We'll need to run some composition tests on the molten mater-

ial, to optimize the laser vaporization."
He shrugged. "Fifteen hours, maybe.
That's a conservative estimate."

"Jenna?" Mother said. Aunt Jenna accessed a series of data files. In the jello, a
graphic of *Courier* crept toward a graphic
of *Exodus*, the interstellar probe, parked
at Icarus, the antimatter production plant
that trailed Mercury in a solar orbit.

Numbers flashed as she changed the
display and studied the readouts. Finally
Aunt Jenna looked up.

"*Courier* reaches *Exodus* in four days,"
she said. "Exodus has already completed
its antimatter fuel transfer. Once the last
eight astronauts arrive at the antimatter
plant, *Exodus* will debark. Once we
launch we'll need several hours to outrun
any pursuit while gearing up for the takeover. That means we need to launch no
later than midday, three days from now."

"So we need that fuel by no later than
midday, day after tomorrow." Mother
turned back to Mara. "Your team *must*
find a way to get it into Joe's hands by
eight P.M. tomorrow."

Mara made a nervous noise. "We'll try,
Mother."

"Trying's not good enough. I'm very
disappointed in your failure." Her face
was stiff with anger. "Remain after the
others leave. I'm taking over. I'll devise
another plan for you to carry out. And
we'll discuss your punishment."

Then she looked at Uncle Byron. "You
left me a message that you'd had a breakthrough. Report."

Uncle Byron's forehead had deep
creases and he was twisting his thumb

Buddy's attention sharp-
ened as Aunt Jenna's
words penetrated Pablo's
shield. Four more days.
That was it!

Buddy looked at Mara
through the corners of
Pablo's eyes, and shud-
dered. Her hair hung be-
fore her face, and her
shoulders were hunched.
Everyone else—including
Pablo, the bastard!—was
avoiding looking at her.

ring. He didn't look like a man who'd had a breakthrough. "My group has managed to improve the omni circuitry and coding to gain ten light-milliseconds of distance in range. That's a huge leap in sensitivity over the current technology."

Mother made fists and bared her teeth. "Light-*milliseconds*? Don't crow to me about light-milliseconds, Byron. I need two light-seconds, minimum!"

"I know." He shrugged again. "We've been over this before, Patricia. There's nothing more we can do. We're out of time." He sighed, heavily. "I hate to be the one to tell you this, but the original plan just ain't going to work. We can't use omni signaling the way we planned. It's time to come up with an alternative."

"I'll worry about alternatives. You worry about a breakthrough." Ignoring Uncle Byron's muttered protest, Mother looked at Pablo. "Report."

Acid assailed his gut. He didn't know how much Buddy had told her last night. "I have assigned one of Uncle Sam's people to bring Carli MacLeod in. He made an attempt last night, but she pulled a gun on him. I'm sending him back out as soon as Medical clears him today."

"Damn it, Pablo! We need MacLeod *yesterday.*"

"We'll have her on the six A.M. shuttle from White Sands tomorrow. I swear it."

How the hell he was going to do that, when he couldn't even get Buddy's cooperation, never mind Uncle Daniel's or any one else's, was a big mystery, but if he could just keep Mother off his back for a few more hours, maybe a miracle would happen.

He wanted to pound Mother's face. It's not her fault, you malevolent bitch!

Buddy couldn't completely shield his relief from Pablo. If nothing else did, Mother's ferocity made clear that even without his help, they probably weren't going to be able to pull this insane scheme off.

"Marsh," Taylor said. "Report."

Uncle Marsh stood. "All the fizz-psych systems are in order. The last of the surgical and emergency medical supplies have arrived and are being stowed. I've been directing the younger children in battening everything down. We should be ready in time."

"Good."

Mother adjourned the meeting, after a last admonishment: "We're not giving up. There's still a chance we can do this. We're going to steal *Exodus*. Or die trying." She remained silent for a moment to let her words sink in, then walked out, with a sharp "Get back to work" tossed over her shoulder.

=Damn you, Buddy, I *need* you,= he thought, switching them back to Krueger's proxy. Back at Krueger's office, he walked to the glass wall and pressed his palms against it, looking out at the courtyard, with its groomed gardens—its leaves and flower petals sparkling with dew, its cobblestone walks and marble benches.

Buddy didn't reply right away.

But Pablo's pleas, and the lonely desperation behind them, wrenched at Buddy's resolve to remain silent.

=Why do you hate her so much? What are you hiding?=

=She's crazy, Pablo— can't you see that? If we don't stop her, she'll kill us all!=

He sat down on the bed and bent his head into his strong, plastic hands, pulling at the artificial strands of hair rooted there.

=You're wrong. You are so wrong. She loves us. She's trying to protect us. She's just irritable, that's all.=

Buddy's words tore holes in the world. Things tilted and stretched—turned strange, distorted, like a balloon; color washed out of his awareness till all seemed grey and soft blue, riddled with billowing dark holes. Nausea. Fear.

No. Nothingness. Numbness. Pablo put his hands on the big, ugly balloon of stuff that tried to surface. He grappled it and shoved it down.

I'm going back to sleep, he decided, with a sort of dazed precision. He wandered back to Krueger's quarters, where he curled up and drifted off and, for a while, even managed to forget Buddy's existence.

="Irritable." Go back to Kaleidas in an hour and visit Mara's crèche, and listen to her crying her heart out. Then come tell me how wrong I am—how much Mother loves us.=

Deep sadness washed over Buddy, regarding Pablo's struggle.

=You don't remember, do you? All those times . . .=

And then anger came. He left me alone, the fucker, left me alone in there just the way she did.

=Fuck you, Pablo—I hope you scream in anguish when you find out how I've betrayed you.=

He twinned the face and went in search of his crèche-mates.

DAMAGED GOODS

Dane was floating; music filled her mind; faces floated before her—not-human faces that she knew and didn't know; sinuous bodies slid over her, caressed her, buoyed her in the pool. Water dripped down from gleaming rock, sent ripples everywhere. The sound of dripping was music.

Bubbles tumbled upward around her, tickling her as they burst; she pinched her nostrils closed, nudged another body aside with her snout—

—dove deep, beneath the other grey, smooth bodies. Fins flurried past her face; more laughter effervesced through her mind. The world was green, blue, dim—rocks and fissures deep beneath her; schools of silver-scaled fish darted among them. She looked up at the others, shouted a song that sounded inside and outside her, whipped her tail and sped upward—

—broke surface—for an instant she paused at the top of her arc—then plunged deep into the pool.

The sensations faded. She lay on her side, blissful and quiet. The dreams, joyous dreams, had chased the evil men and the horrible pounding sound away. Her body was human again.

Someone was pulling something from within her neck; she jerked at the touch, and the object slipped from the hand of the other. The object, a crystal, caught the light as it fell, slow motion, to the pillowed floor.

There had been a piece of crystal inside her neck.

She looked down at herself and saw a stranger's nude body, pale skin and hair, female.

Dane Elisa Cae looked around.

She was in a room with soft flooring and walls. Words flowed around her, songs—a stream of them on many levels of hearing. Many people all about: some she saw, some she couldn't see. Bodies surrounded her, faces and eyes and mouths and legs and arms . . . knowing her, touching her. Everywhere. Someone tried to slide another crystal into her neck. She shoved the hand aside and sat.

I was among enemies, she thought. She shook her head, suddenly dizzy. *They were hurting me. Where am I?*

My name is Dane Elisa Cae. My name is—

Concerned faces surrounded her. *What's wrong? Sing with us, sing* . . .

She shoved them away, lurched to her feet. She was too light; her push carried her to the ceiling, where she struck and bounced. Sinking, she stumbled over bodies and bounded up again. A wall met her. She bounced and fell back. Her name—she was—

—sitting bolt upright among covers, fighting them. She fell on her face on the floor with a heavy, painful thud.

She rolled over and sat. Her arms were thick and hairless; she had small mammaries, a great belly, and baggy shorts that held a bulge. Frowning, she slid her hand into her shorts, and jerked it back out with a strangled scream. She had a man's genitals.

She struggled back onto the bed, retreated into the corner, huddled there in the dimness, stared at a bedside clock that blinked 7:07 A.M. She looked around. The cluttered room was familiar. She knew this place.

Her name was, her name—she—

—was hurting. A steady motion rocked her back and forth on a heap of hard, sharp objects. She lay half propped against something solid, perhaps a wall. Parts of her body were islands of numbness, surrounded by annuli of pain: the right side of her face, her right arm, her left leg.

She muted the hurt as much as she could, and opened her eyes. The sun was high in the sky. Her body was her own again—she was Dane Elisa Cae, in her own tormented, blessed body.

She lay in a wooden cart. Over its edge a cloaked figure's head and shoulders hunched, bobbing up and down. The figure was pulling the cart down a rocky path. He breathed heavily, and said something once, in a loud voice, when a cart wheel caught on a rock. That was how she knew it was a man, by the timbre of his voice.

She tried to sit up, but the angle she was at and the jerks and starts of the cart threw her off-balance. Her right arm and left leg were torn and bloody, and she couldn't bend her leg very far. It didn't feel broken, though. There was only a dull pain when she moved it.

She gripped the edge of the cart and struggled to her knees. She formed the words in her mind and then spoke.

"Where are you taking me?"

The man started, and turned, wearing a strange expression. He spoke; she focused all her energies into understanding him.

"What's this?" was what he had said. He stared at her. Dane had seen him before—in the market. It was the sunburned man with all the gadgets. "So, the robot speaks. Remarkable."

The words came hard to her lips. She hesitated, laying the words out in a row in her mind, like blocks. "Robot! I'm not a robot. I'm a refugee. From Florida. My name is Dane Elisa Cae."

She moved into a more comfortable position and cradled her right arm in her lap.

"Dana Cae, a petey from Florida!" He laughed. "Someone's got a sense of humor." He shook his head. "I scavenged you. The boundary patrol thought you were human, and left you for dead." He hawked and spat. "Animals. Idiots." He went on, "Quite a sophisticated piece of equipment, you are. I had to get up close to tell. I've done a few repairs, clamped off a few hydraulic leaks and rebent your limbs as best I could." He gestured broadly at her. "But you need more work. You're a quart low, at least."

A horrid, sick feeling filled Dane. For a moment she only looked at him. The speck of machinery in her neck, the dreams, her first memory of awakening in that laboratory, with probes and instruments attached to her—

Her head shook violently. "I told you, I'm not a machine. I'm as human as you."

"Then that's one hell of a prosthetic you have there," he said, gesturing with his chin at her arm.

She looked at it more closely. Inside the long gash, the layers of blood-soaked flesh were suffused with fine strands and plastic tubing. Clamps hung from the tubing in three or four places, and the bone underneath glinted. No—not bone; something else entirely.

She touched the flesh, the infrastructure beneath it, and felt nothing. She dug her fingers into the wound. At the elbow joint, she felt some kind of pulley, a round surface, wires. The interior of her arm felt her fingers then, but not as pain, only as a pressure.

Dane Elisa Cae jerked her hand out and looked up at the man. Her fingers were smeared with red.

"You think that's something; you should see your face."

She reached up—the whole lower right quadrant of her face was hanging from a flap; she could feel clamps, and wisps of fiber at its edges. She glanced right, and at the edge of her eye socket, her fingers touched taut strands of wire, which moved a plate behind the eye.

Was this not, then, how human bodies were constructed? She probed down into her mind for the other one she vaguely remembered being—the male, who knew it was OK to have a machine body, who believed this was all a game. Phantomlike, he retreated from her.

The other, then—the face. Mentor. Captor. The one who had sent her here. Mentally she pled for him to come to her aid. Only silence met her inner cries.

A machine. Was she merely a programmed machine? Was that why she had no memory—why she was driven, guided? How she knew things without knowing how she knew?

She scrambled over the clutter, leaped out of the cart.

Dane Elisa Cae could still run. The man chased her. "Hey, come back—I can repair you! I *order* you to come back. I found you; you're mine!"

Even limping, though, she was faster than he. She left him far behind in the foothills, pursued by rhythm—thump, thump, thump—damn those horrible drums and that awful, croaking little voice, and when she finally slowed, she saw him below her on top of a hill, watching her ascent toward the peaks.

MOTHER OF PEARL

Carli stepped outside into startling sunshine and slid her netspecs down over her eyes, at maximum polarity. Traffic had lightened on the streets; Phase One rush hour was over. Only envie-suited sorts were out and about. While heading for the train she sorted through her e-mail.

(A) *** Genie Specials!
(1) 5 Puppies—2F/3M 10 wks old. Hi-temp-
tolerant and hi-intelligence gengineered
Gt. Dane/Shepherd Mix, $8500 EA.
(2) Assorted reclaimed, hi-temp farm stock
good for breeding/cloning. $900–25500. Call
2522-45280 Days/Mail 6449-99201 Eves—MIKE
OR VANESSA *** (A)

(T) TIME @ TEMP @ HUMIDITY :: 08:55:03 @ 32.2C
@ 69.2% (T)

Above the peaks, the morning sun had broken through the clouds, and the air was filled with brilliance and lifting haze. Last night's storm front had dropped the temperature to something tolerable. The stiff, warm breeze that rolled down from the western cliffs of the Sandias, a couple of miles beyond the concrete stanchions that supported the Tramway express loop, at least didn't burn the sinuses. A steam bath, but not a furnace.

(A) ***** Winter's coming—we're overstocked and
we're desperate! Take advantage! Half-price
special: photolucent mini-canopies just right
for smaller homes or additions. A wide variety
of colors and options. While they last. We
finance!

JunoCool Home HVAC Supplies, Wyoming East of Indian School. *** (A)**

(P) PSA 0620 HRS: COOL FRONT EXPECTED TO DROP TEMPS BY UP TO FIFTEEN DEGREES C TODAY. HIGH EXPECTED LOW 30s. MORE WET AIR MOVING IN FROM GULF WILL RESULT IN SCATTERED THUNDERSTORMS BY EVENING. (P)

Fall had fallen! Finally! A smile welled up inside Carli. She switched on her suit, but left the hood and mask off and the zipper only half up, and dialed up a geometric pattern in fall colors. Then, remembering, she scanned the pedestrians' faces. But the young man who had followed her yesterday, Daniel, was nowhere to be seen.

Electric collovehicles sped past on the street. Among them she caught a glimpse of white paint on the pavement: outlines of the four bodies left on the street by that vigilante last night. That put a couple of smudges on the shine of her mood; fortunately, the smudges faded quickly.

**(C) correspondence sent 13 hrs 0 min 49 sec ago ::
4113-66401 [theresa] -> 3910-10003 [carli.dauber]
hey carli,
can you believe it's really been ten months since I've
been in touch? how've you been? gotten your phd yet, or
are you still procrastinating on writing the dissertation?**

**btw, i've wanted to let you know what an inspiration
you were. when ben's and my marriage contract
expired a couple months back we decided to renew
with a permanent contract like yours.how is jere
doing, anyhow? give him our regards.and drop a line!
love, terry. (C)**

She caught a train heading downtown. Phase One rush hour was over, and few other passengers were in the car. She settled onto a bench and clung to the rail. The train accelerated toward city center.

(!) (PSA!) 0902 HRS: * ALERT *** ALERT *** ALERT ***
ALERT! CHOLERA OUTBREAK. FIVE CONFIRMED**

**CASES, ONE DEATH. CONTAMINATED WATER
SUPPLY SUSPECTED, POSSIBLY CITY-WIDE.
USE PURIFIER PILLS OR BOIL WATER AT LEAST
20 MINUTES BEFORE DRINKING. (PSA!)**

At the Central and 2nd Street station, she debarked and climbed the steps to street level, then dashed across the eight lanes of electric- and human-powered vehicles. She pushed past the milling group of licensed beggars to enter the downtown canopy lock.

Her office was in a commercial complex several blocks away from the lock. She entered her office to find Fox hammering nails into the wall to hang a jelly on the wall.

The front office was tiny and had real wood paneling. Against one wall were a couch littered with magazines and periodicals and an end table with a phone on it. A palm tree, two hanging spider plants, and a large begonia with pink blossoms took up space on the floor in the middle of the room. Sunlight from a semipolarized glass wall streamed in and lit up Fox's desk, which, like the area around it, was stacked high with boxes and clutter.

"Let me guess," Fox said. "We got the contract—or you got poked."

Carli frowned. "What?"

"You're smiling. Has to be a reason."

"Oh. Actually, I had a rotten night. Jan called—that asshole Fraser put me off with some bullshit about a merger." She tossed her satchel onto the couch and glanced at her pendant kelly. "You're in frightfully early."

"And you're in late. Sure ya'n't get poked?" He grinned at the face she made. "Three messages for you."

"You're too efficient, Fox." At the door to her office, she turned. "Straighten up those magazines and bring them in to me, would you?"

"I never touch your things," he said. "Y'accuse me of losing them."

He referred to an earlier incident, when she had misplaced an article and assumed Fox had thrown it out.

"Do you want to be paid this month?" she asked him. He blew her a kiss.

Carli depolarized her office window and then sat down at her desk and played back her voice mail.

The first one was from her agent, a duplicate of the call at her home last night. The second was a new call from her mother, reminding her again about dinner tonight. The third was a brief business message from a former colleague.

She set her elbows on her desk and bent her head into her hands for a quick massage, thinking about her mother. Screw it, she thought. I'm not going. She tapped out her parents' number on the keypad, and in a second her mother's face appeared in the display cylinder.

Alison Almquist looked like her Danish and German forebears. Her silver-blond hair was simple and uncurled, her face was square in the jaw and freckled; her eyes were large, a speckled blue. Other than a touch of discreet charcoal eyeshadow around the eyes, she wore no makeup. She appeared scarcely older than Carli, and the resemblance between them was striking enough that people often remarked upon it. Unlike Carli, though, she was petite, and had an air of daintiness, of the Old World, about her. She looked as though she had been transplanted from the nineteenth century.

"Oh, honey, I'm so glad you called! Your father is stuck in Washington; an important vote was postponed till today, and Dad won't be catching the scram back after all."

"That's too bad."

"Oh, it's all right. He's decided to rent a waldo and attend by skinlink. I've moved dinner back to about seven to accommodate his schedule."

"Mother, I . . ."

Carli hesitated. Her father and Jere had been friends since before he and Carli had met. Jere's parents and Carli's had known each other since college—Carli's mom had met her dad through Jere's father.

Neither of her parents would say anything to her, not now or ever, if she decided not to go. But she was going to have to face the situation sometime. She wasn't going to be able to avoid it forever.

She sighed. "I'll see you at seven, then."

She went through her periodicals, caught up on her correspondence, sent out more copies of her research proposal, and made some phone calls while Fox put things away. Then—with an excited and nervous feeling in the pit of her stomach—Carli got the MacLeod notebook back out.

She carried the notebook over to her desk, opened it, and removed the first data crystal. After inserting it into her comunit, while the program loaded, she leafed through those cryptic notes she'd made so long ago. Then for a while she stared at the data and sketches that rotated down through her sensor field.

She had some catching up to do on current research, if she was going to make any sense of all this.

Shame on me, she thought; Jan Wilson—and OMNEX—would have two-headed kittens, if they knew. With a happy sigh, she pulled on her netspecs and gloves, booted up her favorite search engine, leaned her chair back, and dove into the *virtu*-nets.

Just before lunchtime, Paint stuck his head around the door. Carli had just finished sorting out some hard-copy reading materials, while downloading some large files; she waved him in.

He shedded several layers of his baggy *natureil* garb and tossed them on the floor. Then he dropped the materials she had just sorted through onto the floor, and flung himself into the chair by the desk.

"Paint! I just went through those."

He looked down at them. " 'T's your twitch? They're still there." At her baleful look he gathered them up and set them on the corner of her desk. "There. Better?" Then he collapsed into the chair again and gave her a grin.

"Ya get done with your boyfriend," he said, "I want him."

"I knew she had a date!" Fox said from the other room.

"It wasn't a date, and he isn't my boyfriend." She fixed a look on her nephew. "I thought you were tired of the body carousel, anyhow. That's what you told Jolynd."

"Jo's jink about it. I've had the one-two-three series." He dismissed his mother's objections, and the possibility of disease, with a wave of his hand. "Besides, I'm not serious about your date. Not that serious. He *was* pretty, though, nespah?" Paint clutched his chest and sighed. "Was something trey jade about him, though."

"You're telling me." Then she sat forward and leaned on her elbows. "So what did *you* find strange?"

Paint's eyes narrowed. "I'n't know, to point to. Mostly his movements—when he crossed his legs, took a drink. He seemed stiff, or too deliberate. His facial expressions. Something off about them. Not quite right. The gross movements were all right, but most of the small-muscle-group movements were missing, except the hands, and even them . . ." He shrugged. "Should be impossible." Then he smiled at Carli. "Ya've a jade look on your face, Auntie."

Carli chewed her lip. "Last night he told me he was with some secret organization that's out to save the world. I figured he was with one of those extremist groups, so I pulled a pulse gun on him and chased him off. And he ran faster than my eyes could follow."

"A genie?"

"Maybe, but genetic engineering wouldn't explain the lack of fine motor movement."

"Then maybe he really *is* an android," Paint said, but Carli was already shaking her head.

"The AI people are nowhere near being able to produce a syntellect that can interact so well in real time, the way Daniel did." She shrugged. "Maybe I'm wrong."

"A waldo?"

"I thought of that, but it doesn't seem likely there'd be human waldos and nobody'd have heard of them. Besides, the waldo interface isn't sophisticated enough for the kind of muscular control he has." After thinking about it a moment further, Carli shook her head. "I think I'm being paranoid. I think that he *is* a genie, who maybe suffered DNA damage during the splicing process that wasn't discovered early enough, or his parents didn't want to abort. Or maybe he was born with some congenital brain damage, or some other disorder that's been repaired with prosthetics.

"Anyhow, I haven't seen him since I chased him away last night, so he's not a problem anymore. I hope."

"Which, in a way," Paint said, a touch wistfully, "is a shame."

Carli burst out laughing. "Sometimes I despair of you."

"Despair's unschick, Carli. Feel joy."

"I don't have much excuse for joy today. Tania's staying with me." A light came into his eyes, and Carli regretted saying anything. But he shrugged.

"Definitely unschick, Auntie. She uses."

"She's self-destructing. What am I supposed to do?"

"Tell her to find someone else to nack on," Fox said from the door. His arms were folded across his chest, and his expression was stern. " 'S her own biggest jig, anyhow."

"The girl needs someone to take care of her," Carli said. "I can't just send her out into the street."

"Whatever." With a noise of disgust, Fox went back into the front office.

Paint said, "I'll stop by tonight."

Carli glanced at the door, wondering whether Fox had overheard. Wouldn't he be jealous? Though she supposed that the degree of their relationship's openness was none of her business. She shook her head. "I don't want her latching on to you again. It wouldn't be good for either of you."

"I know how to handle Tania."

"She's still stuck on you, and you don't know how to say no, Paint. You know you don't."

"Guess that makes two of us, huh?" He gave her his best raised-eyebrows look, idly kicking the leg that hung over the arm of the chair. She glowered at him.

"All right, then," she said after a moment. "I'll transfer some money to your credit account so you can take her to the hospital. She's got a good case of the Mold, and I didn't trust her not to use any money I gave her to go out and buy a spinner of sprite."

"Right." Paint's gaze smoldered. "The cow."

"Don't say that."

" 'T's truth." At her expression, he said, "Better go. Fox and me're manging." He unfolded himself from the chair and moved to the door, lithely, like a cat.

"Paint—" She sighed, giving it up. "Enjoy your lunch."

"Stay jink." He closed the door.

She put her netspecs back on, called up her log-in icon, and dove into the net again to continue her research.

After a while she happened to notice the time: 1:43 P.M. The NASA Phoenix probe dove into the sun at 2:36 P.M., Mountain standard time. If she left now, she could get home in time to float the probe with her higher-resolution linkware.

She hadn't floated a NASA probe in almost a decade—since she'd withdrawn from NASA's interstellar exploration program, in fact. It hadn't been an easy choice, to leave the program. And after things went wrong with OMNEX, she hadn't wanted to dredge up painful memories of lost opportunity. But *Courier*'s launch, as had her note-book, had stirred things up inside: like a grain of sand, it had worked its way through the cracks in her shell and lodged itself amid the soft tissues, itching and irritating.

"Damn it," she said, "damn you, Paint," and then sighed. "Oh, what the hell." She logged off.

SAVAGE CHILDREN MURDERED; FILM AT ELEVEN

He woke with a jerk, a scream lodged in his trachea, his hands crushing a child's throat.

Sitting up, Daniel leaned over his knees and caught his breath. Only a nightmare.

But it wasn't—not *only* nightmare. He shoved the covers aside and covered his face. Morris. God, Morris. He'd have been much happier if that particular memory had stayed good and buried.

Medical had removed him from the crèche, disconnected him from his beanlink lead, and put him to bed. Afternoon sunlight from the glass wall bathed the room in brilliance. He was sweating. The sunlight that fell across the bed made him too warm, despite the room's chilled air.

I just killed four people, he thought. Children. Four savage children.

It was no good. He knew he should care. But last night's events didn't feel quite real, somehow.

Daniel stood, stretching, and then groaned. He itched. His body hair had trapped little balls of adhesive all over, from where the electrodes had been taped, and he had three days' growth of beard. Daniel furiously scratched his scalp, ran his fingernails lightly over the puckered skin that swallowed the metal jack at the crown of his head. That only made the itching worse. He smelled like an entire football team, *after* the big game, and he itched so badly it felt like tiny bugs were crawling all over him.

With another moan, he stumbled into the lavatory for a quick ultra-shower and a facial and scalp depilatory.

Afterward, feeling marginally less itchy and infinitely more refreshed, he pulled on his jeans and a shirt, drank a quart of fruit juice to take the edge off his hunger, and then keyed into his console to check his mail.

Touch and smell seemed overpowering: the console keys against his fingertips; the pressure of the seat against his back and buttocks; the seam and fly of his jeans pressing against his crotch; the smell of soap and deodorant on his skin; even the air stirring against his arm hairs. It was all intensely distracting.

Krueger and the facility medic had both left him messages in his inbox. The medic's was a typed request for a medical exam within an hour of awakening. Krueger's message was audio only. "Call me as soon as you're awake."

Might as well get it over with, Daniel thought, scratching his underarm absently. He tapped in Krueger's number.

Krueger was a pilot in addition to being the facility manager, and lately he had been spending most, if not all, of his time in proxy. This couldn't have had much to do with vanity. His proxy was essentially identical to his own body, and Krueger was not a pretty man. Large, pale, and bald, with an intimidating stare—he reminded Daniel of a hairless gorilla.

When Daniel entered, he was pacing the floor behind his office couch, through a misty projection column that displayed a large jello of the Earth, complete with satellites and colonies orbiting in 10X real time.

The shadows, cloud systems, and firestorms that moved across the globe's face were real. The Waldos, Inc., business ventures were computer-enhanced. They lit up across the continents and oceans and swarmed around the translucent globe like plagues of insects: work-share communities in rippling greens, joint ventures with the government or other multinationals in orange and red, undeveloped real estate in blue, manufacturing plants in yellows, satellites in yellow, the Waldos, Inc., manufactories-in-orbit in purple.

The walls were covered with bookshelves, which had six or seven sizes of smart books. Sculpted shapes, mostly vases and urns, filled the remaining shelf space and portions of the floor. They ranged from antique American Indian and Greek clay to bronze and brass, to twentieth-century abstracts, to surrealist statuary in mahogany, oak, and cherry wood. The arches and curves and handles and bowls usually drew Daniel's attention for the few moments Krueger occasionally kept him waiting, but today was not a day for delays.

Daniel picked up a midsized book, and the cover displayed a scrolling set of choices that would fit this book size. He chose one of his favorites—a classic, Dorothy Sayers's *Gaudy Night*—and the chosen book's cover layout appeared.

"Sit down," Krueger said, gesturing at the couch, and Daniel caught a whiff of warm plastic and oil, and the sickly sweet smell of air freshener-fungicide. He caught himself trying to mute his olfactory inputs.

"Look, I know what you're going to say."

"No, you don't. Sit."

Daniel sat. Krueger stood with his fists at his sides and eyed Daniel. Flares of light soared past his face, unnoticed. He reached into a pocket and tossed a data lozenge into Daniel's lap.

"Read it," he said. Daniel pulled out his kelly and inserted the lozenge.

REFUGEE RESCUED BY UNKNOWN VIGILANTE!
MYSTERY HERO VANISHES AFTER SINGLE-HANDED
BATTLE WITH WHIP PACK.

Color close-ups of the corpses appeared and hung beneath the headline. The images hit him like a punch in the gut. Their expressions when they had first met his eyes came back to him, and reawakened the screams from his nightmare. A wave of nausea gripped his stomach; bile rose in his throat.

Yeah, it stinks, he thought, grim. But I'm never going to stand by and watch while innocents are murdered. Never again. Daniel ejected the lozenge without reading the article, and tossed it back to Krueger.

"And?"

"I can't bring myself to lay into you for saving someone's life, in spite of what that action might have cost us."

Daniel opened his mouth.

"Shut up. I'm not through yet. I've seen the playbacks; you did what you had to. But we just barely escaped detection—that woman's testimony is all over the nets. We can't afford that kind of publicity, Sornsen."

"I know that."

"Do you?" Krueger sighed. "I wonder if you know just how great a catastrophe it would be if we made the evening news." He propped himself against the back of the couch. Daniel had a hard time concentrating on what he was saying. They *were* just kids, though, Daniel thought. Kids.

". . . those Kaleidas people said," Krueger was saying. Then he stared at Daniel, awaiting some kind of response.

"Excuse me?"

"I said I don't care what those Kaleidas people said. We should have captured the renegade while we had the chance and brought MacLeod in."

"Oh. Right. Ummm." Daniel collected his thoughts, and then frowned. "You didn't have a lot of choice, boss. Rasmussen was insistent and it would have been dangerous to brush him off, with all the clout he's got."

Krueger frowned, hunching his massive shoulders. "I know. He gave me a call after we returned from Shasta yesterday and put the heat on me again." He shook his head. "It's a perfectly idiotic idea, chasing the remote around this way. But he wouldn't listen to reason."

"Any luck on locating the originating signal?"

Krueger gave him a terse shake of the head. "Not yet." Then he erupted, "God damn it, it just doesn't make sense! I've had the pilot frequencies scanned throughout the entire possible range. We didn't find a trace of the signal. No anomalies, no hidden source code, nothing. I myself checked the interface security programs, twice."

"So it's not someone in Austin or Kaleidas."

"It *has* to be. But it's just like the last time—the originating signal can't be located. Which means the pilot must be broadcasting from somewhere else. But where could the renegade have gotten all the interfacing equipment, the proper waldo unlocking code, the crèche, for Christ's sake?"

"They could just be using a beanie and some squish."

"Doesn't seem likely. I don't know. Maybe."

"Well, regardless, it has to be someone connected with the project," Daniel said. "Or someone who *was* connected with the project."

Krueger gave him a sour look. "No shit. I've already checked. Seven people have left the project since the latest beanjack upgrade two years ago. No one who left before that had enough of the right brain centers tapped to interface efficiently with the current model's piloting software. And all seven possibles are verified inactive. Without a doubt."

Daniel nodded. But the memory of the night before intruded again. *I really killed four people.* His hands scratched his head again, then wandered over his chest and arms. Krueger's abstracted frown slowly homed in on Daniel.

"Damn it, Sornsen, stop that scratching."

"Sorry." Daniel let his arms drop.

"So we're left with an insider. Scott and Teru have run a check on every single damned crèche-link in Medical, and I've done the same at Kaleidas. No extraneous signals. I've had everything double- and triple-checked, to avoid the possibility of subterfuge. Nothing. And yet the renegade exists."

He glared at Daniel as though it were his fault. Then he went to the window and looked out at the bird feeder hanging from a tree limb, which was filled with sugar water. A hummingbird and two bees hovered at the feeder nozzles. Daniel attempted to adjust his vision to view them more closely before he remembered he couldn't. He looked back at Krueger.

It had to be said. "Is it possible that Teru, or Scott—?"

"You think I've been sitting here trimming my hangnails while you were out there? I've run thorough checks on both of them. Clean as Canadian corn."

"And me."

"Naturally. No offense." Then he said, gruffly, "You know I wouldn't have you on MacLeod if I thought there was any chance of you being the renegade, Daniel."

"In my copious spare time."

"Right. But I had to check."

"No offense taken. But maybe it'd be a better idea to take the risk of letting some others in on this. Or send Scott or Teru out, instead of me." He thought about the killings again. He could do without any more of that. "I don't know what I'm doing, boss, and that's a fact."

Krueger turned and looked at him. His tone was flat. "Then you're just going to have to rise to the occasion, Sornsen. Because Scott hasn't been piloting long enough to keep his legs moving and keep from drooling at the same time, and I need Teru on the crèche interfaces. You're all I've got for the job."

"Right."

"And stop scratching."

"Sorry."

Krueger went to the window again. After a pause he said, "You know what really gripes my ass, Sornsen? I keep asking myself. If the renegade ends up killing someone, will Kaleidas get any heat? No, Austin will. Because we'll be right up front with our asses hanging out, ready to be cooked. God damn that idiot, he's going to bring everything down around our ears, and I'll be the one to take the heat." He shook his head with a growl. "I'll be damned before I'll take that quietly. Those Kaleidas people sit up there in their little tin can. They forget just how vulnerable we are."

"What are you planning to do?"

"We can't let the renegade pilot do any more harm—we have to get that stolen proxy off the street before whoever is piloting it kills someone. I've had Scott on cameras monitoring MacLeod all day, but we still haven't located the renegade; it must be in the city now."

"*What?*" Daniel leaped out of his seat, shocked into outrage. It's never politically astute to yell at your boss, but the words were out before he could stop them. "*You didn't send somebody else out?*"

Krueger's face went slack. Daniel started to grow concerned when Krueger continued to stare at him; Daniel's anger ebbed.

"Boss, what's wrong?"

Krueger blinked. A scowl spread across his face; he growled as if shaking off a fit of inattention. "What? Nothing's wrong. Relax. Scott got into the security visuals in MacLeod's home and office complexes and has been monitoring the corridor just outside her office. She hasn't left her office all day, and the renegade hasn't come in. And if worse comes to worst, we can alert building security and the police."

Daniel shook his head, but didn't respond. This was about the worst breach in Krueger's usually impeccable judgment that he'd ever seen.

". . . is this," Krueger was saying. "I want you to pull in MacLeod, now. Rasmussen's due for a comeuppance. I'll let the Board find a way to put the heat on him."

"You want me back out there, then?"

"How do you feel?"

"Fine." Daniel resisted the urge to scratch.

"OK, then. Yeah, I want you back out there. I put a rush on repairs to your proxy this morning. If it isn't repaired yet, get a loaner." He paused. "Just bring MacLeod in, immediately. I'll take care of the authorization."

"Right, boss."

"Now get out of here."

The medical center was a honeycomb of cubicles that wandered away from the entry lounge—each filled with sealed crèche baths, monitoring equipment, examination tables, data collectors, and a host of tangled wiring attached to machines with banks of lights, whose purposes were obscure to Daniel.

The receptionist glanced up. "The doctor will be with you shortly."

Daniel settled himself on the sofa, picked up last month's issue of *Time* magazine, and read about the secession riots in Alaska, Thaxton's early cabinet choices, and the surprise return from retirement of Tom Cruise as the great-grandfather in a musical-comedy remake of *Top Gun*.

"Daniel, why don't you come on back?"

He looked up. His physician today was Leanne. She stood by the reception desk, her arms folded. Daniel stood and followed her into the maze of cubicles. From behind, Daniel watched her walk. Leanne had a nice ass and well-shaped legs, and he couldn't help but admire them. She was in proxy, and a delightful one it was, too.

Leanne was an energetic woman who laughed easily, had a Texas lilt, and was, she liked to inform people, a quarter Indian. She looked like a full-blood, with a proud Cherokee nose and black hair down past her buttocks. Her outfit, beneath her lab coat, was a double-breasted, western-style shirt, black cowboy boots—made of real leather—and worn Levi's. This had more to do with the fact that she had grown up a local, rural girl than it did a sense of theater. She slowed and he caught up with her.

"Well," she said, "you're looking a lot better than when we pulled you out of the bath this morning."

"I feel a lot better. But I itch like crazy."

"You must be having a reaction to some of the drugs we gave you. That should pass on its own. But I'll go ahead and give you an antihistamine injection after the exam.

"We did a pretty serious metabolic purge on you, son. You were almost toxic with epinephrine overdose. What the hell were you doing out there, anyhow? Gettin' in a barroom brawl?"

Daniel stretched his lips into what was probably a pretty unconvincing smile. "Right the first time."

He could tell by her expression that she didn't believe him. But she merely nodded. "Are you feeling OK now? Any aftermath?"

"Actually, other than the itching, I feel fine."

She eyed him skeptically.

"Really," he said. "I wouldn't lie to you."

She laughed. "Like hell you wouldn't."

They had reached a cubicle with an examination table; she pulled a drab green robe off a hook and tossed it in his face.

"Strip and lie down," she said.

"Why, Leanne, I'm flattered."

"Yuk-yuk. You proxy-jocks, I wish y'all'd think of a better comeback." But she was smiling.

She strapped him down at the head, chest, arms, and legs, then pulled the Agnostic from its station in the hall and positioned the multipurpose medical scanner to display the results of her testing so he could see it.

"Thanks."

"It's been a few months since your last full-body checkup, so I'm going to give you the works today."

"I can hardly wait."

"You won't feel a thing, I promise."

She injected him with a set of micro-waldos.

"I'm leaving the needle in place for removal when I'm done."

Daniel tried not to squirm. He hated needles.

"Don't hit the laser scalpel trigger by mistake," he said.

Leanne grinned at him and then slipped into the Agnostic's pilot chair and beanlinked into the unit. He watched on the jelly display while she navigated the micro-waldo troupe through his blood vessels and tissues, and gave him a running commentary on her findings as she collected and analyzed samples.

"I'm doing a spot check of your leads and connectors to ensure that no inflammation or short-circuiting is going on. . . . I'm checking your neurotransmitter levels. . . . Now I'm checking your optic nerves. . . ."

Then she mapped his heart, lungs, liver, kidneys, spleen, major glands, digestive system, and limbs. Finally she removed the beanlink and then the needle, pressing a dab of Liquid Skin against the crook of his elbow. It gelled instantly.

"Well, the job hasn't given you an ulcer yet," she said. "Overall, I'd say you're healthy as a horse."

"That's nice to know."

Then she pushed the scanner aside and had him sit up. She pulled a tray of implements over, prodded at his liver and appendix, listened to his breathing, and tested his reflexes. The pungent alcohol she used to swab the skin around his beanjack cooled the heat from the itching.

She stuck a syringe into his right arm. At his expression she said, "Anti-histamine. Should start to work right away."

"God, I hate these exams."

She gave him a little smile as she removed the needle and applied a dab of Liquid Skin to the puncture. "Well, you can relax, hon. I'm all done."

She gave him little jars for urine and stool samples.

"Couldn't you just take samples while you were in there?"

"And give you nothing to do?" She smiled. "Takes too long. I've got two more jocks waiting for a checkup, and rounds to make. Fill 'em and return 'em by tomorrow morning."

Daniel shook his head. "Can't. Sorry. I'm out again as soon as my proxy is back up."

She eyed him, her expression flat. Then she shook her head, so thoughtfully that for a moment Daniel was unsure whether she meant it as a contradiction. "Not till we get the lab results back, you're not."

"Krueger's orders."

"He knows the rules. Sorry."

Daniel pulled on his jeans. "*I'm* sure not going to argue with him."

Her eyebrows went up. "Then I will. He has no business sending you out till you're fully recovered. No field experiment is that crucial, I don't care how top secret it is."

Daniel shook his head. "It's important, Leanne. It's not just Krueger being an asshole—I *want* to go back out. And I'll be careful." He smiled his best smile at her. He couldn't compete with his proxy for looks, but he was not without a certain charm. After a couple of seconds, the vertical lines between her brows eased.

"Well, all right. Bring 'em back within the hour and I'll run them for you, personal-like."

"Thanks."

"But stay out of trouble, hear? I don't want to get dragged into the crèche chamber in the middle of the night to pull you screaming out of the bath like I did this morning. You hear me? I mean it."

He took up her hand, kissed it. "You bet."

"And get those sample jars back to me right now—I want the results before you go."

He was already on his way. "I promise."

Teru was waiting for him by his crèche in the main crèche chamber. The chamber held sixteen tubs—one for each of Austin's proxy pilot-testers—each with its own monitoring and control equipment. Here and there, technicians were checking the readouts of the different crèches. Everyone was supposed to take a day *in corpus* after six days in proxy, but no one enforced it. They were all guinea pigs, anyhow, and their monthly fizz-psych testing sufficed to tell whether they'd been *ex-corpus* too long for their own good.

Down at one end of a long bank of lidded, bathtublike crèches, Krista pushed the lid of her crèche open and stepped out, dripping glycerin.

"Hey, Daniel!"

He waved. "Hi."

She peeled the thicket of leads off her limbs, head, and torso and, with a grimace, removed her IV before wrapping herself in a towel. A technician hurried over to help her.

Daniel met Teru at the far end of the crèche bank. Teru had her proxy back now, and it was done up as a male—a black teenager with a scarf tied around the forehead. The proxy was clad in cotton draw-string breeches and Daniel's old Hindi torture thongs. They had brass spools for toe grips which were mounted on a wooden platform, and they had inflicted several days worth of pain on him before he had given them to her.

"Like your outfit," Daniel said. Like hell he did.

She-he tilted her tall young man's head back to gaze at him. Her-his hand rested on Daniel's crèche board, whose banks of LCDs all shone red. Dangling from the circuitry board was the crèche interface lead.

The crèche was a large bathtub with a lid, three-quarters full of warm solution: they cycled saline, glycerin, and soapy water through, in turn; right now it was salt water. Next to the crèche were a Lung and an air tube with a floating ball. A thermocouple and level indicators at the tub's side were connected through a control system to the heat-exchange pump on the floor.

Various physiological monitors lined the tub's edge, as well as an auto-drip IV filled with a nutrient solution hooked to a computer, and a mess of green, yellow, and black wiring. The wires were electrodes that, when taped to his arms, hands, torso, thighs, and calves, would monitor his body functions, or run a mild electric current through Daniel's muscles to stimulate them and keep them from atrophying.

Next to the apparatus stood Daniel's proxy. The remote appeared to be a better-looking version of Daniel, several years younger than he, and substantially better muscled. It stood dressed in casual clothes, with its arms hanging down, staring glassily at the wall opposite. He walked around it and looked it over. The skin of its face, chest, and arms showed no signs of tear.

Daniel set his suitcase down by the proxy and gave its cheek a good, hard pinch. It was always a weird sensation, to be eyeing himself—his other self—from the outside. He felt like a voyeur. He slapped the cheek.

"Good as new, eh, bud? Takes a licking and keeps on kicking."

"Don't be flippant," Teru said. "I'm not in the mood."

Daniel looked at her-him askance. "You're full of charm today."

"Making you feel good isn't my job. I've a lot of other things to do and I haven't time to baby you." Less sharply, she-he said, "Let's get the diagnostics out of the way, shall we?"

"Right."

"Did you take your purgative? Have you shat?"

"I haven't eaten since I woke up. Only clear liquids. I took a small dump."

"Good. Because I'm not cleaning up the mess."

"Relax, would you?" He stripped his clothes off, climbed into the bath, and hooked up the outlet hose to his penis.

The air was a tad cool for nude comfort; gooseflesh crawled up his legs and he folded his arms, shivering a bit, while Teru taped the sensors and electrodes onto him.

Then he sat and Teru attached the crèche connector lead to his beanjack. The red LCDs on the crèche circuitry board all went off and a bunch of green and yellow ones came on. Several digital displays lit up. Teru examined them, made a couple of modifications with the toggles. The yellow LEDs, one by one, turned green.

"Looks good. Go ahead and recline."

He did. Warm water took him, cupped his face.

He pulled the breathing mask down, slid the foam pinchers over his nose, and bit down on the plastic mouthpiece, while she poked his foot with a needle and sought the vein. He stared at the ceiling and tapped his fingers on the side of the crèche. Air, tasting of plastic and antiseptic, slid in and out of his lungs. Teru's failed attempts with the needle began to send pains shooting up his leg.

"Sorry," she-he said, at his flinch. Teru finally found the vein, and taped the needle down.

"How's the air flow?"

He nodded, made an OK sign with his hand.

Finally Teru stood, tapped a program into the drip-mixer computer to begin the initial dose of tranquilizer-and-neurotransmitter cocktail, and raised her-his eyebrows at him in query. Daniel gave her-him a nod and slapped the lid.

"Right." Her-his gaze held him for an instant, and as the lid went down, Daniel heard her-him say, "Good hunting, Danny," and it was dark.

"Don't call me Danny!" he tried to say. It was hopeless, anyhow. Him as *Danny* was permanently etched in her forebrain.

He began relaxing his muscles as he floated, tuning out the itchiness, all the clinging tape, the needle in his foot, the mask and tubes and electrodes. His breathing was controlled by the Lung, and the rhythmic sounds of the air in the tube and the warm, bubbling circulation of the water lulled him.

A moment of jumbled sensation—the tart taste of green squirted into the back of his eyes, the squirms and twitches of his proxy body crawled across his sight like worms—the smell of someone's voice tickled the back of his throat; that must be Teru.

Then the confusion passed. He opened his proxy's eyes, and he was staring at the teenaged boy who stood by the crèche with his arms akimbo.

"You there?"

"I'm here."

While Teru checked the readouts, Daniel lifted each arm, each leg, rotated his head, squatted and stood. In comparison to his own body, he felt wooden—a little numb—and congested.

"How do you feel?" Teru asked.

He sought his voice. "Great."

Sound reception was exterior only; to his proxy ears, his proxy voice didn't sound anything like his own. He made an imitation of clearing his throat and picked up his suitcase, which felt much lighter to his proxy than it had to him.

He didn't look back at the crèche or think about his unconscious body curled up inside it. Thinking too much about it gave him the creeps.

"Well. I've got work." Teru gave him a quick flick of the hand, and was through the swinging doors and out of his sight.

As he made his way through the labyrinth of the Austin facility's corridors, he brought up a time readout and a display of the airline schedules. If he got the 2:43 bus into Austin, he could catch the 3:50 flight to Albuquerque.

CARLI

There Once Was a Woman Who Tasted the Sun—

"Hello . . ."

Carli nudged the door shut with her foot and looked around. Tania was easy to spot: half buried in Carli's squish-chair, muttering, eyes obscured by Carli's nethood visor, which was set at maximum polarity. Her head swung back and forth and she moved her hands in the air, pointing, dragging, grasping things.

Carli shook Tania gently by the shoulder. "Time to log out, dear." No response. Carli walked over and unplugged the nethood's and gloves' leads from her desk comunit.

Tania sat up suddenly, flailing, and lifted the visor of the hood. "Hey!" And, as she recognized Carli, "Oh . . ." Her eyes had trouble focusing. Drugs again? Maybe just postlink disorientation. She smiled sleepily. "Hi, Carli. I'n't expect you back so early. Ya jink?"

"Yeah, everything's fine, but I need my netset. Could you log off?" she asked, plugging the leads back in.

"Sure." Tania lowered the visor again. In a moment she removed the hood and gloves. "T's going?"

"The Phoenix probe reaches the sun today. I want to float it."

"You were going to Santa Fe. . . ."

"Not till later. Should be plenty of time to ride the probe and still catch the five-thirty bullet shuttle."

She took the hood and gloves Tania proffered and looked them over with a frown.

"Listen . . ." Carli pulled some bills from her pouch. "Could you run down to the corner store and pick me up some corn chips and a Diet Pepsi? I've got the munchies."

"Sure." Tania took the money and slipped out the door.

Once she was gone, Carli took the hood and gloves into the bathroom and disinfected them. The last thing she needed was a case of the Mold.

Then she climbed into her squish-chair and made herself comfortable in the cushioning gel. She slipped on her gloves and pulled them up her arms, and fitted the mesh hood over her head. The metacloth mesh was cool and damp on her hands, arms, neck, cheeks, and mouth, and the sweet-acrid scent of disinfectant stung her nostrils. Carli pulled the visor down and then adjusted the transceiver embedded in the mesh at her mouth and the microprocessor chip at the base of her nose.

"Boot linkware," she said.

Shiny blue, block-letter icons resolved themselves in front of her, while GridLink's signature tune chimed:

COMMAND FILE CONNECT UTILITIES MACRO

She touched CONNECT. As her fingers slipped across its hard surface, the word began to glow a soft blue-green. Beneath it appeared several pictographic icons: a metal caterpillar for hardware link, a phone handset for modem link, a satellite for radio link, and a comunit for local mode. When Carli touched the caterpillar it grew until it filled most of her vision. Electrons pulsed back and forth inside it. Her perspective became that of an electron that left the chip and sped along a wire, swooping and diving, till she reached a graphic foyer.

Its pillars and arches were a translucent glaze smeared across her apartment. Only the words on the backlit crystal banners strung throughout the foyer, and the twodeos and jellos that played in the background, suspended in the air here and there when she moved her head to look around, obscured her view of her living room. Sounds trickled in through her earphones: music, muted voices, mechanical and animal sounds, depending on which way she turned her head. The largest banner, stretching all the way across the foyer, read "Welcome to North America On-Line!" At the top edge of her vision, in muted tones, there remained her original GridLink icons.

With a quick set of touches on her GridLink icons, Carli polarized her visor and cranked up the volume in her earphones. Might as well get the full *virtu* effect. She'd be paying enough for it.

A syntellect approached her from the shadows. It was asexual, bald, and, though rendered in great detail, not quite real-looking. In some indefinable way, it *looked* like a graphic projection. It was smiling. Briefly, its appearance made her wonder whether Daniel had been a holographic projection of some kind. But that idea was even more outlandish than the alternatives.

"May I direct your signal?"

She licked her lips, dry-mouthed. *I can't believe I'm doing this.* The muscles in her chest tightened, making it hard to breathe. *Here goes nothing.*

"Yes," she said. "Connect me to the Phoenix probe transmission."

"You refer to *NASA presents: Phoenix One Enters the Sun's Atmosphere?*"

"That's it."

"Very good. This sequence has been rated AG-five. Suitable for general audiences, classified as science-educational with an action-oriented element. Not recommended for pregnant individuals, individuals with heart problems or other serious cardiovascular diseases, or children under the age of five. To access the sequence requires Time-Walker One-one or greater, or JazzTronix Four-oh or greater. For an additional cost of fourteen hundred sixty-nine dollars and fifty cents, you may purchase JazzTronix Six-oh-four right now."

"I have TimeWalker One-one."

"Very good." The syntellect paused. "Please prepare yourself for signal transfer."

It spread its arms wide and the foyer depixilated, falling away in an avalanche of multicolored snow. "Thanks for choosing NAOL!"

Carli fell into a void. Words ticker-taped across the center of her vision: "Awaiting probe omni signal emergence, please hold . . . Awaiting probe omni signal emergence, please hold . . . Awaiting probe—"

—And then the probe made contact and, using TimeWalker's linkware, she poured herself into the probe's control template.

At the bottom of her vision was a series of icons, for links to scientists and control centers around the world, analyzing or related in some way to the probe's descent. For now, she ignored them. Like slipping into cool silk, or diving into a luminous pool, she moved through the probe's information centers, stretched her awareness into the nooks and shadowed corners of the probe software, perceived and tried to match the rhythms of the machine's quicksilver processes. Her linkware began to shunt incoming data from the telescopic cameras and other detectors, its antennae, spectrometers, photometer, magnetometer, and radiometer, to her perception centers.

How easily it all came back! She felt the corners of her mouth curving up.

A river of free electrons streamed past—the solar wind came to her as both sight and sound: a ringing, sighing whisper in her hearing centers, like the distant cries of a banshee; and magnetic eddies swirling around about her, wraiths of glowing energy. Colors she couldn't name exploded about her. She turned her head this way and that, gazing at the spectacle. Space was fluid radiance, punctuated everywhere by swirls and sparks of brilliance.

Sources of vision came from several instruments, and her visual spectrum extended, with gaps, from radio wave into X ray. Her visible-spectrum eye—one of the probe's cameras—currently faced away from the sun, focused on a star. Carli couldn't access the probe's data files and didn't want to leave the probe or distract herself chasing links; she would wait until the waldo pilot or the probe software used the star's position for a course correction to learn which star it was.

Through a series of colored filters that flicked over and away from her vision, the other eye honed in on the fully lit, blazing sphere of Mercury. The planet, millions of miles away and greatly magnified, became visible over the shoulder of some part of the probe—of her—and changed colors as the filter combinations changed.

She noted, as the pilot's commands accessed the Mercury data, the ways in which the data were being processed. On-board computers were transmitting some last information on the planet. Mercury's surface appeared very like the moon's—scarred with pits and deep craters. It was a dead world. The main telescopic camera was taking a series of highly magnified shots of a huge impact basin near the horizon, a dark circle surrounded by concentric rings of mountains that made it look like the center of a bull's-eye. The basin edge disappeared over the horizon; its diameter must have covered several hundred miles.

As the camera panned away from Mercury, at the periphery of the probe's highly magnified vision were the solar arrays of Icarus Station: a vast, floating patchwork of dark and silver squares that orbited the sun in Mercury's wake, soaking up sunlight for use in antimatter production. She wished she could also have caught a glimpse of *Exodus*, which trailed Icarus.

Carli tracked the radio transmissions. A command was being repeatedly issued to rotate the probe, which did not respond. Something was wrong with the probe that the device's syntellect couldn't repair. She observed the pilot moving throughout the centers, checking for bugs. The pilot cleaned up an error missed by the on-board debugging system. Condensation moved through tubes, and a cloud of gas escaped into space; slowly she rotated—to face directly away from the sun, she realized, listening to the calculations and interpretations. The star she had seen was Pollux.

She sensed a jarring, as though some piece of herself had broken away. A shape tumbled away: it was the casing that had protected the probe's parabolic mirror shield from meteor pitting. More gases were spewed, and the turning ceased.

The myriad colors around her began to shift in tone and intensity; wraiths of streaming electrons, sheets of liquid, magnetic luminescence, darted around her. She was entering the chromosphere. The probe, shielded in its mirrored cup, would plummet into the upper layers of the sun's blazing atmosphere: the chromosphere and the outer edge of the photosphere.

The Phoenix probe had extensive cooling systems, and highly sophisticated ablative and reflective shielding, but its primary survival tool was its velocity. Brief moments after the probe reached the sun's photosphere, the detectors and central core would vaporize. The probe's velocity was 420,000 miles per hour; speed had begun to drop slightly due to drag. They had two or three minutes to collect data before the probe went blind. A few seconds longer, perhaps, for the computers housed in the craft's interior to finish processing and transmit the last of the data.

She felt an arm uncoil itself and extend, and then her eye that looked at Pollux saw it: a spindly, multijointed rod was telescoping out, locking into place as it unfurled a silver sheet that appeared the size of a sheet of computer paper—though sizes were misleading. Meanwhile the camera eyes were shifting around to look out over the shoulder of the cup. Carli felt a bit like an insect coming out of its cocoon, extending its eyestalks and legs.

Two tendrils detached themselves from farther down the arm. The probe controller activated the silver sheet. It would collect molecules and break them down for chemical analysis. One of the tendrils tested electrical conductivity. The last was a pitot tube, to monitor pressure gradients.

The touch of the outer fringe of the sun's atmosphere was a warm breeze against her metal skin, which she felt on her arms and face and neck—ambient pressure fluctuating around 0.0024 pascal, the probe whispered, and climbing slowly. The subsurface cooling system was straining hard to keep interior systems operational. Ambient excitation and ionization temperatures were nearing 500,000 Kelvin and climbing sharply. The probe's sunward surface was at about 680 Kelvin and climbing slowly.

With one heavily filtered eye she looked down, into the gravity well into which she plummeted—and gasped. The sky was filled with sun. No curves, no hint of horizon. Only an inferno, vast and incredible, hazing into a tinge of dark space at the periphery of her vision.

She felt her own body recoil. But she had no choice but to continue to stare: the camera could not be withdrawn, and she certainly couldn't tune out the sight of what lay below.

The telescopic images shifted back and forth—there a dark area, sunspot activity, spewing wild bursts of radio energy. Below, a vast field of bladelike, pink-tinged spicules jetted up from the opaque surface of the photosphere, waving in the eddies and currents of the magnetic field: a windswept, burning prairie. A prominence—hundreds of thousands of miles toward the solar pole—arced up; lazily, like a cat stretching, it reached out to infinity, jets of glowing gas and energy tumbling along its arch. It could incinerate a world and not even register a change in shape.

Horrifying, the immensity of such power. And mesmeric.

She realized then that her stinklink microprocessor was assimilating some of the probe's inputs, rather arbitrarily translating them to sensory language she could understand. She could smell the sun.

Vague, teasing aromas wafted past. She had no names for them, though she tried: tartness; a cloying, musty-sweet scent; something so bitter it made her gag. Underneath these changing currents there developed an undercurrent, a smell like old leaves, chlorinated solvent, and maybe a touch of jasmine-scented shampoo. . . .

As the probe plummeted toward the photosphere, the sun's banshee song crescendoed, a terrible sound: it fell on her mind's ears as a mourning, rageful scream. It took all her will not to disengage from the probe to escape the sound. The probe rocketed down among the towering spicules—a crowd of blazing phantoms, a thousand miles tall—and the photosphere loomed below, close now, a roiling fog bank. Then white-gold brilliance engulfed her.

Her sense of touch vanished as the probe's thermocouples went inoperable. According to extrapolations from interior temperatures, ambient excitation and ionization temperatures were dropping, but the projected black-body temperature outside had risen above 8,000 Kelvin.

The silver sheet vaporized in a blast of light. Reflexively, futilely,

Carli lifted invisible arms to shield her eyes. The probe's arms that held the cameras turned molten, and briefly, before the connection was lost, she had the sense of falling over the edge of the cup into the blast. The banshee's scream cut off sharply. She was locked in the machine mind of the probe, blind and deaf. Meltdown of the core would commence, the probe clock informed her, in approximately eight seconds.

She knew she wasn't really there. But her mind told her she was trapped in a dark box, plummeting into the heart of a giant nuclear explosion—about to be burned to death—

The internal temperature figures tumbled upward. The NASA controllers were shouting at the waldo pilot, *Thomas—pull out, man, you're waiting too long—! *Heat singed her hair; the skin of her face and arms burned—she heard screaming, far away. It must have been her own voice.

A wrench. She was torn loose from the probe. She screamed again, abruptly embodied and buoyant. Hands were on her neck, tugging at her, jerking her head around.

Dark. Icy cold. Shock waves.

Carli opened her eyes, disoriented. The room's ceiling wobbled drunkenly above.

She had returned to her own body. Tania held the nethood and its lead in her hands, and knelt beside Carli's squish-chair, looking at her with a worried expression.

Carli shivered and rubbed her arms, sitting up. The cold was an illusion; the gel of her squish was body temperature. Tears were streaming from her eyes. She trembled and her heart still pounded.

Somewhere deep inside, a tiny bud had sprouted. She didn't want to look at it too closely, just yet; it might wilt under too intent a gaze. Instead, with a laugh, she wiped more tears away, slapped the edge of the squish-chair, and hooted.

"Ooo-*ie*, girl! That was a ride."

HE'S NOT THE ONLY ONE PENETRATING SECURED PERIMETERS

The trolley squealed to a halt and exhaled chilled air as the door seals broke; three or four more people crowded onto the steps, jamming Daniel back against the rear window. A metal bar pressed into his buttocks. He clutched the overhead rail and craned around people's heads for a glimpse toward the front, spotted the back of Carli's head.

He'd be helpless to hide if she should turn, but the likelihood she would spot him in this crush was remote at best. He squirmed and elbowed commuters until he faced outward, palms and nose pressed against the cool, double-walled pane. Then he shut tactile input down as low as it would go. His sense of being cramped faded. He gazed at the receding street scenes.

He had visited this city once with his parents, when he was ten, a five-day stop on their move from El Paso to Denver. Santa Fe was smaller than he'd remembered.

Dusk had settled over the town in the few minutes since he had boarded the trolley. He saw that they had left behind the high-tech squalor of Cerrillos Road, whence he had followed Carli's homing signal from the underground bullet shuttle. The trolley car was now trundling along some other major avenue.

Pedestrians crossed the street in the trolley's wake; sleek electric vehicles with mirrored surfaces and eye-dazzling license displays swarmed past.

The few bare buildings he saw had a Spanish or Indian flavor to them—adobe, clay block, or stucco walls, heavy wood posts for support, and stone or clay sidewalks leading to their doors. But the majority of these appeared abandoned, and they were the exception among the rippling environment canopies that clustered along the road in assorted colors, trembling in the evening breeze like half-inflated balloons.

Little evidence of vandalism scarred the buildings and yards, and the street was clean. He caught a glimpse of a small, open area by a stream. It was a park, muddy and unkempt, with monster cacti and yuccas rising from the lush, knee-high grass.

He'd remembered the landscape as being much drier, but the climatic change was no big surprise. And anyhow, some of the old vegetation remained. The cacti and piñons, crabbed dwarf pines, made seemly companions in a high-altitude valley folded between mountains and what had once been high desert.

As they neared the next stop he turned and glanced again at Carli. She'd found a seat. If he craned, he could see her shoulder.

The trolley turned at a traffic signal and rumbled down a street that wound toward the Santa Fe Plaza. He spotted the state capitol. The building was a monument in the Greco-Roman style, gradually becoming visible within a silvery, photolucent canopy as the sunlight faded. He had a vague memory of touring the building with his father; was it really twenty-three years ago now? That was before the canopies and city walls had gone up.

Several stops after he had boarded, the trolley entered the town plaza and lurched to a halt. By now, more people were getting off than on. Carli's head turned in his direction. He spun and moved to put a group of men between him and her. They gave him a strange look; he shrugged with a smile.

"Austin." His lips moved as he broadcast. "Are you monitoring?"

"I just got here." It was James Scott. "What's the word?"

Daniel activated his compass and checked the readout. "I'm on a trolley with MacLeod; going northwest on"—he craned his neck for a street sign—"Paseo de Peralta. We're past the town plaza now."

"I'm floating you," Scott acknowledged.

"*What?*"

"I thought it might save time—"

"Get out of my face, Scott. I'll tell you if I need you to scan something." Daniel was trembling. Serious bad netiquette. Poking idiot.

Scott's voice quavered. "Sorry, Daniel, I'm sorry. I'm no longer floating you."

Daniel pinched the bridge of his nose. "Forget it, Scott. You didn't know."

He glanced at the icons at the top of his vision, musing, but he didn't want to take his attention off of Carli to do a *virtu*-net search for maps. Let Scott handle it.

"Tracking her manually is becoming difficult," he subvoked after a short pause. "I need backup. Can you project both our signals onto a city map and guide me that way?"

"But you're in the same trolley with her. Krueger said to bring her back right away. What are you waiting for? When are you going to make the approach?"

"It's not going to do any good to talk to her till she talks to her dad and finds out we're for real. Until then she'll never agree to come with me. So till I have some verification she has, I'm sticking to tailing her."

"But Krueger said—"

"You want me to kidnap her, Scott?" Daniel asked.

"No . . ."

"Then shut up about MacLeod and find out if you can project our signals onto a map."

A long pause. "Give me a couple of minutes."

The silence in Daniel's head lengthened. He noticed he was clenching and unclenching his fists at his sides, and forced himself to stop it. Lighten up, he told himself.

The trolley made another stop. Daniel looked above the canopies. Coppery, crepuscular rays fanned out from the horizon; a brilliant blue star shone near the young moon in the garnet-shot sky.

Several more people got off. Perhaps two dozen people were left in the cab. Her back was still mostly turned, and there were people Daniel could dodge behind if she turned toward him, but for the moment he had a clear view of the left side of her face. She looked pale in the light from the fluorescent tube banks.

Scott woke him from his slow study of MacLeod's eyelashes and jawline. "We could do it if we had the right maps, but Teru says we haven't got Santa Fe maps on hand, and she's too busy to do a net search right now. Sorry."

It would take her all of three or four minutes to download the necessary maps.

"Why don't *you* do it?"

"I—don't know where to look."

Daniel swore. But of course, James didn't. He'd just come out of the camps; they were lucky he was computer literate at all. "All right. I'll do it myself. It's not like I have anything else to do. Jesus. In the meantime I want you to find out who MacLeod knows in the north end of town. Check her file."

"I'll run a check."

Daniel called up a menu; a new string of icons spread across the top of his vision. He selected the *virtu*-net log-in protocol, on the low-profile option so he wasn't too distracted, and responded swiftly to the string of questions and promptings and iconic images that flicked in front of his eyes, spreading like changing graffiti across the faces of the other passengers.

In the University of Southern California library he found the street maps he wanted. At the prompt he chose a download protocol and dumped the compressed graphics file into his proxy's memory.

Meanwhile, the trolley stopped near a Moorish temple inside a smoky canopy. Several more people got off. Carli swung onto a bench seat and slouched down, clutching her satchel under an arm. Daniel saw now her cool suit was unzipped; sweat-dampened white stretch cotton showed underneath. She seemed moody and distracted; her gaze was focused inward. But if she turned her head again, he had no place to hide.

There was no choice. He shoved the doors outward as they started to close, and stepped off of the trolley. Once it started moving he trotted after it, at a pace faster than humans normally went—though he hoped not conspicuously so.

Meanwhile he loaded the maps and the access software. At his request the program displayed a topographical street map of Santa Fe, a grid of faint blue lines, and showed him where he was with respect to various landmarks. He appeared on the map as a tiny, blinking dot when he stood still, a tiny blinking green arrow when he moved. He fiddled with several grades of resolution, and then requested to be guided along the trolley line B route. In his vision a series of streets lit up red. His little green arrow wormed along the red line as he trotted along. He shrank the image into a corner of his vision.

No one was on the street in this commercial-residential area. The stars were all out now, and the last of the sun's light was a subtle violet hue on the sky beyond the western mountains. Daniel continued to follow the trolley, ducking inside storefronts or into alleys each time it made a stop. But Carli always remained on board.

Headlights came up behind him; he immediately slowed to a human-normal pace and moved to the side of the road. Intense light blinded him—he dampened the light receptivity of his proxy's eyes and turned. Three multimegawatt spotlights were trained on him.

Police waldo.

Probably too late, it occurred to him to blink and shade his eyes. The hair on the back of his neck felt like it was standing out. The dark shape that loomed before him was the size of a military tank, he realized; what was this, wartime? It was hard to tell exactly how big the waldo was, as the bulk of it was barely visible behind the glare of the spotlights. But it was definitely *big*.

"Go on, assholes, go catch some criminals," he muttered, and stepped up backward onto the sidewalk. "Austin," he subvoked, "I think I'm in trouble."

No one answered. Daniel swore silently, put a smile on his proxy's lips.

He could feel the controller's eyes drilling into him—he didn't know enough about current enforcement technology. If the waldo vehicle had certain types of enhanced vision and if the cop who piloted it looked closely and knew much about physiology, he might be able to tell Daniel's body was a machine.

"Good evening, Officer." Bless whoever had done the voice programming for this mechanical contrivance—his proxy software modulated his voice so it came out even and normal-sounding. Then darkness swallowed him, and at the same instant he heard the vehicle's passage, felt the rush of wind, and smelled ozone. With a sigh of relief he reactivated his night vision. Sight returned.

By now the police waldo—and the trolley—were out of sight over the top of a hill. He jogged to the crest and came upon a three-way fork. Three sets of trolley tracks branched out to follow the streets. He checked his inner chronometer. Two minutes and eighteen seconds had passed since the trolley had come this way. The map showed that the B line dead-ended here. An out-of-date map. Shit. He killed the map. The faint blue and red lines shattered and the bits faded.

Squatting, Daniel strengthened infrared reception and studied the tracks. A trace of a heat signature from the wheels' friction lingered on the center set of tracks. He looked around—no one in sight.

Daniel straightened, cranked up his leg speed to near maximum, and prayed for a paucity of cops.

"Sornsen?" Scott again. His voice sounded excited.

Daniel slowed his pace to a fast job. It was hard to avoid potholes and fire hydrants at fifty miles an hour and hold an intelligent conversation at the same time.

"I'm right here," he said. "Where the hell have you been?"

"What happened?" Scott sounded poised to drop another load of apologies. "Did you need something while I was gone?"

Daniel turned a corner and spotted the trolley about half a mile away. It was slowing as it neared the base of a hill on the northern edge of town. The road continued up the side of the mountain; in the hills above them, Daniel caught glimpses of the city perimeter wall among the pines.

"Never mind. What did you find?"

"I think I know where she's going. Can you give me the nearest major cross streets where you are?"

Daniel called up the map again. This development didn't even appear. The map must have been a good five years out of date. Disgusted, he killed the image again.

He looked around. This street had several residential-sized canopies, most photolucent, all billowing in the evening breeze. The light coming from the homes within them opaqued the canopies somewhat, making them glow like Japanese lanterns. The homes were blurs of light and shadow, jello-images out of focus. But two or three residents had already furled their canopies for the winter. By contrast to the canopy-shielded homes, the unshielded houses seemed brazen, naked.

The trolley rolled to a stop at the track's terminus, and the last dozen or so people debarked. There were no street signs. Daniel triangulated on Carli's signal, spotted her silhouette. She had just stepped onto a lighted slidewalk that moved up into the foothills alongside the road.

"The last time I saw a street sign," Daniel said, "I was still on Paseo de Peralta, but that was some time back, and I've done a lot of twisting and turning since then. I think I'm in a residential district now. A rich one, from the looks of it."

"Yeah . . . Let me see . . ." There was a pause. "I think you must be near the end of the trolley route. There's a terminus at the base of the St. John's residential district. It's a wealthy neighborhood, and her parents live there."

"Good work, Scott. I'm going to follow her. And while you have her records out, give me what you've got on her family."

"It's quite a large file, actually; her father is a public figure. Hold on while I access the long form. . . . Oh—Krueger has a flag here on your information request. You asked about the man she visited at The

Protein Bomb. He was her nephew, Jackson Brennan DuPont. Nick-named Paint. I have a short file on him; he's an ex-convict."

"Oh, really?" Carli had a good head start up the hill now; Daniel stepped onto the slidewalk and started after her. "What for?"

"Draft evader. Served forty-one months of a five-year sentence in the New Mexico State Penitentiary. Paroled almost a year ago."

"Ah." Daniel digested that tidbit. "How about some details on the rest of the family? I know that she has a sister who's much older, and both of her parents are living. Her father's a congressman."

"A Fiscal Democratic senator representing New Mexico, serving his—I guess it's his fifth term. He's on tons of committees. Hmmm. This is interesting—one of his major positions in the Senate is chair of the congressional Global and Eco-Adaptation subcommittee."

"He's the head of GAEA?"

"Right. He's been on numerous ethics panels in the past. And—wow, impressive. Listen to this. Two consecutive presidents selected him as the primary U.S. representative to the United Nations Environmental Programme! I remember that from when I was a kid," Scott was saying. "I wanted to hop a scram to Nairobi and join UNEP ever since I was five."

But Daniel had stopped listening. Carli's father was chair of GAEA? Almost half of Austin's funding came from GAEA. Nearly all of Kaleidas's did. And the renegade pilot was trying to kill the chair's daughter.

Your father has heard of us, maybe, once in his career, he'd told Carli. And then Krueger's response, *he knows,* when Daniel had told him they'd have to leak some information to her father.

The man not only knew; he had been around long enough, he could have been one of the initial sponsors of the proxy-humans project.

Daniel made a small choking noise.

Scott misinterpreted the noise. "Oh, sorry. Rest of the family . . . Let's see. Her mother is a Cosmo, and is heavily involved in volunteer community and religious programs. Oh, here's something. MacLeod had an older brother who died in his late twenties, thirteen years ago."

Concentrate, Sornsen, he told himself. Older brother died.

"Let me guess," Daniel said. "He died in the war."

"No, but you're close. Cause of death isn't listed in this summary, but he spent eighteen months in a veteran's hospital before and up to the time he died, so presumably he died of war-related injuries. That was around the same time as all that biogenetic shit. Maybe he was infected."

"Go on."

"Her sister is forty-five years old, lives in Los Alamos, has two children besides DuPont, by a different father. Both are school-aged. She recently contracted a four-year term marriage with—Shall I go on with this?"

"Just give me the interesting bits. Skip the trivia."

"Heck, I don't know what parts of this are going to interest you, Sornsen. How about I crossload this over to you?"

"I won't have time to read it. I'd rather have you feed me info so I can keep my attention on other things. Just keep the file available, and if I have any questions, I'll ask you. But if you have any images of her family on hand I'll take those."

"Just a sec . . . No, not in this file. Do you want me to do some more digging?"

"Forget it for now. I'll record shots of everyone there, and if we need to match them up later, we'll be able to."

The house's canopy was partially raised. The home of Carli's parents was a two-story, Spanish-style dwelling of white stone block with a sloped roof of red clay tiles. It rested on the side of a hill at the end of a cul-de-sac it shared with three other palatial homes. This house fit right in with its companions; it must have had at least forty rooms— not counting the bathrooms and storage spaces.

Daniel had his IR on. Glowing air, jettisoned from great fans mounted on concrete slabs, rose around the copper coils of six separate AC units and poured upward over the edges of the canopy. Probably about 30 percent of that energy being extracted from the house's interior was pouring right back in the other side. He was facing the back of the house now, but moments earlier, before he had left the street to work his way up the forested hillside alongside the house, he had seen the enormous picture windows that faced the cul-de-sac spill a plume of cool, dark air onto the ground like a pool of fog.

You could always tell the wealthier homes in a neighborhood. Wasted energy meant money to burn—coolth equals status.

The house stood on about an acre of undeveloped mountainside land covered with regional grasses, wildflowers, cacti, and juniper and piñon trees strung with globe lights. Surrounding the property was a wall seven feet tall and about a foot wide, whose top was studded with broken glass. Just inside the wall were the canopy support poles, swathed in furled strips of semireflective canopy cloth; the lower two canopy tiers had been taken up.

On the side of the house near the street, he spotted two men on a scaffold detaching the last section of the second-level tier from the overhead tier. A spider waldo staggered under the burden of one of the deactivated canopy HVAC units, and disappeared behind the house. So there must be a third worker somewhere, the waldo's pilot.

Daniel spotted her, sitting in the cab of the truck in the driveway, wearing a ratty tank top and an old-model control helmet and gloves. The power coils hung out the window and disappeared into the bed of the truck. She must have been plugged into the diesel generator in the truck bed that was coughing and outgassing in puffs of black and infrared; Daniel wondered whether the canopy company could really afford the license fees, or whether Carli's parents were so far above the law they could risk hiring an illegal combuster.

At least the pilot wasn't beanlinked. Second-generation waldo linkware was pretty limited in its capabilities; Daniel wouldn't have to worry much about tripping the spider's sensors.

Daniel viewed all of this dangling from his hands from the warm blocks of the perimeter wall. He had his arms crooked so he could see over the wall's edge, and he was being careful to avoid the glass and keep his head from crossing over the wall's edge. He eyed the house again, made a noise.

"How many people live there?" he subvoked to Scott.

"Both MacLeod's parents, half the year. Just the mother, the other half."

"One point five persons at ten thousand square feet, let's say; that makes for a dwelling density of . . . Ouch." He fell silent and scanned the wall's edge, first for magnetic fields from hidden capacitance wires, then for traces of IR or UV.

"I'm not picking up any unusual magnetic or electromagnetic patterns on the wall. Monkey me for a double check, would you?"

"Look, maybe you should just hang out on the street. The renegade couldn't know MacLeod is in Santa Fe tonight." Pause. "Excuse me, but isn't that broken glass I'm scanning on the wall?"

"The glass isn't that dangerous; I'm being careful. And I'm not going to sit out on the road like a trained dog. The renegade might have resources we don't know anything about and know right where she is."

"Krueger said to keep a low profile." Scott's voice carried a frightened edge.

A minute ago you were telling me to haul her in, Scott. Make up your mind. But with a mighty effort, Daniel refrained from sarcasm. "I promise I'll be careful. Would you please scan?"

Daniel's vision flickered, refocused, and his head turned slowly, scanning the wall and then the yard, at Scott's control. After a second Scott said, "I don't register anything unusual, either."

Daniel gnawed his lip. "I don't buy it," he said finally. "There's got to be something."

He lifted himself a little higher, amplified IR again, and this time turned off all visible wavelengths except a touch of blue to triangulate on the wall's position, and stared down the length of the wall, which was now nothing but a faint shadow. First one way, then the other. Nothing. He switched over to only UV with a bit of visible red.

And had it.

"Look there—at the corner. Do you see it?"

"What?"

"At the corner down there. I see a glint of UV."

"I don't see it."

With a grunt, Daniel dropped to the ground and ran to the corner of the wall. He snatched up a handful of dirt, flicked the pebbles out. Then he leapt up, caught the top edge of the wall, and lifted himself up with one hand.

Mounted on a skinny metal pole, nine inches above the wall, a mirror the size of a half dollar was mounted, set at an angle tangential to the two branches of the wall. And at the mirror's surface hovered a trace of UV, a dim blob of light. He pursed his lips, took control of the piezoelectric fan in his chest, and blew dust in front of the mirror. An angled beam of coherent UV light flickered briefly, reflected in the mirror among dust particles.

Daniel lifted himself higher, saw that the two men in the yard were now leaning against the cab while the pilot guided the spider waldo in disassembling their scaffold. He'd have to go around back.

"What are you going to do?"

Daniel grinned. "Watch me and learn."

He dropped to the ground and headed to the back end of the property. After backing away from the wall a good twenty paces, he started running, gauged his leap, vaulted over the wall. His body passed well above the UV beam. He landed, rolling in pine needles, stood, and headed toward the house.

Moments later, among the branches of a pine tree, settled in a crook of the tree, Daniel looked at the house. He had chosen a spot just outside the dining room. The light spilling from the windows fell on rows of marigolds and posies planted in rich, dark soil. They caught Daniel's eye. An expensive indulgence, keeping the canopy temperature low enough to grow flowers during the hot season. But beautiful.

Two people were in the dining room: an older woman, buxom and thick in the waist, and a slender woman in her early twenties. Both were Hispanic, the younger dressed in jeans and a shirt of thin stretch cotton with bunched-up sleeves—she had small breasts with dark nipples which showed faintly through the cotton and made Daniel restless in his perch. The older was dressed in a semiformal black dress covered by a white apron.

They were in the process of setting two tables, a large rosewood table close to the window which looked like an antique, and an oak table on the far side of the room.

Daniel called up a video capture window and zoomed on each of the women, stored a few seconds worth of images in quick recall for later reference, and indulged himself with a slo-mo replay of the younger woman's upper torso in a window at the center of his vision.

A movement at the periphery caught his attention; he canceled the slo-mo window and zoomed on the dining room again. A small, blond woman wearing a formal dress of blue silk had entered the room. *Floated* might have been a more apt description, though—her gait was smooth and her whole bearing seemed lifted, like a dancer's. Though the woman had to be in her mid- to late forties, she carried the dress well, and its close fit and side slits didn't seem inappropriate. In fact, as he zoomed in on her to record her, Daniel's penis struggled to escape the clutches of the pee-tube, seeking the vertical again.

Damn, he thought. This is getting ridiculous. I gotta get laid.

"Carli's sister," Scott said. "She'd be the right age."

"Maybe. I wish I could hear."

The blond woman spoke to the older woman. The older woman, Black Dress, nodded and left the room through a door opposite the one through which Blue Silk had entered. Blue Silk and Jeans spoke at length, then Blue Silk left. Jeans pulled out her kelly and spoke into it. She sat down at the table. Black Dress came in with a pitcher of iced water and began filling the glasses on the table.

Daniel called up his recording of Blue Silk's entry and placed the image in a window at the center of his vision, both eyes, to study it. He froze an image and enlarged it, did a 3D projection, observed it from all angles, called up and constructed a similar image of Carli and studied them side by side.

The woman in blue silk definitely bore a resemblance to Carli, with the prominent cheekbones and broad face. Her face had quite a few wrinkles. She didn't wear much makeup. She was wearing a small handmade bag of cocoa-colored velvet around her neck, embroidered with red, blue, and yellow cross-stitching, and looped with blue ribbon that matched her dress. He'd seen the like a couple of times before. God-bags.

"She's older than forty-five," Daniel said. "And she's a Cosmo. I think she's Carli's mother, Alison Almquist."

"Really? Wow. My mom *never* looked that good."

Daniel stored the close-up in quick recall and then canceled the image and returned his attention to the dining room. Jeans and Black Dress had been joined by two robotics: a butling unit and a server table. Jeans watched, offering brief remarks into her kelly, as the butler carefully draped a white linen towel across its double-jointed, foremost appendage.

The robot looked, if anything, like a steel bug lying on oversized wheels, with six arms waving in the air and a basket on its belly. It installed a corkscrew attachment on one of its arms, gripped the wine bottle with a rubber-coated vise, screwed in the corkscrew, and pulled. Then it filled a goblet with a dark red liquid; maybe a burgundy, Daniel thought, and his mouth watered. He would love to know what burgundy tasted like.

The butler rolled around the table to extend the glass to Black Dress, who looked surprised, and then opened her mouth in a laugh. She took the glass, sat down and took a sip, and squeezed Jeans's arm, who shared the laugh, showing a lot of teeth.

Then Jeans spoke into her kelly and the serving table rolled forward, picked a crock of soup up off of itself, and overturned it in Jeans's lap. There didn't seem to be any soup in the bowl. Jeans frowned and spoke into her kelly. Black Dress drained the wineglass, wiped it on her apron, and gave it to the butler, which rolled out of sight with it. Then she stood up and went out the door she had earlier entered.

Near the front of the house, Daniel saw that all three of the canopy

HVAC workers were carrying the last pieces of scaffolding to the storage shack behind the house. The two men had stripped off their work coveralls; Daniel spotted a pair on the driveway, a dark smudge against the white concrete, that had fallen off the back of their truck.

Daniel dropped down from the tree.

"What now?"

"I'll fill you in later," Daniel said.

He took hold of the doorknob, gave a last tug at the crotch of the coveralls, which insisted on crawling up his proxy's crack, and pushed the back door open.

Black Dress looked up at him from her stainless steel bowl, a chopping board covered with *real* fresh vegetables in her hands. He caught a faint whiff of onion, fresh bread, and spices. A line of gleaming cookery robots crouched on the counter. The creatures had long, serpentine arms with spoons, tongs, and ladles on the end, and they lifted lids, freeing tendrils of steam, flashing numbers and codes while they combined ingredients, cooked or blended or baked in their muffled innards.

Daniel gawked. These people were *loaded*. He'd known it, but the reality of it hit him in the chest at the sight of the robotic chef platoon, and he froze. The look of surprise on the woman's face became a frown.

"You aren't supposed to come in here," she said.

No time for regrets. He put on a contrite expression and cleared his throat.

"No, ma'am, excuse me, I mean, pardon the interruption. But we still need to deprogram the canopy HVAC controller." The words came out sounding better than he'd expected. He tried a more helpless, winning expression, one that had always worked on his aunts, if not always his mother. "I forgot to finish the sequence before we disconnected the units, and my boss is going to have a fit if the house AC cuts out. Which it will unless I make the changes.

"It'll take all of twenty seconds to finish. Not even that long. Can I use one of your kitchen terminals? Please?"

Black Dress scowled at him, wiping vegetable juices from her hands onto her apron, but the temperature of her expression rose maybe a degree or two above freezing.

She said, "If the mistress comes in here, we'll both be in trouble."

Then she sighed and gestured toward a comunit set in the wall by the door. "OK, just hurry up about it. OK?"

"Right. It'll just take two seconds, honest." Daniel touched the kelly on. A CRT display requested the log-in code. He turned back toward her. "I need you to log me in."

She sighed again and tapped in the code. He stashed the log-in code in quick recall as she typed it in, making a mental note to try not to feel too much remorse later for being such a mendacious snake. At least she wasn't being too nice to him; he doubted he could have gone through with it otherwise.

She went back to her soup, and said, "Hurry up; I'll be serving supper in a minute and you can't be in here then."

"Thanks," he said. "Thanks very much. Can't tell you how much I appreciate this."

Shielding the display with his body, he accessed the modem software, recorded the phone number, prepared the modem to receive a call, and then logged back out.

"Thanks a million," he said, slipping out the door. Hopping, he stripped off the coveralls, then wadded them under his arm and made a dash for the wall as the canopy-company truck pulled out of the drive.

Once he was safely hidden among the trees on the hillside above the house, he turned his radio back on and called Austin. It took several tries for Scott to manage to sputter out a reproach.

"—no answer—scared the holy fire out of me—!"

"You can holler at me later, James. I need your help. Float my proxy and keep watch."

He called up his menu over his right eye and selected "outgoing call"; in seconds, the log-in prompt for Carli's parents' house systems appeared. Scott had the good sense not to ask questions while Daniel logged in and accessed the house programming layout, I/O locations, command files, and so forth. He quick-called an image of the butler from memory, zoomed in, and tried to read the serial number on its side. He could read nine of the ten digits. He'd have to run a simple trial-and-error iteration to get the last digit.

"Give me a heads-up if someone stumbles over my proxy," he said. He replaced the vision of both eyes with a multilevel programming screen, wrote a shell script using i-Runner 6.2 source code, compiled it, and then crossed mental fingers and ran it.

A second later he was rolling through a room, navigating among shelves of books and laser crystals to where several—quite outsized—strangers lounged on huge squish-pillows and a likewise impressively proportioned couch. He stared into someone's enormous knees and, with metal arms, extended a goblet filled with wine. A fleshy hand descended and accepted the goblet.

"Jesus. Where are you? I'm getting some weird readings here. What's wrong with your linkware?"

"Nothing. I'm floating the butler. Shut up for a minute. I'm going to try to monkeyback it."

Daniel overrode the robot's programming long enough to scan for Carli; she stood near a wall of glass panes. She had changed into a dress of pale blues, with darker blue shimmer-tubes—one about the waist and another cowled about her neck. They glowed like veiled stars through a range of hues. She wore Chinese-style flats and no jewelry he could see. Subtle; nice.

The robot, with Daniel floating, rolled over to her and offered her a goblet of wine. She looked down, directly into Daniel's eyes, it seemed. Daniel felt like a six-year-old, looking back up at her. She shook her head at the wine goblet; her gaze returned to a man sitting on the couch and she seemed wistful, even sad.

The robot continued to hold the wine out. After a second she looked down again, and seemed surprised to find the robot still there.

"Some wine?" the robot asked again.

"No, thanks. I thought I said that." Her voice sounded metallic and oddly resonant, through the robot's auditory interpreter. Then she said, "Well, what the hell," and grabbed for it, just as the robot started to take it back. "I meant yes, dummy; let go."

The robot froze with its claw out, trying to calculate what to do next when no means yes. Meanwhile Carli took a large swallow, glanced at the couch again, and then turned to face the windows. She grimaced and eyed the glass, took another gulp.

"Run along," she said, when she noticed the robot wasn't moving. "Go serve other guests."

The butler understood the last part, and so Daniel's awareness was carried away from her again.

"Dinner is served," someone said, and the guests all looked toward Black Dress, who stood at the door.

"Heads up," Scott said sharply in his head. Daniel's awareness snapped back to his proxy. He came to his feet; his senses swam. Ducking against the tree trunk, Daniel made quick adjustments, looked and listened around.

Something big—and clumsy—was crashing through the trees down the hillside.

He crept closer. Two—no, three—human-sized IR signatures were stumbling through the undergrowth. They were too noisy and graceless to be the renegade—though they might be hirelings. Or possibly more whips.

They were heading too far west on the mountainside to be aiming for the Almquist/D'Auber home. He followed them down the hill and listened. They said nothing, though he could hear their heavy breathing. They crept down to the street, and in the pools of light cast by the streetlamps he could see them finally: three men, dressed in a dirty version of *natureil* dress, trailing loose tatters. They were barefoot, or sandaled.

Peteys.

"Sit tight till I signal you," Daniel subvoked to Scott, "but don't go off-line, OK?"

"You got it."

The three skulkers passed the parked cars and the fire hydrant, disappeared around the corner. Something struck the streetlight, which shattered with a tonal cry. This didn't inhibit Daniel's sight much, but plunged the street into human-visible darkness.

He saw curtains flutter across the road. Great. Someone would probably call the cops. Ought to jig off, he knew, but he could run fast if he needed to, and he was curious. He ran down the cul-de-sac to the corner and peered around the wall's edge.

Two of them used a crowbar to break the padlocks on the Dumpster. They began hauling out bags of garbage while the third broke into the salt station. Tiny white pills poured out of the box, bounced onto the sidewalk and into the road. He scrambled after them, stuffing handfuls into his baggy garment. The other two sorted through the trash, whispering excitedly as they tucked things down their outfits.

Then headlights appeared around a curve lower down the hill, and the three men made a frantic grab for a few items and then bolted back toward Daniel. He had no time to hide; they ran past him and dashed up the dead-end street. Then the car was blazing a light show, blaring a sound like bells—police waldo. Lights played across Daniel's face.

"HALT," a voice boomed. That was all it took.

Daniel's dash carried him to the base of the hill on the heels of the peteys. The man farthest behind gaped back at him, face pale in shock. He stumbled; Daniel picked him up. The lights from the waldo shone up the street at them.

"HALT. POLICE," the voice boomed again.

"Go on." He shoved the man toward the trees. It was the salt thief, a white man in his mid-thirties. He stumbled again, stared at Daniel as if he were a cop.

"It's a waldo," Daniel said. "It's too big to go crashing through the forest. He's calling for reinforcement." He knew because Scott had tuned in to the police broadcasts and piped it through to him.

The man needed no further encouragement. Daniel headed across the hillside, flanking them. His enhanced vision gave him the advantage; they couldn't see him.

The three men came slam up against the city wall, and leaned against it, panting. Daniel crouched behind a tree nearby. The wall was a good twenty feet high, and all the trees within jumping distance had been chopped down.

"Nowhere near our rope," one gasped.

"Head for it," the salt thief said, and stumbled blindly along the wall. They'd never make it.

"Get out of there now," Scott said in Daniel's ear. "The cops are coming."

Daniel already knew that; he heard the voices down the hill, and lights flickered among the trees. He stayed with them, though, shadowing them. The salt thief found the rope, started up it. "Come on! Come on!"

Daniel dodged into darkness when the police spotlights burst on, flooding the trees, creating sharp edges of light and shadow. The two men on the ground turned, blinking, arms raised.

"Don't shoot," one of them said. They were both middle-aged.

Voices yelled at the man on the rope to drop to the ground and surrender. He didn't stop. Shots were fired, and then he was over the top, and gone. Daniel thought he might have been hit, but perhaps not. Several policemen entered the clearing, threw the two remaining men to the ground, beat and kicked them for a minute or two, and then slapped restraints on them. Others shone their lights among the trees.

"Spread out, spread out," one said. "The fourth one's still out there."

Looking for *him*.

"Christ."

"Daniel, get out of there!"

"For stealing garbage," he said. "Christ."

He ran.

DINNER PARTY HELL!

About halfway through the chilled tomato-mint soup, Carli decided that if she had to smile one more time at another one of Mother's guests, she would scream.

Eighteen people attended the dinner party in all, eleven of them adults. One of the adults had waldoed the party—not her father, after all, who was there *in corpus*, but Fred Alvarez, a Washington friend of his who had missed the scram shuttle that he had just barely made. The waldo was a sophisticated model, a large jello-tube in which the man's head and shoulders appeared, mounted on a three-wheeled circular base. The waldo had two miniature cameras on its shoulders, metal bars that rose up on either side of the tube, that also supported two arms with three-fingered, rubber-tipped claws for hands. When Alvarez moved his gloved hands, the three-fingered claws moved; when he turned his head, the waldo turned.

Jolynd's two younger children, her husband, Michael's, three, and three others Carli had never met sat across the room, at a table near the fireplace. The children ranged in age from four to eleven, and they were giggling and teasing the robutler, which had been programmed to keep them entertained and fed and out of trouble.

Carli almost wished she were sitting with them. Or better yet, eating in the kitchen with the house systemskeeper, Belinda, a young woman with whom she got along quite well. Instead Carli was trapped at the grown-ups' table between a Santa Fe city councilwoman and a man she introduced to Carli as her term-husband. The councilwoman, Joan Fall's, new term-spouse, whose name Carli had forgotten twice already, was a lanky, grey man with hooded eyes and onion-skin lips who answered Carli's questions in rusty monosyllables.

Carli shivered. Mother always kept the house cold, and the presence of guests ensured an assault of refrigerated air. Carli had come prepared, though, this time. She pulled her tubular shimmer-wrap down over her shoulders and rubbed her forearms, which were crawling with gooseflesh. Then she forced herself to pay attention to Joan, who was talking to her again.

"Your mother tells me you're getting back into commercial communications research," Joan said. She brushed at the carefully styled and polymer-coated Greek curls on her forehead; beneath the light of Mother's antique cut-tin chandeliers, the swirls of rainbow-tinted plastic with which she had styled her black hair reminded Carli of a slick of crude oil. Her nervous flick tolled the huge gold bracelets on her arms like bells. "Have you found any business yet, or are you still developing proposals?"

"Actually I have a couple of proposals out," Carli replied, "but—"

"Ah, good!" *Toll.* "I have a number of connections in upper management at OMNEX in Dallas that might be—But what am I thinking? That wouldn't do for you at all, would it? Still, give me a call next week and perhaps I can put you in touch with someone. They wouldn't hold that court battle against you for this long, surely?" *Toll, toll.* "Speaking of legal matters, I must say, I'm so glad to see you and Jeremiah here on good terms, so soon after your contract expired! It's only been a month or two, hasn't it?"

Carli felt the color drain from her face. She pulled her lips across her teeth into a strained little smile and said, "The divorce was final last week. But it wasn't—"

"And you, Jere!" Joan drew him in with a clanking sweep of her arm. "Thank the goddess for term marriages, eh? They're so painless; everything is settled ahead of time. None of that nasty legal infighting that goes on when traditional marriages end. I personally think term marriages ought to be compulsory."

Carli clutched her napkin into a ball and eyed Joan. A hush had fallen over the table; Joan in her magnificent faux pas had drawn the attention of all the guests.

"Jere's and my marriage *was* traditional." Carli said it mildly.

Joan looked at her. She opened and then closed her mouth. Then she leaned back in her seat with a pinched expression. A general air of embarrassment settled over the room.

On Joan's far side, Jeremiah quickly shoved a spoonful of soup into his mouth. The magnitude of the blunder—and Joan's expression—finally overcame Carli's humiliation, though; she wrestled a sudden, feral grin to the ground and gazed deadpan at the councilwoman.

"Oh, my, well—" Joan rallied, smiled, dabbed at her lips with her napkin, and said, "Then it's all the more pleasing that the two of you are on good terms. Ah, thank you."

She made a show of selecting the right croissant from the server table that crouched at her elbow, and the moment passed.

Good terms. Ha. Carli sighed again, took a sip of soup. The marriage may as well have had a time limit written into the contract. Nine years, four months, seventeen days, and a handful of hours.

The hour tally wasn't firmly set in her mind; she couldn't decide whether to start the count from when she had found the letter or when she had actually closed the front door behind her. It mattered, somehow. And she must have spent a good three or more in that old rattan chair in the attic, barely able to breathe in the stifling, musty air, wearing an old T-shirt of Jere's, cutoffs, and her hair bound in a cloth.

Three hours. She remembered the old box at her feet, and how she sat there holding a letter in her hand. The one addressed from the federal marshal to Jeremiah MacLeod. Thanking him for being such a patriotic fellow. Reading, rereading it over and over, and finally just sitting and staring at it.

She had sat up there while the sun moved across the hazy sky and set. And on her way out, she had taped the letter to the hall mirror downstairs.

Carli swirled her soup with the celery stick, bit down hard on the stalk, dragged the wet fibers between her teeth, and exchanged a brief, meaningful look with her sister, Jolynd—whom Mother, for reasons known only to her, had seated between Colonel Rodrigues and Carlotta.

Carlotta was an old high school friend of Mother's, and Carli's sort-of-namesake. She wore many strands of polished stones, leather, feathers, and wood, and a proud array of wrinkles and age spots. She smelled of patchouli and dressed in the *natureil* fashion, in the layers of loose, gauzy shawls and wraps, the baggy, Japanese-style trouser-skirts.

It had to be a statement of principle, not lifestyle. Carlotta couldn't possibly be a *natureil* for real, except in winter; her age and her mass were too great. She was probably about sixty-five years old or so, almost six feet tall, and weighed close to two hundred pounds. In the 125- to 140-degree heat of summer, without a cool suit she'd die of heat stroke in an hour, max.

In spite of her mass, though, she carried an air of ethereal, catlike elegance that made her strange and beautiful. Her grey and chestnut hair flowed over the chair seat in back of her, almost to the floor. She had told Carli once, when Carli was a very little girl, that scissors had never touched her hair. Tonight, as always, she wore her leather circlet with the fiery opal at the brow. She called it her third eye.

Ever since she was a very young child, Carli had believed that Carlotta, her eldritch godmother and namesake, had a touch of Real Magic about her. And that old belief had lingered long into adulthood, had infiltrated Carli's agnosticism.

Carlotta was a licensed spiritual guide, and Carli's sister, Jolynd, hated the New Church of the Cosmos almost as much as she hated Carlotta. Carli figured Mother must have succumbed to an evangelical impulse to seat Jo next to her childhood nemesis. Jo might even go so far as to call it mental cruelty.

Carli eavesdropped on their conversation. Carlotta was doing all the talking—mostly to the colonel, as Jo was chewing the inside of her lip and casting dark looks at Alison, totally ignoring Carlotta; something Mother had done was really eating at Jo tonight.

If Carlotta's intention was to convert Colonel Rodrigues, she was wasting her time; the colonel was, if possible, an even more devout atheist than Jo, and the best Carlotta could get out of him with her talk of cosmic connectedness and psychic balance was grunts and mutters, and perhaps an occasional outraged snort. Carlotta smiled gently at his explosive sighs of protest, which seemed to irritate him even more.

Then Carli glanced back toward Jeremiah and her father. They and Mrs. Rodrigues were carrying on a discussion about the possibility of war with Mexico over the refugee crisis, and the international environmental conference under way over reclaiming the ruin of postwar Antarctica.

Jere must have sensed her gaze, because he looked up. After a pause he smiled at her, and after an equal pause she found herself smiling back. Their eye contact lingered for a mere instant after the smiles faded, and then Carli looked away—to catch Jo's husband, Michael, giving her a knowing look.

Jo was his fifth term-wife, and he thought he knew far more about some things than he actually did. She stared back until Michael twitched and looked away. Then she slurped another spoonful of soup.

She spotted the robotic server at her elbow. It had repeated itself at least once already, offering her a roll. Its sterling silver pincers hovered over a mirrored tray spread with steaming, freshly baked crescent rolls. Iced butter floated in silver cups; dollops of spread the same pink as the sun's chromosphere, which might have been crab meat or salmon, filled a crystal saucer.

"May I serve you?" the robot repeated, yet again.

"Help yourself to the croissants and spreads, lovey," Alison said. "You're holding up the server."

Carli took a croissant and looked at her mother. Alison was slim and stunning—in a slit-leg Oriental dress of midnight over royal blue silk, blue-on-blue. Her silver-blond hair was simple in style and unwaxed. Enveloping her ears were intricate ear chapeaux of smoky quartz crystals thonged with blue satin cord. She wore her little, embroidered God-bag at her neck, and Carli noticed her touching it occasionally. She exuded class—elegance and simplicity.

Carli looked down at her own dress of powder and sky, with the shimmer-tubes she had added at waist and neck to dress it up. It looked like a dime-store version of her mother's outfit. She wiggled her toes inside her favorite cloth shoes. Her fingers reached up for her locket pendant, the one Dennis had mailed her from Australia for her fifteenth birthday.

Underdressed, Carli thought. What the hell.

When Alison saw Carli watching, she gave her a shining, gentle smile. She was so beautiful. Carli had to lower her eyes. She swallowed, and it felt like a handful of razors going down.

Next time I really will say no, Carli vowed silently, and tore a bite out of her roll.

About the time supper had wound down to coffee and lime sherbet, Jolynd's eleven-year-old daughter, Tess, came up to Alison's elbow and asked solemnly, "Can we be excused, Gramma? Please?"

Alison nodded with a smile that crinkled the corners of her eyes. " '*May* we be excused?' Yes, you may. But stay off of the banisters."

The older children ran out of the room amid a great deal of cheering and laughter. The two littlest, Michael's Andy and another little boy, climbed into the bed of the butler's transport basket and squatted in it while Willis, Jo's eight-year-old hell-raiser, hauled it out by one of its arms. Alison summoned Belinda, the systemskeeper, via her wrist kelly, and told her to take them to the library and keep an eye on them.

"You're such an anachronism, Mother," Jo said. "That attitude went out with the turn of the millennium."

Everyone laughed, and Alison smiled, but Carli gave Jo a sharp look. She knew that tone. Jo persisted, "Belinda is a *virtu* programmer, not a baby-sitter. . . ."

"She's a *servant*, dear. She's expected to perform other tasks besides maintain the kelly service."

Carli recognized the look on Jo's face and braced herself for an explosion, but Jo's voice was quiet. "Tess is almost twelve. She's perfectly capable of keeping an eye on the younger ones."

"That's enough, Jo," Chauncy said. His tone was even more flat and final than Alison's had been. Then he broke out his Capitol Hill–style, oil-on-troubled-waters smile and cast it about the table, meeting everyone's eyes.

Carli returned her father's glance with a plastic smile pasted to her face. I can't believe it, she thought. During a dinner party.

"It's been a stressful day for everyone, I'm sure . . ." Chauncy said, and let the sentence taper off.

Joan, her term-husband, Alvarez-waldo, and the Rodrigueses were shifting in their chairs. Jere's face was impassive; then, when Joan leaned forward for her coffee cup, he quirked an eyebrow behind her back at Carli that tugged a reluctant smile onto her face. Michael coughed.

But something dangerous was building behind Jo's eyes. She stood.

"Excuse me, Dad, am I getting it right? Did you actually have something to *say* about the way this household is run? Pardon me while I get my kelly; I want to mark the date in my calendar."

Jo turned on Alison.

"Oh, and speaking of having a say, Mother, the way I raise my children is Michael's and my concern, not yours. And let me tell you, I don't appreciate your interference, your exposing them to that, that"—words failed her briefly; she flung a hand toward Carlotta— "*crap* you call a religion."

"You're still angry about last night, darling; I can see that," Alison said. The thinness of her lips when she smiled was all that revealed any distress or anger. "Let's discuss this later."

"Dear me," Jo said. "I'm frightfully sorry to make your party guests squirm. You might explain to them how you've cut me off the three times today I've tried to speak to you in private. I will have my say, Mother. Here it is.

"One. I don't want Tess growing up thinking she can solve all her problems by burning moss in a clay bowl and wishing them away. I told you specifically when I dropped her off yesterday not to involve her in your evening meditations.

"And two, I don't want her thinking that Belinda—or any other household employee—is to automatically take on such assorted roles as mommy, waitress, nanny, or whatever, simply at your whim."

"Jo, please," Alison said. By now the stiffness in her smile had spread; her facial muscles might have been chiseled from stone. Simultaneously Chauncy said, "Jolynd!"

Jo met Chauncy's gaze. She shook her head sharply, frowning. Michael came to his feet and stood behind Jolynd, placed his hands on her shoulders.

"We'll be going now," he said.

He followed Jo out of the room. Dramatic. Carli's "I hope you'll excuse me," as she made her own escape was anticlimactic.

She dashed up the stairs to the split-level landing, paused at the archway to the library. Belinda was sitting cross-legged in the lounge area between the couches, on the big Indian rug spread over the marble floor. With netgloves and some guidance from her, Tess, Michael's nine-year-old twins, Douglas and Lisa, and the two older of the three children Carli hadn't met were assembling three-dimensional shapes of various geometries from a series of colored shapes in a jello-tube. Willis was chasing Andy and the other preschooler among the rows of bookcases that separated the lounge from the entertainment area. The kids must have turned on the jelly and then abandoned it; from beyond and between the books came faint, strangers' voices and movement.

Jo stood in the center of the big room, a tiny cool suit over her arm. She grabbed four-year-old Andy as he darted past. As she squatted next to him she dashed tears from her eyes, looking up at Michael. "Why do I let her still get to me? Damn it! *Why?*"

"Mom, look over here!" Willis cried from among the bookcases.

"Because you love her," Michael replied.

"Yeah. But sometimes, Mike, sometimes I hate her. I just hate her."

She was trying to get Andrew into his cool suit. He struggled in her grasp, totally absorbed in dodging the other preschooler, who was trying to tag him with his clearie light-dye pistol. Willis had come up and was tugging on her arm. "Mommy . . ."

Jo bared her teeth. "Willis, go get your cool suit *now*. Andrew, stop it!" She gave the younger boy a shake.

Michael laid a hand on her arm. "They don't need the suits, Jo; take it easy on them. It's cool enough out."

Tess was struggling into her cool suit. She stopped halfway, came over, and wrapped her skinny arms around Jo's neck. Jo hugged her back, then broke down and started crying in earnest. The rest of their children looked at her and grew quiet.

"Come on," she said, wiping away tears; "Boys, Lisa, get your suits. Let's go home."

As they filed past Carli, Jo touched her arm and said, "I'll call you, OK?"

Carli nodded and gathered her into a quick hug. "She means well, you know."

"That's not enough anymore, Carli."

They shared a long look. "I'll call," Jo repeated.

Carli followed them down through the foyer to the front door, and waved as they descended the stone steps and disappeared among the trees. Then she grasped the worn brass handle, swung the old oak door closed, and leaned against it with her eyes closed.

After a moment she straightened with a deep inhalation, smoothed her dress, and went back upstairs to the library. Belinda waved to her from the viewing area; she and the three children remaining had settled in front of the jelly.

French doors of cut glass with lace sheers opened from the glass wall onto the balcony. She pushed them open and the house AC propelled her out into the warmth. She closed the doors against the pressure, padded across the wood slats to the railing. Her goose bumps disappeared and her skin relaxed in the warm breeze. Sweat formed between her breasts and under her arms.

She leaned over the edge and looked down. The headlights of Jo's car lit up the rosebushes and the white blocks of the house, as they backed silently down the hill to the gate.

Behind her, the lighting changed. She glanced back through the doors. Her father led a procession of guests into the library: Fred Alvarez-waldo, Jere, the Rodrigueses, and Joan Fall. They settled in the lounge-area couches, and shortly a server wheeled into the room carrying drinks.

Carli turned her back on them again and lifted her face to the breeze. The air current carried a scent of pine. In the distance she heard sirens and a dog barking. The wind rattled the branches of the trees. Then she heard the door open.

"I thought you might be out here."

Carli turned. The voice was Jere's. The warm light from the library streamed around him, shadowing his face and form. Laughter and clinking crystal spilled out also; her father and the others were raising their brandy snifters in a toast.

Jere held two snifters himself. He extended one to Carli and she took it, then turned back to lean on the railing, to gaze down at the heat-distorted city lights and the scattered spots of light from the pete camps among the foothills. The door clicked closed. He came up beside her.

Carli swirled her cognac. The fumes that rose from it stung her nose. She sipped; warm, almond fire slid past her palette, down her throat. A trickle of sweat traced a slow line between her breasts. Other trickles coursed down from beneath her arms. She pulled the tube off of her shoulders, over her head, and clutched it in her hand.

Her heart was pounding, but she was sitting above it all, in her mind, breathing slowly.

"Ah," Jere said, and leaned on the wooden rail. "They've finished raising the canopy."

Carli lowered her head in a nod. "They were just finishing when I arrived."

She looked down at his arms. His stocky hands were clasped on the rail and his left forearm was inches from her right. She saw a glint of metal on his hand—he was wearing his wedding ring.

Carli glanced at him, swallowed a sudden pang. But his gaze wasn't on her. He was looking out at the pines. They were all strung with globe lanterns, clear out to the property line, to the support poles that arched up over the house.

The lower tiers of the house canopy, bright nylon tarps, were wrapped about the poles like furled sails. The overhead tier was the only one left in place. A shadow of dull red and umber, it blotted out the stars overhead and made snapping noises in the breeze.

"For the winter," she added. "Carlotta says the summer heat has broken. Sure feels like it."

Jere nodded. He gestured at the lights with his chin. "Beautiful, isn't it?"

Carli heard the dog barking in the distance again. The sirens had gotten louder. She wondered whether whips were in the neighborhood. But the house security system was good; it'd hold. She took another sip of cognac.

"Yeah," she said.

"Did you watch the launch?"

"Yes." She bit the word off a little too short, then forced herself to draw a slow breath. She glanced at him; a tentative smile flickered on his lips.

"So did I. I thought of you." He took a breath, and she was sure he was going to ask her why she hadn't returned his most recent call, but instead he said, "I regretted—you know. I mean, I wasn't sorry for *my* sake you dropped out, but sometimes I feel guilty. . . ."

"I let that go a long time ago, Jere. Like I told you then. No regrets, no looking back. It was my decision, after all." She shrugged. "It seemed like the right choice at the time."

The words left her mouth before she considered their impact, and Jere looked hurt. She regretted them. She had a sudden urge to kiss him at the corner of his mouth, as she used to do when he was hurt or sad, or to lay a hand over his.

"Quite a scene, at dinner."

"It was that." Jere barked a laugh, accepting the change of subject.

"Mother sure knows how to orchestrate the fireworks. She seats me next to Joan Fall, and Jo next to Carlotta. Where is Mother now, anyway? In meditation?"

"Yes. With Carlotta and Joan's husband, what's-his-name—Richard?"

Carli shrugged. "He was awfully quiet. I wonder what to make of him. He seems a strange match for Joan."

"He's a Cosmo; I know that much. He looks like some kind of dusty old librarian or something."

Carli gave him a look and laughed. "Such a maligned breed, librarians. From what I hear, he's actually the art director at the O'Keeffe Memorial Gallery."

"Hmmm."

They were quiet for a few moments.

"What was with Jo, anyway?" Jere asked. "She was really on the edge tonight."

"She had every right to be! Mother's always trying to manipulate everyone to get her way. And Jo's the oldest, she gets the worst of it. I don't blame her one bit."

Jere's expression was skeptical. As much as if he had said the words, his silent dissent infuriated her.

"God *damn* it, Jere, it's right in front of your eyes! Why do you always stick up for her?"

"Easy, easy." His hands went up. "I'm not trying to pick a fight, Carli. I don't want to get into what's going on between Jo and Alison." He turned to look at the view again, then shook his head. "You always assume the worst of me."

Carli started to speak, hesitated, then said it anyway. "I have good reason."

"Yeah, and you won't let me forget it."

"I thought we weren't going to fight."

"Right." He turned away and took some deep breaths. "But god damn, it hurts, Carli. You never gave me a chance to make anything up to you." She watched muscles jerking in his jaw. "You never let me explain."

He turned abruptly and his hand brushed her arm. Carli started, and stepped back. His face was half lit, half shadowed. His visible eye was the color of forest moss; the dark one, a mere glint. The angle of the light made his normally smooth cheek craggy, his nose a ridge. His breaths came quick and shallow.

A band across Carli's chest tightened till she could barely breathe herself. She thought, Now we come to the real issue. And perhaps it was time. She found herself with lots to say.

"Explain! What was there to explain? You lied to me. All those years, I blamed myself for what happened to Paint, *and you never even told me*. You let me believe that it was my fault he went to prison."

"He broke the law, Carli; what was I supposed to do? I protected your name, at least; no one knew you were involved. Jesus." The word was torn from him—his eyes were dilated and moist. "This is tearing me apart. Can't you see that?"

"Yes, I can see." She bent, pressed her fingers to her lips, looked up at him again, and her fists rolled into balls. Her voice came out flat and toneless. "Paint was raped in prison, did you know that? Repeatedly. Over three years of his life, he spent in hell. And you couldn't even be honest with me about what you'd done."

He was chewing on his lip. "I—didn't want you to leave me," he said.

"I deserved the truth."

"His number came up. He should have gone gladly. Willingly!"

"Like Dennis, right?"

His fists slammed against the wood. "Exactly like Dennis! Men like him were giving their *lives* down there." He broke off and stared at her. "You worshipped the man, Carli. How could you do what you did, after Dennis?"

She shook off his words with a growl. "You're wrong, Jere. It was a pointless war—no one should have had to fight it. I lost my only brother to that goddamned piece of polluted, melting ice, and I was not about to lose my nephew, too."

"You treat him like he was made of glass. But he's no different from anybody else. We all took our chances. It was cowardice to evade the draft, plain and simple. It's not my fault he had to suffer the consequences. He deserved whatever he got."

He leaned forward, suddenly fierce. "Let me tell you something, Carli; I don't give a damn about your nephew. He probably *liked*—" Then his eyes went wide and he reached for her. "I didn't mean that."

Carli barely refrained from smashing her fist into Jeremiah's face. A nasty smile spread across her mouth. But she merely turned and left him there at the railing, and opened the doors. When she glanced back, his head was bent into his arms.

Chauncy was perched in the corner of the couch, his arms spread across the back, his legs crossed wide, ankle on knee. He looked to Carli like some kind of wise and friendly Buddha, with his brown eyes radiating compassion, his slight paunch and his balding pate. He was talking about the goings-on in the Senate, and the others were gathered around, silent, rapt. Carli sat down in the middle of the couch between him and the colonel.

". . . the chair was so angry by this time, she threw the entire entourage out without their 'due process' anyhow. You should have viewed the Congo-net releases the next day!"

Everyone burst into laughter. Jere entered, turned his back to close the French doors, very carefully, like an old man. He came over to the cluster of people. Carli glanced at him briefly; his face was colorless, waxy—all but translucent, like marble in the midday sun. He gave Chauncy a wan smile and didn't look once at Carli. Give me a fucking break, she thought.

"I have to get back to Albuquerque, Chaunce. Thanks for the invitation."

Carli felt her father's gaze. She shifted in her seat, folded her arms about herself, and met his look as he said good night to Jeremiah. Then Chauncy smiled all around and picked up with his story where he'd left off.

Alison, Carlotta, and Joan's husband entered, and the conversation effervesced into a confusion of voices. Carli heard the front door close, and released the breath she had been holding. She started to stand.

Her father touched her arm. "I wonder if I could have a word with you this evening before you leave."

The loom room up in the attic had been her bedroom for most of her childhood. The lights came up when she entered. The room's air was still and hot, and smelled of must.

"AC up," she said, and climbed onto her old brass bed. She shoved the pillow off—it was too hot for fabric cushions—and then looked out the bay window at the dark, wind-whipped canopy, while cool swirls of air pushed the dead heat across her legs.

Carli had gotten the room the day she'd graduated from fifth grade, after years of lobbying. It had been a major coup.

It was of a normal width for a bedroom but twice as long. The ceiling above the two outer walls slanted inward. The bed was near that corner of the room, so Carli's head brushed the ceiling when she leaned back against the brass bars of the headboard.

Each of the three bay windows had seats with drawers beneath them. When she was young she had used one of the two bay windows on the long wall for stargazing, and the other for her various science experiments. The one on the short wall had been for her pets.

For years the "science" bench had been covered with assorted experimental clutter—with the microscope and piles of little glass slides, and jars of chemical and preserving fluids and crystal and plant and mold growths, in a weird profusion of colors that had spilled over and blistered the white paint of the benches. The window bay on the short wall, which had deep shelves on two sides of the bay instead of benches, had housed her menagerie—the pair of guinea pigs, her hamster and the bull snakes, the maze-running mice she had raised for a school science project, and the parakeet before it had squeezed between the bars and escaped.

The animals had always made so much noise she had often had trouble sleeping at night, with their diggings, scratchings, and chirps, and their cages usually stank, too. Bits of newspaper, cedar chips, small-animal droppings, and various types of seed, wilted lettuce, and carrot peelings had littered the floor.

All the benches were now smooth, painted a determinedly pastel blue, and covered by translucent, cobalt-blue squish-cushions. A spider plant and a wandering Jew thrived on the shelf where the rodents had resided. Other plants hung from the sloped ceiling and grew from large brass pots on the floor.

Other than her bed, only one item from her youth remained: her cherished four-incher refractory telescope, a cylinder of white enamel, chrome, and glass on a squat tripod. It rested on the floor in the second bay window, the one nearest the head of her bed. She occasionally wondered why her mother had left it there. Perhaps as a kind of memorial to Dennis, who had bought it for Carli, so long ago. Or perhaps a memorial to Carli's own brief NASA career, which ended a few years after Dennis had returned from Antarctica, after he had finally died. Carli would never have expected it of her, but among all her non-NASA friends, acquaintances, and relatives, only Alison had tried to talk her out of leaving the space program.

At the time Carli had assumed that Alison's motives had more to do with Dennis than with her. But now, this decade and more later, Carli doubted. Maybe she knew me better than I thought, Carli mused. The notion provoked a strong, not entirely pleasant, reaction in Carli's gut. Whether the ascendant emotion, ultimately, was alarm or comfort, she couldn't decide.

Besides Carli's bed and the plant pots, the only other piece of furniture in the large room now was Alison's loom, strung with the web of a half-woven rug that had not changed size or shape in the last ten years, and Alison's old pine chest. Carli and Dennis had built it for her when Carli was twelve and Dennis sixteen—a huge monstrosity loaded with splinters, with leather straps and brass rivets for hinges, and for a handle, an old lion-head door knocker Dennis had found at a garage sale, with the brass ring in its teeth.

As she looked at the pine chest, remembering, a smile grew on her face and a hard knot formed in her throat. She swallowed hard and scooted off of the bed, went over to it, tugged on the lid and pressed it upward. The lid's raising sucked an acrid insecticide/antifungal into her face. Carli coughed and pinched her nostrils with her fingers. All Mother's old patchwork quilts and heirloom comforters must have been in there.

She pulled out one of her favorite quilts, a patchwork quilt made by her great-grandmother, and draped it across her lap; the room had grown cool enough now that she didn't mind the touch of textiles. She ran her hands over the soft cotton, tweaked the wadding. The chemical smell was strong.

Carli left the lid propped open.

"Increase air circulation," she said distinctly in the direction of the control panel at the door. It was an older model, and other than a few simple commands, didn't understand spoken English too well. But after a second the smell began to dissipate.

Then Carli laid the quilt back in the chest and went over to the bay window with the telescope. Back when, she and Dennis had sat on these very benches and gazed at the planets and stars, and in serious whispered voices, with all the earnest belief that children could muster, had sworn to join the space program together, and someday visit the stars.

God, how I miss you, Dennis, she thought, bowing her head. Why, goddammit? When the draft notice came, why didn't you run away? So many others were hiding; why couldn't you?

It was an old and tired thought, and by now an unwelcome one. Impatient, she flicked the teardrops away, shoved one of the squishcushions aside, and set the scope on the bench. After fiddling with the tripod stand and the scope's focus, she pointed the business end of the scope toward the flickering lights on the hills west of the house. She bent over the eyepiece and adjusted the focus. Dim forms on the hillside—dark piñon trees as misshapen in the rocky soil as ancient bonsai—leapt about as she rotated the scope on its bearings.

Then she heard her father's slow, heavy footsteps on the stairs, coming up from the third floor.

She didn't turn her face toward the door when he entered, only continued her search for the lights on the hillside. Her heart was pounding.

"Does that thing still work?" Her father's voice held a smile.

"Of course," she said. She located a light source on the dark hillside, a pete's shack about half a mile away, beyond the city's periphery. A window of waxed paper resolved into focus. Beyond it, inside the house, blurred shapes moved. She stood aside when her father approached, and he took a peek, changed the focus.

"I always wondered if you were using it to spy on the neighbors," he said, straightening. In spite of herself, she smiled back.

"I didn't, back then. The canopy blocks the stars now, most times. And there's too much light pollution. People's houses are all you can get. But I guess I'd better change it."

She aimed the scope at the yard three stories below. "There. No more peeping. No one will ever know. Care to verify?"

"I'll take your word for it." Chauncy sat down next to the scope on the bench. Carli sat down on her bed, facing him.

"I didn't expect to see you, per se," she said. "Mother said you'd be waldoing here for the party."

He shrugged. "Today's session got out in time for me to catch the six-thirty scram from Dulles. I wanted to see you. Person to person."

"Oh? Why?"

Chauncy shook his head and chewed on the inside of his lip, eyeing her.

"I didn't invite Jere to torment you; I hope you know that," he said abruptly. "He insisted. You must know he still—"

Carli exhaled explosively. "Dad, don't." At his expression she said, "What did you expect? The divorce wasn't an amicable one, you know."

"There seems to be a lot more hostility on your part than on his." Carli pressed her fingers to her lips and only looked at him. "And it looked to me like you said something out on the balcony that upset him terribly."

Carli clenched her hands in her lap, nodded. "Yes, I told him the truth. That's always hard for liars to swallow."

He leaned forward, his forehead deeply lined. "I just don't understand why you're so angry with him. Jere is a fine man, and he obviously still loves you. Ten good years of marriage, you were talking about children, and now all of a sudden everything's gone to hell."

Carli lowered her head, fought for several seconds for composure. "He just blew it. There's no going back."

Her father was silent for a moment, staring at her. Then he puffed his cheeks out and pinched his lip.

"Won't you at least tell me why?"

Carli looked at him, bit her lip to keep from bursting out laughing. She knew that was inappropriate, but there it was.

Tell you that your precious protégé, son of Amos, Mother's first sweetheart and your close friend since college, is the secret informant who turned Paint in?

She wanted to hurt Jere, oh, she did. But not her father. Not Jere's parents, whom she adored. Not even, bless her, her mother.

Jere hadn't told anyone that he was the informant, and there had been a tacit agreement that no one in the family would ask too many questions. No one would think about it. Everyone assumed one of Paint's acquaintances had turned him over, for the reward money. Or that Carli—who, everyone knew, had known where he was hiding—had fucked up and let it slip somehow.

If she told them—told anyone—what Jere had done, the repercussions wouldn't die down for generations. This family of hers contained so much buried pain—decades of unshared remorse and secret angers and hurts; they clutched it all like ugly scars to their abdomens, kept it quiet for all they were worth. One slipup, one careless word, and everything she valued—and she did value them, for all their often unbearable behavior—would erupt in a cascade of escalating emotional violence. She'd seen it happen before.

"No," she said.

He frowned and she clenched. Here it comes. But he sat down next to her on the bed with a strange look on his face.

"I really scorched it, tonight, inviting him, didn't I?" he said, and put an arm across her shoulders and looked hard into her eyes. "I hurt you. I'm so sorry, Coo."

At the sound of the pet name, a brief spike of anger came—she didn't want to feel this pain. Then something hard and tangled uncoiled inside her. Grief surged up, burst out through her throat and eyes, surprising her and her father both. She buried her face in her father's chest and he held her, rocking her like a small child, while she sobbed.

Eventually the sobs tapered off, and she wiped at her nose and eyes. Chauncy smiled at her and brushed some of the tears away, then handed her a handkerchief.

"You've been holding that in for a while, I bet," he said. She nodded. "Well, it was a mistake for me to press about what happened between you and Jere.

"I—I wish it hadn't happened to you; I wanted you to be happy, Coo. I so hate to see you hurt. I thought maybe things would be good for you, you were going to escape all the craziness. . . ." His voice tapered off. Carli shook her head against his shoulder; her mouth twisted into a smile.

"Nah, I just hide the insanity better."

He laughed and gave her a squeeze. She sat up, wiped at her eyes and nose.

"How long are you in town this time?"

"Heading back tomorrow morning." At her expression, he said, "I know, it's absurd. But the session ends next week, and things are really heating up on my revised air-quality bill. The Populists are threatening to filibuster over a rider attached to it, and that would be disastrous for everybody."

"You probably wouldn't have time for *huevos rancheros* at Tomasita's, then, early."

"Sorry, honey; my scram is at six-thirty A.M."

"Oh well." She gave him a shrug and a smile. "Next time. Once the session's over."

He was all the way to the door before she remembered. "Oh, yeah—have you ever heard of a group called Kaleidoscope before?"

He didn't turn away from the door right away. She thought, My God, there really *is* such a thing, and as the pause lengthened she began to grow alarmed.

"Dad?"

Finally he turned around. The way he looked scared the shit out of her.

He looked shocked. Old. And gaunt. And the look in his eyes was like some fire had burned out everything inside—all love, all hope—and all that was in him was ashes.

"Where . . . where did you hear of that name?"

"From some nutcase on the street—I thought." She leaned forward. "I can tell you're upset."

"*Who?* Who told you?" He came back to the bed, gripped her wrist.

"Dad, you're scaring me."

He looked down at his grip on her hand, and released it. She rubbed at the wrist. But his gaze didn't soften. "I'm sorry. But I have to know. It's very important, Carli. Tell me all the circumstances, anything that might be relevant."

She told him about how she'd been followed, about her encounter with the strange young man in the body bar.

"And you haven't seen him since?"

"No. What's this about, Dad?"

He rubbed his face, and didn't speak for a long time.

"Dad?" she said.

He looked up at her again. "I can't tell you, honey, and you should never have heard about it." Then he took both her hands in his. "I need to extract a promise from you. If you see the young man again, string him along, tell him whatever he wants to hear, and then call a number I'm going to give you. They'll bring help. Will you do that?"

"Of course I will, if that's what you want me to do. But what's going on?"

That look grew in his eyes again. "I can't explain right now, and I don't know if I ever will. You'll just have to trust me."

"But—"

He gave her hands a shake. "Trust me."

"OK. And Dad," she said, when he reached the door. "Thanks for helping me cry."

The stark lines of his face softened. "Night, Coo," he said.

"Night."

After he'd left, she bunched the pillow up and propped her elbows on her knees. "Interesting," she said, and her eyes went narrow.

What was Daniel trying to sell her, and what was her father trying to hide?

Hell, at least it gave her something to think about besides Jere and the divorce.

Coup du Corps

Danger. 419. Wait.

Dane cradled her damaged arm in the half darkness. She crouched in a puddle of steaming water, inside a storm tunnel that smelled of must, rot, and fungus. Shadows flickered across the tunnel mouth. She listened to the dripping of water; the scrabblings of tunnel creatures; the echoes of footfalls and car wheels on pavement overhead; the gusts of wind that played the mouth of the tunnel like a wind instrument.

Occasionally a train would surge past below, and the sound built in intensity till it drowned out all others and made the walls of the storm tunnel tremble, then died away.

The inner voice was with her now, the voice with the face she should know: a second presence in her mind.

344. Wait. 151.

She was trying to ignore the voice, trying to think. But the voice made it hard to concentrate.

She had climbed the ridge of the mountain till the fence ended at an empty guardhouse at the base of a cliff. She had scaled that cliff, and another, and even then she had climbed the forested mountainsides and granite-strewn washes, a mile into the sky. Till she had reached the peak, and knew she was safe from the men in the Jeeps, the men with billy clubs and guns.

98. Enemies near. Wait.

She had scaled down the western face of the mountain, and in that time the sun had crossed the sky and set, beyond a bank of distant thunderheads that discharged blue lightnings to the land beyond the volcanoes.

Wait for darkness. Wait for silence. 15. 34. No one must see.

It was damp here, and a little cooler than it had been while she was scaling down the granite cliff in the glare of the afternoon sun. She had stumbled into the outskirts of the city, through the residential district with its quiet gardens and fountained parks, into the noise of the streets.

People had crowded the streets, more people than she had ever seen before, pouring up from underground, out of buildings, rushing by in vehicles. She hadn't known there were that many people in the whole world.

The people moved swiftly; many ran. A storm had built up in the skies to the east and gotten ensnared in the mountaintops, and now threatened to spill its waters down the cliff face. The winds had come up, blowing trash and tumbleweeds down the streets toward the center of town.

Wait. 3. 34415. 19. 98.

But even in the crush, she had begun to draw stares and silence on the street. Her face. Her arm and leg, with their wounds, their dangling tubes and clips.

When she had been unable to bear it any longer she had leapt from a bridge into a storm culvert, and had hidden in this tunnel. The others in the tunnel, the tattered ones, had fled at the sight of her.

I'm still dreaming, she thought, rocking herself. Those other visions, too, seemed real until I awakened. But surely if it had been a dream, she would have awakened by now.

The storm clouds were nearer. She couldn't stay down here long if it rained. But the inner voice seemed adamant.

Wait. Wait for darkness. Wait for silence. 34415198. Wait.

She bowed her head, bowed to the certainty in the voice.

"OK," she said. Her own voice echoed in the tunnel. The strangeness of it silenced her for a moment. Then she spoke again. "OK, I'm doing what you tell me."

She laid her wet head down on her knees.

The winds outside had grown steady, screaming at the tunnel mouth. The fading sunlight outside the tunnel was now gone. Dane lifted her head, looked around. All the cars, footsteps, and other street noises had ceased. She hadn't heard them in a while.

Dane stood. It was time to go.

The air exploded, exploded again, in mind-splitting noise and intense light, and she stumbled and fell headlong into the water.

She regained her footing, looked outside the tunnel. Raindrops the size of fists struck the ground. Another flash, and thunder jarred her teeth, boomed past her in receding echoes.

A roaring swelled behind her. She turned—a wall of water surged around the curve of the tunnel. It knocked her off her feet. She tumbled out into the culvert in an angry swirl of dirt, debris, and water, taking water in her mouth and nose. There was no up.

The torrent spat her onto a sheet of steel mesh that blocked the entrance of a tunnel a ways downstream. She clung to the mesh, varied her vision across the spectrum, trying to see in the liquid. The water was too dark, too particle-ridden. Dane clawed her way up the mesh till her eyes were above water. Her head scraped the tunnel ceiling.

A little more light shone here. She saw the tunnel opening a few meters upstream. Beyond it was the uncovered culvert—along with the logs, planks, and other flotsam that the flood was hurling at her. She dodged them—or tried, at least. She deflected one or two with her legs. But the logs were too many and the tunnel was too small, too full of water. She took several hits in the ribs, one in her right shoulder.

Dane bunched her legs onto the mesh and leapt into the face of the current, flailing her arms and legs in a clumsy dog paddle. Twice she was knocked back to the mesh. On her third try she grasped hold of the concrete lip with the fingertips of her good arm. She hauled herself out of the water and onto the top of the tunnel.

The rain came in pummeling gusts. She pushed the mat of hair off of her forehead. The lowermost supports of a culvert bridge were about two meters above her head. She checked her purchase on the curved concrete of the tunnel, then frog-leaped up and grabbed a beam, and swung herself up into the network of supports beneath the bridge.

A sudden gust nearly knocked her off. She caught her balance by throwing herself onto a downwind strut, and climbed up higher to where the wind was more broken up by the structure.

She climbed as high on the supports as she could and used the wind to keep her pinned to the structure while she stretched up and reached the edge of the footbridge. She pulled herself up so her eyes were level with the surface.

The footbridge was suspended over the storm drain. All she could see of the streets that bracketed the culvert was a slick of fluorescent lights on hard-driving rain. Overhead, a tangle of great copper coils, disgorged like snakes from the building walls, dripped scalding water on her head and her bare skin, in counterpoint to the cooler blasts of rain.

A good thirty feet up, a stripboard spanned the street, announcing a curfew, along with the time, temperature, and humidity. Distant shouts underlay the barking of dogs and the sound of rain crackling on hard surfaces. No one in sight. She scrambled onto the bridge.

She had discarded the shredded remnants of her plastic foot covers during her climb up the mountain. Her white jacket was in tatters now, too. She stripped it off and dropped it into the dark tumult below.

She studied her surroundings more closely. Floodwaters surged through the streets. Then she realized she knew this street. The buildings, the signs—they had been in her dreams last night.

Impossible.

She left the bridge, ran splashing down a street. At a corner down the hill, a blurred street sign glowed green. Rain and distance made the sign illegible. But she knew.

The street was called Summerville. No—Something Summerville. General Summerville. Or maybe—something about a dance.

She ran to the street, stopped on the corner across the way. The sign resolved into focus through the sheets of rain.

General Somervell.

A building of brick, copper, and glass stood on that corner: 103 General Somervell NE, the sign above the door said. SHALAKO DANCE APARTMENTS. Vacancies. Call 7998,240073/C-N # J420-(UU1-OGDEN)/GridLink # 2222-01012.

"No," Dane said. "Not real."

Go to the door, the voice told her.

She ran across the street, leapt up over the grille that led to the front door—a wide entryway of glass and metal. Dane wiped water from her eyes. A keypad glowed green numbers at her. The display screen blinked, "ENTRY CODE:__"

34415198.

She punched in the number with a hand trembling so badly it took three tries to get it right. The door seals cracked and the door opened inward. A rush of cold air swept past Dane Elisa Cae into the street. She stood staring at the hallway beyond the door until the door closed again. Then she shook herself.

Dane punched the code in again, and this time slipped inside as the door opened. She hunched over in the hall, panting and not panting—that unnerving duality of sensation.

Something went off inside her like an explosive charge, separating her from herself; she was suddenly a passenger in her own body. Her legs carried her stumbling into the lift, and she watched her hand rise and press the number 10 on the backlit board. Tenth floor, she thought. The lift stopped, doors opened; her body limped down the hall to apartment 1062.

The hand again rose. No, she thought suddenly. This isn't a dream. This is my body. Mine.

Another number floated into her mind as the hand typed it: a six-digit code, 140926. She focused all her attention on that willful hand—it quivered, stopped, then finished the code.

She had made it hesitate, though. That was something.

She rode her body into the dark room on silent feet. A small infrared glowing on the couch. Animal. She was unfamiliar with the species. It made a low sound and jumped off of the couch. Danger? But her body ignored it, approached the door opposite, looked inside the bedroom.

The animal came up and sniffed at her leg as she stood there, and rubbed the side of its face against her, two strokes with each cheek. Then it turned and went back to the couch.

Dim light came from a half-closed door. Two large heat signatures writhed on the bed—they must be humans. They were too close together for Dane to tell clearly which glowing warmth was which. Soft voices, moans, movement. Someone somewhere was sifting the voices, breaking the words down, making them into squiggles and lines, comparing them to other squiggles she hadn't known were stored within her mind.

They weren't the same. Not the one she sought.

Anger erupted like another explosion. Dane flung herself against her invisible constraints—her awareness split—her body went still/she flailed wildly in a bath of glycerin.

The presence was railing—*Not her. It's not her!*

She screamed back, *Get out!* She jabbed at the intruding presence, shoved the other away, out of her mind, slammed an inner door so hard she could feel its reverberations in her teeth and jaw.

Abruptly she was back in her body, standing in the middle of the dark room. The sudden shift struck her hard—she tottered. Her body went still. Somewhere else, she felt her heart hammering, felt her lungs heaving deep breaths. She felt moisture on her cheeks and touched her face: it was dry—still savaged, all feeling on the one side dead.

She backed up awkwardly, slid down a wall, huddled beside the couch and hugged her knees. Words fluttered to her mouth from somewhere deep inside.

"Forgive me," she whispered to the empty silence inside her mind. "I can't. I just can't. Forgive me."

Faintly, on the far side of that inner door, she could still hear the raging of the voice.

The voices in the other room started again. This time Dane listened to what they said, concentrated on the words and made herself understand them. The other coiled deep in her mind was quiescent now, uninterested; therefore listening was her own action, her own choice—if a small one.

". . . must have fallen asleep. . . . What o'clock, Tender?"

There was a pause, rustling.

"Almost midnight."

"Mmmm. When's Carli back?"

"She said 'fore midnight. 'Be the party lasted longer than she thought it would."

Another pause.

"Guess I better trek 'fore she finds me in her bed. . . ."

"With me. 'T's what you were going to say, isn't it? You're jerking me."

"C'mon, Tender—"

"Don't call me that. Get out. Let me go. *Let me go!*"

"I'm sorry, I'm sorry. Stop yelling! Christ. You haven't changed one poking bit, Tania. 'N't know why I bothered."

The bed creaked, and footsteps crossed the floor. The woman's voice broke, and strange sounds came from her.

"Come back to bed, Paint."

"No way. I got to go." After a pause: "You're always maxed out, Tender. You cry too poking much, and you stick too much shit up your nose. You're a mess, nespah?"

" 'Be I have reason." Pause. "Say hi to your boyfriend, Fox. That's where you're going, isn't it? Back to his bed. Aren't you?"

"That is none of your business."

Things got quiet for a moment, except for the soft sounds coming from the woman. Then the bed creaked again.

"I'm sorry, Tania. I'm sorry. I'n be such an asshole."

The woman's noises got louder. "Go away."

"I give up. Look, I really do have to go, Tender. Not just making that up. I'll call you tomorrow. I really will."

The noises stopped. "You will? Promise?"

"Promise."

Dane drew back into the corner behind the couch when a bare-chested young man came into the room. His hair streamed like a glowing, ginger-colored waterfall down his back in the fluorescence that came in through the window; he wore baggy pants and sandals, and as he crossed the room he wrapped a great, gauzy cloth about his chest. The animal leapt off of the sofa and twined itself around his legs, making noises.

"Night, Gyle, you old man," he whispered, stroking its head, then paused for a glance back toward the bedroom. A young woman stood silhouetted in the door, wrapped in a blanket.

"I," she said, and then stopped. " 'Bye."

"Later," he said, and left. The woman turned and went back into the bedroom. She made more of the noises Dane had heard her make earlier.

Dane got up and went out into the hall. At the end of the hall was a stairwell, above which an orange EXIT sign glowed. The door floated closed and latched, but not before she heard, faintly, the young man's footsteps echoing up the stairwell from below. She glanced at the elevator, but the other in her mind would not let her leave the apartment. Her legs carried her back inside.

She went over and looked out the window. It was still raining out, though not quite as hard as earlier. She waited at the window for several minutes, but she never saw him leave the building. Dane went back to her spot, sank to the floor, and mused over that fact while she waited.

FLYING FECES

He bounded over the D'Aubers' wall, struck the ground, and rolled. And lay there a moment with his heart pounding and a tight, quivery feeling in his stomach.

"That was too close," Scott said in Daniel's ear. Teru seconded him.

With a rude, radio-transmitted noise, Daniel bounded to his feet and scrambled for the storage shed behind the D'Auber-Almquist house. He shoved the sliding door open, picked his way among the clutter, and crouched among the rakes, hoes, piping, and yard and garden robots.

The cops had probably gotten a good look at him back there in the forest, and from their radio transmissions, they were still searching. He was going to be here for a little while.

"I'm here to spell Jamie," Teru said.

"Let me wrap this up real quick," James Scott added. "Daniel, I've been scanning the police frequencies. It sounds like their search is carrying them down the hill, away from you."

"What possessed you, Danny? You should have let those whips be. This is twice in two days. Every time you go out, you get into trouble."

"I don't need a critique, thank you," Daniel said, crouching amid the tools. "And they weren't whips. They were peteys."

"Whatever. You should know better."

Yeah, yeah, he thought.

"I'm off-shift," Scott told him. "I'll talk to you in the morning."

Daniel slumped over his knees. The adrenaline had gone by now, and he felt weak and sick. The feeling of violence just ended resonated; images of those kids he'd killed last night came to him.

Murderer. Murderer! What choice did I have? They'd've killed that old woman. Morris. Never again. Never just stand by when I can help.

The inner voices tumbled past in a murmur, arguing. With a shudder, he shut them out. His head spun from fatigue.

"God, I'm beat. What time is it?"

"A little after eleven. What's been happening? Scott didn't brief me completely."

Daniel shook his head. "Too poking much." He hesitated. "Do you think you could spell me for a while, Teru?"

After a silence, she said, "Danny, I've gotten two hours' sleep in the last thirty-six. I'm all in. And I'm not calibrated for your machine. It's bloody awful running an uncalibrated machine, love; have a heart."

"Yeah. I understand." He laid his head on his knees. "Just can't go on like this much longer." Then he took a deep breath, back in his crèche. "But I guess I'll have to. Let's get back into the D'Aubers' house."

"As late as it is, perhaps she'll decide to stay the night."

He scoffed. "Don't torment me with the hope of getting sleep tonight."

". . . If you see the young man again," the senator was saying, "string him along, tell him whatever he wants to hear, and then call a number I'm going to give you. They'll bring help. Will you do that?"

"I'll be damned," Daniel said softly. "Jackpot."

He rocked back on his heels, nearly knocking the leaf blower over. He switched his vision over and caught at the machine and righted it, then settled back onto his heels and switched back to the house-system camera.

It had taken him a good hour, and a lot of effort, to crack the audiovisual routines and find Carli in the attic. And it was a good thing he'd decided to make the effort. He was getting an earful.

"At least she knows I was on the line with her about Kaleido-Scope," he broadcast to Teru. "But he made me sound like a criminal."

"The shit's really about to fly," Teru said.

"Get me Krueger," Daniel said. He popped another menu.

For once, Teru didn't argue.

The senator left Carli in the attic. Daniel made a quick set of modifications to his subroutine, and video-hopped the senator from the attic stairway back to the lounge. Senator D'Auber said good night to the two couples remaining and exchanged a couple of words and a cursory peck on the lips with his wife. Then he headed up toward his private office on the second floor.

Daniel's awareness flicked into the room a few seconds ahead of the senator's entry. He scanned it quickly, storing quick-recall images right and left. The room held an array of jellos of several kinds, mostly photographs of the senator at various functions across the years. A lot of them were him with other famous public figures.

The most prominent one had him talking to the president of several terms before, Celia Shyner, and some NASA official. Beside the senator stood three kids—a girl about seventeen, a boy in his early teens, and a young girl whom Daniel immediately recognized as Carli.

They were at some sort of NASA function. The kids were wearing shorts, T-shirts, and NASA visor caps, standing beneath the belly of a supershuttle: the *Callisto*.

That would have been the first orbital-colony launch. Daniel had seen the launch, too; now he even recognized the cube shot. It had been used on the jello-net and in the *virtu*-net. Daniel had been four or five years old then, and had watched the launch sitting atop his father's shoulders, standing in the rain outside a store in El Paso, along with a crowd of other peteys.

Carli must have been nine or so, open-faced and freckled. She was holding the hand of the teenaged boy, looking up at the shuttle with an awed expression, reaching toward it with a hand. The boy's hand was on her white-blond head, his gaze on her. He was laughing, his lips parted. Daniel guessed the boy was Carli's older brother, and the other teenager must have been her sister.

There were no more shots of the children, but several other jellos of D'Auber: one where he, a very young man, was casting a fishing line with Rosenfeld—back in the thirties, that must have been; one of him with an enormous pair of scissors, cutting a ribbon at some more recent state function. They were all arranged in midair about the walls and above the desk.

The desk was mahogany with a marble top and had a phone headset on it, a kelly unit and full upper-body netset, a floating lamp, piles of correspondence and memory crystals, and a paperweight made of a cluster of uncut rose quartz crystals. The window covering most of the outer wall was opaqued with a photo mural: a large wave was about to crash onto outcroppings of porous black rock. Translucent, water-tone squish-chairs were set around a low conference table between the desk and the window. A six-foot jellovision cylinder was mounted in the corner.

The senator burst into the room and flung the door closed, at which point the waves on the window splashed in slow motion onto the rocks to the sound of a breaking surf. Bach's Third Brandenburg

Concerto started up. D'Auber walked into the middle of the plush white carpeting and came to a dead stop. His shoulders slumped. Daniel, watching from behind, from the video unit above the door, would have given a fortune to see the senator's expression. The older man's hands rubbed hard at his face, passed and repassed over his bristly scalp. He whispered something that might have been "Damn" or possibly "Dan"; the house's audio reception wasn't very good.

Then he sat down at his desk, slid the netset over his head, slipped his arms into the shoulder-length gauntlets, and pulled the mike close to his lips. He stuck his hand into the field in front of his kelly and accessed the unit. Hurriedly Daniel shut off visuals and isolated the senator's kelly link to the house system. He climbed into D'Auber's matrix and captured the phone number as the senator called it up.

A device on the desk spit out a disruption field, and soon the senator was enveloped by a dark, crawling sphere. Daniel got tossed right out of the senator's kelly and back into the house system.

"Damn it." Daniel traced all the house systems, looking for a way to jump back into the communications network, but security was too tight.

"Daniel, it's Krueger," Teru said.

"What's the problem, Sornsen?"

Daniel exited the house security system. "Give me visual, back there." He wanted to see Krueger's face. "Teru, cover my proxy for me, and keep an eye on Carli."

His vision and hearing whited out; sensations tunneled away. He found himself staring at Krueger's broad, white face out of a video pickup.

Krueger looked surly. Teru's proxy stood nearby, in wax-statue mode. Banks of lights and ghost images flickered in the background; the Classified control room was otherwise empty.

"What is it? Why haven't you brought in Carli MacLeod yet?"

"We might be about to have some serious problems, boss. Watch this." Daniel accessed his proxy's volatile memory and replayed on one of the screens what had just passed between Carli and her father.

Krueger's expression became thoughtful. "He'll contact Thompson, for certain, and several of the BoD members, too, I'm willing to bet." A troubled look came onto his face, one that gave Daniel an uncharacteristic glimpse of his indecision.

He nodded into the camera from which Daniel was watching him. "I appreciate the advance warning, Sornsen. Now, what the hell are you waiting for?"

Daniel took a deep breath. "I want to talk to you about MacLeod's father."

Daniel didn't like the expression that appeared on Krueger's face. "Sornsen, I told you. Professor MacLeod's father is unimportant. The critical thing is to get her here before her life is endangered."

Unimportant? "Carli's safe for the moment. And I'm beginning to think that there's a better way to find the renegade pilot than Rasmussen's renegade-napping idea, boss. But I'm going to have to know. How involved in KaleidoScope is the senator?"

Krueger shook his head. "Fuck the senator! How many different ways do you want me to tell you? We need to get Carli MacLeod here. We'll worry about the renegade once she's hidden, safe and sound. You're wasting your time if you're trying to do anything else."

Daniel felt himself shaking his own head, back in his crèche.

"But I'm convinced there's a link between the senator and the renegade. If we know the senator's involvement with the project, his connections, we might find that link."

Krueger's face contorted as though invisible hands were trying to remold it.

"No," he said. "You're wrong. The renegade has no link with Senator D'Auber. Bring me Carli MacLeod. That's all I need."

Daniel sighed. "Look, what do you want me to do—kidnap her? Because that's what it would take."

Krueger remained silent.

"Boss." Daniel paused. "I can tell you're under some kind of constraint. You know more about what's going on than you can tell me, don't you?"

Krueger didn't answer.

"Don't you?" Daniel repeated.

"I have to go," Krueger blurted, and bolted out of the room.

Daniel called Teru back. Her proxy reactivated and sat down in the chair before the video camera. Daniel could tell from her-his closed expression she-he didn't want to talk about what had just happened.

"You need to get back to your body. MacLeod's in the garage, about to leave."

"I will. But listen. Did you overhear my conversation with Krueger?"

"I did." Her-his expression was still reluctant.

"He knows something, Teru, and we're being kept in the dark. I don't like it." He cross-loaded the buffer file he had created while Senator D'Auber was dialing. "Here's a phone number; I want you to trace it. And see what *real* information you can dig up about the senator, OK?"

"Not a chance, Danny; it's not authorized."

"Come on! A woman's life is at stake." When she-he said nothing, he went on, "You know Krueger's not the type to keep these kinds of secrets when someone's life is in danger if he weren't under terrible pressure. Someone's blackmailing him, or—or something. I don't know what. But I'm telling you, he really *wants* us to find out. That was just his way of saying he can't help us."

She-he scowled at Daniel. "That's such bullshit, Danny."

"Are you sure? Think about how strangely he's been acting. He's shut us all out. The fact is, he's got someone riding him somehow. He needs help.

"There's a lot more going on here than just some disgruntled ex-employee stealing government property. And if we don't find out now, it's more than just that security guard who got killed, or just Carli MacLeod's life at stake.

"You gotta help me, Ru. You've got to. I can't do it on my own."

"Do I?" she-he said softly. Her-his beautiful, boy's eyes were narrowed, close to the screen. Then she-he nodded. "All right, then. I'll see what I can do."

She-he disengaged Daniel's connection in mid-thank-you.

It took him a moment to realize that the lights he was looking at were the headlights of someone's car as it backed out of the garage, and that Carli's homing signal was coming from inside it. He was back in proxy.

Daniel headed for the wall, leaped over it, and crouched in the shadows, waiting for the car to back out of the gate and hoping the cops had called it a night and given up on their search.

MACHINE-HUMAN FACES

With a glance at her mother, Carli nudged the car thermostat lower. She had her cool suit on—without the coolant pack attached, of course; it wouldn't fit on her back in Mother's pricey little sports car. Carli had unzipped the top half of the suit and peeled it down around her waist. It was easier to wear the suit than to carry it aboard the bullet shuttle and subways, but without the coolant unit it made her legs and lower torso swelter while her upper torso, bare except for her stretch cotton halter top, was a tad too cool.

She shifted again, curled up against the armrest of the passenger seat with a hand pillowing her cheek against the glass, and watched the city lights pass. She had this vague sense of unease, considering what her father had said about Kaleidoscope. A couple of times she looked in the mirror set into the sunshade. But they were alone on the streets.

"Thanks for the ride," she said.

Alison was changing into the right lane to get onto I-25. She always bypassed the city streets, when she could. Carli supposed all the refugees and poor people made her nervous.

"I don't mind dropping you at the station."

Alison had thrown on a long vest of bleached leather over her blue silk to protect it, and had on matching bone leather gloves, another anachronism. Carli couldn't help noticing how small and dainty her hands were.

"I'm glad you came tonight," Alison added.

"Mmmmm. Yeah."

Several minutes of silence ensued. Carli didn't try to fill it with anything. But Alison finally said, "I just want you to know that I didn't want to invite Jere."

"Sure."

Carli thought she was keeping her voice under control, but Alison must have heard something in it, anyway. She glanced sidelong at Carli, smiling her gentle smile. "You let too many negative feelings in. It's bad for your health, and it attracts all sorts of dark beings around you."

"I really don't want to talk about it."

"Well. It wasn't my idea. I just wanted you to know that. I told him you wanted to forget all about Jere and the divorce and to leave you alone about it, but he insisted that you two needed to talk, maybe patch things up. Now he can see what a mess he made of things, how miserable he made you! I'm going to have a word with him tonight."

"Mother, please don't. He and I settled it between ourselves."

Alison gave her a close look, her lips pursed. Then she sighed. "I love him dearly, but sometimes he's so unreasonable! Men. I sometimes wonder how I've managed to keep us together for so long."

"I guess it's easy to stay married to someone you have no respect for when you're apart most of the time," Carli said. The undercurrent of sheer nastiness in her remark alarmed her, but Alison took the comment in stride, and appeared thoughtful.

"Yes, I suppose so. But you know, it's not so much a matter of disrespect. I think he's an intelligent man. He's also very caring. Just— sometimes he can be so selfish, so self-absorbed. He can be totally oblivious to the needs of the people around him. . . . Like insisting I invite Jere to the party."

"It was your party. You could have said no." Carli's voice came out almost inaudible, and Alison must not have heard it, because she didn't respond.

"It's the same thing he's always done. The way he would drag the three of you off to Washington every summer when you were kids, away from your friends and your music and dance lessons, showing you off like prize marlins to his Washington colleagues.

"It used to infuriate me," she said, and her hands were gripping the wheel so tightly the leather squeaked. "It was just so callous of him, pretending it was because he wanted to spend more time with you, leaving me alone in Santa Fe. . . ."

Carli frowned. "You didn't want to come, Mother. You were always too busy or something."

Alison looked at her, wan and dark-eyed; Carli immediately regretted her words. He'd never really wanted Alison there. They all knew it.

Carli hesitated.

"Dad can be incredibly oblivious." That was true, too. "I could see how that would be difficult to take sometimes."

Alison nodded, relaxed. "It is," she said. "But I know that he loves me, deep inside." She was silent a moment, navigating a series of turns, back onto the city streets. Then she burst out, "I'm so sorry you were hurt. He didn't mean to, really. It's just his way. Don't stay angry with him."

"I know, Mother. Don't worry."

"We put the light around you during meditations, darling. Everything will be all right."

"Well, thanks. I appreciate the sentiment."

"It's not just a sentiment, dear. The mind and spirit are incredibly powerful, and with meditation you can turn them toward the light. Ah, here we are."

Alison pulled the car over to the curb and unsealed the door. Carli climbed out, then leaned back in to give Alison a kiss on the cheek and grab her satchel and coolant unit from the backseat.

"Thanks again for the ride," she said.

"Be careful going home. Keep the light about yourself."

"I love you, Mother," Carli said, and then the door lowered and sealed, and the grey, aerodynamic vehicle shot away down the deserted street, past the strip joints and bars toward the highway.

And the bitch of it, Carli thought, looking after her, is that I really do.

She didn't have her city residency ID crystal, so technically she was violating curfew. But the subway station was at Moon and Central, and the stairs came up less than a half block from the apartment building. She scanned the streets from the subway opening. No one in sight. A hard rain fell and water rumbled as it rushed through the culvert.

She zipped her cool suit up to the chin and turned off the patchwork pattern. The suit turned matte black. She cranked the temperature down, then pulled the hood on and pulled her pulse gun out of her waist pouch. This time it was charged.

She kept her head moving, listened and watched, as she walked up the hill to the building, pelted by high-velocity raindrops. But even the thieves and whips had enough sense to be in on a night like this.

When she opened the door to the apartment she heard Tania crying in the bedroom. Argyle thumped to the floor with a plaintive meow and looked up at her. He meowed again. It sounded like a question.

"Carli?"

Tania came to the door, wrapped in a blanket, her blond hair all tousled. In the dim light the ravages were invisible; she looked beautiful and young, like years before. "How was the party?"

But her voice quavered, and Carli knew she had been sniffing sprite. And that Paint had been here, been with her.

Damn you, Paint, Carli thought. She tossed her cool suit and satchel onto the couch and came toward Tania, arms open. "Lights up," she said. "Honey . . ."

Then Tania looked past her, and screamed. Carli turned. And her hand yanked her gun out of her waist pouch. Someone stood next to the couch.

First glance said woman, seriously injured. She was six feet tall and totally naked. Three ugly gashes, one on her face, one down her right arm, one slash across her left thigh. Her skin was a canvas someone had spilled buckets of paint on, cocoa and vanilla, like a pinto. Her body was unusually long and slim all over. Wiry. Her hair and facial features, though as varicolored as the rest of her, were Negroid. Her eyes stared at Carli, unblinking, without expression.

A closer look said not human. Machine. The wounds in the thing's arm, leg, and face were bloodless, and in place of veins, muscle, and bone were plastic tubes with clips hanging from them, wiring, meta-ceramic infrastructure.

"Say something else," the woman-thing said. It spoke with a slow deliberation that made it sound artificial.

"Who are you?" Tania demanded.

"Say something," it repeated, looking at Carli.

Carli didn't speak, merely stared back at the thing over the sighting gauge of her pulse gun. *It will look like a woman. Tall. Unusual complexion. Incredibly strong. It has killed before. It's after you.*

She shook her head, trying to think. Machine. Or waldo? Bound to be strong in addition to being fast, so whatever she did had better work the first time.

Shoot it? She wasn't sure her little pulse taser was powerful enough to incapacitate the robot, or cyborg, or whatever it was. And if she shot it without incapacitating it, it might get pissed off.

Get Tania away, that was the first thing. It was after her, Carli. Get Tania out of danger.

But she couldn't tell Tania a thing. The creature was waiting for the sound of her voice like a cat crouched above a motionless rodent.

"Carli will shoot you if you don't jig, whoever you are," Tania said, swaying forward. She was too stoned to tell it wasn't human.

The machine looked at Tania for the first time. Carli went icy cold. The scent of her own fear, strong and bitter, filled her nostrils. Cold sweat beaded on her skin. She grabbed Tania's arm and propelled her toward the door.

"Get out," she mouthed. "Get help."

Tania resisted, gave Carli a puzzled glance. "You're the one with the gun. Why are you whispering? Why don't you just tell her to jig?"

Carli shook her head at Tania, with as much expression as she could, jerked her head toward the door. Tania looked at her with a frown. "She's just a drunk petey or something."

Then, out of the corner of her eye, Carli saw the open doorway into the hall. Still holding her gun on the thing, Carli started backing toward the door.

Come, she thought at it. Come on. I'm your prey. Follow me.

As the woman-thing passed Tania, Tania said, "Don't be afraid, Carli. I've handled this kind of thing before," and moved to take its arm.

Carli shouted, "Tania, *no!*" and the woman-thing struck up at Tania with its right arm.

The blow lifted her off the floor. Her head slammed against the wall and she landed on her back across Carli's desk. All the memory crystals and equipment scattered. Argyle vanished into the bedroom with a howl. A dark stain smeared the wall where Tania had struck it.

Carli fired the pulse gun at the thing: twin lasers ionized the air between them, and an electric current arced toward the woman-thing, striking the floor as the woman-thing knocked the gun from her hand. She hadn't even seen it move.

But her shot had done some damage to its good leg. She must have burned down a segment of its body, starting at the right hip, before it knocked her aim off. Its leg buckled. Then the woman-thing locked its leg and tilted its head at her.

Tania groaned.

"I think you're the one," it said. "You sound like the one I seek. Why did you shoot me? Are you an enemy, then?"

Carli bit her lips. She started backing toward the door again—keep it in sight, don't give it a reason to attack you by bolting. That Daniel person might be downstairs and he'll know what to do—dear God, please let him be down there—

"I've come a long way seeking you," the woman-thing said. They were in the hall now. It was following her, limping badly. Its voice sounded more like that of a lost child than a killer. But its gaze was still flat and intense. Ten more steps to the stairwell. Carli kept backing, edging along the wall.

"I'd know if you'd just say some more words," the woman-thing said. "The voice that guides me needs to know. It's getting desperate. I"—pause—"have come so far. I need help. I'll protect you from the voice. If you'll just tell me. Please tell me what I am. Tell me how to stop the drums beating."

They had reached the stairwell. The door sensed her presence. She felt the air currents change as it floated open behind her.

Here goes, she thought, and dashed.

She leapt down the stairs several at a time. Leap, leap, leap, swing around the landing, leap, leap. She heard it above her running down the stairs, calling her.

Then someone caught her, propped her up against the banister. An urgent voice spoke into her ear. She looked up. It was the young man, Daniel.

"I can stop it," he was saying. "I was watching on camera and I can stop it. Just stay here."

She squinted at him, nodded, tried to catch her breath.

"And don't say anything. It's targeting your voice pattern."

Carli nodded again, heaving breaths.

He started up the stairs, and then there the thing was, on the landing above them.

Carli saw Daniel had something in his hand which he was concealing from the thing. It looked like a memory crystal, only larger and thicker. The woman-thing glanced at Daniel, then looked back at Carli.

"I have so many questions and so many have tried to hurt me. Who am I? What am I? Did you make me? Why did you hurt me?"

Daniel took a step up as the woman-thing was speaking. The woman-thing took a step down. Carli shrank against the railing.

"Please just say something. You're so silent. You're angry with me, aren't you?

"I just need to know. Am I, am I human? Am I real? I think I must be going mad. I have these dreams, and they're real, only they're not. And I can't get away from the pounding. And that awful voice."

Another step up, another step down. Carli gnawed her lips. It was a machine. Not human. A murderer.

(Maybe a cyborg, Carli, maybe an experiment, an embarrassment they're trying to silence; how do you know you can trust him? What if she—it—is the real victim?)

Daniel told the truth about KaleidoScope. And look what the thing did to Tania. It's insane.

(Listen to it! It's terrified. It was frightened. Tania reached for it, and it thought she was attacking.)

And simultaneously, from another corner of her mind—syntellect? Have they developed so sophisticated a real-time-interactive entity? Have they really come so far?

The woman-thing stepped down again. Daniel pressed himself against the wall, unmoving, and the thing passed him, coming down to Carli. Carli stared up at it.

The thing stopped when it reached her. Its hand touched the torn pseudo-flesh of its face.

"Two days ago," it said, "I woke up in a place many miles from here, inside a fence. I thought it was a dream, just a mind game. But then someone tried to kill me.

"And I realized my name. Dane Elisa Cae. But that's all I can remember. I don't know who I am. I have a voice inside, which guided me here. I'm seeking someone. It's you; it has to be."

Carli saw Daniel moving in on the woman-thing from behind. Hurry, she thought.

"This isn't just a mind game, is it?" the creature continued. "I can't be human; I'm just a machine. I'm not real. Am I?"

And it was just too much. She couldn't hold her silence any longer against the pain in that voice. Carli reached up, touched the being's savaged cheek.

"I don't know if you're human or machine," she said. "And I don't know about voices in your head or anything else. But you're not just a thing. You know what pain is. You're real. Pain makes you real."

The being's gaze focused inward, as if it were groping for an understanding. She saw Daniel at its back now, fumbling at its neck. The being shrieked at Carli, *"Run!"* and its fingers went around her neck, and it started to squeeze the life from her.

It was crushing her throat. Her lungs wanted to explode. There was no air. Carli's vision blackened; she flailed and kicked. Dear God, let me breathe!

Then she was looking up into the face of the young man, Daniel. He held her upright by her arms, shaking her, with a scared expression.

Carli's vision still swam; she drew deep, gasping breaths, one after another. Her body didn't believe it had enough air until several volumes had gone in and out and the spots in her vision faded. Then she struggled to a seated position on the cold stairs, clutching her throat, swallowing, and working her jaw. Her windpipe throbbed and it hurt like hell to swallow. The being stood nearby, without expression, perfectly still, as if someone had thrown a switch. She eyed the creature. *What was it?* she tried to say. *What the hell is that?* But all that came out was a rasp. Daniel saw the direction of her glance and shook his head.

"Don't talk. I'll explain things, I promise, but not here."

He helped her up, draped her arm over his shoulder, and they started up the stairs. The woman-thing turned and followed; Carli started, but Daniel shook his head. "It's OK. I've disconnected the unit. It's following my commands now."

Tania was sitting on the desk when they came in. Daniel set Carli down on the couch, but she followed him over to Tania. Meanwhile the being walked inside and closed the door. Carli eyed it, but Daniel was ignoring it, and he should know.

Still, she made sure the thing was always in her range of vision.

One of Tania's pupils was slightly more dilated than the other, and a trickle of blood led from her ear down her cheek.

Daniel gave her a look, a grimace.

"My head hurts," Tania said to Carli.

"I'll bet it does," Carli rasped. She took Tania in a hug, looked over her head at Daniel. "Need a doctor right away," she whispered. "She's got a concussion. Maybe a skull fracture."

"We've got to get you both to a doctor."

Carli's hand went to her throat. She twisted to look at the thing that had attacked her. "What is it?"

He hesitated. "A classified project."

Carli nodded; that made a number of things make sense. Daniel was studying her, tugging on his lip. "A police report will have to be filed," he said.

"A thief broke in," Carli whispered. "We'll leave out the robotics, and you." At Daniel's surprised expression, she said, "You were telling the truth about Kaleidoscope, and you saved my life. I owe you one."

"Thanks." Daniel gave her arm a squeeze, and stood. "I have to return this unit, but if they let me, I'll be back in touch, OK?"

"Do I have your word on that?"

Daniel appeared uncomfortable. "Well, I'm not really authorized to make that kind of decision, but . . . to the best of my ability, yeah. You've got my word."

Carli nodded. "OK, then." She rubbed her damaged windpipe again. Rubbing only made it hurt worse. Her body felt like it had been a die in somebody's crap game. It was almost one in the morning; she wanted nothing more than to climb into a hot bath and sleep.

Hospital waiting rooms, exams, NatMed forms, police interviews . . . She sighed. It was going to be a long night.

With a sheepish glance at her, Daniel picked her cool suit up off of the couch and pulled a small silver thing from the bottom of the cool pack.

"A homing device," he said. "A bug. We won't need it anymore."

Anger touched her, fled quickly. The bug might have saved her life. "Suppose not."

"You'll be calling your dad."

Carli gave him a sharp look, and nodded. "Yeah."

He nodded with a sort of shrug.

"I'm not—" He broke off and looked at the floor, then back up at her. "Whatever they tell you—I don't know why *that* was after you and I don't know if they're going to let me talk to you again, but it was just to protect you. That was all I was trying to do."

At his words, a lump formed in Carli's throat. She nodded.

As he started to turn, she croaked, "Thanks. I shouldn't have spoken. Incredibly stupid. But—so much pain in its voice . . ."

"Yeah. It sounded so sincere *I* almost believed it. You couldn't have known."

She gave him an outfit to put on the woman-thing, and helped him dress it. As he left she started to tell him about the hidden connection to the old subway tunnel in the basement, then thought better of it. She wasn't *that* quick to trust.

When she came through the automatic doors supporting Tania, the nurse at the emergency room desk made them fill out forms. Tania was confused and kept asking in too loud a voice what day it was, what they were doing in a hospital. Finally the desk nurse exchanged a look with Carli and had one of the robots escort her back. Carli finished both their forms.

She hesitated, worrying a bit of lip, when the cursor on Tania's form stopped by the question "Are you currently taking any drugs or medications, either legal or illegal?"

"Sorry, Tania, honey," she muttered, and typed in *1) Sprite. 2) Cocaine. 3) Unknown if others??*, feeling rather like a fink.

Then she pushed the terminal back, and the nurse told her to have a seat.

Hospital patter surrounded her: voices, gurneys, and machines on wheels, whose echoes bounced around the straight edges and tiled floors like hard rubber balls in a racquetball court. It was a busy night at St. Joe's.

Once curled in a chair in the waiting area, Carli slipped her specs and glove on, and spoke a quiet command into her kelly. A silver squiggle appeared in her lap when the connection came through, and a voice spoke in her ears. And at the exact same instant, bells rang out at eighty decibels, followed by a page: *Dr. Baca, report to Room 522, stat.*

Carli pressed the specs over one ear and put the mike close to her mouth.

"Dad?" Her voice cracked on the single syllable; how long was she going to sound like she was gargling rocks?

"This is Senator Chauncy D'Auber's number," the syntellect said. Its androgynous voice chased words up and down the tonal scale, inflected in such a way it sounded vaguely alien. "The senator is asleep. Would you care to leave a message, or may I help you in some other way?"

She'd forgotten about that particular piece of software; she hadn't called her father in the middle of the night for years. "This is Carli D'Auber. Give me an emergency override, please."

"I'm sorry, Ms. or Mr. D'Auber, but your name is not on the list of persons who are authorized to override," the ghost said. "If you would care to leave a message, however—"

"No, I don't care to leave a message, and if you—" With an effort of will, Carli stopped herself in midsentence. Even if yelling at machines weren't pointless, she was in no condition to shout. "If you would be so kind as to check your list again," she whispered, "I'm sure you'll find I'm on there somewhere."

"There is no need; I am infallible."

"Try Carli MacLeod."

Without pause, it replied, "Yes, Carli MacLeod is on the list. Unfortunately, your voice pattern does not match hers, Mr. or Ms. D'Auber or MacLeod, and so, regretfully, I am unable to comply with your request. If you leave a message, I am certain Senator D'Auber will return your call as soon as he is able."

"I'll tell you why my voice pattern doesn't match your records. The reason my voice pattern doesn't match, you electronic moron, is because my larynx has been crushed!" Her voice got progressively louder as she spoke. Pain lanced through her throat.

"I now record that your voice pattern matches at less than a five percent margin of error," the ghost said, "which is within my parameters to accept in the event of an emergency override. Have a nice day."

Carli slumped. An inarticulate sound squeaked out of her mouth. Then her dad's face, blurred and pale and of the same silverish cast, appeared in her palm. He blinked at her.

"Carli? What time is it?"

Her heart rate jumped, though she had no real reason to feel guilty. "About two-thirty," she croaked.

His attention sharpened. "What's wrong with your voice?"

"Throat injury. The—creature—that young man warned me about." She swallowed. "Showed up in my apt."

He looked over his shoulder, presumably at Mother, and a strained, worried look came onto his face.

"Are you OK now?" he asked.

"Yeah. Daniel—he disabled it."

"Good." He rubbed his face, drew a breath, and said something she couldn't hear over a page. She pressed the specs over her ear again. "What?"

". . . are you now? At home?"

She shook her head. "St. Joe's."

She heard her mother's sleepy voice in the background.

"Hang on," he told Carli. Over his shoulder he said, "It's a business call, dear. Go back to sleep."

Then he gave Carli a look that spoke of ashes.

"Hold for a minute," he said, and the silver squiggle came back.

His face rematerialized in front of her in a moment or two and he said, "I"—behind her, someone started shouting for some kind of assistance and she missed some of what he said—"of men out."

"What?"

"Congressional Security is on their way," he repeated more loudly.

"Oh, Dad . . . come on." But his expression was unyielding, and she gave up the argument.

"Are you still in the emergency room?" he asked. She nodded.

"With a friend of Paint's. Concussion."

"You have a concussion?" She shook her head. "Your friend does, then? The unit gave her a concussion?" At her nod, he closed his eyes and muttered an oath; she couldn't make it out. Then he asked, "How bad?"

Carli had to shake her head again. "Don't know yet."

Then she spotted an older, redheaded woman and a skinny girl on the brink of adolescence, a brunette who looked a little like Tania. Carli waved at the woman, who didn't see her and went to the ER admissions desk to speak to the nurse. Carli turned back to her kelly.

"Better go. Need an exam and to report the break-in."

"Wait. What about the, the creature?"

"Daniel took it."

Her father nodded. Some of the tension in his face eased. Which meant, she suddenly realized, it wasn't Daniel's involvement that bothered him. It was her own.

"This," he said, "isn't the time or—" The rest of his sentence was drowned out by another page, but she got the gist of it.

"I understand," she whispered.

He frowned at her. "What?"

She shook her head. It didn't bear repeating. Two men in dark grey sheath suits entered the ER then, followed by a woman in a police uniform.

"Security's here."

"I'll call you in the morning, then," her dad said.

"Afternoon, please. Need sleep." She paused. "It was a robbery. Just a break-in."

The relief on her father's face was palpable. He even broke into a smile. "Good, Coo. Good thinking."

She looked over at the group of people who had gathered at the ER desk. Tania's mother and sister were looking at her, and the ER nurse was pointing her out to the police officer. The men in grey were already coming over to her.

When she was little, she had been afraid of the men in Congressional Security, with their somber faces and their guns and concealed body armor, even when Dennis and her dad insisted they were only there to protect her.

Good thinking. Indeed. With a shudder, she cut the connection and dropped her kelly to hang on her platinum chain. She gave the suits a nod.

"Ms. D'Auber?" It was the taller one who spoke. "We've been dispatched to protect you."

They both pulled out ID lozenges. She slid each into her kelly for a cursory glance at their names—Roy Tennys, and then Donald Gramitzsky—and the head-and-shoulders images that rotated a full 360 degrees, with a red ribbon of ID numbers beneath. She popped each of the lozenges out and handed them back with a nod and slid her hands into her pockets.

Roy, the taller one, had eyes without depth or expression. He gave Carli the creeps. Like, if someone told him to, he'd have not a twitch of conscience about laser-frying her brain right through the retinas, or putting a bullet into her heart. The shorter, thin one, Donald, had a more likable, lived-in-face, though his manner was reticent.

"My voice is gone," she whispered, as the nurse and Tania's mother and sister came up. Carli gave the nurse a querying look, and he shook his head.

"She has a hairline fracture in her jaw and a concussion, ma'am. She's very confused and has lost some memory, we think. That should be temporary. The doctor is examining the results of her X rays now."

"I'd like to see her," Carli said.

The redheaded woman shot an ugly look at Carli, possibly because she'd gotten a look at Carli's response to the drug question. *Don't want to admit our darling daughter's got a habit, do we?* Carli wondered. Or perhaps she blamed Carli for what had happened.

She gave Carli her shoulder and turned back to the nurse. Her voice was high-pitched with strain and she was twisting a Kleenex in her hands. "Take me to my baby."

The nurse led Tania's family away, and the policewoman detained Carli for a moment. She first gave a rather sharp glance to the two suits. Roy explained that they were with Congressional Security, detached to protect Senator D'Auber's daughter, and the policewoman's eyebrows went even higher as she looked first them, and then Carli, up and down. After examining all three of their IDs, she seemed satisfied.

She then handed Carli a police ID crystal, whose image was not nearly as high rez as the suits', which Carli dutifully examined and handed back. She had copied Carli's notes from the ER computer, and used them to ask her a series of questions about the break-in.

"Nothing missing?"

Carli hadn't had a chance to comb the house thoroughly, but she thought not.

"Description of attacker?"

Carli described the creature as a tall white woman, leaving out the exposed machinery and the strange blotches. Just in case Daniel had to use public transport on his way back to wherever he took the creature. Didn't need to make things any more difficult for him.

"How do you think she got in?" the woman asked. "How did she get past apartment security measures?"

Carli shrugged. Having a bruised larynx could be a good thing.

"Have you ever seen the woman around before?"

Carli shook her head.

Well," she said finally, "we'll get someone on it right away, but break-ins are becoming more common in that part of town, and chances aren't good we'll find much. . . ."

"I understand," she rasped. "Thanks."

"I'll contact you if something turns up."

She handed Carli a stylus and asked her to scrawl a signature under the police report she had filled out on her own kelly. Then she left.

Carli, flanked by a man in a grey suit at each elbow, went back into the emergency room, in the direction they had taken Tania earlier. Several of the ER personnel cast disapproving looks at the two government sorts, but Carli wasn't going to quibble with their presence, not after coming within a few millibars of being someone's idea of a murder victim.

Four rooms took up the suite they entered, separated by privacy screens. The first room, being scrubbed at breakneck speed by a robot, gave Carli a quick impression of green gowns and towels, blood-reddened water and sheets. Strips of stained gauze fluttered about. In the next two rooms were patients: an old man lying prone on a gurney, taking long, stertorous breaths, with an IV in one arm and plastic green tubes up his nose; a young woman sitting in a wheelchair while a hospital technician sprayed a cast onto her swollen ankle.

They reached the third room just behind the ER nurse. The nurse pushed the screen aside. Tania's mother and sister must have just entered, too, because they were both looking at Tania, who lay propped up on a gurney, clenching the rails of the gurney, her eyes rolled back in her head.

She was moaning, little soft mewling sounds. Vomit splattered her gown and blankets, and the sour smell made Carli's stomach turn. Tania's forehead and right temple had swollen to the size of a clenched fist, and the skin was turning a sickly yellow green.

Carli glanced at the nurse. A look of alarm came onto his face—he pushed past Tania's sister and mother, forced Tania's eyes open, and then checked her breathing and pulse.

He dropped the wrist, and for Carli the next several seconds registered as a series of stop-action images—the nurse pressed a red button on the wall, his mouth opened to issue urgent commands, Tania's mother staggered against the screen with her hand at her mouth, someone in hospital garb grabbed Carli from behind, shoved her and the others out of the way—

Moments later, Carli sat on a gurney in a different suite of rooms, wearing a grey-green hospital gown with the requisite ventilation at the back. The taller suit, Roy, sat on a stool, looking bored and cleaning his nails with his pocketknife. Donald, who seemed even more disinclined to talk than his partner, stood at the screen, looking out toward the hallway with old memories behind his eyes that Carli didn't ask about. Down the hall toward the NatMed offices and waiting room, Carli could hear the wailing of Tania's mother, faintly. They must have loaned her the nurses' lounge to freak out in.

Carli leaned forward and buried her face in her hands. Let this be a nightmare, she thought. But when she looked between her hands again, she was still in the emergency room, and the voices and crying outside continued unabated.

Things quieted down after a while. The ER nurse came in to let her know Tania had developed an extradural hematoma and slipped into a coma. They were prepping her for surgery, to drain the blood that was putting pressure on the brain. Some whip victims arrived shortly after that and activity picked up again, so it was four-thirty in the morning before Carli was finally examined.

The doctor gave her some heavy-duty painkillers and prescription throat lozenges, told her to go home, alternate heat and ice on her neck to minimize the bruising, ice after forty-eight hours, and to avoid talking for a day or so. Tania was still in surgery, and her mother, sitting in the waiting room, had lapsed into listlessness. She wouldn't talk to or even look at Carli. The teenage girl, Tania's sister, slept stretched out beneath the armrests across the bank of seats. It reminded Carli painfully of Tania sleeping on her couch the night before.

Guilt filled Carli, standing by the ER door looking at them. She was supposed to have been the victim, and it was Tania who got hurt.

The suits gave her a ride home in their slick electric collovehicle with the shaded, bulletproof windshields and crushed leather seats, and nobody said much on the way.

PABLO

IT WASN'T *HIS* FAULT

"Why the *hell* am I getting calls from Senator D'Auber, Chairman Morrison, *and* Secretary Thompson in the middle of the night?" Mother demanded as she appeared in Krueger's jellowall. "What's going on?"

Pablo stared at Mother. It'd been a long night. Once again he had no idea where Buddy was—whether he was just ignoring Pablo's calls, or had gone back to Kaleidas to play face-games with their crèchemates, or what.

"I'd have to kidnap her, then," Uncle Daniel had said, when Pablo-Krueger had told him to bring her in. "Is that what you want, boss?"

Pablo could hardly have said yes.

So he had spent the intervening time secluded in his quarters, ignoring all calls—pacing, worrying, starting to call Mother and then stopping in midaction, and wondering whether running away was feasible.

There was no escaping it now; he had to tell her.

"There was, there was . . . the renegade . . . I mean . . ." Get a grip, Pablo. He drew a breath. "The renegade attacked her. Aunt Carli. A few hours ago."

Rage coalesced onto her face. "*A few hours ago? And you didn't call me?*"

He said nothing. She stared at him, hands clenching and unclenching. "Explain."

He did.

"And why didn't you order Sornsen to bring her in?"

Pablo lifted Krueger's big, meaty hands in a shrug. "I did. He wouldn't listen to me."

"Then you obviously weren't trying hard enough. You have screwed things up royally for everyone. You may have just cost us the mission." Her words struck, tearing like little glass darts. "I'll handle this myself. We'll see about your punishment later."

"No, wait! Give me another chance. Please, Mother . . . *te amo.* . . ."
His voice tapered off as she broke the connection. "Shit."

He called for Buddy once more. Still no response. Dropping into the chair at his desk, he-Krueger tucked a meaty leg under himself, stared out at the darkness beyond the window, and began rocking himself and humming.

CARLI

DADDY'S GIRL

Carli made the suits get a room in a hotel across Central. They argued, but if they were in the apt, she'd never get to sleep, and having them around was a little like buying insurance after the house had burned down, anyhow.

They found a room that faced hers from across Central, made her promise to keep her windows depolarized, and gave her a bug to carry that looked like a class ring. She strung it through her platinum chain, feeling ridiculous. *Hello, this is agent J, come in, Brainiac.*

"Fine," she croaked, closing the door behind them. "Fine."

She put a kettle on to boil and sat down next to Argyle on the couch, absently petting him. He rippled, arching and then flattening himself under her hand like a hamster, and purred in rhythm with her strokes. Static electricity made his long fur come to life under her hand, crackling and spitting. He butted against her thigh, then rolled onto his tummy and grabbed at her hand with his claws, levering it between foreclaws and aft—needles sank into her skin—but he was careful, even then, and released her after a couple of pretend-bites and rough licks. She smiled down at him and tousled his head.

So. Why *did* you let a couple of government agents invade your life, Carli?

(Because I was scared, that's why. Because someone tried to kill me and I was scared.)

And what's the real reason? Come on, we're alone in here.

(Because Daddy told me to. Daddy fucking *told* me to. OK?)

She must have been out of her mind. Temporary insanity. She only hoped she wouldn't snore too loudly, or talk in her sleep. That was assuming she'd be able to sleep.

After making herself some tea, she called Paint. Both he and Fox, unfortunately, had their kellies on auto-message—but they had never been what you'd call early risers. After leaving a message for Paint to call her that afternoon and another message to Fox that she wouldn't be in that day, Carli got undressed and wrapped up in a robe.

From the living room she waved at the opaque windows across the way (she wasn't sure exactly which one they were watching from)—"Hi, guys," she whispered into the class ring—and then entered the kitchenette to fix herself some buttered toast and another mug of chamomile tea.

She found herself so tired she couldn't sleep, so she curled up in the couch with a hot mug cupped between her hands, turned on the jelly, and watched a comedy instead. The plot was as tired as she was, though, and after a few minutes she switched it over to the news, turned down the volume till it was almost inaudible, and gave her eyes a good rub. Grit and inflamed blood vessels made her eyes burn.

No coverage of *Exodus* ensued; the only thing covered on the space-news channel was a brief mention of an odd theft: a large quantity of cesium ingots had disappeared without a trace from Kaiser-Toyota's manufacturing plant on Shasta Station. One employee was injured, and a search of the station as well as all ships that had been at dock during the period of disappearance had yielded nothing. Then a political scientist gave her analysis about the new administration's transition to power, and what it meant in several different areas.

Carli sipped the herb brew, and smoky, bittersweet liquid scalded her tongue; the heat soothed her throat. As a sedative, though, neither the tea nor the political pundit helped much. She was exhausted and achy, but she just wasn't sleepy. She turned off the jelly and set the cup down.

The fact that she could barely walk a straight line notwithstanding, Carli succumbed to an obsessive impulse and changed her bed sheet and straightened the room a little. She took her medications with a cup of water and wrapped a cool pack around her neck, which eased the ache.

Then she succumbed to gravity, slipped into the cool percale envelope, and tried to fall asleep. It was seven in the morning, and the first rays of sunlight streamed in through the unpolarized panes.

When she closed her eyes, against the bloodred screen of her closed eyelids, the face of her parti-colored assailant—the pinto-shaded woman-creature—appeared; not as it had attacked her but just before, when it had touched its cheek and asked for help. Pleading mouth, flat secret eyes: *Help me.* And then the hands around Carli's throat, squeezing off her air—

No. Sleep. She rolled over, thumped her pillow, tried counting prime numbers. But the face formed again, and the dark eyes—whoever was behind them was a long way away, buried deep inside—*help me. Free me.* And the hands—

She sat up, and her hands went to the cool pack. It was too much like being choked. She unwound it, tossed it to the floor. Sleep.

And behind her eyelids, Daniel stood staring at the barrel of her pulse gun, and then he disappeared into the night fog: a blur of motion, then nothing. And her eyes came open with the realization.

Whatever the woman-creature was, so was Daniel.

Syntellect units, then—? No. Emphatically not. Because Daniel was no artificial intelligence. Too much about him defined his humanity.

But precious little had defined the pinto woman as human. Little besides her pain.

You have pain. You're real. Pain makes you real.

Waldo units, then. They were pilots. It must be a classified project that her father had some involvement with. The technology was closer to hand, anyhow, than that sophisticated a syntellect.

So the million-dollar question became: who was the pilot of that runaway waldo? And why did whoever it was want to kill Carli? Because of who she was, or because of her father? Did she know something she didn't know she knew?

She laid all the questions aside with a groan and flung an arm across her eyes to block out the sunlight. There'd be plenty of time for reflection later, and her mind would be clearer once she'd slept.

Cats are psychic, and they choose their moments carefully. At the precise moment Carli was slipping into the long, slow thoughts that precede sleep, Argyle heaved himself onto the bed with an uncatlike grunt and climbed onto her feather pillow. Carli all but levitated off the bed.

Half sobbing with frustration, she shoved him off and pulled the sheet over her head. He came back, digging at the covers around her face, and she tossed him off, three, four, five times, until they reached a compromise: he stayed off her face, and she let him stay on the bed.

But the urge to sleep was gone. She tossed; she turned; she thumped her pillows. It was getting close to lunchtime. She gave up, threw the sheet aside, and announced to Roy and Donald across the way, "Can't sleep, guys. Excuse me while I take a shower."

She slid the ring and pendant chain off, laid them on the stand by her bed, and took her kelly into the bathroom. Only after she had turned the shower on full blast, stripped, and stepped under the curtain of hot water did she deactivate visual and call her father. She also turned down the volume and cupped the kelly close to her ear. Just in case they had sound-enhancement equipment.

Chauncy answered immediately. "Coo. Are you all right?"

"Fine." Her voice, albeit still rough, already sounded better. Or perhaps it was the painkillers. "Tired, mostly. Listen—"

"And your friend?"

"Don't know yet. I'll call the hospital next. Listen, Dad—"

"I've been following up since we talked, and I have some reassuring news. You're in no immediate danger. Everything's under control—"

"Dad, stop for a second. I want to call off Security."

He sounded surprised. "Why? Are they staying at your place? You could ask them to take a room nearby; they don't have to be in your apartment."

"I've already made them check into a nearby hotel, but they're bugging the place. It makes me feel creepy. That's why I'm calling you from the shower."

That drew a chuckle out of him. His soft laugh pulled a smile from inside her. It didn't last. "Well, the number at the hotel is 7984-1816. Please have their boss call them off."

A pause. "That wouldn't be a good idea, Coo. We don't know enough about the situation yet to be sure that you're not still in danger."

"Daniel caught the woman who was trying to kill me."

"I know. But there are still a lot of unanswered questions, and I'd feel better if you'd keep the security men a while longer. Do it as a favor to me, OK?"

She bit her lip, worried it. She had a vision of herself, a bug in a jar—grass blades in the bottom, holes poked in the lid and all, like the bugs she'd caught when she was a kid—with enormous men in gray suits peering down at her through the glass. She drew a sigh.

"For how long are we talking about?"

"It'll only be a few days, at the most. I promise. Call me every morning and evening, and I'll keep you updated."

"All right, then. They can watch through my window, but I don't want to be bugged. It makes me nervous."

He was silent for a moment. "Very well. You can tell them to come pick up their listening devices. I'll give them a call of confirmation."

"Thanks." She continued worrying her lip, pulled a flake of skin loose. "And since we have a little privacy—I was hoping you could en-lighten me as to what this is all about."

His flat-toned "Oh" didn't bode well, but she forged ahead. "Dad—what was that creature? Why was it trying to kill me? Was someone trying to get to you through me?"

There was a long silence. "I wish I could explain, dear," he said fi-nally, "but it's a national security matter, and I can't discuss it. You know how those things are, Coo. One of the occupational hazards of having a politician for a father." A different kind of chuckle, a strained noise. "You know how it is."

That was his way of pleading: *Let it go, Coo.* Or perhaps it was a command. They came almost to the same thing.

"Sure, Dad. I understand."

Let it go. She was good at that, when it came to her father.

Summers when they went to see him, Carli would be so desperately glad to see him; she'd have done anything to please him. So he'd take her up in his lap and he'd ask how Mother was, and she'd tell him—she hates us, Daddy, she picks on us; last week she yelled at me and Denny and dragged Jo through the house by the hair because she waited till "The Doughty Douglas" was over before she cleaned up her room—and he'd listen and make clucking noises and say that's awful and you have every right to be upset, and when she'd say, why don't you talk to her, Daddy; why don't you tell her to stop? he'd say, it's just her way, Coo. She loves you in her own way.

Let it go, he meant. Let it go. Take what I can give you and don't ask me for more.

I understand. What a joke. She didn't understand at all. Carli shut off the water. She had a sour feeling in the pit of her stomach as she toweled herself dry.

Once in the bedroom, she said, "Roy, Donald, I've just spoken to my father. Your surveillance is going to have to be limited to watching from across the way. He'll be giving you a call of confirmation. Come on over and pick up the class ring."

Then she called the hospital and was informed that Tania was still in a coma. Surgery hadn't helped.

Paint called while Carli was getting dressed. Since Roy and Don-ald were listening in, Carli restricted her description of what had hap-pened the night before to the official one.

Paint's face showed shock. "Poke me total. That's just after I—"
He stopped, switched gears. "Um, I'n't know if Tania mentioned, I
dropped by earlier like I said I would, and saw no one then, inside or
out. Wonder how the woman got in. Trey jade."

"Yeah. Whoever it was might have even been there while you
were."

She looked at him directly, reproach settling onto her face. He
read it right, and lowered his gaze after a second. She disconnected
without saying good-bye.

If Paint hadn't been there, hadn't been with her, maybe she
wouldn't have been so high. She wouldn't have tried to stop the pinto-
woman, and wouldn't be lying comatose in a hospital bed with tubes
up her nose.

But that was bullshit. Tania spent most of her time maxed out.
What had happened to Tania was no more Paint's fault than it was
Carli's. But the fact remained that Paint, the prick, had gone and poked
Tania again, whom he so actively disliked, just to prove he could. And
Tania, that self-destructive twit, had been too needy to say no.

Carli sat down at her dresser and brushed the absolute shit out of
her hair, till the ends pulled and snapped like overstretched elastic.
When she slammed the brush down on the glass blotter on top of the
dresser, all the little glass bottles and silver trays of pins danced on
their doilies. Carli saw in her reflection the blackening bruises on her
neck and the haggard lines on her face.

She pushed her hair back with a sigh and rested her chin on a palm.
The woman in the mirror did likewise.

The doorbell chimed. Roy and Donald.

"Just a minute," she shouted hoarsely, and studied her own gaze.

What was really eating her was—even though someone had just
nearly choked the life out of her, she'd never know who, or why. And
why not? Because it was her idol of a father, and because he'd thrown
those two magic words in her face: *national security.*

She pushed the little saddle chair back and stood. She had some
magic words of her own. "Fuck that."

"M-m-raow?" Argyle said. He looked up at her from licking his
belly, in the spot of sunlight beneath the window.

"You heard me," she replied. She snatched up the class ring bug,
went into the living room, yanked the door open.

Donald stood there, hands in his pants pockets. He'd taken his formal sheath off, loosened his cravat, and rolled up his sleeves. His hair had gotten damp and rumpled, and little red spots dotted his shirt and cravat. Pizza, Carli guessed. Maybe spaghetti.

"You shouldn't open the door without checking to see who's there first," he said.

"How do you know I didn't?"

"Your footsteps. You didn't pause at the door." He held out his hand and she dropped the ring into it.

"No offense," she said. He shrugged, did something with the ring, and slid it into his pocket.

"Roy's put out about it. But it's your neck; you should excuse the pun. And we can't get the boot if something should happen, when your father authorized it." He shrugged again. "Actually, we can see you just fine from across the way. We don't need the bug all that much."

Right, Carli thought, and closed the door.

First she made herself a peanut butter and mango sandwich on seven-grain bread and poured herself a glass of ice-cold soy milk. Then she took her kelly, sat down at the desk, and proceeded to empty the drawers, looking for a notepad and pen.

NOW, *THAT'S* PRIVATE PARTS

Daniel awoke at one-thirty in the afternoon, thanks to the alarm, his eyes gluey with discharge, and a furry colony of bacteria on his tongue. Sunlight blasted the colors right off the pavement stones, plant leaves, and ground outside the window. He winced against the brilliance and sat up.

The world had tilted during his sleep in some extradimensional direction—in some indescribable quantum or psychic way. A dull pain throbbed behind his eyes, making him queasy. Other aches and pains plagued his arm, leg, and abdominal muscles, as if he'd been wrestling in his sleep, and he smelled even to his own nose a lot like an old sock.

He had felt like a shriveled prune after climbing out of the salt bath, sometime before sunrise, and hadn't bothered to shower before stumbling back to his room and falling into bed. That had been a mistake.

But first things first. He picked up his netspecs, earphones, and gloves off the bedside table and slid them on. On the menu bar was a security-coded selection that let him check up on his proxy back in Albuquerque. He'd stashed it in a subway tunnel near Carli D'Auber's place.

The unit crouched in a cubbyhole in pitch blackness, exactly where he'd left it. The antimatter reactor was shut down; all systems were on standby. No one would see it unless they knew right where to look. As he touched its circuits, far away he could hear the wail of a train, and nearer, the scratchings and chittering sounds of rodents. A damp, musty smell tinged with petroleum waste wafted past. Satisfied, he logged off.

He'd head back that evening to pick it up. For now, he wanted to tend to his flesh.

The ultra-shower, tooth brushing, and a clean pair of underwear, sandals, gauze drape, and jeans got rid of his headache, but his stomach still lay shriveled and nauseated in his gut like a lump of collapsed matter. He thought he might never want to eat again.

Once in the deserted cafeteria, though, as he moved down the cook-and-serve counter with his silverware-laden tray and the row of chrome arms lifted lids and brandished serving forks, spoons, or ladles for his benefit, he caught glimpses of the stews and fillets, caught whiffs of the spices and aromas and flavorful steam rising from the pots and trays, and his mouth filled with saliva. His stomach growled enthusiastically. Saved from the necessity of further IV feedings.

He packed away helpings of beef-flavored whey spice loaf, buttered *sukuma wiki* leaf paté, half a papaya with lime, a mound of mashed plantains, and a thirty-two-ounce cherry Coca-Cola. For seconds, he chose a slice of rhubarb pie and a cup of café moccha with coconut cream, and carried them back to a table by the window. Then he stared out at the tree-shaded patio and sipped his brew, and let the pie sit for a while.

A group of people from Neurophysiology came in, including Leanne, the medic. They filled their trays with food, laughing and talking. Daniel had a hard time not staring at Leanne as she got her food, because he realized after a second that she was in her own body. Her own body was, as best he could tell, essentially identical to her proxy.

They came toward him.

"May we join you?" Leanne asked, and at his nod slid onto the seat next to his. "Have you finished your classified project yet? Are we actually going to start seeing you around again one of these days?"

He felt himself color, and gave her a smile. Damn, but she was beautiful—those wonderful cheekbones and brown eyes and body-hugging long hair. She didn't need a proxy to intrigue men.

He thought about all the enhancements he had made in his proxy's design to his own stature and muscle tone and facial lines. All vanity. And it accentuated his own, real plainness. He wished Leanne had never seen him in proxy. With his deprivation-sharpened sense of smell, he caught a whiff of soap and calla lily from her hair and skin, and this time his erection swelled right up against the zipper of his jeans—too damn close for comfort.

He blew a breath out and shifted away from her. Down, Fido. Down.

"It looks like we've got it pretty well wrapped up," he managed to say. "My part of it, anyhow. But I'd better not discuss it; sorry."

"That's OK," Leanne said, and stirred her mango juice with a finger. She popped her finger in her mouth to suck the juice off, and gave Daniel a smile. The erection, which had wilted a little, swelled right back to its full extension.

The others chatted for a little while about the various projects and people in N-phys. Daniel, knowing little about either, mostly listened and ate his pie.

Leanne stayed seated when the two men left. Daniel had the sense she was looking at him, but when he turned to look, her gaze was elsewhere. An unnatural silence stretched between them; Daniel started to grow too warm.

"I have to get going," he said, and stood with his tray. She had a look like she wanted to say something, though, so he paused.

"I'm going into town on Saturday to do a little shopping, and maybe catch a play or an allie," she said. "Would you like to join me?"

Joy and panic surged up for control of his mouth.

No! Don't do it—run while you can!

Go for her—she's yours! Do it, asshole—you chickenshit!

What about all the work that's been piling up while you've been running around the countryside chasing the renegade?

I want her—

You mustn't!

I will!

Shut up in there, he commanded. The work argument clenched it. He hadn't even logged into his business directory since last Friday. He'd have to chain himself to his desk to catch up. That fucking renegade.

"This project has put me so far behind, Leanne. I have to work."

Disappointment shadowed her face. Then she gave him a smile that made him feel like melting. "Sure. Maybe some other time."

"Definitely," he said. "How about next week?"

"Lovely. It's a date."

He walked over and separated the contents of his tray at the chutes: plastic into one, metal into the next, food refuse into the third, paper into the last. Remembering the look on her face, he felt like climbing into the third chute himself. Coward. Idiot.

At least the erection had stopped plaguing him.

The Classified Face Lab's dry, refrigerated air poured out of the opening door into the hall and raised gooseflesh on Daniel's arms. He spotted Teru, wearing her teenaged male Adonis proxy, beyond a bank of electronic equipment, seated at one of the calibrating stations near the back. The room smelled of oil and ozone.

As he drew nearer he saw she was bent over her sensor field, weaving inputs that changed the readouts in her *virtu*-tube. Beside her station stood the renegade proxy, with its damaged arm and leg. So lifeless-seeming. Even innocent.

Slabs of the proxy's blotched plastic skin were peeled back. Twisting wire cables were jacked like two bizarre umbilicals into the exposed machinery of its neck and into a socket behind one of its eyes; individual wires snaked between the metaceramic ribs into its chest cavity. Pieces of alloy and composite-resin proxy innards and tools lay strewn around its feet on the glastic tile floor. In the dim lighting, a blur of LEDs in the proxy's chest and gut flickered red, blue, yellow, and white among the translucent strands of blood-tinged siloxane lubricant.

Daniel shivered; he had a creepy, unreasonable fear that the renegade pilot had slipped out of the blind cul-de-sac of the proxy's now-shunted linkware into the interface, and infected the facility *virtu*-net.

Teru, engrossed in her readouts, didn't look at him as he came up beside her-him. His gaze traced the shiny tight mesh of her proxy's hair, the side of its face—whose features were much like her own, though perhaps more classically African—then the thick neck and muscular shoulders, the male pectorals, the muscled abdomen that disappeared into her-his drawstring pants. At that, a sudden urge filled Daniel to shake Teru and shout at her-him. The impulse ebbed when he saw how exhausted Teru was.

Her fatigue showed only in her proxy's posture, which was rigid, and in the way she-he twice misentered and had to repeat her-his instructions to the sensor field in the few seconds Daniel stood watching.

"You should be in bed," he said. She-he jumped and her-his head jerked around.

"Damn you, Danny, don't sneak up on me like that!"

He bit down on a defensive reply. "Sorry." He dragged a chair onto the raised platform and sat down. "Don't call me Danny."

She-he shrugged. Daniel looked past her-his shoulder at the readouts. Teru was running psychology profile similes. Daniel glanced at the renegade.

"So the pilot is still inside?"

"Yeah. The results are fascinating. I'm doing the runs now, not going to analyze them in much depth till I have some more responses. I'm hampered by the lack of physiological feedback, though, damn it! It's making this ten times more difficult."

She-he stuck her-his hands back into the sensor field, and the readouts changed again.

"How long have you been at this?" he asked. "Scott said you had gone off-shift at four A.M. I figured you'd sleep all day."

"I came back in about eight. So I got a few hours' sleep, anyhow." She-he shot him a resentful look. "You might have rung me up and let me know you'd got back. Scott mucked about for almost two hours before I came in. I had to spend at least an hour and a half untangling the mess he made of the linkups."

"You were the one who said you needed sleep last night. I was just trying to be considerate."

She-he started to reply, stopped her-himself. "You're right. I *am* knackered." She-he rested her-his chin in a meaty hand, eyeing the readouts in the jello-tube. "I don't want to stop until I finish this series. They're fascinating, Daniel. Infuriating. Simply inexplicable."

"What have you got so far?"

"Well, the developmental prelims are all I've had a chance to study. I've been summarizing them while the rest of the second series ran. Let me pull up and show you. Put these on."

She-he tossed him a linkware beanie. While he seated it onto his beanjack, with a click that reverberated through his skull, and buckled it on, she-he stuck her-his hands into the sensor field. The instant Daniel accessed the software, a bilateral coded matrix—a double helix of shorthand words, classifications, and numbers—tumbled down across his vision. Daniel studied the readout, but he didn't know the first thing about psychosocial lingo; the symbols were meaningless.

"Here," Teru said, "and here," pointing. "I used EDACS to test the—"

"EDACS?"

"Emotional Development and Coping Skills. A more user-friendly version of the original software Odhiambo and his graduate students developed."

Daniel squinted at the readout. "Those must be the raw data, then?"

At Teru's look of surprise he had the feeling he'd asked a dumb question, but she-he answered amiably enough.

"No. There's a good deal of data reduction there. The latest version also has a very sophisticated interpreter that calculates the likelihood of major cultural influences and gives general information about gender identity, so you don't have to pull up and dig through all those interminable charts and nomographs. That matrix is one of EDACS's standard personality summaries.

"You can tell a deal about a person's early role-model experiences from that," she-he said, warming to the subject, "and a good bit about cultural background. The interpreter module isn't preferred for any sort of detailed analysis as it can be misleading, but the results I'm getting are frankly beyond the pale, even so.

"Look." She-he pointed. "There. And there. This person has no consistent sense of gender identity. The renegade responds to intimacy stimuli as a female, based on the Gilligan developmental model. The anomalies are several, but not outside the transcultural range for women. Yet based on the Piaget model for cognitive development and the Kohlberg moral-development model, the renegade responds in a way that coincides strongly with male behavior, again with odd anomalies.

"I tried to triangulate using Odhiambo's aggression-cooperation model, and I got reasonably non-sex-specific behavior, a little more male than female, perhaps. But with important anomalies. His similes are designed to be highly sensitive to cultural influences, though, and that's hampering me." Seeing the glaze in Daniel eyes, she smiled: a pained grimace. "The upshot is, I'm having serious difficulties in determining whether the renegade is male or female."

Daniel raised his eyebrows. "Really? Is that unusual?"

Teru grunted, cast an indignant look at the coded helix. "It's unheard-of!"

Then her-his expression grew more thoughtful and she-he rested her-his chin on her-his palm again. "Part of the problem is that EDACS has a lie-correction routine based on the subject's physiological responses, which is immensely valuable in getting past the subject's ego defenses and focusing the test responses, and I'm unable to use it because I can't access the renegade's physiological reactions to the tests. And not knowing where the renegade is from, I can't calibrate the routines for cultural influences. It could be that our subject is a male who is highly female-identified, or vice versa. Or that the subject's culture has strong modifying influences either way."

"Ah. But I thought you could use the Odhiambo tests to tell where someone is from."

"I'm running a set of language- and culture-specific scenarios now, in fact, attempting to track that down. Gender identity is such an important ingredient in cultural analysis, though. It's making everything ten times more difficult. English doesn't seem to be her first language. On the other hand, *nothing* in the system seems to be her first language. I'm baffled." She-he sighed and ran a hand over her-his head and face, staring dully at the screen. Daniel touched her-his shoulder. "Leave it for now," he said. "Get some sleep. We have the renegade; he or she—or it—isn't going anywhere for the moment. And you'll do better work once you're rested."

"I suppose. I hate to quit now, but I'm all in. Damn."

"You can let the series finish on its own and program the daemon to keep the renegade in a loop till you come back."

"All right, then. You're right. But keep Scott away, right? He doesn't know what he's about, and I don't want him to muck with things again."

Daniel put a hand on his chest and raised the other, by way of an oath. She-he smiled faintly at that, and set up the program to run automatically.

"What did you find out about that phone number, by the way?" he asked. "Who did the senator call last night?"

Teru had a rueful look. She-he shrugged. "No big surprise—he called the chairman of Waldos, Inc.'s, Board, Morrison. No doubt to raise a frightful ruckus over our chasing the renegade proxy about the countryside without telling him his daughter was involved. I'd not be surprised if the DOEP, the subcommittee, *and* the BoD are in an uproar over all this and that's why Krueger has been out-of-pocket all day."

"Makes sense. So maybe Krueger's problem is just nerves over all the high-powered political pressure."

"Mmmm," Teru agreed.

"And now to bed," he said. "Come on. I'll read you a bedtime story."

She-he stood, and Daniel took her-his hand. It was a comment on the extent of her fatigue that she-he let Daniel lead her-him through the corridors to her-his room.

She-he stopped him at the door with a hand on his chest and, after a pause, leaned over to kiss him on the mouth with her man's lips. The action evoked in Daniel a weird confusion of affection, arousal, and revulsion.

"G'night, Danny boy," she-he said, and the door slid closed.

Daniel laid a hand on the cool metal of the door for a second. His heart twisted and a knot formed in his throat. Flashes of all the old recriminations he'd piled on Teru came back to him, like tired reruns on the J-net.

I'm tired of fucking a plastic doll. I'm tired of you changing your sex on a weekly basis and picking up strange women. Why is it all right for you to do it, but if I do it, I'm a sexist male? Why do you keep calling us a mistake? Why didn't you figure out you prefer women before you made me care about you? Why don't you let me cherish your real body, if you love me?

Why don't you let me love you all the time?

Damn you, Teru, he thought, you and your plastic testicles. Damn your breasts, damn your gorgeous thighs and that warm, wet, aromatic place between them that you've got locked away in a crypt. The renegade wasn't the only one with a confused sense of gender.

He wanted to be angry now, standing in front of her closed door, but all he felt was sad.

Why did he keep getting involved with women who needed rescuing? Or who he thought did.

Daniel turned away from the door, stuffed his hands into his pockets, and ambled down the corridor toward his office/lab, thinking about Leanne and Teru and even a little about Carli D'Auber; thinking what a cheat it was to be so in need.

A MOST VISCERAL REACTION

She found two important historical references to waldos. *Waldos, Incorporated, Origins of.* And *Development of Waldo Technology, 1950 to Present.* Popular Oxford Encyclonet Files E-n56022Jx 82pci and E-n5602h 455dw.

Carli finished the last bite of her sandwich and washed it down with soy milk, then set the sweating glass down and wiped her mouth with the back of her hand. Then she settled into the squish, slipped her net-gloves back on, and adjusted her hood. General information first. She started with the history of waldo research.

The first generation of waldo technology had originated in the 1950s, with the invention of remote-manipulation arms. The user manipulated a series of levers and gears that translated the user's movements into motions produced by a mechanical hand that acted on objects behind a window or screen.

She activated a jello icon, and an image of a man in old-fashioned garb walked up, seated himself before a windowed box that appeared before him, and began to manipulate a series of levers. Inside the box, to the sound of servos, a mechanical hand picked up and put down various objects.

This first-generation waldo technology was used in handling radioactive and other hazardous materials, and also when sterile environments were needed. Thus, waldos were used primarily in the high-technology industries of the time, such as precision machining, silicon and electronics manufacturing, nuclear research, etc.

Robotics and remote-controlled devices grew more popular over the next two decades, and by the 1980s industrial and military uses of second-generation waldos, radio-controlled remote electronic technology, were widespread. Both remote-manipulation and remote-sensing devices were used.

Her father's role slowly became clear as she read. Waldo technology had been heavily sponsored by government funding since the Cold War and New World Order years of the past century, under the aegis of space, military, and more recently, the eco-adaptive sciences. Carli remembered her dad's intensive lobbying for environmental funding, back when she was little—his numerous strategy meetings with then-president Shyner and his fights with certain members of her Cabinet and other senators.

Shyner had bucked severe industrial and political pressure to create a new arm of the government, a Cabinet-level position dubbed the Department of Environmental Protection, or DOEP, in 2028. Within a few years, even her loudest critics had begun to quiet down in the face of all the disease, the firestorms and mud-slides, the famines and droughts, the monstrous storms that ravaged entire continents. Thanks to the DOEP, the U.S. was at least more prepared than it would have been. Consequently Shyner became a popular president, with a reputation for foresight.

And Dad had been close to the president, involved with all the planning. He'd been the first appointee to head the DOEP. His political career had soared. Carli remembered that. She remembered Mom thinking he was having an affair with the president, which Carli secretly thought would be great, because then she'd have a president for a stepmom. She even remembered talk about him having his own shot at the presidency, back then.

He'd been appointed to the Global and Eco-Adaptation subcommittee of the congressional Committee on the Environment, GAEA, during the war in Antarctica, and in the midst of the early global-climate-change panics in the thirties, forties, and early fifties. Third-generation waldo research had been one of the DOEP's research projects, and GAEA had been somehow involved. This was apparently rather odd; usually the two branches of government kept a certain distance from each other.

The largest government contractor for waldo research had been, and continued to be, Waldos, Incorporated, which had the lion's share of the waldo market—though Tokunaga Cooperative and Comm-Tetra, a pan-Eurasian corporation, also had active programs.

Carli jotted down the letters "DOEP" and "GAEA," and turned them into dark, calligraphic doodles. She also took note that early in the development of third-generation technology, a pattern of psychoses and hallucinations on the part of the users had stalled development of direct brain-waldo interface technology for several years. A series of major breakthroughs within the past fifteen years or so had ended the stall and revitalized the field.

Waldos, Inc., the philanthropist Richard Blaine, and Patricia Taylor, a Nobel Laureate in neuronics whose name Carli had encountered, often in scientific journals, featured prominently in those breakthroughs.

The history presented information only on specialized machines, not humanlike remotes. But Carli's numerous attempts to come up with references to humanoid remotes only located one.

Report to Congress—Preliminary Feasibility Study of Applications of Waldos, Final Draft, vol. 3, Congo-Net File LC-r799000 4101.3w. A report to Congress done in 2038 by an independent research firm on various waldo technologies, for the purposes of funding approval. One of the technologies considered was a humanoid remote.

The researchers had concluded that the programming complexities involved and the lack of specialization in the human body made it pointless to develop such a humanoid waldo, when equipment developed for a specific task would be much cheaper and better designed. They summarized with the question "Why develop one piece of equipment that can do many things, none of them exceptionally well, when for the same cost you can design many machines, each a masterpiece of efficiency? Humanoid remotes are economically unfeasible and unnecessary." No references to humanoid remotes existed after that time, in any of the datanets.

Carli frowned, thinking. It wouldn't be the first time information erasures and cover-ups had occurred in classified research. But the total lack of historical references in a major datanet meant that Daniel's secret project wasn't merely classified; clearly it was being carried out under conditions of utmost secrecy. That level of secrecy was almost impossible to maintain for long. She should be able to dredge up something if she just kept digging.

She fell to musing, and an image rose unbidden in her mind: her brother, Dennis, walking around in a body like Daniel's, or the pinto woman's. *Economically unfeasible.* A pillow in what remained of his face, compliments of one of his war buddies, had been a much cheaper solution.

Carli searched for more scientific detail about waldos designed in the last ten years. But most of the histories found by the current search had been developed for nonscientific use, and held few details about the technology itself.

So she called up her primary search engine's syntellect to compile a bibliography of research papers done in the field over the past ten years, with abstracts, and meanwhile started gathering information on Waldos, Inc.

Waldos, Inc., was founded just after the turn of the millennium, the brainchild of Richard Quintelle Blaine, the late trillionaire and philanthropist, along with Dr. Patricia Margaret Taylor, a neural physicist, and a small, hand-chosen team of experts. The technology on which the company was founded was a web of coated nano-wires implanted within the human brain, and the development of linkware that allowed the brain's electrical impulses to be amplified and translated into radio broadcast signals that could control a machine's actions. This technology had become known as beanlinking. Among the primary markets for this technology were the military, as well as heavy industries such as agricultural, transportation, computer, waste disposal, salvage, and space development.

Though initially beanheads tended to be highly educated, a gradual shift occurred toward the poor, refugees, and homeless, who often purchased the technology through the many work-indentureship programs available during the last three decades. Use of the technology outside the developed world—the U.S., Canada, Mexico, Japan, and Europe—was rare, as it was a capital-intensive technology to implement.

Interestingly, Waldos, Inc.'s, work on third-generation technology didn't bring them instant success. Waldo's earliest renown and financial successes during the first three decades of the third millennium were in streamlining second-generation technology. This made waldos more affordable, with ensuing leaps in agriculture, manufacturing, and waste handling that eased some of the food and materials crises wracking the world during the steepest part of the greenhouse curve. It also reenergized the flagging effort to move industries and cities into orbit.

Waldos was perhaps best known now, though, for its leadership role in the development of third-generation space and military waldo technology, and for its involvement in Rosenfeld's New Vision waldo indentureship program of the forties and fifties—both of which came about as a result of third-generation breakthroughs.

Waldo weaponry and craft were decisive factors in the Antarctic Conflict. Also, with Waldos, Inc., as the prime contractor in government-subsidized indenture programs, the worst of the refugee and homeless crises began to ease a bit in most parts of the U.S., and within twenty years of its inception, the company had risen to a position as one of the largest multinational corporations in existence.

The text continued. Carli paced as she read, occasionally calling up a keyboard to take notes, and downloaded large chunks of text and imagery into her kelly.

At some point the librarian syntellect produced a bibliography of links to several hundred research papers, along with a series of design images and specifications for various kinds of waldos. Carli dumped these directly into her kelly for later study and then requested the syntellect to draw up a map showing all existing U.S. waldo manufacturing facilities.

The North American continent spread out across and well beyond the edges of her desk: mountains and valleys, sparkling lakes and oceans and all, even a few wispy clouds for effect, that floated in the air just below the ceiling.

The map displayed provinces, cities, and states for the U.S. and Canada. Canada dimmed. State boundaries for Alaska and the lower forty-eight glowed in orange across the brown and green of the map's surface. The letters of each state's name stretched across its surface in purple letters, and the state capitals and major cities appeared in shadowed hues. Their names shone green above them like tiny traffic signs. Highways emblazoned with numbered shields crisscrossed the continent.

Carli moved her hands over the map, pressing floating hot spots, and twenty-seven plants sprouted like geometric mushrooms in a blaze of colors—white, blue, red, yellow, orange, green—clusters of tiny buildings scattered throughout the continental U.S. and Alaska, with the names of the owner companies shining in yellow letters above them. Carli walked through the map to study the different plants. All but three were owned or jointly owned by Waldos, Inc.

"What about Hawaii?" she asked.

"No manufacturing facilities exist there," the syntellect replied.

"Are these all accurate representations of the existing facility buildings?"

"They are accurate to within approximately the last year, though not to scale. The facilities' dimensions have been exaggerated so that their general features would be discernible to the naked eye."

"Can the buildings be further enlarged to provide more detail?"

"Yes, up to fifty times the current size, within preset tolerances. Which facility would you like enlarged?"

"None, for now. Build me a matrix of personnel and product data for each plant."

A ball formed over the map and then exploded like fireworks in the air above one of the plants. The sparks rained down into a luminous cube: a matrix showing how many people worked at the plant, in what capacities and in how many shifts, what materials the plant purchased, and what sorts of machines were assembled, in what quantities. Fireballs kept appearing and exploding over the map until all twenty-seven plants had a matrix suspended above them. Some of the matrices had more complete data than others.

"Which of these facilities are also associated with research and development?" Carli asked.

"No data."

"Which are located near DOEP offices?"

"No data."

"GAEA?"

"No data."

"Hmmm. Interesting."

Not everything she would have wanted, but it gave her a good start.

"See what financial data you can find on them," she said, and dumped the map and the stats into her kelly.

"No data immediately available in public-access encyclonets," the syntellect said. "Financial nets may be accessed at an additional charge of eighteen dollars and ninety-five cents per minute and one dollar and one cent per kilocharacter, and then the data compiled per your specifications for an additional fifteen dollars per net-second. Shall I multitask the search?"

Carli called up the time: 4:43 P.M. She wanted to visit Tania at the hospital, and visiting hours ended at six o'clock.

"No," she said. "Cancel all searches."

"If you place a marker with your user code and bank code in nonvolatile memory, I can search, compile, and download the information in backtime mode. This also means a ten percent savings in your overall access cost."

"All right, then." She typed in her user and bank codes. "Give me the search, but limit it to no more than four thousand dollars in access charges, and store the data. Don't do the compilation. I have my own software." She looked at her notes. "And give me a bibliography of public information on DOEP and GAEA projects and facilities, as well as any publications by or about Richard Quintelle Blaine and Dr. Patricia Taylor."

After signing off, Carli accessed her commware and called the hotel across the way. Roy's face appeared above her palm, looking surly.

"Yeah?"

"I'm going to visit my friend in the hospital. Do you guys want to come over here, or shall I meet you at street level?"

"You stay right where you are. We'll come get you." His tone was snappish.

"Fine," she said, sharply. "Jesus. Who pissed in your cereal bowl?" But he'd already disconnected.

She called up her own copy of the map, cut to the plant stats, and pulled them into a summary matrix. San Jose, San Francisco, Austin, Omaha, St. Charles, Raleigh, Boston . . . The list went on, rather dauntingly.

There had to be a way to find out which one of the plants housed classified research. Somehow.

She sighed, saved, and went to get her waist pouch and pulse gun. Maybe inspiration would strike, later. The doorbell chimed.

"Coming!" she yelled.

At the door, hand on the grip, she remembered what Donald had said, and flipped on the view screen. *There, I looked,* she planned to say. But the young man there wasn't Donald or Roy. He stood over six feet tall and seemed rather ethereal-looking, with a thin, wispy, blondish beard, and large eyes. He was dressed as a *natureil,* and looked like a friend of Paint's or Tania's.

She activated the mike.

"Yes?" she said.

"Ms. D'Auber?" The man had a tenor voice, and a trace of a New England accent. He smiled into the camera beside the door. "I'm Derek Jonas."

"Yes?" she repeated.

"I'm a fellow scientist and I have some information for you about what happened last night. With the—creature. I wonder if I might come in."

With that she suddenly recognized from the body language that he was a human-shaped waldo. A friend of Daniel's, then?

But discretion seemed the better part of valor, especially since he hadn't buzzed her from downstairs. Another tenant had probably let him in, but . . . Let Donald and Roy handle security. It was their job, anyhow.

"If you could wait a moment," she said, "I'll be right back—"

And then his fist came through the door.

Carli stumbled back with a gasp, tugging at her pouch flap. His hand found the bolt and unlocked it; he shoved the door open and it slammed into the wall with a splintering crack. By now Carli had gotten her hand into her pouch—the handle of her gun pressed against her palm.

In a blur he moved and caught her wrist in a grip that sent pain shooting up her arm. He pulled the waist pouch off of her hand. Its contents clattered onto the floor.

She gritted her teeth and twisted against the weak point of his hold, between the thumb and fingers. It didn't give. He pried her pulse gun loose from her hand with a quick, effortless twist and slid the weapon in among the folds of cloth in his pants. She tried to swing him off balance with a step back and a yank. He met the attempt like a six-foot stone block.

"Sit down," he said, and flung her onto the couch, half lifting her off the floor, wrenching her arm. He closed the door. She panted, clutching her arm, blinking back tears of pain. Pressure had built in her bowels and bladder from the fear. Hold on, she told herself. Hold on. Roy and Donald would be here any minute.

"I want to show you something," he said. He lifted his forefinger. "See this?" He drove the finger like a pile driver into the wall and pulled it back out, leaving behind a neat hole with chips of plaster and paint around it. He blew dust from his finger. It was uninjured.

"That could have been your skull," he said.

She nodded, forcing her gaze away from the hand to meet his eyes, which were an amazing, brilliant turquoise color.

"I understand," she said. Her voice quavered. "What do you want me to do?"

"We're going on a journey," he said. "Don't try to run, don't try to warn anyone, don't do *anything* unless I tell you to. And when I tell you to do something, do it quickly and without resistance. Is that clear?"

She nodded again.

"OK. Let's practice, shall we? Stand up."

She pushed herself to her feet and faced him warily.

"Very good. Put your arm around me."

She did so. He yanked her kelly pendant off her neck, tossed the kelly unit to the floor, and crushed it underfoot.

"You won't need that," he said. He gripped the back of her neck. She turned her head and his hand tightened painfully. "Try anything and I'll crush your spine. Clear?"

She nodded once, slowly. Her heart was racing. Slow, deep breaths, Carli. A step at a time. Think, and stay calm.

"We're going to walk together to the elevator and go to the ground floor. I want you to pretend that I'm your lover. Smile."

She forced a grimace onto her face. He pulled the door open and they walked down the corridor to the elevator. Mr. Montoya, her eighty-year-old neighbor, was carrying his laundry into his room. He waved at Carli and went into his apartment.

"Mr. Montoya," she said after him, her voice desperate in her own ears. But apparently Mr. Montoya didn't have his hearing aid on. His apartment door closed, and the hand at the back of her neck squeezed till the tendons ground against bone and pain made her vision go grey. She cried out, tears of pain spilling down her cheeks.

"That was a warning," Derek Jonas said. "No more talking."

I'm going to kill you, she thought. I'm going to fucking *kill* you. She began to tremble, sick with rage and fear. He pressed the elevator button. It opened on Roy and Donald.

"Gentlemen," Derek Jonas said. "Excuse us."

He made to pass them, forcing Carli forward. Something in Roy's expression warned him, though, and as Donald yanked her from Jonas's grasp, Carli saw Jonas go for Roy's face. Roy crumpled to the floor, screaming: a thin, high-pitched sound. Blood and brain matter spurted from his eye. As she looked at him, hearing his screams, Carli came loose from her moorings and floated up and back, somewhere above her body.

Donald shoved her.

"Run!" he yelled, pulling out a gun. Jonas grabbed him. Carli sprinted for the stairwell. Doors opened and closed down the hall. Shots echoed around her, and screams, blows—the automatic door floated open. She slammed into it and stumbled down the stairs.

A force slammed her into the wall at the first landing, knocking the air from her chest. She turned and stared up into the face of Jonas. Flecks of gore spattered his clothing and face.

She wanted to say something but couldn't catch her breath. She began to think she would suffocate.

"I don't have time for this nonsense," he said in a disgusted voice, and his hand moved. Something stung her neck; consciousness shattered into a million fragments and tumbled away.

IT'S AWFUL, IT'S ON THE NEWS

Scott burst into Daniel's cubicle.

"Daniel," he said, "it's awful. It's on the news," scattering Daniel's concentration. Scott was in his own skinny body in a loin wrap, unshaven, a panicked look on his round, baby-boy's face.

"What are you talking about?"

"The news," Scott repeated. He leaned over next to Daniel's terminal, panting. Amid the blond stubble, the skin-tone plastic protective cap stretched over his beanjack made the jack look like a mushroom, or a tumor. He smelled faintly of locker-room mold and rubbing alcohol. "Face into the J-net. Hurry."

Daniel frowned. "I'm trying to work. Hey—!"

He grabbed at Scott's hands but was too slow to stop him from exiting his software. Over his shoulder Scott logged into the J-net and called up a news jello.

"Would you please *look?*" he said, pointing. Daniel looked.

In the field, a moving cube shot bounced fuzzily around a sheet-draped body on a stretcher, which was disappearing into the tail end of an ambulance. Daniel sat up straighter. He recognized the street.

The voice-over was saying, "—or of his apparent kidnap victim, Carli D'Auber, daughter of Senator Chauncy D'Auber. The two murdered men have been identified as Donald Gramitzsky and Roy Tennys, security agents employed by the Congressional Security Agency . . ."

"What?" Daniel went bolt stiff.

"That's what I'm trying to tell you—"

"Never mind, never mind." Daniel waved his hands, leaned toward the jello-tube. "Shut up."

The announcers launched into a discussion of Carli's and the senator's backgrounds, and started talking about possible reasons for the kidnapping. They said Senator D'Auber wasn't available for questions.

Daniel stabbed at the control, and the picture faded. Then he turned and grabbed Scott by the arm.

"Tell me exactly what you heard and saw."

"An unknown assailant got into the building and smashed through her door. He killed the two security agents, destroyed all but one of the security cameras, and kidnapped D'Auber. No one admits letting him into the building; he might have broken the entry code. They have some security pictures from the undamaged camera, but the shots aren't that good. They also got descriptions from her neighbors and put together a composite portrait. I got that downloaded into my system. Here."

He pressed a data lozenge into Daniel's hand. A strange look came onto his face and his voice went treble.

"I could have kept the visual surveillance on. I shut it off when the renegade boarded the shuttle this morning. I didn't think we'd need it. . . ."

"You couldn't have known. None of us did." Daniel rubbed at the space between his eyebrows with a thumb and took a slow, deep breath; a dull throb had started at his temples. Slowly, Daniel, slowly. Get it right the first time. No time for mistakes. "Go on. Did they have any eyewitnesses?"

"Some of the ground-floor tenants saw him take her out of the building and load her into a car, but it turned out to be stolen; they found it abandoned in an old lot on the West Mesa. They think he must have her stowed somewhere in the city.

"He smashed through the door with his *bare hand*, Daniel. They got that on film."

Daniel stared at James Scott and saw his own realization reflected on Scott's face. Another renegade.

"Christ." Daniel surged to his feet. "Notify Krueger and Security. Then get to Production. Check all the final Assembly and Quality Control queues. Also check the rosters and find out if there's a shortage. *All of them*. Right?"

"Right."

"Call me in the Face Lab as soon as you know."

Daniel pulled out his kelly and called up Teru. She-he materialized in his palm, lying prone, blinking and looking groggy, in proxy as before. She-he passed a hand over her-his boy-man's face. "What is it?"

"Sorry to wake you, love, but you'd better meet me in Classified. It looks like the renegade pilot may have escaped and stolen another proxy."

"Shit." Her-his image blurred as she-he came to her-his feet. "Bloody hell."

Daniel entered the lab. Nothing had changed: the renegade still stood immobile and partially gutted with its face impassive and eyes vacant. It looked oddly vulnerable amid the scattering of parts and tools. The air seemed even colder than earlier; gooseflesh sprang up on Daniel's arms and he shivered.

He called up Teru's simile daemon; it was running through a random set of scenarios. He couldn't tell from the readout whether the pilot was still inside. So he was reduced to pacing the floor, glowering at the renegade proxy.

He remembered the lozenge James Scott had given him, and inserted it into a reader. The security camera mounted down the hall from Carli's apt had captured only a brief, blurred image of the kidnapper, far down the hall, from the side. He blew it up and watched the kidnapper hustle her across the hall into another corridor several times, in slo-mo. She appeared stunned, or unconscious. Then he studied the composite portrait, as it rotated slowly in the jello-tube. He ejected the lozenge and eyed the renegade proxy again.

The kidnapper was no one he knew. It had to be a proxy, from James Scott's description, but the clip didn't give any new clues to the pilot's identity.

Teru entered and, with a brief glance at Daniel, slid into the seat at the calibration station and activated the sensor field. An aurora borealis sank through the air around her-his hands and she-he began a program weave. Daniel watched over her-his shoulder as she-he called up and changed the readouts. Teru ran a series of diagnostics and checks, frowned, said something under her-his breath and eyed the renegade proxy through narrowed eyes.

"What?" Daniel asked.

"The simile arbitration record implies the pilot's in there, simply refusing to respond to symbolic stimuli. But—" Teru shook her-his head. "I don't like it. It gives rise to wonder whether the pilot has pulled some trick with the proxy linkware to feign minimal response while she's off somewhere else."

Daniel squinted at the tube contents. "Is there anything you can do to verify?"

"Let me think." Teru sat staring at the readout, then the proxy, then back. She-he wove a few more commands. Then she-he shook her-his head again with a frustrated grunt.

"The only way to verify would be to shut down the similes and talk to the pilot, see how she responds. But if we turn off the simile daemon, the pilot will realize we've trapped her, and disengage. If anyone is in there now, she wouldn't be for long."

"*Damn it.* What do we do?"

"Get out of my lab and leave me alone for a while. I'll see what I can do."

She-he swung around and hunched over her-his controls. Daniel stared at the back of Teru's head, bit off an impatient reply.

Outside the lab, Daniel called up Scott's number and, with a glance around, thumbed down the volume of his kelly. The day shift had just gotten off and traffic in the corridor was heavy.

Scott took a long time to answer. When his voice came on, he was out of breath.

"Took me a minute to find someplace private," Scott said. "Sorry."

"What word?"

"Nothing yet. I'm only halfway through the week's QC roster. I have the Assembly queue to check yet, too." A pause. "The shift super is asking questions. What do I tell him?"

"I'll talk to him. What about Krueger?"

"He's not answering his phone."

Daniel swore. "That tears it."

"I'm sorry. I couldn't get past the override."

"Stop apologizing. You didn't do anything wrong. I'll take care of briefing him. You concentrate on finding the missing proxy."

Daniel called up an organizational chart and got the name and kelly number of the QC shift super's boss. He punched up her number and, while waiting for her answer, thought up a plausible story.

"We're looking for a possible faulty interface crystal," he explained when her face appeared in his tube. "It was slated for rework, but we can't locate it, and I want to make sure it didn't somehow end up installed in one of the proxy units. I've sent one of our people over to check the Assembly and QC queues and rosters over the past few days. Could you give your foreman a call and let him know what we're doing?" he asked.

"Glad to. You realize that's a pretty stout task," she said, "if you need to check *all* the rosters and the units themselves. Especially since your man is unfamiliar with our system. I'd be glad to assign a couple of people to help him if you'll give me the batch and lot number of the bad part."

"Thanks, no," Daniel said. "Um, James Scott is a little *wet*, if you get my meaning. This experience might do him good."

Her eyebrows arched sympathetically, one supervisor to another. Daniel only just avoided wincing and signed off. Dirty business. But Scott had been the one on duty when the first proxy was lost, so maybe it would balance things out. Or maybe, Daniel thought, I'm just taking out my frustrations on the easiest target.

"Mr. Krueger isn't receiving visitors or calls," the syntellect receptionist said.

"It's an emergency. Please request an override with Mr. Krueger."

"All overrides must be authorized by use of the emergency code. Please pronounce the emergency override sequence, slowly and clearly."

Daniel eyed the machine for a moment, chewing his lip. Then he went up to the door and pounded on it. No response from inside. He pounded till his fist hurt. Nothing.

"Mr. Krueger isn't receiving visitors or calls," the receptionist repeated.

"The hell he isn't," Daniel muttered. He went back to his quarters and called Jacob Martinez, a co-worker in Systems, whom Daniel had assisted in installing the facility's privacy-screening software several months back.

"Hey, how's your latest project coming?" Jacob said. The older man's face hung above Daniel's kelly in his palm: a face with short grey wisps of hair across the forehead, friendly creases, loose jowls, and a large, lippy mouth.

"Fair," Daniel said. Then he blew out a breath. "Actually, I'm calling because I need a favor, sub rosa."

Jacob's eyebrow's shot up. "Oh, yeah?"

"I can't explain, so don't ask me why. I need to borrow your source code for debugging PrivaScreen."

Jacob frowned. Then understanding dawned on his face. "Is this for a practical joke?"

"Not a joke. I can't say what it's for, but it's important."

Jacob looked disconcerted. "I'm not supposed to share it with any-one. Period. Security would have my butt out the door in a minute. . . ."

"Look," Daniel said, "the worst thing I could do with it is inter-rupt someone who doesn't want to be interrupted."

"Yeah, but it's still a violation of the Electronic Information Privacy Act, to use software to intrude on other people's electronic property."

"Like I said, it's important. *Real* important."

Jacob looked at him, long and hard, chewing his lip.

Daniel said, "Don't worry. Your name will never come up. I promise."

Finally Jacob blew air out through his lips, with puffed-out cheeks. He shook a finger at Daniel. "You owe me, Sornsen."

"Thanks, Jacob. Thanks."

"Do you have BorderLAN Five-three?"

"I have version Five-two."

"It'll do. Disconnect and load BorderLAN, and set up the desti-nation path exactly where you need the debugging code to go. I'll transfer the source code and executable batch file. The files all start with 'PSD'; you'll recognize them."

"Thanks a bunch."

"They'll be set up to decay after half an hour, and they won't be duplicable, so don't even try."

Pity. Daniel, though, wasn't one to stare into the mouths of gift ponies. "Thanks again."

"Don't mention it. And I mean that."

Jacob's image disappeared.

The debugging software Jacob cross-loaded to Daniel's kelly was designed to change the parameters and options of facility personnel's privacy screen routines. And, since it could actually change the lines of programming in those privacy-screen routines, it could also be used to change a person's emergency override codes.

Which was exactly what Daniel did to Krueger's receptionist, with a data lozenge and five minutes worth of searching through Krueger's privacy-screen routines.

Then he triggered the door and stalked into Krueger's office.

Krueger looked up, surprised. He was crammed into a chair by his desk. Facing him, projected in his jellowall, was a man standing in some crowded public place. In the background an announcement sounded for a shuttle flight.

"Carli D'Auber's been kidnapped," he said, interrupting the man on the phone in midsentence.

"I'll call you back," Krueger told the other, and disconnected. The man's image vanished. Krueger gestured at the couch. To Daniel's surprise, he didn't ask how Daniel had gotten past his privacy screening.

"Sit down. Tell me what you're talking about."

Daniel declined the invitation to sit.

"It's all over the national news, boss," Daniel said. "Someone has kidnapped D'Auber. And I think it might be the renegade. Teru left the simile controls on automatic a couple of hours ago and went to bed; the renegade may have escaped and stolen another unit."

He went on to describe what he'd seen and heard on the news. Krueger listened without comment, looking grave.

"Scott's checking Production and QC for missing units," Daniel finished. "Teru is running some diagnostics on the renegade proxy to see if the pilot somehow escaped. They'll probably both be at it for some time."

"Good," Krueger said. Daniel looked at him expectantly, but Krueger remained silent.

"Well?" Daniel prompted.

"Well, what?"

"What do we do next?"

Krueger looked uncomfortable. "It sounds like you've got everything under control. Give me regular updates," he added, with a faintly bemused look.

Daniel sighed, frustrated. "I'll keep you posted, then."

Krueger made another grunting noise and waved him out.

He went back to the Face Lab.

"Did you brief Krueger?" Teru asked.

"Yeah." With a sigh, he sat down on a stool facing the renegade proxy. "Talk about a total wash. I couldn't even get him to focus on the problem. I don't know what's with him anymore." He gestured toward the proxy with his chin. "What's the word on that?"

Teru sat back from the sensor field, pulled off her-his mesh-gloves, and tossed them on the counter with a look of disgust. "I can't tell if the pilot's in there or not. She won't respond to any stimuli. I'm out of ideas."

Daniel stared at the damaged proxy and thought.

"I've got it." He grabbed a beanie from the workbench and put it on, *ka-LICK.* A menu of connect choices scrolled across the top of his vision. "Put me in there with her. As Carli D'Auber."

Teru frowned. "What on Earth . . . ?"

"Just do it." He grinned at her. "Trust me."

DANE ELISA CAE

DRUMBEATS EXPLAINED

After a chase down a tiresome array of shadowy stairwells, halls, alleys, and empty streets, Dane had lost the woman she sought, and stumbled upon a street festival. Now she wandered, staring about herself.

Great, blazing wheels, chains, and bulbs spun through the air on tethers, neon-bright against the steamy night sky, flinging screams and laughter like spray. Gurgling screams and dull red lights issued from dark doorways set into wheeled houses; snarling, bloody-toothed, nylon-furred beasts leaned from the windows and slashed at the air with plastic claws. Laughing clowns with cotton candy hair teetered toward her on stilts and bent down to thrust balloons in her face. Noise and smoke blasted from booths—hawkers' voices teased young women; wooden balls clattered against walls and bumped each other; coins jingled in jars; wild strains of music clashed against each other like stormy waves. The smells of sweets and frying foods—sausages, doughnuts, potatoes—fought trash and sewage for dominance.

Humans crammed between the booths, milling past each other, elbowing her in their hurry; she caught snippets of their conversations. She saw people from many lands, and heard many languages spoken—many different brands of gibberish. Dogs and cats and rats and hand-sized cockroaches scavenged discarded food and debris, beneath feet and at the edges of the crowd. Laughing and sullen faces flowed by. Bizarre creatures she knew couldn't be real—mythical beasts and dinosaurs—appeared and faded: holograms, projected against mist squirted from jets on the midway's sides.

Dane wandered through the crowd, searching for the woman, refusing to engage with any of the hawkers or spectators, though several beckoned, spoke, or tried to grab her. The festival seemed to go on forever.

Then she saw her! Just a glimpse, amid a sea of others. The woman turned and ran. Dane ran, too, shoving her way through the crowd, and then down a darker, less populated side street. She called out.

"Stop! Please."

The other woman stopped, and turned, regarding her. Staring at the woman, Dane grew dizzy; the woman's face floated, briefly—an image painted on an invisible balloon. Finally the woman spoke, and Dane strained to understand.

"What is your name?"

Dane hesitated. "I'm Dane Elisa Cae." Her hands opened and closed. At the sound of the woman's voice, an urge to kill this woman washed over Dane—so powerful it made her breath grow short. She swallowed, hard. "Who are you?"

The other woman shook her head. Again she spoke, and again Dane strained to understand. "Why did you try to kill me?"

The voice filled her with such need! She couldn't contain it. Dane sprang at the other—who wasn't there, suddenly; Dane's hands closed on emptiness. She spun. The woman stood nearby, a look of contempt on her face. "You'll have to do better than that, I'm afraid."

And she sprang again. And caught nothing—and sprang again—and caught nothing. The woman asked *why? who are you? what do you want with me?* over and over. And gradually, as it never had, Dane's machine body began to tire.

Finally she crouched near the other, numb with fatigue, panting, sweating, her heartbeat pounding in her ears.

Panting? Sweating? How could that be?

"Why?" the woman repeated, softly. Dane remained silent.

I don't know. All I know is that you must die.

Thump, thump, thump. Her heartbeat grew louder with every breath she drew. Thump, thump.

The woman cocked her head and narrowed her eyes, listening. "You hear something, don't you? Drums, is it? A heartbeat?"

Thump. Thump, thump, thump. An irregular rhythm; not a heartbeat. It was growing still louder. And a tiny voice, like a doll or a toy, filled the spaces in between. Dane clamped her hands over her ears.

"Stop it!"

She started to run.

The woman followed her, and so did the beating, and the tiny voice. Cobwebs—sticky, white, diaphanous curtains—loomed into her way. Dane fought her way through them, and at last broke through into a huge room filled with banks of large capsules, all hooked to machines and pipes. The other woman materialized in a corner nearby.

Dane collapsed on top of a capsule, trembling. The capsule trembled, too, with each beat, BOOM, BOOM, and the voice inside was screaming, *Let me out! Jesus fucking CHRIST—I'll die! Let me out!*

With a shriek she scrambled away from it, staring as the lid slowly opened. Amid billows of white smoke a large man emerged: naked as a newborn, with eyes burning and red like coals.

She gasped. "I killed you."

The naked man shook his head. "No, not me. I'm only wearing his body."

Then she looked into his eyes, and knew him: his name was Buddy, and he was the voice in her head. The one who'd controlled her. He was part of her, somehow. Or she was part of him.

"I wondered where you'd gotten to," he said. Dane lowered her gaze, remembering.

"You're the one in my head, telling me what to do."

"That's right."

She frowned deeply. "We sealed a man into his crèche and killed him. I remember now." Buddy nodded, gravely. "His screams birthed me, didn't they?"

"They did."

She gestured at the woman who had been chasing her. "I was supposed to kill her, too, wasn't I? You sent me after her once before. But they stopped me, and so you got me another body and sent me out again. Right? That's why I thought I was a man—you hid me inside your body for a while, betweentimes."

He glanced at the woman with a faintly surprised expression, and nodded at Dane. "That's close enough, I suppose."

After a second of pondering it, she shook her head. "I'm still confused."

"That's normal." He looked again at the other woman standing there, eyes narrowed, and then held out his hand to Dane. "You're trapped in a simile. Come on. I'll take you home."

PEOPLE SOUP

Daniel-as-Carli watched a glowing-eyed simulacrum of Krueger emerge from the crèche. *Krueger?*

The Krueger simulacrum exchanged a few words with the piebald woman. Then they took hands, merged into a single being, and vanished, leaving Daniel-as-Carli standing alone in the simile. From somewhere, faintly, he heard Teru say, "Shit—we've lost her."

He pulled off the beanie. The simile faded; he frowned and blinked. "Were you watching?"

"Uh-huh." She-he sat back and took off her-his own beanie. "I was tracking the fizz-psych readouts. Something you did got up her knickers in a big way. All the readouts went berserk. What happened?"

He shook his head. "I'm not exactly sure. I provoked her into attacking me and it triggered some sort of memory she was trying to suppress. She re-created a version of the crèche chamber. *Austin's* crèche chamber. A crèche opened and Krueger stepped out. They took hands and merged, and then vanished." He hesitated. What the hell was Krueger doing in the renegade's simile? "They talked about having killed someone."

Teru mirrored his frown. "Odd."

"Very odd. I have a bad feeling about all this."

Teru grimaced. "Don't go spooky on me. Things are bad enough as is."

Daniel stood. "I'll call you later."

He turned and walked slowly away, musing. The renegade . . . the kidnapper . . . There had to be a link between them. And somewhere, it seemed, there had to be a link with Krueger, too.

As his hand touched the door that swung open onto the corridor, Daniel realized the man on the jellophone with Krueger had been the man in the news lozenge. The one who had kidnapped Carli D'Auber. He'd been at White Sands. And he'd been talking about a shuttle flight.

We killed a man in his crèche.

He froze as it hit him, a shock, like a face full of ice water. He gasped. "Oh my God." Then he yelled. *"Oh my God!"* And he bolted down the corridor.

Teru came running out of the lab and followed him, shouting, "What is it, Danny? What?"

He ran, shoving people out of his way, to the crèche chamber. Leanne, *in corpus*, stood a few slots down from Krueger's crèche, doing a check of someone's readouts. A few other technicians, both in proxy and *in corpus*, were also scattered about, doing maintenance on empty crèches here and there, while the attendant proxies stood immobile nearby, empty-eyed sentinels. Daniel laid his hands on the lid to Krueger's crèche. If he was wrong—and God, he hoped he was wrong—Krueger would wring his neck. Intruding on a pilot in his crèche wasn't done.

He glanced at the readouts on the control console. EKG, breathing, hormonal levels, EEG, all normal. I am wrong, he thought. At least, *someone* is alive in there.

But Krueger would never be involved in a kidnapping. Not no way, not nohow. And that was only one way in which the man's actions hadn't been normal over the past couple of weeks.

There was only one way to be sure, and that was to open up the crèche and talk to Krueger in the flesh.

Leanne had come over, smiling. Then she got a look at his face. "What is it?"

Teru caught up with him. "Danny, would you please tell me what you're on about?"

Daniel tried to catch his breath. He gestured at Krueger's crèche. "When was the last time anybody saw Krueger *in corpus?*"

Leanne and Teru looked at each other.

"I gave him his last fizz-psych clearance about a week ago," Leanne said.

"About a week? Can you be more precise?"

"Sure." She called up a data screen on Krueger's crèche control console. "Hmm. November sixth. Closer to two weeks, I guess."

Two weeks. *"Damn it."*

"Wait—what are you—"

She reached out to grab his arm, but Daniel threw the lid open before she could stop him.

A highly concentrated stench, feces and the sweet-foul odor of decomposing flesh, billowed out. Daniel clutched at his nose and blinked furiously, eyes watering. He and Leanne staggered back, gagging, retching. But not before he'd caught a glimpse of the crèche's contents. And a glimpse was more than enough.

The contents of the crèche had been human once, but intestinal bacteria, with the help of assorted fungi, had gone a long way toward converting them to simpler compounds. The body floated in warm saline, amid a scum of yeast and fungus. Skin and subcutaneous fat had come away in large strips, gobs, and patches; the intestines had spilled out in great grey loops. A large enough patch of skin had eroded away across the chest to reveal several ribs and a lung. The face was bloated, eyes bulging, skin flayed. There was enough distortion of the features to raise doubt about whether this could truly be Krueger.

At the smell, the other technicians looked up, yelled in dismay and alarm, and joined the stampede toward the door. Only Teru remained, staring down at the contents of the crèche. Daniel watched through the door's window as Teru reached in gingerly and touched something. Then she-he went over to the sink, washed her-his hands, and came out into the hall, bringing a cloud of foulness with her-him as the door opened.

With a grim expression Teru said, "It's him. He was clutching his rosary. He always kept it with him when he was piloting."

"Rest in peace, boss," Daniel said softly, looking in the direction of Krueger's crèche, and closed his eyes, letting his forehead touch the cool glass of the door's window. He could look forward to nightmares about this for a long time to come.

Leanne turned away and emptied the contents of her stomach, as two or three others in the hall were doing. In death, as in life, Krueger's presence was making itself felt throughout the facility; the smell was spreading via the HVAC system so rapidly that before too long the whole building would have to be evacuated.

CARLI

UP THE GRAVITY CURVE

She heard a humming, and sensed motion. Voices murmured. Footsteps, hundreds of them, shuffled and tapped and clattered, going by in all directions. Bongs chimed and PA announcements echoed. After a few seconds she realized that her eyes were open. She blinked rapidly, to soothe their burning.

Sight, a soft watercolor haze, coalesced slowly. People clutching bags were hurrying past on slideways. Sunlight streamed in through tall windows. Luggage and cargo machines lumbered past on the scramways outside; beyond them were commercial scram jets, being jockeyed about by traffic waldos.

Her head, supported by a cervical support, lolled to the side. She tried to straighten it. No luck. Her body, as best she could tell, didn't exist. She could see it, seated beneath her with its hands folded neatly in the lap, but it wasn't responding at all. Drool leaked out one corner of her mouth; it tickled her cheek and cooled the collar on her neck.

At least she could feel *that*.

The waldo chair she sat in had a pair of mechanical arms set into the sides. A comm jelly was mounted on a tripod that was attached to straps at her shoulders and waist. She had a beanlink cap on, whose wires led to the comm jelly and the chair's control console, a lingual pad that rested at her lower lip. When she tongued the pad's main lever, nothing happened. She tried each of the six hot keys. Nothing.

A sign overhead revealed that she was at White Sands, heading for the Orbital Flights terminal. As she neared the security screening station, the chair slowed. Security types were querying the passengers, searching bags, and scanning people for weapons. Before her was a large man's back. He slung a bag onto a belt and stepped through a detector. A security guard spotted her and came over.

"Destination?"

Of its own accord, her comm jelly's audio replied, "Shasta Station."

"May I see your exit visa, flight confirmation, and one other form of identification?"

"Of course."

Her waldo chair's right arm pulled a packet of papers and an ID lozenge from a pocket built into the chair behind her legs, and extended them. The guard inserted the lozenge into her kelly, looked over the contents, flipped through the papers and stamped a page, and then handed it all back. "Very good. We'll have to do a manual search of your chair."

"By all means," her comm jelly replied. The guard misinterpreted her desperate stare; with an apologetic "It's standard procedure," she reached behind Carli's back, then around and slightly under her buttocks and legs. Carli couldn't feel the touch. She fought to move but only managed a sigh. Meanwhile the guard had finished her search.

"Go right on through," she said, pointing. "Around that way."

The chair obliged.

The flight took eleven interminable hours. Her seat was near the back, affording Carli a decent view of the passenger cabin. Only a dozen or so passengers were scattered throughout the large compartment, and most of them spent the time, best she could tell, maxed out of their gourds with antinausea drugs and/or faced into the *virtu-* or jello-nets.

She had no way to signal for help, anyway. So, seated next to the window and unable to do anything to help herself, she merely sat and watched the Earth slowly shrink outside the window.

She thought about the e-mail she'd gotten from her friend Sid after *Courier*'s launch, and she thought about the last time she'd been in space—coming back from Pinnacle City, the L-5 platform where she had spent three years training for the *Exodus* mission and doing freelance communications research. And how waiting for her Earth-side were her new love via a net-side friendship-turned-romance, Jeremiah MacLeod, and a miraculous, totally unexpected grant from the Angler-Phipps Foundation to pursue her idea for an instantaneous communications device based on the latest and most bizarre results in particle physics.

She used to wonder whether she would have left the NASA interstellar program for Jere alone, or for the research grant alone. No, it was both together that had decided her. How drastically lives are changed by simple serendipity.

After a while more mundane matters began to consume her attention: the hunger pangs knotting her stomach and a growing thirst. The attendants made a point of visiting her frequently, offering in increasingly baffled tones some food or drink or assistance in using the lavatory, but her comm jelly declined on her behalf, politely but quite insistently.

She did eventually manage to control the drooling. She also gained a minute amount of head control, and rediscovered some sensation in her innards . . . but, after several hours of mounting bowel and bladder pressure, wished she hadn't.

Shasta Station. She was probably the first to spot it. Even in her current state she couldn't take her eyes off it. It was a good deal larger and had a different configuration than Pinnacle City.

Conversations died away as others noticed; heads craned.

Virulent sunlight glinted off the solar arrays as the shuttle passed alongside them—a vast field of silver rectangles linked in a series of branches that fanned out far above and below. Carli blinked. The intensity of the reflections left bright patches on her vision. Their orientation shifted slightly, tracking the sun's face like a field of angular, metallic sunflowers. Far beyond, parent kissed child: the Earth and moon touched—glowing moonstone gem; sapphire globe, striated with swirls of cloud. Then they were past the arrays and approaching Shasta Station.

The barbell-shaped habitat was visibly spinning, and had an enormous, netting-sheathed sphere and a docking node at its center of rotation. The shuttle slowed and reversed its direction as it neared the station. Tail first, with steering thrusters spitting tiny gouts of purplish flame, the shuttle backed around the orbital in a wide arc, past the spherical microgravity habitat and the slowly whirling, windmill-like latticework and canisters of the main habitat. Lights flickered along the habitat's sides, making it resemble nothing more than the world's biggest, most complicated carnival ride.

As the shuttle passed the end of the canister, a set of marquee arrow-lights far below pointed to the docking slip at the habitat's center of rotation. The shuttle decelerated further, rolling. Carli moaned; the motion made her empty stomach churn.

The shuttle's maneuverings went on for some time. The dock slip inched nearer. Meanwhile, as they crept toward the dock, a small craft grasping three big cargo pods detached from a point out on the latticework. The other craft's steering jets and main thrusters flickered, and it dropped swiftly away. Another big commercial shuttle was moored next to the dock: nose pointed down, tail high, cargo bays open to space, it was being unloaded by robotic cranes. Other machines crawled along the enormous latticework cylinder, insectlike. A pair of hard-suited humans jetted past in the middle distance, tethered together, holding hands.

Once the shuttle's nose was pointing at the dock, its steering jets began to fire, and the shuttle began to rotate to match the station's rotation. They also adjusted cabin pressure; Carli's ears popped. She sucked on her thirst-parched tongue, hard, till she had enough spit to swallow, and the pressure in her ears eased a little.

Finally an announcement came over the PA system: "We'll be arriving at Shasta Station momentarily. Please verify that your restraints are properly secured, and return your seat backs, viewers, and dispensers to their locked, docking positions. Thank you."

Meanwhile, a flight attendant pulled himself through the passenger cabin, grasping the hand holds on the seats' sides to propel himself. He stopped in range of her view.

"Ms. Talbot, your chair will be available for you inside the docking bay."

Help, she thought.

"Thank you," her comm jelly replied.

"Will you be needing assistance to deplane?"

"No," her comm jelly said. "Someone is meeting me."

Fresh, raw fear wrenched her out of the numbed stoicism she'd settled into.

"Very good," the attendant said.

As the other passengers debarked, the flight attendant accompanied a young woman to Carli. The woman wore white overalls and had longish, honey-brown hair that floated around her face.

"Welcome to Shasta Station, Ms. Talbot," the woman said.

"Thank you," her comm jelly replied. "You must be Mindy Phelps. I'm glad to be here."

"Your quarters are all set up as you ordered. I'll escort you."

The woman unbuckled Carli from her seat and, tucking her feet into a foothold beneath the seat in front, lifted Carli up.

"Your comunit will interfere with the transport. May I remove it for the duration of the transit?"

"Very well," the jelly replied.

With the flight attendant's help, the woman removed the tripod, harness, and jello-tube, and strapped Carli into a larger, canvas contraption with metal handles, labeled "Personal Transport Harness." She grabbed one of the handles and propelled Carli before her toward the shuttle's open airlock.

Two habitat workers took hold of Carli as she emerged into the docking bay.

"I've got her, gentlemen; thank you," the woman said, and shoved off from the edge of the shuttle.

One of the workers said to Carli, "Enjoy your stay, ma'am."

Carli and her captor floated to a nearby line of open-faced, ski-lift-type cars that crawled on tracks along the floor of the docking bay. The woman caught hold of a handle set in the car's side, hooked a leg around a bar lower down, and swung Carli into the seat. Carli rebounded gently. The young woman swung in beside her, catching Carli as she started to tumble slowly up and away, and lowered the containment bar.

The bay was spherical, a noisy cavern of a place with a large shaft running through its center. Sounds wobbled and echoed throughout; servos whirred, magnetic boots and clamps clattered; gears clanked and ratcheted. Cargo pods moved back and forth on cables through the middle of the bay, and dockworkers swam through the bay from web strand to web strand, or clung to moving handholds strung along the bay's bulkheads. Some used compressed air jets, either hand-held or strapped to their belts, to steer themselves.

The main habitat elevators neared. About twenty feet before the car reached them, the woman grabbed a handle on Carli's harness, lifted the car's containment bar, and kicked off, propelling them both outward. Two dockworkers rose out and stopped them in midair. For an instant, hope welled up in Carli, but they exchanged furtive looks with the woman and took hold of Carli by the handles of her harness.

"Hurry," the woman said. "They're waiting. I'll doctor the arrival roster."

She pulled a canister of compressed air from her belt, pointed it, and jetted off through toward the elevators.

The two men hauled Carli, inert sack of uncooperative flesh, to an area on the far side that was obscured by crates and small cargo pods. While one held onto her, the other keyed in a sequence on one of the spherical pods. It opened as a spider waldo crawled over—like the ones she'd seen crawling around on the outside of the structure. Its ten legs were equipped with magnetic attachments. Carli stared in horror as the men guided her toward the pod's interior, and tried to yell and struggle. It was no use, of course; all she managed were a couple of feeble bleats and twitches, while they folded her into the pod in a very businesslike way.

Then he typed something in and the pod closed, shutting out light, and she heard the locks engaging.

She had no idea how long she was in that cargo pod, in pitch blackness. First she hung for a while inside the pod, then there were dull thuds and clanks, and the pod began to move. She was banged and jostled about inside, weightless goods. This went on for about an aeon. Eventually she settled gently to one curved side, and realized that they must be transporting her along the outside of the spinning latticework cylinder toward one of the habitats at the ends of the barbell.

Another aeon passed while the tug of rotational acceleration increased gradually to maybe half Earth's gravity, and then motion stopped; more dull clanks and thuds vibrated the hull of her pod. She sat some more. More clanks and thuds, more motion.

Light pierced in. She winced. Indistinct figures bent in and lifted her out.

She was laid on a couch and something stung her neck. Sensation seared her, wildfire-fast, fanning out from the point of that needle prick into her arms, her chin and ears, her torso, her legs. With a shriek of pain and anger, she arched, leapt to her feet . . . collapsed . . . pushed herself back to her knees.

There were three of them: a young woman with blue-black hair, another woman with silver hair, also young, and a stocky, middle-aged man, bald as an egg. The two women were human waldos; the older man was *in corpus.*

When it became clear they weren't going to attack her, Carli shoved herself to her feet again with half-dead stumps for arms and scrambled around the small room on pinprickly legs, looking for an exit. There were two doors, and she saw no way to open either. She turned and scanned the room for some sort of weapon: a table lamp, a pair of scissors, anything. Other than a few pieces of bolted-down furniture and a counter with a tray of food and some liquid-filled tubes, the room was barren. She grabbed a fork and brandished it at them.

They merely looked at her. Carli, still breathing hard, felt a little absurd. The fork trembled in her hand; she had a hard time gripping it. But the fire in her limbs was subsiding, slowly.

She lowered the fork. "Who are you and what do you want?"

Then she recognized the man.

"Byron? Byron Kowalski?" For some reason, seeing her former colleague pissed her off worse than anything that had happened so far. She threw the fork down. "What the *hell* is going on here? Is this some kind of elaborate gag?"

Byron went red and mumbled something. The woman with black hair came forward, extending a hand. "Ms. D'Auber, we owe you a most humble apology."

Carli held up her hand. "Save it. I need a toilet. Now. Or we'll both regret it."

The woman pointed, and a door slid open, revealing a toilet, sink, bidet, and shower. "Make yourself at home. Please." Then she gestured at the food, an array of sandwiches and other food and some drink tubes. "If you'd prefer, we'll give you some privacy while you refresh yourself and have a bite to eat."

"No. You stay right there."

She closed the door, stripped down the khaki coveralls she'd been dressed in, and peed and peed and peed. The burning pressure in her pelvis ebbed. Her bowels emptied, too, explosively, at length, and the spasms in her abdomen slowly subsided. She washed herself in the bidet. Then she scrubbed her face and hands, and her underarms, which stank, and drank several handfuls of water.

She pulled off the phony beanie and tossed it into the corner. In the mirror was a stranger—they'd painted her face with a gold, tan, and white Nautilus shell that centered high on her right cheek. She scrubbed at it, but it didn't come off. A tube of Mask Dissolve lay on the sink. They think of everything; how thoughtful. She squeezed the paste into her hands, rubbed it in all over her face, and rinsed the offending mask off. Then, drying her face, she went into the other room.

The two women had seated themselves on the couch. Byron stood beside the counter. The smell of food made her mouth water. What do I have to lose? Carli thought. She tossed the face towel in a corner and headed for the refreshments. They waited silently as she stuffed several crackers with some sort of paté into her mouth and followed with a handful of raisins.

She could feel the pressure of their gazes on her back. After a few more bites of food and several slugs of juice, she swallowed hard and turned to face them, a by now half-eaten soy-and-spinach sandwich clutched in one fist and a mostly empty fruit drink tube in the other. Byron avoided directly meeting her eyes, but the gazes of the other two were direct. The dark-haired woman stood and extended her hand again. "I'm Patricia Taylor, chief scientist and administrator of Kaleidas."

Carli eyed the outstretched hand. As conciliatory as they were acting now, her life was in their hands. That had already been made amply clear. She should be circumspect.

She did manage not to spit on the hand.

After an awkward pause, the other woman turned the outstretched hand into a gesture toward the others. "This is Jenna Sternberg, my chief programmer. Byron Kowalski, you already know."

Byron lifted a hand in a wave. "Carli, it's good to see you again."

"Oh, spare me, please." She tossed the sandwich and juice onto the counter and wiped her hands on her coveralls, angrily. "I've been threatened with evisceration, drugged, and hauled off the goddamned planet against my will. Two men were murdered trying to protect me. Now you three are trying to act like I'm here by invitation. Give me a fucking break."

The woman's tone was mild. "You have no idea how fortunate you really are. We stand at the brink of history, and you have a ringside seat."

Carli refrained from rolling her eyes. "Why don't you explain to me just how fortunate I am." Then the woman's earlier words struck Carli, and she gasped. "*You're* Patricia Taylor?"

The woman nodded, somber, eyes narrowed.

"*The* Patricia Taylor?"

The woman nodded again.

Carli stared at this sex bunny of a machine-being. *This* was the woman whose advancements in waldo linkware had transformed telepresence technology? Who must be at least eighty years old, if not older? Carli reached back for the chair by the counter and lowered herself into it.

"I've studied your work. *Retrofitting Humanity* was required reading in my graduate telepresence courses." Carli rubbed at her face. "I've always—" She stopped, looked up at Taylor, blew a deep breath out. "You have no idea how much I wish I could say I'm glad to have this opportunity."

Taylor nodded. "Let me say that *I've* always wanted to meet *you*. Your achievements in instantaneous communications have made so much possible." She paused. "Please forgive the drastic methods we used to get you here. We had no choice; we're out of time and out of options. We need you." She gestured at the other door, which opened onto a corridor. Her colleagues stood. "But before I get into that, let me introduce you to the rest of my staff and give you a tour."

Together Again for the Very First Time

It seemed only an instant before, in her own body, she'd seen a dead man emerge from a crèche and announce himself as Buddy. Now Dane was perched inside a very strange, humanoid but not human, body.

I killed a man's flesh, she thought. No—Buddy did . . . ? A dust devil of confusion swirled up. And fear. She thought instead about Buddy. He must have brought her here and then left. Where was he now? She wanted answers.

The body she rode in was, of its own volition, pacing across a big, invisible platform above a wide savanna. Beneath their feet, a pride of lions sprawled, watching a herd of wildebeests graze nearby. Crooked, spiked trees sprouted up across the hills, on whose leaves giraffe grazed. A herd of elephants sprayed themselves and trumpeted at a water hole in the middle distance. A thunderstorm smeared the horizon, and its moist winds stirred and cooled the air.

The body she rode in was a gigantic lizard man, and his hand gripped the other wrist behind the body's back. Most of the rest of the meeting attendees were also strange beasts: she spotted a centaur, a ten-foot-tall stick creature with a clown face, a giant wolf, a glitter-skinned, flitting fairy, a drool-dripping insectoid alien in a space suit, and so on. About two dozen strange creatures were listening to the speaker: some seated, some floating, some standing.

A floating, jeweled fish with arms and an almost human face whose eyes glowed blue-green spoke at the front. A three-dimensional map of an orbital platform floated beside the talking fish, and the map changed as the fish pointed at it. Animated figures moved around inside the map, doing things she didn't understand.

Someone was impatient; someone else, though equally intent, was not as restless as the first. The impatient one interrupted the speaker. "How many Marines are there? And how many other personnel?"

The fish replied. As usual, it took Dane a second or two to translate. Forty-seven, she'd said. Forty-seven Marines and 479 non-Menagerie technical and support staff. Dane wondered what a Marine was. As she wondered, a picture of a man in a uniform came to her. She realized that the fish was actually a young girl named Amy.

How do I know all that? she wondered, and grew afraid again.

=You know because I know.=

=Buddy?=

He was the impatient one she'd sensed.

=Yes. Now, hush. Pablo mustn't detect you, and I need to concentrate on this conversation.=

So she hunkered down and watched. Words washed past in trickles, streams, torrents, but she was content to let them go by without straining to understand them; Buddy would handle that. Instead she studied the faces and bodies and hands. She noticed that the hands spoke as much as the mouths did. Each creature had a characteristic set of gestures that made him or her identifiable, even in disguise. Even the person piloting this body.

And with that, she realized that she shared this body with someone. No—some*ones*. With Buddy, and someone else.

=You're sensing Pablo. He's the first of us three, and usually prime. Settle down, now.=

Prime? she thought.

=The dominant one,= Buddy replied. =The one who commands the face.=

=Are there others?=

Others sharing this body, she meant, and he knew it. A hesitation ensued.

=No. I don't think so.=

=Does he know about the man?= she asked. =The dead flesh?=

=Not exactly. I handle that memory. Now, hush.=

Dane grew afraid of Pablo.

=Can he hear us?=

=He will if you don't be quiet.= A pause. She could tell Buddy was trying to figure out how much to tell her. He thought of her as a very young child. She resented that. =He doesn't know about you.=

Why was her existence a secret? What if he found out? She sensed his presence, huge and pervasive, all around her. If he ousted her, it would be a death sentence; where could she go? She scrunched herself up as small and as quiet as she could.

The meeting broke up after a bit, and then Pablo changed linkware settings and took them to a small room, where he spoke with a sublimely beautiful woman with plaited black hair almost down to the floor. *Mother.* Mother. Dane grew excited, and curious, but Buddy pushed Dane back from the interface.

=She's poison. Let me and Pablo handle her.=

Cautiously, from her tiny corner, Dane tunneled her way through the cracks and crannies in Buddy's and Pablo's presences, and peeked out at the woman. She couldn't keep up—things kept fading in and out—but it seemed Pablo and the woman were talking about a performance Pablo was going to give. Buddy was biding his time, exchanging a thought or two with Pablo, and in his own private space, thinking about something that needed to be destroyed before it was used to do great harm. Trying to figure out how to get to it when no one else was around.

Dane caught a glimpse. The thing in Buddy's thoughts was a body—the woman Dane had spoken to, briefly; the one Dane had pursued. She saw now that her great desire to destroy the woman had actually not been *her* desire at all, but Buddy's, flowing through her.

You know what pain is. You're real. Pain makes you real.

Dane had been so alone, so desperately afraid, and she'd just hurt the woman's friend, but still the woman had found those words of comfort for Dane.

=I don't want to hurt her, Buddy.=

Buddy knew what she meant.

=It's necessary. Otherwise she'll help Mother do something awful.= At Dane's wordless protest, he added, =Don't worry, it won't be like the other time. We're not going to harm her flesh, just her body.=

DANIEL

WORD SPREADS FAST

A crowd was gathering. Word would spread faster than the stench.

"Leanne, would you call Security?" he asked, when she'd straightened and wiped off her mouth. She gave him a grim look and nodded. Daniel tapped Teru's shoulder. "Come on."

He headed down the hall at a run. Teru loped and caught up. "Where are we going?"

"To the Face Lab for an Odhiambo simile crystal. Then Krueger's office." At Teru's puzzled look he added, "There's a chance he doesn't know we're on to him yet."

But when they got there, Krueger's proxy stood unpiloted at the office window, palms on the glass.

Daniel felt something break inside. Morris's eyes, lifeless, staring. Another innocent life taken.

With a roar he slugged the proxy in the ribs; it barely moved. He hit the plastic flesh again and again, as hard as he could. "You bastard! *Murderer!*"

Teru grabbed him and pulled him away. "Ice it, Danny-boy. Nobody's in there. You're wasting your anger. Save it for the one at the controls."

Daniel stared at the proxy, then looked away, trembling with rage. He took several deep, calming breaths. "You're right," he said finally. "You're right."

Watchfully, Teru let him go. Daniel gave her-him a reassuring wave; "I'm OK now. Honest."

"I'll bet the crèche had a trip thread," she-he said. "That's what I would do. He knew the instant Krueger's body was found."

Daniel circled the room, then dropped onto the couch. The room was saturated with Krueger-abilia: statuary, books, furniture, paintings, holograms. It was hard to imagine him gone. A dull ache began to burn behind Daniel's eyes. He wiped moisture from them. His voice came out thickened by the tightness in his throat.

"He could be such a son of a bitch. But he was good to me."

"It's over, ain't it?" Teru said, sitting down next to Daniel and taking his hand. Daniel gave Teru a look.

"This scandal will be all over the nets by tomorrow," she-he said. "There'll be an outcry. Thaxton wants to ax us anyway, and our congressional support is tentative. Waldos, Inc., and the DOEP and the Pentagon will dive for cover, to avoid being sullied by the bad publicity. We'll be shut down."

"Yeah." Daniel sighed and leaned forward, closing his aching eyes and pressing cool fingers against his lids. He looked up at the empty proxy again, and his glance fell on the linkware beanie that sat on a head-shaped stand at the corner of Krueger's desk.

You do what you have to, he thought. He crossed over to the desk again, detached the beanie from its leads, lifted it off its stand, and tucked it under his arm.

"Do you know where I can find a tube of Seal Strip?"

"Sure. I was using some on the renegade a bit ago." Teru reached into a pocket and handed it to him. "What are you doing?"

He stuck the tube in his pocket. "I think I can help Carli, but I have to move fast. Federal agents are going to descend on this place like locusts in about twenty minutes, max, and they'll detain everyone. It'll be days, at least, before they're done interrobanging around."

She-he grabbed his arm. "Let them handle it, Danny."

He shook his head. "I don't trust them to do it right. They don't know what's going on, and they don't have the technology to deal with our proxies. Not without a lot of things getting smashed or blown up, or a lot of people hurt. Delays may mean Carli's life. I have to help her."

Teru rolled her-his eyes. "Always the hero. Why? Don't put yourself at risk this way."

On impulse, instead of answering, he gave Teru's proxy—male or no—a brief kiss, and then cupped her-his cheek with a hand. "It was good between us, for a while, nespah? Friend."

Teru laid her-his hand over Daniel's. "Friend. Be careful, right?"

"Right. I'll be in touch. And, uh, tell Leanne I'll be in touch with her, too."

Teru's lips quirked. "She *is* nice, eh?"

From the door, he waggled a finger. "Uh-uh. I have dibs."

A smile like sudden sunshine broke on Teru's face—the first un-strained smile she-he had given Daniel in a long time. Maybe I should have let go of us a long time ago, he thought.

"You have dibs," Teru promised.

I LOVE A PARADE

They pulled out all the stops. They showed her labs that were better-outfitted, with more really cool equipment, than she had seen since her NASA days. Byron seemed quite proud of his communications labs, and talked about some of the improvements he'd made on their original design.

Then he showed her to a room outfitted with skinlink sets. It was a large room, by space standards, maybe ten feet by twelve. The skinlink suits hung from hooks along the walls like Peter Pan shadows, dark and shimmery, wired to individual control units built into the wall. She fingered one; it felt like spandex, only stiffer and thicker.

"Have you ever tried one?" he asked.

"No."

"They're supposedly almost as good as a beanlink."

Someone had been giving them a *lot* of money.

Then Dr. Taylor took her to a different set of equally impressive labs and introduced her to Marshall Sullivan, whom Taylor called "Number Two"—an old man with a warm, genial manner.

"I'm honored to meet you," he said, pumping her hand with great enthusiasm. Like Byron, he was not in a waldo body. She learned from him that they called human-style waldos "proxies."

Dr. Sullivan gave Carli a tour of the medical facility and several proxy testing labs, at which people in waldos—or rather, in proxy—were performing various activities and being tested in different ways. She asked numerous questions, and Dr. Sullivan answered them with a straightforward demeanor. But, child of a politician, she could sniff out deception in the most sincere of countenances, and she sensed evasion somewhere around the edges of his answers—particularly when she asked questions about the pilots themselves.

Afterward Dr. Sullivan escorted her to a conference room with a large table cut from lunar rock, on which was mounted a huge, fancy jello-tube arrangement. More refreshments were laid out. Each place at the table had its own comunit. Seated at the table were the woman named Jenna Sternberg, in proxy; Byron Kowalski, *in corpus*; and another man in a brawny, dark-haired, Caucasian proxy, whom Taylor didn't introduce.

"Please, help yourself to the refreshments and make yourself comfortable. I've prepared a presentation, to give you some background."

Carli got some water and chose a spot at the table well away from the others. She lowered herself into the seat with a sigh. Beneath the vigilance that stiffened her spine and tautened her muscles, fatigue was building up. She wondered when—if ever—she would get to rest.

Taylor was cueing up a title animation loop on the main jello-tube and the others were speaking quietly on the table's other side. Partly concealed by the smaller jelly display before her seat, Carli checked the comunit. The lens came on when she laid a finger on the touch pad, but when she tapped on the linkware icon, nothing happened. With a sigh, she sat back. It never hurt to check.

"This is a version of a talk I recently gave for the secretary-elect of the Department of Environmental Protection," Taylor said. "A talk at which your father was present." Carli's eyes widened. Taylor nodded. "That's right—your father has known about our research effort since its infancy."

"Then he can't be too thrilled that your people kidnapped me and killed the men he assigned to protect me."

Taylor shrugged, looking annoyed. "There are some things your father doesn't understand."

Carli surprised herself. "Like what?"

With a visible effort to curb herself, Taylor said, "I'll get to that in a bit. But first, let me give you the background on my research."

Carli sat back. "By all means."

Taylor leaned forward, spreading her palms on the table. "I'm about to tell you some things that will make you uncomfortable. I'm going to be blunt about some difficult choices we've made, and you'll find them no easier to face than I have, I'm sure. But if you bear with me, I'll be able to demonstrate how not just our nation, but also the crèche children themselves, have benefited tremendously from my research."

Crèche children? thought Carli.

The ensuing speech, while long and technical, engaged Carli's interest despite herself. Taylor paced the room, gesturing and speaking, while in the tube on the table, jellos zoomed around, illustrating various waldo feats, and carefully crafted graphics sprouted, bloomed, and spread: revealing all the ways in which humanity had gained over the past thirty years from waldo technology.

Law enforcement—military applications—hazardous-materials handling and other dangerous work—space exploration—transport of goods—miniaturization and maximization—advancements in prosthetic technology—expanded opportunities for the disabled and ill— the list went on and on. It was nothing Carli didn't already know, but it was an imposing recital nonetheless.

"In short," Taylor said, "telepresence, waldo technology, and the jello- and *virtu*-nets over the past thirty years have transformed society. They have improved our standard of living in thousands of ways. They promise to be an important contribution to solving the ever-worsening environmental problems that plague our planet. Telepresence, more than any other single technological development, has opened the frontiers of space to us. And all due to our research here."

Carli was sure she hadn't made a sound, or any motion to indicate her reaction, but Taylor paused, and her gaze burned. "I am not exaggerating when I claim credit, Ms. MacLeod. Our research has built the very foundation on which some critical *virtu* technology rests. We wouldn't have been given tens of billions of dollars over the past eighteen years if we weren't producing results.

"What would the average person back on Earth have to say if you told him you invented a device that has completely transformed space telecommunications? And your research wasn't even classified."

Carli frowned, then sighed. Point granted.

"So. I've gone on at great length about how wonderful waldos are. What's the bad news?" Taylor ticked the points off on her fingers. "First, waldos are expensive to build. Even a few waldo losses can put a company out of business, or sound the death knell to a research project or exploration. Our nation's employee indentureship program has softened the blow of waldo loss by transferring part of the burden for protecting the equipment to the pilot, but this has not eliminated the problem.

"And because waldos are primarily used in dangerous-environment settings, losses are all too likely if things go wrong. The leading cause of waldo loss, accounting for an appalling seven percent of the GNP in 2052, is pilot error.

"Why do I quote such out-of-date figures? Because I want to stress that the impact of waldo loss on the GNP *has dropped three percentage points* in the sixteen years since, due to advances in interface technology that can be traced directly to my crèche-born research."

She paused. Carli lifted her eyebrows. It *was* remarkable, if true.

". . . leading contributing factor to pilot error is interface failure," Taylor was saying. "Interface failure is caused by two things: insufficient bandwidth, leading to signal loss and corruption; and lags in signal transmission and processing. Let me first talk about lag."

She went on at length about the several sources of lag, and where her group had achieved major reductions therein, and where she anticipated further room for improvements—with a nod to Carli for the MacLeod device's dramatic reduction in signal lag over great distances. Carli couldn't help her sudden, sharp pleasure at Taylor's use of the word *MacLeod*, instead of omni, however much her stomach twisted with dissonant feelings.

Taylor did point out, though, that the MacLeod signal's great expense made it useful only in certain applications, such as space communications and military applications.

"This means that the *fastest* a waldo can react right now," she summarized, "using current technology, *is only about two thirds as fast as a typical human*—which, by the way, is about four times as fast as it was sixteen years ago when I started my research. About sixty percent of this reduction is due to the development of MacLeod communication; the remainder is directly or indirectly related to the crèche-born studies. The potential this lag creates for pilot error is much lower than it used to be, and we've improved the interface with plenty of syntellect to get past the rough spots—but the risk of error is still substantial.

"And we are nearing a point of diminishing returns. A great deal of money would have to be invested in further research, to obtain more than a few more microseconds of lag reduction."

Here it comes, Carli thought, the coup de grâce: their reason for this dog and pony show. But Taylor switched gears instead, displaying a graphic on bandwidth.

"I mentioned signal degradation earlier. In the short run, signal degradation is not as serious as problem as lag. Signal loss and corruption have been found not to be significant contributors to pilot error," she said. "Pilots appear to be able to extrapolate and 'fill in the blanks' almost automatically. However, over time, signal degradation leads to feelings of dissociation and disorientation, resulting in more serious long-term problems."

Beside her, as she spoke, jellos from a recent, highly publicized murder trial appeared, of a waldo pilot who had gone berserk with an automatic weapon in a mall. These were followed by some disturbing images of people endlessly washing their hands, lining up pieces of silverware and growing enraged when someone tried to change them, and hospital beds lined with people whose lights, as they say, were on, but nobody was home.

"You might have heard the term *beanie-burn*," Taylor said. "Long-term waldo pilots end up suffering a host of mental disorders with alarming frequency. Everything from aggravated phobias, depression, drug and sex addiction, bipolar disorder, and obsessive-compulsive disorders to hallucinations, catatonia, fits of rage, paranoia, and delusions.

"In the long run—though lag can result in enormous losses that put companies out of business and shut down research efforts—signal degradation is a much more serious problem than lag. The psychological cost is immense. The American Association of Waldo Pilots estimates that the impact on the industry of beanie-burn is on the order of ninety billion dollars *a year*."

Carli frowned. With all the talk about lag and its obvious connection to the MacLeod transmitter, she had assumed that was why they wanted her, and that they were about to hit her up for help along those lines. She didn't have a clue, now, where Taylor was trying to lead her.

"So. Are we stuck with these limitations, pilot error in the short run and mental disorders over the long term, or is there some way to transcend them?

"That," Taylor said, "is where the crèche-born come in."

DANIEL

TIMES YOU HATE THE NETS

Daniel flashed his badge at the guard and slipped into the underbrush beyond the fence, just as some large, ominous-looking collocars hissed up to the guard shack. After that it was a short walk in the evening heat—or rather, a sprint, amid swarms of assorted flying insects and, later, a sea of migrating brown male tarantulas that fortunately took little notice of him, in their single-minded hunt for females—over a wooded hill, to Highway 290. Then a bus trip to Austin's airport, and an uneventful commute to Albuquerque by plane. At the Sunport, he caught an express train on the Heights-Central line.

While the train rocked along, wheels spitting white-blue fire at the darkness, Daniel logged into the jello-nets via his kelly. As he was checking the news, a highlighted item appeared: "TOP SCIENTIST MURDERED." He eye-clicked on the headline and read the excerpt.

(News) November 21, 2067, Austin, Texas—Dr. Samson Krueger, well-known scientist and administrator of a robotics research center in Austin, Texas, has been found murdered. Dr. Krueger was dead for some time when the body was discovered.
An APB has been put out on Daniel Sornsen, believed to have knowledge about the murder. If you see him, please click [HERE] to report his whereabouts. (News)

And there was Daniel's ID jello.

The story went on, but he stopped reading and put his kelly away, mouth suddenly dry, looking around. Two or three people in the car were wearing netware. Daniel slouched down and turned away from the others, looking out the window. He was sure they were eyeing him, comparing his profile to the news jello.

The next stop was Eubank. He forced himself to step casually off the train, and it moved away. His heart thundered and sweat trickled down his torso.

There were times he hated the nets.

Few people were in the station, though there were three hours till curfew. The subway attendant in the glass booth beyond the turnstiles read a book and paid no attention to him. At the far end of the platform, after making sure no one was looking, he jumped down into the darkness and headed for the spot where he'd left his proxy.

It was still right where he'd left it, in a dark nook off the main subway tunnel. After pulling the proxy's shirt off, Daniel got the Seal Strip out and removed the Strip end cap. While feeling along the invisible seams of the proxy's chest panel, he applied Strip in a line behind his touch. The solvent had a sweetish smell, and felt slick on his fingers.

After a few seconds he peeled the skin away and worked his fingers through the web of lubricant-filled capillaries, pushing them aside. A light inside the chest cavity came on, illuminating the workings. The switch box inside was metal with a hinged panel; he pressed a button and it, too, opened. Daniel changed some settings at the switches. Then he closed up the inner panel, moved the lubricant tubes back into place, applied sealant from the Seal end of the tube, and pressed the skin back down. Then he wiped his hands on his jeans.

Now to find a quiet spot somewhere, a spot with the right kind of hardware setup that he could modify, to make use of the beanie he'd taken from Krueger's office. Perhaps he could find something appropriate at the university. Not bloody likely he'd find what he'd need, without an exhaustive, highly risky search. But it was his best chance—he had to try.

As he was straightening, something hit him in the back and knocked him down, banging his head on the ground. A knee pressed into his back and a hand at the base of his skull shoved his head down. He tasted dirt and oil. Pebbles ground into his cheek. Daniel bucked and tried to throw his attacker. Futile. He could barely breathe, much less fight.

"Stop fighting or I'll break your neck."

"Paint, what are you doing?" another voice said. "You said talk, not break."

"Stow it. *I'm* on this," the man with his knee on Daniel's back said.

Paint. Paint. Carli's nephew?

"Listen," he said, and groaned as the man shoved his head and neck down. Rocks dug into his cheek and nose.

"Shut up. I want to know where you took her. Or you're a grease stain."

"It wasn't me who—"

Another sharp jerk cut him off. "Don't poke my ass. I saw the jellos. I saw the door and the wall. That was no human attacker. I've met your machine-man here, and Carli told me what it could do." He shoved his knee into Daniel, who groaned again. "Why did you take her? Where is she?"

"There are others," he grunted. "Here to help . . ."

"Soft moves—soft," the other one urged. "Let him talk. 'Be we take him down after, if needed."

A pause. Then the knee lifted and the hand released his neck. "All right. Talk."

He rolled over and got up, spat dirt from his lips, and brushed pebbles from his face. It was dark, but enough light from the streets above filtered down through an overhead grating for him to recognize the man he had met at The Protein Bomb a couple nights back. Paint. The other, he didn't recognize. Both stood between him and the main tunnel. The other man cradled a two-foot iron bar in his hands.

"I'm not the kidnapper. I was assigned to protect her," Daniel said. "I'm with a secret government project." He broke off. "It's kind of complicated."

Paint stared at Daniel, arms locked across a broad chest, a face that might have been chiseled from marble. "Night's young. We've the time, nespah, Fox?"

"Vraymon."

A train roared by. Its wheels struck seams in the rails and emitted flashes that limned the two men facing him in weird, strobelike, electric auras. When it had passed, Daniel said "Look . . . why don't we go someplace a little more congenial? I'll tell you everything."

After a whispered exchange, Fox said, "Follow me," and moved past Daniel into the dark cul-de-sac. A flashlight winked on. Paint, behind, gave him a shove, no doubt a gentle reminder that he wasn't free from the threat of grease-staindom yet. Daniel snatched up the beanie and followed.

At the end of the cul-de-sac was a crawl space. Hunched over, he followed Fox through the long tunnel, amid spiderwebs and scurrying rodents and insects, through clouds of choking dust and dark, rank-smelling, squishy pools. It wasn't quite as bad as a sewer, but it came pretty damn close.

At the tunnel's end were some gratings. Fox removed one of the gratings and squirmed in; the light disappeared, blocked by his body.

When Daniel hesitated, Paint shoved him again. He pulled himself into the concrete-lined tunnel. It was barely big enough to belly-crawl through and seemed to go on forever, though—thankfully—it was marginally drier and cleaner than the one they'd just been in.

Finally he emerged into a dark space and stepped through an open panel door. Something smelling of plant decay squelched beneath his shoes. Paint emerged from the big metal box and closed and locked the panel door. The place they'd emerged from was an old machine: some sort of ancient dryer, or air-conditioning unit, or heater, whose guts had been removed.

They were in a basement. Fox led the way out of the back room, which was full of clutter and boxes and indistinct objects, and calf-high mounds of dry blue mold, and slime the color of lime Jell-O. That was what Daniel had stepped in earlier. They dodged around clusters of enormous brown and grey mushrooms, which fanned out like parasols from the walls and sprouted from the clutter on the floor. After passing through a dim, not-quite-as-moldy hallway past other rooms, they reached a set of stairs. A long climb later they emerged on the floor of Carli's apt. Her door had a big hole in it with frayed edges, and yellow tape across it with red lettering, "No Entry! Police Barrier!"

Paint carefully peeled the tape aside.

"Umm, are you sure we should be doing this?" Daniel asked.

"They stripped the tape off, aim-side," Fox said. "The bastards left a mess. They were just going to leave the big hole in the door, too. So"—he grinned—"we *reappropriated* the tape to keep thieves and whips away till we'n get repairs made."

Daniel wondered how much good the tape would do, but kept his doubts to himself. Paint plugged in the code and they went inside. A big, orange-striped cat with a white chest and paws came running, meowing noisily. Paint picked him up.

"Hey, old man." He tousled the cat's head and then turned to Daniel, gaze hardening. "Sit down and start talking."

Daniel brushed off some more dust, mold, and cobwebs, and sat, crossing his legs. His palms and knees were sore, scraped up. So was his face.

"I don't know who kidnapped Carli," he said, "but I think I know where he's taking her. One of the platforms, or maybe the moon."

"Explain."

"I caught a glimpse of the kidnapper talking to someone—"

"Who?"

"It doesn't *matter* who!"

Their expressions didn't yield. He sighed.

"All right, all right. He was talking to someone impersonating my boss. Never mind the details," he said, when Paint started to speak. "Surely that can wait. The point is, the kidnapper was calling from White Sands Skyport; I recognized it. And they were announcing a shuttle flight in the background."

" 'Be 't's coincidence," Fox said.

"Maybe. But I *think* the kidnapper was saying something about her being about to board a shuttle when I barged into the room. My mind was on other things and I didn't know then he was the kidnapper, but . . ." He shrugged. "I'm almost sure of it."

Paint and Fox exchanged a look.

" 'F you're lying—"

"I know, I know. I'm a grease stain."

"All right." Paint took a breath. He sat down in a desk chair, and Fox sat down next to Daniel on the couch. " 'N we catch that flight?"

"No, it was two hours ago. I think we need to get a copy of the passenger list and destination of that shuttle. There can't be more than one shuttle launch at a time; they haven't got the facilities for it."

"What o'clock's the call?"

"Let's see—it must have been just before seven. Er, six P.M. here."

Paint turned to Carli's desk and slipped on her netspecs and a mesh-glove. He twiddled his fingers in midair, muttering, and then turned back.

"A shuttle departed for Shasta Station from White Sands Skyport at five fifty-seven."

Daniel stared. "Shasta Station?"

"What is it?" Fox asked. "What's wrong?"

"Another branch of our secret project is housed there. Something real jade is going down." He spent a moment eyeing the two of them. "This could turn into some pretty heavy shit. How far into this are you two willing to go?"

"Define 'heavy shit,' " Fox said.

He sighed. "I don't know. I don't know who's involved in the kidnapping, or why. All I know is that some very powerful people have their asses exposed right now, and the stakes are high. People have already died. We could end up in a corner we can't get out of."

Another look passed between Paint and Fox.

"Carli needs help," Fox said, with a shrug. A smile flashed onto Paint's face, and he squeezed Fox's shoulder.

"We're in," Paint told Daniel.

Crèche Kids in the Center Ring

They were all watching her, waiting for her reaction.

"The crèche-born?" Carli repeated. "Is *that* what all this nonsense is about?"

Taylor pursed her lips, eyeing Carli, and her colleagues exchanged glances. Hit a nerve there, Carli thought, suppressing a fierce smile.

"They're at the heart of our research," Taylor replied, with a slight edge to her voice. "Twenty-four years ago, pilot error and mental breakdown were endemic—close to suffocating waldo technology in its infancy. At that time I was a private consultant to Waldos, Inc.'s, research arm, along with other clients, such as the DOD. After some initial research for the DOD, I persuaded the then-CEO of Waldos, Richard Blaine, to approach the U.S. government with a proposal to create a cooperative venture to study the interface-failure problem in depth.

"We added Dr. Sullivan to our team early on, and made some important advances over the next several years. It was this early linkware work that earned me the Nobel Prize. But we realized that in a couple of decades the technology would be bumping up against some constraints that were simply unavoidable. So we came up with another approach."

A jello of three brains appeared beside her, each turning slowly in the vertical and horizontal directions. As she spoke, one by one, the brains' regions lit up in different colors, as captions described what their functions were and how they were affected by environmental influences.

"Our brains are highly adaptable when we're young. While the largest-scale structures tend to be built-in and not very changeable, the smaller structures are extremely malleable. We allocate our mental resources to various skills over the first sixteen years of our lives, especially the first five years, depending on the demands of our environment.

"Dr. Sullivan"—with a gesture at her colleague—"and I did extensive research in this area eighteen years ago, before our crèche project began, and showed a clear correlation between piloting skill and exposure to the nets from an early age. Pilots who have regularly faced in since childhood show a correspondingly stronger ability to compensate for lags, as well as a resistance to disorientation. The earlier the exposure, the greater the ability to compensate for lag and resist disorientation.

"Unfortunately, lag and disorientation had been seen as at the root of some serious social problems back in the teens and twenties. In a well-intentioned—but terribly misguided—attempt to protect children, federal laws were passed setting thirteen as the minimum age at which the beanlink could be implanted, except in extreme cases of total physical incapacitation. Many states had—and still have—laws severely restricting minors' access to the *virtu*-nets at all.

"I don't know whether you've followed the issue—"

"I haven't," Carli replied.

"Well, that perception, that facing in is responsible for an increase in teen apathy and violence, has since been thoroughly debunked in some well-documented studies," Taylor went on. "But it was too late. The public perception was there, and the laws were already in place."

Taylor gripped the back of a chair. "Ms. MacLeod, our crèche children are not only beanlinked, they have lived in protective cocoons for years—most since infancy. They live a very different life than most children do. So, as a moral and compassionate woman, you must be concerned about their welfare."

She paused. They were all scrutinizing Carli now. She looked down at the table and took a few seconds to try to absorb the impact of what Taylor was saying. Beanlinked babies? Children locked in pilot crèches since infancy?

Your life's in danger, D'Auber. Be careful.

But this woman was an idol—a role model. She found herself unable to dissemble.

"I'm recently divorced," she said finally. "It's D'Auber, not MacLeod. And if you're telling me that your secret research involves illegal experimentation on children, 'concerned' is not the word for what I'm feeling."

Sullivan and Jenna Sternberg shifted in their seats and made soft sounds of protest.

"First of all," Taylor said stiffly, "let me assure you that we've proceeded with the children's welfare as our first criterion for any action."

"You're able to substantiate that claim, of course."

A flash of irritation. "Of course."

"Because I find the idea of using human children as research subjects in this way horrifying, no matter how great the scientific need."

Her words hung in the air like a foul odor. Taylor started to reply, but Sullivan came to his feet.

"You are leaping to judgment without knowledge." He gestured at the young man who sat silently beside him. "Our crèche children have enjoyed opportunities none of us can even imagine! If it weren't for the Face Laws—which I regard as *criminal*; those laws deprive kids of the ability to fully adapt to an important part of their world!—kids everywhere would share—to at least some degree—the abilities of our children."

"And you can't really be so naive about studies involving children," Sternberg said. "It's done all the time. With no harm to the kids."

Carli shrugged, arms folded across her chest. The others exchanged more glances.

"She's useless to us like this," Sternberg said in a low voice to Taylor, who had started clenching and unclenching her fists, staring at Carli without blinking.

Marshall Sullivan intervened. "Let her ask the hard questions. She's earned the right." To Carli he said, "You're a scientist. I beg you to keep an open mind. Give us the chance to prove ourselves to you."

After a long pause, Carli released a breath. "Very well—I'll try."

"Let me first correct a misconception," Taylor said, her tone sharp and her face taut with hostility. "Our research with the crèche children is legal. Under the National Securities Act Amendments of 2012, 'line item' exemptions can be applied to state and federal laws in force, even if those laws don't specifically call for exemption and even if we are not in a state of general emergency, if national security is deemed to be at stake.

"President Shyner was fully briefed and approved our launching the crèche-born research in 2049." Signature pages appeared in midair in the jello-tube. "Note that both President Nightingale and President Kennedy have extended the exemption, based on our substantiation of the enormous benefits this nation has enjoyed, and the advantaged position the crèche-born themselves enjoy."

"What about Thaxton?"

Again, glances were exchanged. "He hasn't been briefed yet," Taylor said. "And he won't be." Then she shook her head. "I'm getting ahead of myself again. Before I go on any further, I'd like to introduce you to Pablo."

The man who hadn't been introduced yet stood up.

"Wait. Before you begin any demonstrations, let me ask a few more questions about the children."

Taylor nodded to the man, who sat back down. "By all means." There was a sarcastic edge to her voice, which Carli ignored.

"How many are there and what are their ages?"

Sullivan answered. "There are twenty-seven: fourteen girls and thirteen boys. We recruited in two waves—the first ten are between fourteen and sixteen years old now, and the rest are between seven and ten years old. Pablo here is the eldest."

" 'Recruited.' Hmph." Carli looked at the man, who returned her gaze impassively. Sixteen? He looked at least several years older. It was hard to get used to, this body-swap stuff. What effect must this have had on his development, spending his childhood in an adult body? Or had he?

She asked.

Sullivan said, "Actually, for the First Wave kids, we gave them baby, then toddler, then preschool-aged proxies, to simulate physical growth. Budget cuts forced us to abandon the approach after a few years. It *has* made for some differences in their development, I believe, though we've compensated as best we could with an extensive series of age-appropriate *virtu*-similes, programmed by Jenna with the aid of a team of psychologists and programmers out of our sister facility, Austin."

"The very idea of the human proxy was developed initially to give the children a sense of their humanity, in fact," Taylor added. Carli's string of nonjudgmental questions had apparently calmed her down. But this was obviously one extremely volatile woman. "After studying the matter, we no longer believe that human-style proxies are strictly necessary. The similes serve the same purpose. But by this time the infrastructure is in place, and they do have some other advantages over nonhumanlike waldos."

"Where and how did you 'recruit' the kids?"

"We identified a group of children who have serious immune deficiencies, or certain other kinds of life-threatening immune-system oddities," Sullivan replied. "Infants, mostly—none older than two and a half. Are you familiar with 'bubble kids'?"

Carli shook her head.

"Kids who live in sterile environments. That's what the majority of our kids are. They can't be exposed to any environmental toxins or pathogens, or they die. Their immune systems are completely dysfunctional, or even nonfunctional. The kids' parents were too poor to properly care for them. A few had been abandoned to the system. We explained as much of our program as we were allowed to their parents, those who still had parents, and they gave the children up as wards of the state. We implanted beanlink technology and brought them here."

"Most—if not all—of our children would be dead by now, if we hadn't intervened," Sternberg said.

How noble. How much did you pay their parents for them? She didn't say it.

NET-SIDE SKULLDUGGERY

The three of them came up with—for lack of a better word—a plan. Paint hauled out Carli's archaic mike-touch-pad-and-keyboard setup and hooked it up to the comunit's jello display, to crack the commercial jellophone service lines and gain illegal access to an omni connection. Daniel spent the next couple of hours soldering and tinkering, jury-rigging a beanlink hookup to Carli's comunit.

He had almost all the tools he needed to upgrade the beanlink; Carli had plenty of spare connectors, jacks, and wiring about. But he wanted a few odds and ends, and Paint wanted to take his own comunit, to set up on Shasta. Fox appointed himself gofer, and left to see what he could scrounge at Carli's office, then to drop by his and Paint's place and pick up Paint's comunit, plus toiletries and a few changes of clothing for the three of them.

Once Daniel finished the upgrade, he beanlinked in to run some tests. The linkware crashed on him numerous times, but eventually he managed to diddle the settings so the software cooperated, grudgingly. Performance was not 100 percent. It wasn't even 80 percent of what he was used to. But if Paint could pull off an omni line eliminating signal-response lag, it'd do.

"I'm ready when you are," he said, eye-clicking to close his debugging gridwork.

"Your omni line is set up," Paint said, still working. "Password *gutterbug.*" He spelled it. "One word, all lowercase. Hold—I'll transmit the account settings to your in-box."

After a moment, Paint gave him the signal and he called up his e-mail. There was a message from Paint with an attachment. He hooked the icon with a finger and dropped it into his beanlink utility directory, and then booted up the linkware. And there, among the other icons, was a little lightning bolt. The omni connection.

When he eye-clicked the lightning bolt, then spoke and spelled the password at the pop-up query box, his proxy control face appeared. Omni connection confirmed. He tweaked the settings, ran a couple of utilities to further improve performance, and then slipped down into his waiting plastic-and-metal body.

This could end up being a disaster, Daniel thought, flexing his proxy's hands. The jury-rigged connection wasn't so great; fine motor control was poor. His fingers felt almost completely numb. Sense of smell was severely degraded. Even visuals and sound had a grainy quality.

Switching on amplified light reception, he made his way—carefully, getting used to the differences and gaps in his proxy's responsiveness—from the cul-de-sac, through the crawl spaces, to the basement, and up the stairs to Carli's place. Fox had entered the apartment and was about to close the door. Daniel hurried to enter, as Fox dropped a duffel bag onto the floor by the couch.

When Daniel saw his flesh-self cradled in the squish, it jarred him loose, and suddenly he was looking at his machine-self with his flesh-self's eyes. He was tired enough that the abrupt shift in perspective rattled him.

"Got everything we need," Fox said, and went over to Paint, slipping his arms around Paint's neck in a light embrace. " 'Be you made good?"

"Working on it." Paint fended Fox off as he tried to nibble his ear. "Not now, Foxifox." Paint spared Fox a quick, piquant glance. " 'Be later."

A flash of annoyance crossed Fox's face and he dropped his arms, but he said, "Later. OK. Hungry?"

"Yes, please."

"You, Daniel?"

"I could eat a bite."

Paint turned back to the comunit, and Daniel worked some more on improving his beanlink, while Fox banged around in the kitchen. Occasionally Daniel glanced over to see how Paint was doing. At one point, Paint captured a jello-image of Daniel's proxy.

"What's that for?"

"Virtually all secured facilities use smart systems to ID intruders," Paint said. "Your machine-man's image is going into their 'harmless animals' data file. White Sands's smart system is going to think you're a species of deer."

Daniel stared in reluctant admiration. "How do you know so much about security systems?"

"I designed smart systems for a living, pre-ice. I'n't do much about the other systems, though. You'll be on your own for the rest. But I *can* tell you what else you'll be up against."

A while later, in the jelly, strings of text and code and other odd bits came and went as Paint's fingers danced from the keys to the touch pad and back. Then, though the display didn't appear any different than it had, Paint straightened suddenly.

"I'm in."

"You are?" Daniel removed his beanie and sat up in the squish to get a better look at the display. Fox came out with cheese-substitute sandwiches, and passed one each to Daniel and Paint.

"Switching over now." Paint set the sandwich aside and touched a key. The text was replaced with a 3D "White Sands Skyport" graphic, which blasted off, dissolving.

"First we get seats." A passenger list came up. Paint selected at random three people traveling together. "Sorry, folks, ya'll catch the next flight," he said, and bumped them off the list, inserting his and Fox's legal names in their place, plus a false name for Daniel. Then Paint went back to the main menu. "Hold while I set up a few dodges and firewalls." Text flashed through the display. After a bit he said, "Now let's hook their bully ops."

A jelly-foyer, studded with free-floating, three-dimensional icons, faded in. In the center of the foyer was a big eyeball gyrating in a circle. A ribbon of glinting red and orange letters circled beneath the eye: "Watchful Eye Security Services."

"I've built in some dodges, but we don't have much time before they detect us. Better move fast." Paint pointed, clicked, and dragged, scanning a series of grids, maps, and screens too quickly for Daniel to follow, and talking either to himself or his linkware; Daniel was unsure which.

"Jink—here it is." Paint gestured.

Daniel and Fox looked over Paint's shoulder at the live data being shown on the airport map. The skyport perimeter was surrounded by a concertina-wire barrier; an inner electrical fence charged with 50,000 amperes, also used as a conductance-wire alarm; and on the grounds, a gridwork of IR-enhanced visual-light sensors with smart ID systems. A team of fourteen security waldos roved the perimeter, as well as the scram jet runways, VTOL craft liftoff and landing platforms, and hangars.

Paint captured the image and saved it to disk.

"Fifty thousand amperes—that's lethal, isn't it?" Fox asked.

"Bohcoo petes and whips in the area." Paint did some more with his hands. Interfaces came and went. Then he sat back with a sigh and a nod. "There. You're in. Now officially an unusually large deer."

"Will it be enough to fool their system?" Daniel asked. Paint flashed him a wry grin.

"Ya'll know by tomorrow, nespah?"

As he spoke, the screen dissolved. Fox pointed with an exclamation.

"They spotted us," Paint said. "No big jig; I've put a firewall in— What? Shit." Paint slammed fingers onto the keys as the display changed. "They're over the wall—tracing our netpath. Tracking us." A tense second or two later he sat back and ran fingers through his red hair, which had fallen into his face.

"Did they find us?"

"Doubt it. I had other dodges in place. Pretty sure we lost them at the University of Minnesota." He flashed a smile. "Guess we'll find out, nespah?"

Daniel drew a breath. "Damn."

"Hey, a little skullduggery's de rigueur, net-side. Be a Ritz, not a saltine."

Paint's casual attitude was contagious. "What the hell."

Paint slapped Daniel's thigh. "That's a schick tude."

"A what?"

"Attitude. A schick attitude." Paint finished his sandwich and stood, yawning. To Daniel he said, "You'n have the couch. Pillows and extra blankets in the cabinet." He pointed at some doors set into the wall next to the kitchen. "Less you want to join Foxifox at me." Then he laughed, head thrown back, at Daniel's expression of disgust. The ferocity of the gesture reminded Daniel of his dance the other night. "Night, Gutterbug."

When Fox didn't stand, Paint said, "Coming, Foxifox?"

"In a bit," Fox said, not getting up from the couch. Daniel had no idea where the sudden tension in the air had come from. He looked from Fox to Paint and back again, and wondered if Paint was jealous. Of him. Or of Fox being with him. Then he was gone.

" 'S just twitching you, you know," Fox said, after a few moments. "He doesn't mean it. Don't let it get to you."

Daniel, still annoyed, pretended not to hear, and went back to work on his proxy.

Fox finished his own food, watching while Daniel reseated his beanie and put the proxy through some test moves. Finally Daniel decided to stop fiddling with it and piloted the proxy into a seated position on the living room floor. Fox eyed it.

"Quite a piece of work, that."

"Yeah."

"What powers it?"

Daniel hesitated. "Antimatter."

Fox edged back. "Oh."

"Relax." Daniel slapped the proxy's chest. "The reactor and magneto-bottle are well protected. Everything's triple-foolproofed." He paused. "Besides . . . well, if containment *did* fail, this whole quadrant of the city would be a big, empty crater long before we could get out of range."

"Antimatter . . ." Fox shook his head. "That's heavy enough shit for me. 'F we're nabbed, we're yeti for life." Then he sighed. "The hell. 'T's for Carli. 'N I touch it?"

"Sure."

Fox leaned forward and pinched the proxy's skin. "It's warm. Feels like real skin."

Daniel grinned. "It's supposed to." Then he gestured at the tools and parts lying around. "I could use your help packing up."

With Fox's help he got the tools and parts packed into a large tackle box. Fox lifted it experimentally, and grunted.

"Hefty. Baggage costs bohcoo to ship."

Daniel shook his head. "Which reminds me. I don't have much on my card. How about you guys?"

"Paint says we'n use Carli's account. 'S got bohcoo bucks."

Fox dropped the toolbox beside the duffel bag. Then he stretched, catlike. Muscles rippled along his arms, back, and legs. "I'm to bed. See ya aim-side."

"See you." Daniel yawned, rubbing at his eyes. It was almost 1:00 A.M. Sleep. What a fine idea.

Fox paused and frowned. "Think we've got a chance?"

"Hope so." He decided to be optimistic. "Yeah. I do. They won't be expecting us."

CARLI

AND FOR OUR NEXT TRICK . . .

"Let us show you what our kids can do."

Sullivan picked up a box and put it on the table. In the box was a large, analog clock with only a second hand. Or rather, a microsecond hand; the clock's face had one hundred large demarcations, with ten small ticks between each two large marks. He flipped a large switch on a box by the clock, and the hand swept around the clock's face, one revolution per second. Then he switched it off and hit the red button next to the switch. The hand reset to zero.

"This clock is what we use to test our proxies' basic reflexes," he said, and held up two insulated wires, with tiny alligator clips on the ends. "When you close this circuit, the timer hand stops moving. Like so." He started the clock and then touched the clips together. The hand stopped.

"Now you do it," he said, and handed her the clips. He concealed the switch from her with his back. "As soon as you see the hand start to move, touch the clips to each other."

She did so. The hand stopped its sweep at 159 microseconds. He looked at it in surprise. "Let's try again." On her second try, the hand stopped at 153 microseconds.

"Interesting. You have fast reflexes. The average untrained person's response time is closer to a hundred seventy microseconds or so.

"Now. Let's have Jenna do it. Jenna, as you'll note, is in proxy. Her crèche is nearby"—Carli noted that as Sullivan mentioned Jenna's crèche, the one they called Pablo made a quick, furtive gesture with his right hand—"so signal transmission lag will be negligible. However, the interface, processing, and translation lags will still be there. Jenna?"

The silver-haired young woman stepped up and did the same thing Carli had done. The clock showed 232 microseconds. Sullivan also had her repeat. This time it read 235 microseconds.

"Jenna's been trained for speed, as are all waldo pilots these days, and her baseline response is one hundred fifty microseconds," Sullivan said. "This means that on average, it took an extra"—he paused and scribbled on his touch pad—"eighty-four microseconds, on top of her own body's reaction time, for the proxy interface to implement her response. About half again as much time as the average human body could react.

"And now Pablo. You'll note that he's also in proxy."

Sullivan had him stop the clock twice, also. His times were 186 microseconds and then 180.

"Pablo's baseline reflexes clock at one hundred fifty-five, five microseconds *more* than Jenna's. His software and hardware are identical to Jenna's." Sullivan looked at Carli, eyebrows lifted, waiting, while Carli puzzled it over.

"But then . . . but that's impossible. If he's not reacting more quickly, and if the equipment is identical, he's about fifty microseconds too fast! Where is the extra time coming from?"

Sullivan exchanged a grin with Taylor, who came forward. "Because it turns out that there is an additional lag in the interface—one that couldn't be isolated until our kids came along.

"Our kids have been in proxy most of their lives. Their mental organization is different. Our mental commands to act are geared to go to our own, physical bodies. The beanlink implant interposes itself between our thought and our would-be action, and translates and delivers that message to the waldo instead. But our brains are set up to interface with our own bodies—not with machines. Our kids were given the opportunity to adapt to the face at a time when their brain wiring wasn't set yet. They have a much more direct and efficient interface with the linkware."

"And a correspondingly weaker interface with their own bodies."

Sullivan frowned. "True. But as I believe I already mentioned, these kids probably wouldn't even be alive, if not for our intervention. . . ."

"I'm just trying for a complete picture here. Please continue."

He exhaled, noisily. Taylor had started pacing behind the chairs, scowling.

"Very well," Sullivan said. "Another demonstration. Dr. Sternberg, if you'd be so kind?"

The young woman went to the far side of the conference room. Sullivan tossed a baseball into the air and caught it a couple of times.

Then he threw it at her, hard. Sternberg, set to catch the ball, missed entirely; she overbalanced and nearly did a face plant on the table.

"An instant replay," Sullivan said, and in the large jelly, the ball flew from his fingers and struck Sternberg's chest just after her hands grasped at it. A readout beneath the image gave some numbers.

"As you see, the ball struck her two hundred and forty-six microseconds after it left my fingertips. Plenty of time for even a waldo pilot to react. But she didn't put her hands in the right place at the right time.

"Now Pablo."

He repeated the experiment with Pablo, who caught the ball easily, one-handed, as it neared him, and tossed it back. Sullivan showed the replay in the jelly. Pablo's hand came into the correct position much earlier than Sternberg's, in plenty of time to catch the ball.

"The crèche children have not only quicker proxy reflexes overall, due to more efficient mental organization around their beanlink; they also automatically compensate for the lag that can't be eliminated."

"In other words," Taylor said, "their eye-hand coordination is geared for lag, while we have to think about it and correct our natural impulses."

"And there's more," Sullivan said. "How familiar are you with the *v*-net?"

"Pretty familiar."

"What cruisers do you use?"

"Depends," Carli said. "TimeWalker is my favorite for floating probes and otherwise waldoing around. For net cruising, I tend to use GridLink Gauntlet Five-one. It has its shortcomings, but it's a good generalist's cruiser."

"Hmmm. Most people don't want to mess with what kind of net face they have. You're clearly one of the few who are net-savvy and take an interest in shaping your net face. Then there are the beanheads and the hatchets, the hackers and crackers, who use much more specialized stuff I doubt you've even heard of. And then there are our kids. Jenna?"

Sternberg, having a quiet exchange with Byron, perched on the table now and spread her hands. "To most people the nets are an electronic extension, or reflection, if you prefer, of the real world. They're a message-transmitting device, or an easy way to get the shopping done, or do research, or slip on an avatar on evenings and weekends, and play or chat with friends." She shook her head. "But to our kids the nets *are* the real world.

"They wear their cruising software like clothes. They're constantly immersed. You could almost say that English is a second language to them; programming languages, mathematics, logic theory—these are their first language. They have no fear of technical subjects. They hold immense logical structures in their heads; they see flaws in code where a body-bound programmer would spend years hunting and never see it. I've been a programmer since I was a teenager, but I can't come close to doing what they do." She frowned, her focus inward. "They're never distracted by the demands of the flesh. They have phenomenal powers of concentration."

"We've tracked them," Taylor added, "tracking down bugs and worms and honing in on crackers—it's amazing. It has to be seen to be believed. They have all of the creative and adaptive abilities their humanity gives them, and vastly superior mental organization as well."

"On their own initiative," Sullivan interjected, "they've created *virtu*-proxies—personality subroutines that are as far beyond net avatars as our proxies here are beyond spider waldos. Waldos, Inc., is currently gearing up to sell these next-generation creations to the general public, and we expect them to make a huge splash in the marketplace."

"And as a follow-up, just because they were curious what would happen," Jenna said, "they tinkered with their code, expanded on it, and have ended up creating prototype logical-thought engines that we believe, based on initial tests, approach real artificial sentience. We've sent some of these engines to be tested by the syntellect development teams at MIT and UCSC, and they are flabbergasted. Absolutely stunned."

"And the kids have done all this out of a sense of play—simply to improve their face-games," Sullivan said. "Think what they'll accomplish over the rest of their lives, if we simply give them the chance."

Carli held up her hands as Taylor started to say something else. "Whoa. Look, the results of your research all sound very impressive, and we can argue the ethics till the cows come home, but what does this have to do with me?"

They all looked at her. There was a long silence.

"We haven't held anything back," Taylor said finally, "and I'm going to level with you now. Thaxton's secretary of the environment,

Enid Thompson, has made clear that our days are numbered. We're about to be shut down." She pressed index and middle fingers to her lips. "I've worked with the government for a long time. I know what they're like. Despite our successes, despite the fact that some people in power have benefited greatly from our accomplishments, we are an embarrassment to them."

Carli remembered her father's reaction when she had asked him about KaleidoScope.

"Except for Byron," she went on, "we have worked with these children since they were babies. They are our children. They call me Mother. In many ways—in all the important ways—I *am* their mother." Her voice grew hoarse. "I am gravely concerned about their fate. I believe that the very best they can hope for, if this project is shut down, is to be locked up in some institutional hospital for the rest of their lives. Ignored, neglected—or worse. Treated like bugs, to be studied without regard to their own desires. If they're not quietly gotten rid of altogether, to avoid the possibility of scandal." At Carli's expression she said, "You come from a political family, Ms. D'Auber. Don't claim a level of naïveté you can't possibly have."

It *was* true that dreadful things could happen. When power brokers didn't set a strong example in terms of personal integrity—which few politicians did—their underlings often went even further over the line. Carli's quiet horror over the bizarre and complex ways political power could be abused, over the things she saw as a child when she spent summers in Washington with her father, had led her to abjure politics, early on.

But incidents as extreme as Taylor spoke of were vanishingly rare, and she wasn't about to give Taylor the satisfaction of granting her point, in any event.

"We study them ourselves, yes," Taylor went on, "but they are our babies. We also care for them and provide for them. *And* they are the centerpiece of our work. They are much more to us than just experimental subjects." Her voice had risen in pitch as she spoke; now she clenched her fists and shook them at Carli. *"You must understand!"* Carli thought Taylor was going to grab her, and jerked back. Just as suddenly, Taylor turned away, her proxy body gone completely rigid.

The others stared. Sullivan laid a hand on Taylor's shoulder.

"Hang on," he said. "Don't lose it now."

Taylor laid her own hand over his and nodded. The look in her eyes when she turned back was terrifying. "I'm not going to let anyone hurt my kids."

Carli's lips felt numb. "What do you want from me?"

"We're going to steal *Exodus*," Taylor said. "We need your help."

DANIEL

THINGS PROCEED APACE

Paint and Fox woke him at five. Fox made them all coffee, bacon, and toast, and after they ate, Daniel climbed into the squish and bean-linked in. They three—his proxy, Paint, and Fox—caught a bullet train to Alamogordo/White Sands.

At 7:03 they debarked at the White Sands Skyport station and rode the long march of escalators up to ground level. The terminal, a big five- or six-story building, lay across several lanes of honking, jockeying spaceport traffic linguini.

While Fox went inside the terminal and Paint stayed with the luggage, Daniel looked around.

Beyond the bullet-train entry lay a large parking lot and a highway. Daniel zoomed in on the view. Beyond the four-lane highway was a barbed-wire fence. Wan, sandy hills, covered with grass tufts, cholla and prickly pear cacti, and an occasional small shrub, rose and fell away into the distance. Mountains rimmed the horizon to the east, west, and north, beneath a great dome of cloudless turquoise.

White Sands? The sand's not all that white, Daniel thought. What's the big deal?

The air was warm and dry; in the heat waves, the mountains seemed on the edge of evanescence; insects buzzed and whirred in a noisy chorus that underscored the traffic noise; a spider crouched at the corner of a web in the nook of a bus stop; a lizard—impending road jerky—sunned itself on the asphalt. On this side of the road, some distance to the west, mostly obscured by a series of hangars, were the liftoff scaffolds and scramways.

Fox had returned by the time he got back to Paint and the luggage.

"It's gate Four-B," Fox said. "Orbital Flights wing."

Paint and Fox picked up the duffel bag and tool kit.

"Meet you in the passenger lounge," Paint said. "No later than seven-forty."

"Right."

The other two headed for curbside check-in, and Daniel made his way across the parking lot toward the highway.

CARLI

Nobody's Fool

Carli came to her feet with a shriek. *"What?"*

"You heard me."

Carli put the chair between herself and them, gripping its back, her heart racing and her mouth dry. Taylor's civil façade had fallen away; she stared at Carli in stark aggression, lips thin and whitened, hands gripping her own chair back and trembling under her intensity. The others in the room were staring at her—Taylor, not Carli.

They're terrified of her, Carli realized. Choose the wrong words and she was a dead woman. She saw it in Taylor's lizard-dead gaze. She had used up any tiny reserves of tolerance the woman might have had. It was clear—she had no choice but to cooperate.

But her mouth had a mind of its own.

"No fucking way. Find yourself another patsy."

Byron buried his face in his hands with a groan. The whites of Taylor's eyes showed all around, and her teeth were bared. Jenna put a hand on Taylor's arm and said to Carli, "Your options are limited at this point." Taylor shook off the touch with a snarl.

"Maybe so," Carli replied. "But I have friends aboard that ship, and even if I didn't, I'm not about to sabotage our first—and maybe only—peopled mission to the stars."

Byron cleared his throat. "Look, Number One, perhaps I could talk to Carli privately. There's so much we haven't explained yet, so much she doesn't understand."

But Taylor had leapt over the back of her chair onto the table as Byron spoke, and now crouched on it, baring her teeth as if she wanted to tear Carli's throat out. Her voice came out in taut bursts. "Get her out of here. Now."

Byron pulled Carli hurriedly out of the room and closed the door. As they started down the hall, faint, muffled noises—screams and thuds—issued from behind it.

DANIEL

SKYPORT SKULLDUGGERY

Daniel squatted across the highway from the spaceport perimeter's barrier, in the shade of a shrub, and surveyed the area. He had made his way west along the highway to a point about a third of a mile from the terminal. From up here on this hill, he could see a startling line of white to the north and west: the leading edge of White Sands National Monument's gypsum dunes. Now, *that*, he decided, was sand white enough to get excited about.

In the distance, south of the spaceport terminal, a single shuttle rested within a rack of metalwork, nose skyward. The rows of hangars were rather closer, the nearest of them perhaps a quarter mile away. A scram jet moved past, picking up speed. At the end of the scramway, far to the west, it shot out and up, lancing the sky, shattering the silence with a sonic blast that startled birds out of a nearby shrub.

Daniel called up the diagram Paint had saved, then zoomed in and overlaid the diagram on the reality to compare the two. Rolls of stacked razor wire, a cleared area a few yards thick, and then a twelve-foot electrical fence with cameras every ten yards, that was all as shown on the diagram; inside, sensors were mounted on poles every twenty yards. And then there were the roving security waldos. He hoped there wasn't some extra bit of security that hadn't shown up in the software.

It was 7:20. Time to get started.

He took an IR read on his surroundings, and then called up his systems menu and shut down his coolant systems, which shed through his skin the heat generated by his reactor. He pulled the spray bottle out that was tucked into his belt, and began spraying himself all over.

Depending on how much he exerted himself, he estimated he should have around twenty minutes before the forced shutdown and emergency venting kicked in, when the proxy's core temperature reached 200 degrees Fahrenheit. That wasn't nearly as much time as it sounded like.

Daniel shut down all unnecessary systems and remained still while waiting for his surface temperature to cool down to match the pale, heat-reflecting dunes. Median dune temperature—his target skin temp—was about 82 degrees. He watched the little red core-temperature indicator needle creep up the right side of his vision, ever faster, while the skin-temp indicator crept down on the left, ever slower—

Core temp at 108.6, skin temp at 100.0 . . .

Core temp at 114.0, skin temp at 93.8 . . .

Core temp at 124.1, skin at 90.8 . . .

After fourteen minutes the spray bottle was empty, and his skin temp hovered at 84.2 degrees. Core temp had climbed above 140. With his own IR he could see that his outstretched hands were a shade brighter than the surrounding terrain. But he needed every remaining second to make it to the terminal before systems shutdown.

It'll have to do, Daniel thought. He dashed across the highway and crossed the drainage ditch. After making sure no cars were coming in either direction, he sprinted for the rolls of razor wire, leapt over them, and—steeling himself—grabbed hold of the fence.

When hand touched wire, the idea of touching barbed wire juiced up with 50,000 amps of instant death overcame his rational mind. Fear threw him back to his own body. He was breathing shallowly and sweating, despite the room's comfortable temperature. Come on, Sornsen. Get your butt back there. He sank back into the squish and concentrated.

Contact. Download. Barbs dug into his skin. He held on carefully, so as not to tear skin. Muting the pain, he scaled up the swaying strands of razor-edged wire.

Core temp was around 157. That gave him just a few minutes to get past the grid and into the building. Enough time, if he hustled. He jumped, landed ankle-deep in sand, and started running.

The IR sensors didn't move, but he felt horribly exposed under their silent black glare. Core temp 161, skin temp 83.9. He heard something, and ducked behind a low rise, rolling, as a large security waldo lumbered past. He lay silent and tried to calm down—from its behavior, it wasn't looking for any IR anomalies, just making its rounds—but the damn thing took forever to move out of range, past the shoulder of a hangar. Then Daniel got up and started to run again.

Core temp accelerated upward: 168 . . . 180 . . . 192. He dodged past the sensors. Fifty feet to go. I'm not going to make it. *Fuck.*

Onto the concrete, with less than a second to spare. Core temp above 198, and still in view of the last row of IR sensors. He hit the emergency vent manually—no choice; better to stay mobile—and luck blessed him. A scram jet, which had just landed, passed him within several yards as the core cooling systems kicked in: his skin temp soared and steam erupted from his mouth, ears, and anus. Muting his hearing, he darted over beneath the scram and ran along beneath it till he reached the terminal, then ducked inside an employee entrance.

By the time he reached the main baggage-handling area, fortunately, the steam venting had tapered off. The baggage handling was all automated, but he did spot a worker or two in a set of glass-walled offices overlooking the conveyors and sorters. He kept his head down and kept equipment between him and them. Core temp down to 165, and slowly falling. Skin temp was above 115. He'd better not bump into anyone. His shirt and pants were soaked; he prayed it would be attributed to sweat.

The spaceport schematic gave him the right door; Daniel slipped out into the corridor amid the other travelers. He checked his internal chronometer: it was 7:40 on the nose.

At Gate 4B he slouched down into a chair beside Fox. Fox started and held his hand above Daniel's forearm, which lay on the armrest, then touched it and swore, softly.

"Ya jink?"

Daniel grinned. "Fine. Where's Paint?"

Fox gestured with his chin at the line of people waiting to get boarding passes. Paint was nearing the head of the line. At the very front, a couple with an older child and a baby was creating a scene. In a loud voice the man said, slapping the counter, "What do you mean we don't have seats? Our reservations were *confirmed!* Our tickets are right here!"

"I'm terribly sorry, sir," the attendant behind the counter said, "but there's been some confusion. You'll—"

"You're damn right there has! I demand to speak to your supervisor."

The woman with him tried to calm him down, but he brushed her away and the baby started crying. The attendant was making a call. Daniel was half afraid the man was going to slug someone. In a moment a woman in a Lagrange Spaceways uniform came up. She listened to the man's explanation and looked at their paperwork.

"I agree that there's been a terrible mistake," she said. "There appears to be an error in our computer system. Unfortunately I can't get you on this flight. Weight intake at the orbitals is carefully controlled, and we can't bump any of the other passengers. But I can take your names and resubmit your flight application automatically. I'm afraid it'll be another six weeks before—"

"*Six weeks?*" the woman repeated. "We've sold everything we have! We have no place to stay!"

"You'll get us on that shuttle," the man said, shaking a finger in the supervisor's face, "or I'll have your job."

By this time a security guard had come up. The man took a look at him and then turned to the woman.

"Come on, Brenda," he said, and stormed off. The woman followed, crying quietly, trailed by the older girl, and the baby had started to wail.

Paint looked over at Fox and Daniel with a nano-wince.

After all that, liftoff was—almost—a letdown. They had seats in almost the exact center of the spaceliner. The engines' roar deafened them as the shuttle started to rise, and flames licked at the windows' exterior. Acceleration pressed them into their seats. They shook and rocked and jiggled. Nothing like sitting atop a prolonged explosion to give you a bit of a thrill.

Daniel reconsidered. A letdown . . . ? Na-a-ah . . .

As soon as they'd gained enough velocity to attain orbit and acceleration had tapered off, making speech possible again, Daniel told Paint and Fox, "I'm going to unplug and get some rest. See you in a couple hours."

He closed his proxy's eyes, called up the linkware, set the proxy on autopilot–sleep mode, then pulled off his beanie back in Carli's apt and rubbed his scalp around the jack. He thought about the family that they'd bumped, and felt bad. The cat lifted its head and eyed Daniel.

"Mrrraow?"

"You and me both, pal," he said.

CARLI

WHO SO BELIEVETH IN TAYLOR

"Byron, wait up," Carli said.

He turned and paused; she bounded up to him and grabbed his arm—partly to regain her balance and keep from shooting past him in an arc toward the ceiling, partly in entreaty. He grabbed a handhold and stabilized them both.

She gestured back toward the conference room. "Byron, how could you go along with this scheme? The woman is completely deranged. Stealing an interstellar probe ship . . ."

He shrugged. "It's complicated. You start down a path; you don't always know where you're going to end up. This way." Holding her arm, he led her around a corner. "But she's not deranged. She has some kind of hormonal imbalance. Her moods are affected. Not her intellect."

" 'Affected'?" She scoffed. "I guess that's one word for it."

He opened a door and gestured for her to enter. It was one of his labs. Two technicians were running some sort of test using an oscillating sensor field.

"Take a break, ladies," he said.

"Ay, ay, sir," one said, snapping him a mock salute, and they hustled out of the room, leaving Byron alone with Carli. He sat down on a lab stool and studied her.

"Are you afraid of death, Carli?" he asked.

She scowled. "What does that have to do with anything?"

A long pause, while he gazed into the air over her head, fingers locked behind his neck.

"I don't know if you heard, Lisa died four years ago."

Carli winced. "Oh, God. I hadn't heard. What happened?"

"Yellow fever. Contaminated water supply. A mutated form, completely resistant to treatment. And Rosie died a year or so later, of an aneurysm we didn't know was there." Rosie was his wife, who couldn't have been older than her mid-forties; Lisa, his little girl, who would have been two or three at the time.

"That's rough. I'm very sorry."

"Rosie's and Lisa's deaths hit me hard, Carli. I was left with a huge emptiness inside. Death robbed me of everything that mattered."

Carli thought about her brother, Dennis, about his lingering death. She remembered his blue, lizard-skin hands twitching on the covers, that last time she'd seen him, and she drew a long, slow breath. "Yeah. I think I can understand that."

"And from—oh, about the age of twenty-eight or so," he went on slowly, "I've been watching my own body's systems slowly wind down. And you know what? I don't want to die."

Carli looked at him for a moment. "But you *are* going to die some-day, you know. You'd better find a way to make peace with that fact. Not waste your life kowtowing to a madwoman, chasing wild dreams."

He cocked a finger. "And *that* is where you're wrong. Dr. Taylor isn't mad, and her research isn't just about waldos and the nets. It's about extended life."

"Oh?"

"Mm-hmm. She'll go on at great length about how she and Dr. Sullivan are doing a legal study of the crèche-born to improve the waldo face. What she won't tell you is that in tandem, they've been pursuing a highly *illegal* study of life-extending drugs. Nanotech drugs that clean out all the debris and repair the damaged DNA in our cells. She and the kids have all had the treatments. I put all this together a year or so ago, shortly after I joined the Menagerie, and Marsh admitted it when I confronted him with what I'd found. They'll be giving me a beanlink and starting me on the treatments after we launch."

Carli gave him a skeptical look. He gestured at a computer termi-nal. "Look it up yourself, if you like. You'll find Marshall Sullivan's name on all sorts of research papers, back in the twenties, thirties, and forties, looking for nanotech drugs that keep the body from aging. Sul-livan was on the trail of a series of treatments that would lead to ex-tended life. Suddenly he disappears from the literature, and a year or two later he's here, doing this highly classified waldo research with Patricia Taylor. Why do you think that is?"

"I have no idea."

"I'll tell you why, and it's also why the project is in even bigger trouble than they're letting on. The powers that are funding this project have been investing in life-extension research on the crèche children—research that wasn't included in the presidential briefings, hasn't been approved, and who knows if anyone other than Taylor or Sullivan knows about it? . . . Though I'm betting *someone* in power does. They couldn't have gotten this far without that level of support."

She thought about Dennis again, and her father. Drugs that cleaned up damaged DNA. And the project had started up during the war, sixteen years ago. Which meant that the timing would be just about perfect, for a man desperate for a way to save his slowly dying son, back then.

Her dad knew.

"Jesus, Byron."

"This project gets shut down, and all that will come out."

"How do you know all this?"

He shrugged. "I'm a nosy SOB. Kept digging till things started making sense. This whole project started because Richard Quintelle Blaine didn't want to die, forty-five years ago. He kicked things off back in twenty-two by giving Marshall Sullivan a private grant to figure out how to keep him alive forever. I found the funding approval in an obscure electronic archive."

"Blaine? The trillionaire who spent all that money on Brainsicle technology, in the oughts?"

"Yep. Founder and first CEO of Waldos, Inc."

"Wait a minute, wait a minute. You're telling me that there are drugs now that'll make you live forever—?"

"Not forever, for certain, but definitely for a long, long time. They're not sure just how long yet. Marsh told me that Taylor has been taking the drugs for almost thirty years. She's a hundred and twenty-four."

"She's *what?*"

He looked smug. "A hundred and twenty-four. You can look that one up, too."

"I can't get used to these bodies that aren't people's real bodies."

"They're real. Just not flesh and blood."

Taylor, 124 years old. Carli shook her head, trying to clear it. "Those machines are no substitute for flesh and blood. Surely you can't be blind to all the things those kids have been deprived of."

"They've been deprived of *death*, Carli! Their immune systems don't work!"

"Maybe that was true thirty or forty years ago, but there've been gene treatments for most immune disorders for almost two decades now. Those kids needn't have been taken from their families, deprived of a normal childhood. Sullivan was dissembling."

"Hideously expensive treatments, yes, maybe. Treatments that their families couldn't afford."

"And how much has been spent on them this way?"

He stared at her.

"Besides. They could still be given those treatments now, if the project were shut down, and be gently reintegrated to society at large. Maybe Taylor and Sullivan will be in deep shit if the project's shut down—I would hope so!—but I certainly don't buy her melodramatic assessment of the *kids'* fate."

Byron grimaced. "Well, actually, they've spent their developmental years immobile, in a low-gee environment, with just enough electrical stimulus of their musculature and nervous systems to keep their bodies from failing. Their bodies haven't grown normally. And they've been altered surgically and biotechnically. They can't survive outside their crèches anymore."

Carli groaned and slapped hands over her face. "Oh, please. I can't take this! I've stepped into a nightmare!"

Byron touched her arm; she jerked away.

"It just takes some getting used to," he said. "It's really not horrible at all. Just different. Haven't you read any of Hans Moravek's work, or Marvin Minsky's, or Li Chan Thunder's? We're not our bodies. What makes us unique is our intellect. Information, sentience. Intelligence. That's what defines us as human."

"Oh, bullshit."

"Are you saying a quadriplegic is better off dead than beanlinked?" he demanded.

"Of course not." Carli leaned against the counter and rubbed at her eyes. Fatigue was making it hard for her to think. "This is too weird for me. Look, I don't care what you guys' motives are; this is wrong."

"Why?"

"Why? *Why?*" She sighed, exasperated. "All right. Let's leave aside the whole question of the kids, for now, and even my kidnapping—I've been fucking *kidnapped*, Byron! Two federal agents were killed trying to protect me! That's a major felony!"

He colored. "I feel badly about that. I'm sorry."

"That makes me feel much better; you have no idea. But never mind that. Let's pretend I'm not bugged as shit about being dragged up here against my will, about the two men killed in the process, about what's been done to these kids. Byron . . . have you ever heard the term *grand larceny?*"

He smiled, slightly. "Grand Theft, Space Ship."

"God *damn* it—I'm serious! You guys are planning to steal something that took decades of effort on the part of hundreds of thousands! You want to steal a one-of-a-kind ship worth many billions of dollars, *and* all its contents—not to mention the fuel it's taken years to stockpile." She cocked a finger and put it to his head. "You're putting a bullet right into the head of the interstellar space effort. *Blam!*" She pulled the trigger. He jumped, slightly, and pushed her hand away with a frown. "There's no way it'll survive this," she said.

"You don't understand," he protested, but she lifted a feeble hand, suddenly exhausted. "Please. No more. I need to rest. May I rest for a while?"

He chewed his lip and didn't say anything for a moment. "Carli . . . OK, yeah, you can rest. I'll take you back to your room."

At the door to her quarters, he said, "We only have two days. We can't afford for you to spend a lot of time pondering whether our cause is just. You have to make up your mind quickly. In the next six hours, Taylor's going to need an answer." He held out his hands. "Help us, Carli. Help me. Please."

"Enough, already. Good night." She pushed him back and closed the door. When she tried it, it was, of course, locked.

She leaned her head against the cool metal and closed her eyes.

FREEZE!

They found him.

It was only moments after he had unplugged. He had just made himself some more toast and tea and was coming back into the front room, intending to take it all to bed and nibble while reading a magazine. His plans changed when a police waldo broke down the door. It rolled in, crushing wood beneath its treads, bristling with weaponry, its camera and weapons platforms scraping wood and paint from the doorjamb.

"FREEZE," it boomed. Daniel froze. The cat yowled and squirmed under the couch. Daniel thought, eyeing the damage, Carli's going to be *pissed*.

The waldo scanned Daniel and the rest of the room, and then four men swarmed around it and jumped Daniel. Toast went flying. Hot tea sloshed on the pants of one of the cops, who swore and cuffed Daniel. Bastard—it's your own damn fault, Daniel thought. He got carpet-burn on his already raw face while they searched him, read him his rights, and handcuffed him. Then they hauled him to his feet.

This being-jumped business was getting old, fast.

The local FBI office was downtown. They raced him there in a screaming, flashing, hybrid electric collocar—all the way from the Heights to the Valley, zooming across multiple lanes, dodging all number of human- and electric-powered vehicles—and hissed up to the curb at 8th Street.

They pulled him out of the car. The air was cool and breezy. The downtown canopy was in the process of retracting across the enormous, transparent metaglass frame that arced high above. The cops hustled him around the canopy locks, which were being dismantled by a crew of assorted waldos, and across the square.

Instant celebrity. Bystanders crowded around, craning to see him amid his cordon of federal bully types; hovering news waldos and reporters shone lights and stuck microphones toward him and the lead bully, asking questions. It was clear from their questions that they thought *he* was the kidnapper.

"No comment," the lead bully said, pushing them aside. "Make way, please. No comment."

They ushered him into one of the scrapers surrounding the fountained square, through a foyer whose granite floor was polished to a high gleam, and up in the elevator to a floor with a big shield and sign on its wall: "Federal Bureau of Investigation." He was hustled through a reception area and bull pen, and into a small room with a table and three chairs, where they sat him down and left him alone.

Out the window, across the square, was Carli's office building. Beyond the fringe of buildings was the upper edge of the metaglass bones that made up the canopy frame. In the distance, beyond the train lines and the freeway, rose the twin crests of the Sandia Mountains: a matte painting of purple mountains' majesty against the weird, dark blue of the sky and cloud stacks of cotton puff and kitten fur.

It had been incredibly stupid to leave Austin, and even more stupid to stay at Carli's place. They could easily have traced him to Albuquerque from Austin, and where else in Albuquerque to start looking for him? Maybe he'd be framed for Krueger's murder. He chewed at his lip and worried at the handcuffs with his wrists. What were Paint and Fox going to do with his proxy? If he didn't get back there by the time the shuttle reached Shasta Station, the spaceliner crew would assume his proxy had suffered a heart attack or something, and cart it off to the habitat's hospital. He could just picture the look on the examining physician's face.

Forever later, an older man in an expensive envie suit came in, accompanied by a bully in a Congressional Security Agency uniform. Daniel stared: The older man was Senator D'Auber. Live and in person.

"Remove the handcuffs, please, Mike," the senator told the bully, who did so.

Daniel rubbed his wrists with a sigh.

Senator D'Auber pulled out a chair and sat down across the table, looking rumpled and tired. He nodded at the bully, who set a disruption-field generator on the table and turned it on. A crawly black torus expanded from the generator's emitter, changing shape as it did so. It swallowed them like a swarm of bugs; in a second, they three were inside a silvery sphere a meter and a half in diameter. A soft light issued from the generator and reflected off the sphere's inner surfaces.

Daniel's eyes widened. Could D'Auber really get away with interfering with the feds' electronic monitoring devices, right in their own headquarters?

The senator smiled wryly at his expression.

"Daniel Sornsen?"

Daniel nodded. D'Auber stuck out his hand, and Daniel took it. The senator had a warm hand and a firm grip.

"I'm desperate to find my daughter," he said. "I need your help."

Daniel sighed, eyeing D'Auber. Can I trust this man?

"How can I help?"

D'Auber sat forward with an intense gaze. "Tell me everything that has happened."

BREAKING UP IS HARD TO DO

Pablo handed prime to Buddy and ducked out as the door closed behind Aunt Carli and Uncle Byron.

"I'm floating surveillance on you," he radioed Uncle Byron, who gave him a dental-auditory acknowledgment. Pablo tracked them, jumping from one security camera to the next—

And spotted Marines, a pair of enlisted men, heading right for them, around a bend.

Pablo scanned for options. There was a hall on the right, up ahead.

"Turn right," he said, "hurry!"

Uncle Byron did so, hustling Aunt Carli aside and into one of his high-security labs . . . out of harm's way. Barely in time.

With a sigh of relief, he returned to the conference room.

Buddy took prime as the door closed behind Aunt Carli.

With the door's latching, Mother completely lost control. Shrieking invectives, she grabbed the massive, stone conference table and tried to overturn it. And *it moved*.

Buddy leapt forward to restrain her, but couldn't keep a grip. She threw him off and scrambled across the table toward Uncle Marsh.

"Fucker!" she screamed. "I was *fine* till you came along! You're poisoning me!"

Uncle Marsh stumbled back out of her reach, knocking over a chair. Buddy grabbed for an ankle and missed. Jenna pushed in front of Uncle Marsh as Mother lunged again; Mother struck her, and the two proxies slammed against the far wall.

He sensed Pablo's return.

=Look at her. Tell me she's not crazy.=

Pablo stared at Mother, unable to bring himself to reply.

He had just figured it out. She was dying.

"Stop it!" Aunt Jenna yelled. She finally got Mother in a solid hold, and slammed her against the wall. It did no good. She did it again, and again, till Mother stopped surging toward Uncle Marsh. "Patricia, *stop!*"

The fight went out of Mother all at once, and her rage shriveled as quickly as it had bloomed. She shrank into the corner, out of Aunt Jenna's grasp, and her eyes hollowed out. She was going far away, someplace none of them could follow.

Finally Pablo's thought penetrated.

Mother. No. I don't want you to go.

=Dying?=

=Dying.=

A doubt formed, quickly suppressed. =We should be so lucky.=

Pablo snarled. =I've had enough of you. Let go.=

Pablo grabbed at the face linkware—

—and took prime.

And Buddy—

—relinquished control.

The door burst open. There stood Uncle Alan.

"What the hell is going on in here?" he demanded.

=Take it. Who needs you?=

=Get out of here. Get out of my head. You make me sick.=

=I've got news for you, Mama's boy. It's my head, too.=

Buddy vanished. And good riddance.

He threw shields up.

=Dane?= he called. =Can you hear me? Come on out. We've got work to do.=

PLAN B

Everyone but Mother turned to look at Uncle Alan, who stood at the entrance with arms akimbo.

"Well?" he said.

Uncle Marsh cleared his throat. "Alan."

His voice roused Mother, still huddling in the corner; she filled her body and stood, stiff and awkward: unfurling like an embattled flag in a powerful wind. Holding out a hand to restrain Uncle Marsh, she replied, "Just a staff meeting, Alan. Surely you're familiar with the concept." He scowled. "What do you want?"

"I heard shouting."

"Shouting?" Her eyebrows went up. "I didn't hear anything. Did you, Marsh?"

"Not a thing."

"Jenna?"

"Me, neither."

"Pablo?"

He shook his head, not trusting himself to speak.

"Hmmm." Mother turned back to Uncle Alan with a shrug. "It must have come from somewhere else. Perhaps there's a mechanical problem down in the electroplating area. Or one of the troops had his radio turned up too loud."

Uncle Alan gazed at her suspiciously.

"Is there something else I can do for you?" Mother asked, baring her teeth.

"I want your weekly report immediately. You're late with it. Don't think I haven't noticed that you've been avoiding me."

"It's nothing personal, I assure you. I've been busy."

"Busy or not, you have an obligation to keep me apprised. I'll expect you in my quarters at noon."

"Very well. In half an hour, then."

He left. She melted into a chair and laid her head on her arms.

Pablo went to her, hesitated, touched her shoulder. She didn't look up. He withdrew his hand but remained close.

"Good thing he didn't happen by a couple minutes earlier," Aunt Jenna remarked.

"Yeah," Uncle Marsh said. "Patricia, this is a small habitat. The place is crawling with Marines. We can't keep Carli Mac—D'Auber away from them forever."

"It's not for much longer."

Aunt Jenna sat down next to her. "Realistically. What can she do in a day or two? Even if she *does* decide to help us, I don't care how brilliant she is, two days is not enough time to get familiar with the labs, much less make a breakthrough."

Mother sighed and lifted her head as if it weighed a ton. "All Byron needs is another pair of eyes on his work. He's no genius, but he's no idiot, either. He's made real progress. And I've read the write-ups; I believe they were close to a breakthrough years ago, before she lost the technology to OMNEX." A pause. "And, to be crude about it, even if she doesn't give us a breakthrough, she's useful in another way."

"Because of her father," Uncle Marsh said. "As a hostage."

Mother lifted a hand in a shrug. Uncle Marsh groaned. "How did we come to this pass?"

Uncle Byron reentered, closing the door. "I gave her six hours to rest and think it over." He looked around. "What's wrong?"

"Uncle Alan came in," Pablo said in a low voice, as Aunt Jenna said something to Mother, "just after you left."

"Oh, God." Uncle Byron dropped into a chair, eyes wide. "Did he see or hear anything?"

Pablo made a wavering motion with his hand. "It was close."

"And I'm telling you, Number One, we can't overcome a human crew of forty-four with an eleven-second signal lag," Aunt Jenna was saying. With a glance at Uncle Byron she added, "And no offense to Byron, but at this late date there's no way we can count on him and MacLeod, I mean D'Auber, to come up with the breakthrough we need."

Uncle Byron frowned. "I still say there's a chance we can pull it off. I'm certain we're just overlooking something incredibly simple, some really stupid design flaw. . . ." At Aunt Jenna's expression, he said, "You haven't seen Carli at work. If OMNEX hadn't pulled the stunt it had, she'd have found the solution years ago."

"Maybe. But I still say we need a Plan B."

Mother said after a moment, "All right, then. You may as well know. There's a Plan B."

"Tell us," Uncle Marsh said, when she didn't go on.

"I've had a couple of the kids studying *Exodus*'s systems. They've found an alternative, if we can't use omni technology." She paused. "We can infiltrate the ship's syntellect systems using plain-vanilla radio technology and disable the life-support systems, and just blow the air out the locks. We'll clean up when we—"

Aunt Jenna cut her off with a shouted, "No!" and Uncle Byron came to his feet. Pablo looked from one to the other of the adults, confused.

Uncle Marsh shook his head. "We can't. That's going too far. Patricia . . ." He sighed heavily. "Your judgment is affected by your illness. Two people have already died; that's two too many."

=More than that,= someone whispered. =More than two.=

=Who is that?= he asked. =Buddy, is that you?=

No answer came. Pablo grew scared. No way. Two had died: the bodies of the federal cops protecting Aunt Carli from Mother. Only those two.

"The deaths are regrettable, Number Two, but I'm quite serious when I say I won't let harm come to my kids. We've come too far to turn back now." Mother was on her feet suddenly, pacing. "It's not just the kids. We've got eternity in a bottle. You know as well as I do we can't let it get into others' hands." She faced him across the table. "Think about it for a minute, Marsh. They find out we've developed extended-life treatments and they'll go insane with lust. We'll be the subjects of a search the likes of which no one has ever experienced. There'll be no place to hide."

His shoulders slumped. "I took an oath to protect life."

"You'll be protecting life. The children's lives." She walked to the end of the room, turned, and planted her palms on the table. From there she looked at each of them, and her passion, her utter conviction, was an almost palpable force radiating from her.

"Let's face facts," she said. "More people are going to die. I've done everything I can to engineer a low-casualty plan. But the fact is, even if we oust the Marines and support staff from Kaleidas without a single casualty—which ain't likely, folks—when we launch, *people will die.*

"It's unfortunate. But we have no choice. *Exodus* is our only hope of saving our kids and protecting our work. We have to proceed. Even if it means the probe astronauts have to die, too."

She met each of their eyes in turn. Pablo met her gaze calmly. He didn't understand why the others were so distressed when it was just bodies they were talking about killing. But that was the way it worked in the similes, too, so maybe that was just how they were supposed to act.

"Is there a way to disable the ship without killing the astronauts?" Jenna asked.

"Even if we could, we'd then have to deal with a group who out-number us and would have had time to prepare for us," Mother said. "The crèches could be put at risk that way. I won't brook putting the kids in any danger."

"Look, guys," Uncle Byron said. "Give me a chance with Carli. There's still a chance we can solve the omni problem."

Mother thought it over and gave him a nod. "All right. We don't have to commit ourselves to an alternative till late tomorrow. But I want a definite commitment from her in six hours, Byron. Or we go to Plan B right away."

"All right."

"Now, if you'll excuse me," she said, heading for the door, "I have a phone call to make."

PEEKABOO . . .

Buddy wouldn't listen to her repeated pleas to spare Carli. Dismayed, feeling helpless, Dane retreated to her own little corner.

She didn't want to watch Carli's body die.

Instead she observed the operation of the linkware menus, closely, peeking out through the gaps in Pablo's and Buddy's concentration, while Pablo programmed his simile and Buddy piloted a body using the twin set of linkware. I can do that, she thought.

So she waited till Buddy and Pablo were both occupied, and darted up to the linkware—set up another face twin, made her selection—and tapped into the station's monitoring control systems. It was an arrangement Pablo had already set up, so all she had to do was make a selection from the menu. From there she could hop around to all the different views.

Dane wandered from camera node to camera node, getting a sense of the system's extent and structure. The place Pablo and Buddy thought of as Home had three big areas. The first was a place where long, clear tubes carried glowing red and orange liquids to bubbling vats where blades scraped dark stuff off the top of the bright liquid, and troughs where bars and rods were formed from this liquid, then plunged into water, causing billowing explosions of steam, and where those rods and bars were loaded into cargo pods.

The second big area was a place where automata made body parts and other, more arcane devices. The third was a warren of many large and small labs, where technicians and waldos performed experiments both on various pieces of equipment and body parts, and on people Dane was coming to realize were the crèche-mates who inhabited Pablo's and Buddy's thoughts. In addition there were also some smaller areas: banks of private quarters and offices.

So many nooks and crannies to explore!

She spent some time in the body-manufacturing area, watching the body parts being made. Rods, tubes, and other parts of various shapes and sizes were dipped in vats of amber fluid. They went in dull silver-grey and came out as if dipped in essence of liquid rainbow: be-decked in colorful swirls and whorls. Holes were bored in these parts by machines, sending sparks flying, and nuts and bolts and wiring were inserted. In other areas, sheets of plastic skin and musculature, riddled with tiny tubes, were rolled off big skeins and shaped around frames of metal or metaceramic. Eyeballs of every conceivable color were con-cocted and assembled, and sent rolling down conveyors, bouncing into bins where they waited to be fitted to small metal plates. Jaws were fitted to metaceramic skulls, skeletal hands and feet fitted to arm and leg bones.

So that's how our bodies are made, Dane thought. She thought about the others—those like Carli and the people she'd met during her wanderings; the ones whose bodies were constructed differently—and wondered what process was used to manufacture those bodies.

In one location, inserted into a circular section where ceilings and floors had been cut away, was a monster of a machine: a very, very tall titanium tube with a grid at its open base and dark boxes attached down its length. On top of this enormous tube sat a big, complicated mechanism, to which flexible piping ran from an arrangement of vats on the floor above. She tweaked the views and saw that three of the vats' lids were open, and machines were loading massive, whitish-silver bricks into them. The big tube dangled from cables above a titanium-reinforced floor.

In the quarters and offices, she eavesdropped on a number of events. Four men were playing cards in one room; two people were playing with each other's skin surfaces and genitals in another; people were eating in a cafeteria. A man that Pablo knew—he called him Uncle Alan—was having a conversation with a jello projection of an-other man.

They were talking. She made a recording of their conversation, summoned all her concentration and listened, though of course it took her much longer to decode the conversation than it took the two men to hold it; since she was forced to listen, play back, and listen again, every few words.

". . . Sam Krueger's murder," the other man was saying.

"Oh? What *is* the latest, then?" Uncle Alan asked.

The other man shook his head. "The FBI is investigating. One of the Austin people appears to be implicated, a Daniel Sornsen."

Uncle Alan showed surprise.

"You know him?" the other man asked.

Uncle Alan shook his head. "Not exactly. I met him the other day. He and Dr. Krueger waldoed up to give us a status report on the most recent proxy theft from Austin. Do you think Taylor and her cronies are involved?"

"I doubt it. But it doesn't much matter for our purposes, does it? Fact is, someone somewhere obviously has it in for the Kaleidas program, and they're doing a lot of our dirty work for us. We may be able to just sit tight and let the FBI uncover all the dirt D'Auber and Taylor have been hiding. Everything is going to come apart for them, fast and hard, without any help from us." The other man templed his fingers, silent for a moment. "The one wild card here is D'Auber."

"The senator."

A nod. "Mmm. He has enough influence to complicate matters. He has strong connections in certain segments of the administration from way back. For instance, I've been told he and Boczek graduated from Harvard together, and are close acquaintances, if not friends."

"Manuelita Boczek? Head of the FBI?"

The other man nodded again. "So it would facilitate matters if the investigators could get their hands on documents that directly implicate him, sooner rather than later. Think you can help there?"

"Hmmm. I'll do some digging and see what I can turn up," Uncle Alan said.

AT THE BOTTOM OF THE FOOD CHAIN

Some indeterminate amount of time after Carli finally fell asleep, something woke her. She lay there in the dark, wits slowly converging. A pattern of phosphorescent colors flickered across the wall and ceiling. The colors hadn't been there when she'd gone to sleep.

With a frown, she sat up. In a jello-tube that also hadn't been there before—it must have been hidden behind a panel in the wall—was a jello. Carli threw off the covers and padded barefoot across the cool tile floor to examine it.

It was a schematic of part of a building. Given the apparently cylindrical structure, it seemed likely to be the habitat. A small, blinking blue square was in an interior room. Red triangles studded the hallways and rooms around it, and at one location was a gold circle. As soon as Carli neared the jelly, the blue square stopped blinking and left the room. It moved through the hallways, avoiding the red triangles— some of which were moving—till it came to the gold circle. When the blue square entered the gold circle, the circle erupted in a flash of light and the map dissolved. Then the schematic reappeared with the blue square back in the room. The jello ran through the same scenario again. Then again.

She heard a whisper of sound and turned. The door was open. Someone was helping her escape.

Unless it was a trap.

But what did they have to gain? She was already in their control. They could kill her at any time, if that was their aim.

Besides, it beat sitting in a locked room. Or wandering aimlessly through enemy territory on her own.

She turned back to the map.

Out the door and left, go ahead five doors, turn left again, up a shaft for sixteen floors, ahead four doors, right, eight doors forward, pause for . . . some kind of signal? the blue square waited there till red triangles got out of the way . . . then across a tee, and ahead two more doors. Carli turned it into a mantra: left, ahead five, left, up sixteen, ahead four, right, ahead eight, pause for signal, across tee, ahead two. She breathed it to herself as she pulled on her jeans and shoes, and slipped out the door.

An ovoid hatch was on her left, five doors down from her room. She opened it and stuck her head in. It was a vertical tunnel with a ladder mounted on the wall. Painted on the far wall in large white letters was the designation "18E." The tunnel extended many stories downward, and perhaps a third as far upward. She grabbed hold of the ladder, closed the hatch, and ascended. Oddly, the next floor up was 17E. They must use a numbering system that started at the habitat's "top" floor: the one closest to the orbital's center of mass. Even at less than half a gee, at the top of her long climb she was heaving great breaths, exhausted and dizzy. Altitude sickness, probably. The air was quite thin—substantially thinner than Albuquerque's at five thousand feet, or even Santa Fe's, at almost seven thousand. Though she imagined that, as during her stint in orbit, they probably used a substantially higher oxygen content than the Earth standard of 21 percent.

She cracked the hatch open at level 2E and listened. Voices were talking, growing louder. Red triangles? It must be. Once the talkers had passed and their footsteps had faded, Carli opened the hatch further and stuck her head out.

No one was around, though she could still hear noises, faintly. Voices, and machine sounds. She bounded out of the hatch—too hard—struck the other wall, and grabbed at a handhold to steady herself. Then, straightening, she crept down the hall, toward the sounds.

Ahead four, right, ahead eight, pause.

She had reached the tee. To her right was the source of the noise: voices and, not machines—or rather, not only machines—but cutlery against plates. She'd reached a cafeteria. She caught a glimpse through the open doorway of at least a dozen people seated at long tables.

Something was coming. Carli ducked into a doorway. A waldo or robot cruised toward her, then turned toward the cafeteria, loaded down with clean flatware and cups. Two men in uniform crossed the intersection, doing the low-gee shuffle and laughing as they headed for the cafeteria.

Marines! She stepped out and started to call out after them, when a figure across the tee waved at her. It was the young man-proxy from the meeting. He put a finger to his lips, then signaled her again. She looked both ways, and hurried across the tee.

"This way," he said in a low voice, and took her arm. At the end of the short, shadowed cul-de-sac was a door labeled: "Employees Only—DO NOT ENTER!"

They ducked inside as more people passed through the main corridor behind them.

The kitchen was large and completely automated. Mechanized ovens, tubs, and other devices stretched along one aisle; cleaning implements and tubs were spread out along the other. Robots bustled past, carrying tins filled with food, or loaded down with dirty dishes, cups, and cutlery.

"Come on," he said, hurrying her down the middle aisle, past the cooking and cleaning robots, with his hand grasping her arm above the elbow.

"Wait," she said. "Why are you helping me?"

He shook his head. "I'll explain later. Come on."

Near the back was a rubber-lined door that ended at knee height. It was labeled "CAUTION—Food Recycler—Throw Scraps Here. FOOD ONLY!"

The door opened as they approached. Carli tried to brake—"Wait! What are you doing?"—but he continued to propel her forward. His grip was unbreakable.

"In you go," he said, and she had only an instant to see the slashing blades in the shaft below, before he shoved her headfirst into the chute.

FURTHER DISRUPTION

It was the man's obvious distress over Carli that decided Daniel. He told Senator D'Auber everything.

When he reached the point at which he and Teru had discovered the abandoned Krueger proxy, D'Auber said, "It sounds as though Carli's kidnapper must be based in Kaleidas, then, not Austin."

"That's how it looks to me. I think someone from our sister project killed Samson Krueger and took his place, and used his position as a cover to try to kidnap or kill your daughter."

Senator D'Auber, a deep frown bunching his brow, sat back. The chair creaked. The bully cleared his throat. "A squad of Marines is stationed up there."

"True . . ."

"We can contact General Utney at the Pentagon."

"Not just yet, Mike. There are too many other possibilities; there could be people from both facilities colluding on this. Before we act, I—"

D'Auber's kelly chirped. "Encrypted omni call from Dr. Patricia Taylor at Kaleidas," it announced.

"Oh?" D'Auber's eyebrows shot up, and he eyed Daniel thoughtfully.

"Do you think she's involved, somehow?"

"Hmmm. I don't know. It's hard to believe, but it's equally hard to believe she wouldn't be aware . . ." He sighed, frowning. "Kelly, patch the call through."

So saying, he set his disc-shaped kelly on the table. Its jello-lens extended itself upward and expanded to twice its original size. A moment later Dr. Taylor appeared: a small, ephemeral presence on the tabletop.

"Senator."

"Doctor, I believe you know Daniel Sornsen."

Daniel lifted a hand in greeting. His heart beat hard at the sight of her.

"Why, yes, one of Sam Krueger's people," she said.

"Now, what can I do for you?" D'Auber asked.

"Umm, perhaps we should speak privately," she said.

The senator's glance followed hers to Daniel. He grunted.

"Daniel, will you excuse us? Mike, perhaps you'd better step out, too."

The bully looked surprised, but nodded. Daniel followed him through the disruption, the electric swarm. He went over to the window. The bully stood by the door, using his pocketknife to shave slivers off a small piece of soapstone he'd pulled from his cool-vest pocket. Nine stories below, tiny people milled around the square. In the street, miniature bikers, trikers, skaters, and ricky drivers passed by. The canopy was completely retracted now, and the early afternoon sun blazed down on glass, metal, and the fountain pool in the square, spawning reflections that burned his eyes. There was no sound, except for muted footsteps and voices outside the door, and the crackling hum of the disruption. Time passed.

"Mike, Daniel."

He turned. Senator D'Auber had shut off the disruption. He wore an oddly affectless expression.

"What happened?" Daniel asked.

"It was an unrelated matter," D'Auber said. "Well, I suppose we're finished here." He stood. "I want to thank you for your time, Mr. Sornsen."

Daniel's head spun. "Whoa . . . what about Carli? What about Kaleidas?"

D'Auber paused and looked at Daniel for a long moment. Then he went to the door. Hand on the knob, he said, "I've decided to handle things a different way. But thanks again for your cooperation, Mr. Sornsen."

"Wait." Daniel grabbed his arm. "You can't just drop it this way. What did she say to you? Did she threaten to hurt Carli?"

D'Auber gave Daniel a hard look that made him release his arm. "Don't get mixed up in this any further. Stay out of it."

Daniel started to protest. D'Auber leveled a finger at him. "*Drop it.* You're in way over your head already. If you aren't careful, you could find yourself in deep trouble. There are people who believe you are complicit in Sam Krueger's murder."

Daniel stared, stunned to speechlessness. A warning? Or a threat?

D'Auber's expression thawed a bit. "Go home, young man. Not to Austin—KaleidoScope is finished. Your real home. Or better yet, somewhere else altogether. Disappear. Start a new life. They won't come after you. I have that much clout left." He paused again. "Carli told me how you saved her life the other night. I'm grateful. Now forget all this and go home."

And he exited. The bully pocketed the disruption-field generator and followed, closing the door behind him. Daniel had, just barely, the presence of mind to wonder what his fate would have been if D'Auber *hadn't* been grateful.

BLACKOUT

While he was making some last adjustments to his latest simile code, the module they'd use in tonight's prep session, his top-level linkware menu lit up across his vision, sending the code to the background. The link settings were suddenly different—then back to their original settings—then reset again.

=What the hell are you up to?= he asked Buddy.

No answer. He tried to take prime, and suddenly he was staring at his coding again, confused.

A blackout. A big one; he'd lost at least twenty minutes. He hadn't had one of those for a very long time—not since he and Buddy had negotiated their careful, formal division of power, years ago.

Something strange was happening. From a long way away, he felt the surges of adrenaline, the thundering heart, the rapid breathing. Buddy's triumphant glee, and someone else's dismay and aversion, came to him as an image flashed through his mind: the soles of Carli D'Auber's shoes as she fell into a shaft with blades flashing at the bottom.

=Buddy—*what have you done?*=

Firing an alert to the other crèche-born, he bullied into the thicket of Buddy's defenses.

HERE'S TO THE REPTILIAN HINDBRAIN

Reflexively she tucked into a somersault as she fell, then forced her body to go straight and rigid so her feet dragged against the chute's far wall. At the same time she arched her back, expanding her arms and upper torso so that her arms, shoulders, and upper back dragged on the near wall. This slowed her low-gee fall to a slide down the narrowing chute.

She skidded to a halt maybe a foot, maybe less, above the blades. Their swift, metallic snick-*chop*, snick-*chop* sounded just beneath her buttocks.

Later, remembering, she couldn't believe how flawlessly right her response was. Good old reptilian, integrative processing.

A disinfectant smell mingled with the overpowering stench of spoiling food. Her left shoulder had gotten wrenched, but it wasn't so bad that it couldn't be ignored, for now. She looked up. Her attacker was gone. Food scraps came tumbling down from an upper level, pelting her face and torso. Spitting, shaking reconstituted mashed potatoes, lettuce, and ketchup out of her eyes and nose, she prayed no one dropped anything heavy.

Come on, Carli; you used to climb rock chimneys and cliff faces in the Jemez foothills as a kid. You can do this.

Pushing with hands and feet, she crept back up the shaft, inch by inch. Twice she slipped on food that slicked the sides of the chute, and nearly fell. Food hit her another time or two, slowing her ascent. The chute gradually expanded as she went up, till only her upper back touched the wall with her legs almost fully extended . . . and, fortunately, no further. By the time she reached the hatch, her left arm and back were throbbing, and she was trembling and sweating heavily.

The hatch was closed. With her right hand she felt along the lip as far as she could, up, down, and sideways. No catch, no way to open it from the inside. She wouldn't be able to hold on like this for long. Chop, chop, chop.

She hung there beside the door for what seemed like an eternity,

her yells for help echoing through the chute, but in reality it was probably only a minute or two before the hatch opened.

It was her attacker.

"Bless the crèches!" He reached in and grabbed her shirt. Twisting
his hand in the fabric, he pulled, and she lost her precarious purchase.
Carli screamed. Clamping a hand over her mouth, he hauled her out
of the chute, not bothering to fend off her blows and kicks, and
dropped her on the floor. Then he squatted next to her.

Hand still clamped over her mouth, he said, "I'm so sorry."

As he spoke, a coterie of man- and woman-proxies clustered
around. Behind them Carli thought she saw Marines gathering. Someone slapped a patch on her neck. The man-proxy released his hold on
her mouth and she called out to the Marines, but realized even as sight
and sound faded that she'd been drugged, and her pleas for help
emerged as nothing more than mutterings.

Her last thought was that maybe the Marines were in on this, too.

"STICK A SOCK IN IT" IS NORMALLY A FIGURE OF SPEECH

They let him go—didn't even tell him to stay in town in case they had further questions. The reporters and news waldos outside the building barely gave him a sniff.

He checked his kelly as he approached the subway station. The nets were crackling with the latest release: Senator Chauncy D'Auber had just been contacted by the kidnappers of his daughter, a Southeast Asian terrorist group nobody had ever heard of. Daniel snorted.

"Yeah, right."

There were further news breaks about Krueger's murder as well. Daniel skimmed them, shaking his head. KaleidoScope's power structure was about to come crashing down, from a very great height. Maybe D'Auber was right and Daniel should take this opportunity to get far, far away from falling shrapnel. He thought regretfully about Teru and Leanne, and his other friends.

But he had some unfinished business. After hopping lines twice, each time watching closely and finding no evidence he was being followed, he returned to Carli's place.

The entry to her apt had been amply retaped with "Police Barrier!" tape, and the door still lay on the living room floor. The cat was in the hall, sniffing at the elevator. Daniel picked up the cat, carried the animal back to the apt, and removed the tape. One of Carli's neighbors came by and peered in.

"Repairs," Daniel said, dropping the cat, who went over to a scratching post and began to tear at it. The woman, seeming satisfied, moved on.

Privacy was the first order of the day.

Tire tracks had gouged the door, but it was still in one piece. The hinges had been torn out of the door rather than the jamb; most of the screws still dangled in the hinges' holes, and a couple lay on the floor. The jamb and the locking bolts were still mostly OK.

He knocked a few loose chunks of wood off the jamb and door, sanded the worst of the splinters off, then put the door back in place, bolted it, and secured the hinges using longer screws that dug in past the damage to good wood. It'd do for now. Using her hole saw, he then cut around the area smashed through by her kidnapper, and cut a piece of thick plywood out of a crate in her storage closet, forming a circular wedge. The wedge he lined with wood glue and then pushed it into the hole in the door. Finally he cleaned his hands, sat down on Carli's squish-chair, and switched the netset to jelly mode.

The cat jumped in his lap. He petted the animal, absently, while he called up Carli's account to check for messages—they'd agreed that Paint and Fox would use her account for communications, in case Daniel's was tapped.

There were two messages. First, a man with a stethoscope dangling from his lab-coat pocket appeared in the jellowall, looking grave. "Ms. D'Auber, I'm Dr. Tardis. It's about Tania Forrest. I wonder if you could give me a call right away."

Then an older woman came on. The tear-streaked cheeks and moist eyes didn't conceal the meanness in her face. Holding a hanky to her nose, she said, shrilly, "It's *your* fault she's dead! You and your crazy nephew and his friends . . . abusing her, giving her drugs! I'm going to sue you for everything you've got!"

Daniel grimaced. The young woman had died. Damn.

He beanlinked in and canceled his proxy's autopilot, then dropped into proxy and opened his eyes. Paint and Fox eyed him.

"That you?" Paint asked.

"It's me," Daniel said—or tried to say. Something was blocking his speaker, inside his throat. And for that matter, his mouth felt strange. Something bad-tasting was packed in it. He poked a finger into his mouth, hooked fabric, and pulled it out . . . and out . . . and out.

It was a large tube sock. He stared at it, baffled.

"That's mine," Paint said, taking it.

"Why did you stuff a sock down my throat?"

The corners of Paint's mouth twitched. "You seemed to enjoy it at the time."

The remark pissed him off. Fox saw it in his face, and slugged Paint. To Daniel he said, "You were snoring really loud. People were complaining and we couldn't wake you."

"Don't worry," Paint said, deadpan. "Nobody saw. I put a blanket over us while I did it."

Daniel closed his eyes with a sigh and rubbed the bridge of his nose.

"Ice it," Fox told Paint. " 'S torqued enough."

"What took you so long?" Paint asked Daniel. "We were starting to worry."

He told them what had happened. Their expressions grew grave.

"Vile old shit," Paint said. "Abandoning Aunt Carli like that."

"He may have had no choice," Daniel said. "He seemed pretty messed up about the whole thing. And he kept my ass out of jail, which he didn't have to do."

"Probably figures this way ya'll put your pretty ass in danger trying to save Carli, while he'n claim no-fault. Minute it's jink for him, we're ice." Paint's gaze smoldered. "I've known him a long time. 'S a calculating, manipulative bastard."

" 'M on, Paint." Fox forged on in the face of Paint's glare. "You know he loves Carli."

"Then he should be up there himself, helping her, not interfering with *us*."

On arrival at Shasta Station, they and the other passengers were directed to the main concourse, where they were met by a young woman who showed them the habitat's emergency procedures. They were given the locations of Shasta's multitude of evac airlocks and the emergency stations, where they were to go if they heard the evacuation horns. Then they learned how to don a life bag.

The metacloth life bags, in bright red lockers at emergency gathering points all along the concourse and in corridors throughout the habitat, were made of reflective gold material. The bags had zippers inside and out, a large canister of air, which the user or someone outside the bag could open to activate air flow, a temperature-control unit, and some emergency food and water rations in a small box. There were also a couple large, one-size-fits-all diapers for the obvious purpose. Supposedly the bags were good for up to twelve hours for a single occupant, and had a radio beacon that was automatically initiated when the air canister's valve was opened.

Then they checked into the Shasta Hilton. Their room was maybe eight by ten, with a low ceiling, a set of bunks built into one wall and a tiny bathroom and even tinier closet on the other. The lower bunk was supposed to be a double bed, the higher one a single. A desk with jacks for assorted net connections was set into the wall beneath the window, which wasn't a portal but a jelly that projected a scene from outside the station. Next to the entry was a built-in, relatively low-tech jelly comunit.

"Cramped quarters," Daniel remarked, dropping the duffel on the floor.

"Yeah, but what a view." Paint bounded over to the jelly and looked out at the Earth and moon, both full. The moon was just now moving out from behind the Earth. Both wheeled lazily through an arc overhead, about to move out of view. Beyond, stars blazed. In the foreground, antennae, radio dishes, and other equipment were visible at the scene's periphery.

Paint unpacked his own comunit and peripherals from his carry-on bag while Fox unpacked the clothing and toiletries.

"I'm going to reconnoiter," Daniel said.

"Give me a minute and I'll go, too," Fox replied.

Daniel thought he caught a frown on Paint's face, but Paint's hair fell like a curtain, obscuring his profile as he knelt next to the bag. A moment later, when they were ready to go, Fox gave Paint a kiss and whispered something to him. Paint shrugged rather irritably, but seemed mollified.

First Daniel and Fox visited the Tourist Information kiosk and spoke to a rep about the assorted tours available, and then they headed up to the interhabitat elevators to watch the passenger- and cargo-handling processes and schedules. Fox took surreptitious notes. After that they grabbed some fast food at McDonald's and sat down at a table overlooking the carnival down on the main concourse.

"Queers jade you," Fox said, as they munched Soy Macs and fries, "nespah?"

Daniel frowned and played with the straw in his chocolate shake. "That's not it. I don't care who bangs who, as long as they don't come on to me."

"Paint just likes to tease."

"I wish he wouldn't."

Fox shrugged. "I don't think he's ever gotten over the things that happened to him in prison. 'S jiggy."

"Jiggy?"

"Nervous. Insecure. It fucked 'im up, all the torture and rape and that. Doesn't believe 's got much to offer."

"That's nuts. He's quite attractive. Good looks, well muscled, in-telligent, graceful, all that."

"Yeah." Fox smiled, wistfully. "Thing is, *he* doesn't believe it. Has to keep proving himself on other people. Sad."

For him *and* you, Daniel thought. "Does it bug you?"

"That's not a one-man man? Nah. I knew how he was." Fox fell silent. "'Be someday 'll get it out of his system," he added after a mo-ment.

"You married?"

Fox nodded. "Short-term, open contract, renewed quarterly."

Which meant the contract would expire soon. Daniel wondered whether Fox would renew. He probably would. Fox obviously got the short end of the deal, when it came to Paint, but he was also, obviously, hooked.

COLLABORATOR

Byron was pressing a damp cloth to her forehead. Carli sat up, pushing his hand away. She was back in her quarters. And her attacker stood near the door.

"Relax. It wasn't Pablo who pushed you into the chute," Byron said, when Carli started and stared. "He was the one who rescued you."

"Someone stole my proxy while I was doing something else," Pablo said.

"We think it's the renegade," Byron added.

"The one who tried to kill me before?" The other two nodded. Carli frowned, eyeing Pablo. "How can you be sure, Byron?"

"Jenna personally checked the proxy rosters. We keep a log of everyone's signal, and Pablo was found to be faced into a programming environment at the time, producing code. There can be no error."

"How do you know Jenna checked the rosters?" Carli demanded.

"I stood right there while she did it."

"And how do you know it was her, and not the renegade hiding in her proxy? For Christ's sake, how do you know *anyone* is who he says he is, in those damn things?" Carli said, waving a hand in Pablo's direction.

Byron said, "Relax. We have ways to trace the data. We're looking for the renegade right now."

Carli buried her face in her hands and exhaled. I want to go home, she thought.

Byron sat down next to her on the couch. "I know this is hard for you. But we have to know now whether or not you'll help us. Dr. Taylor can't wait any longer for your answer."

"And what if I say no? Will you kill me? Or maybe just let the renegade do your dirty work for you."

Byron looked offended. "Of course not. If you decide not to help us, we'll keep you here till launch, and then you'll go into a life bag with the other non-Menagerie staff, to be picked up by Shasta rescue teams. I'll see to it that no harm comes to you."

"But . . . ?"

"But." He paused. "If you don't help me find a way to expand Mercury's omni radius to Icarus Station within the next thirty-eight hours, Dr. Taylor has decided we're going to have to kill the probe astronauts."

"That's insane! You know it is! Even if I agreed to help—it's too little time!"

"It's very little time," he admitted. "But it's the only hope they have, so we shouldn't be wasting time arguing."

"Besides," she said, calming down a little, "why should I believe you? How could you possibly pose a threat to them?"

Byron winced. "It's a relatively simple process, actually. We're one of the nation's primary sources of omni communications software, and we have clearance to provide upgrades to secured operations."

Carli's hope sank. "Such as *Exodus*."

He nodded. "We're scheduled to beam a set of software upgrades to *Exodus* before its departure this afternoon. Software with a few added features, I'm afraid."

Carli stared at him for a long, silent moment. God damn you. God damn you all straight to hell.

She sighed, and stood. "All right. Let's get to work."

MOTHER-NOT

Mother? . . . Mother? . . . No, that name didn't seem right for the woman who slumped in a chair by her bed, staring blindly at a sensor field filled with graphics and numerics. Dane studied the black-haired woman-proxy from her vantage point in the room's corner. The sight of her filled Dane with such longing. Longing for someone, or something, this woman might have been, or tried to be.

A memory surfaced—Dane didn't know whether it was real, or merely something she'd seen in a simile—of being cradled in the arms of a giant, enfolded in those warm, bare arms, looking up at a woman's face, a woman with dark, dark skin and rich skin smell, of grabbing at the black, tightly curled locks of hair that tumbled down, barely within reach. A woman who murmured comforting words in a strange language as she unbuttoned her shirt.

No llores, Pablito. Un momento. Te amo. No llores.

Don't cry. I love you. Don't cry.

She remembered, suddenly, nuzzling that delicious skin, seeking the black circle of flesh—taking that flesh into her mouth, and the warm milk that squirted against her palate, quenching thirst, taming hunger.

Someone somewhere was crying.

The tears weren't hers; she wasn't Pablito. If she was anyone's child, she was Buddy's.

An alarm went off. Mother-Not roused herself, with obvious difficulty, and ordered the door to open. Standing there was the woman Pablo called Aunt Jenna. They spoke, and as always, Dane had to force herself to pay very close attention to understand them.

"You wanted to talk to me?"

"Yes." Aunt Jenna's gaze was drawn to the jelly, in which a set of alphanumerics hung:

T-00:08:42:21

Aunt Jenna grimaced. "Less than nine hours."

"That's just the earliest we could launch. We have a few hours' flexibility to finish critical tasks." She smiled. "And my grandmother always said, whatever doesn't get done didn't need doing."

"Hmmm. I suppose." Aunt Jenna drew a breath. "Couple of things. D'Auber appears to be all right—a little shocky, but she's bearing up all right. Byron reports that she's agreed to work with him on the omni range problem. They've been at it for several hours now."

"Good. And the other thing?"

Aunt Jenna looked grim. "I've been running checks on the kids' signals to see who the troublemaker might be."

Mother-Not's eyebrows went up. "You've found the renegade."

"No. Weirder than that. I've uncovered some odd anomalies in the logs that I can't account for."

"Explain."

"I can't, yet. It's all very subtle stuff. But there's a characteristic set of changes in the data. On a hunch I pulled up the longitudinal data we've collected on the kids and I've checked the past two years, so far. The alterations are there in many, if not all, of the files."

Mother-Not appeared annoyed. "I don't have time for this. What's the bottom line?"

"The bottom line is, they've broken into our systems and have been tampering with the research data. I haven't had time to analyze the alterations for any kind of larger pattern, but one thing is clear. They're manipulating our perception of them. Two hours ago I would have been able to tell you with complete confidence what and who they are. Now . . ." she shrugged. "I haven't a clue." A bitter laugh. "Years of research, down the tubes. And what's worse, if they were able to penetrate our file security, who's to say what other secured systems they've gotten into? They could be watching us right now."

Both women glanced at the camera Dane was viewing them through.

"I think you're going overboard with this," Mother-Not said.

"Am I? I don't think so."

The phone rang. Mother-Not touched a key, and Uncle Alan appeared in the jelly.

"These cancellations and postponements are unacceptable. I want you in my office *right now.*"

"I'll be right there," she replied, and cut him off. To her kelly she said, "Refuse all future calls from Alan Rasmussen."

"Acknowledged," the kelly said.

To Aunt Jenna Mother-Not said, "Keep investigating, and let me know what your findings are."

"I don't have time! We have only a few more hours till launch and I'm up to my hips in last-minute crises! What the hell are we going to do if we get out into deep space with these kids and find out they're malevolent, twisted somehow? What will we do then?" She pressed fingers to her lips, cutting herself off from whatever else she wanted to say.

Mother-Not waved Aunt Jenna's words away like a bad smell. "You're being paranoid. They're just kids. Get back to work and don't worry about the data alterations right now. We'll deal with this development after we launch."

Aunt Jenna left, looking very troubled.

The alarm sounded again. Mother-Not's kelly said, "Encrypted omni call from Chauncy D'Auber."

She took a deep breath and straightened, smoothing her hair. "All right. Enter decryption sequence and patch him through."

An old man appeared in her jelly. "Dr. Taylor."

"Senator. To what do I owe the pleasure?"

Anger gathered on the man's face. "Don't get cute. I've diverted the murder *and* kidnapping investigations, as you required. Now I want my daughter back."

"Not quite yet." Mother-Not sat back, interlocking her fingers across her belly. "I still have a need for her, for a bit longer."

"Damn you!" he exploded. She remained impassive. With visible effort, he quieted. "You and I both know you don't need Carli. You've had me in your pocket for years."

She wore a tight little smile. "A little extra insurance never hurt anyone. Besides, I need her technical skills."

"Let me speak to her."

"I showed you a jello. That's enough for now."

"It's not enough! If you want me to show any mercy when this is all over, you had better—"

"Senator, you're in no position to threaten me. I'll be back in touch shortly to let you know what else we want."

Mother-Not touched a key. The senator's image dissolved in mid-word.

"Kelly, refuse all further calls from Senator D'Auber," she said, "but take a message, if he cares to leave one."

"Acknowledged."

And she touched another key. Uncle Marsh appeared. "Number One?"

She slumped. "It's getting bad again. I can't go on."

"Are the mood swings getting to you? Or is it pain?"

She shook her head, covered her face. After a moment she spoke, haltingly. "The pain is so bad. I can't think. I can't keep up appearances."

"I can increase your pain medication dosage again."

"It'll cloud my thinking. I need to be sharp."

Anguish and ire appeared on his face. "Then there's nothing I can do. I've told you that. You should have allowed another round of surgery, and gene and chemotherapy, when it might have made a difference."

"The timing was bad. It would have meant abandoning the project. You know that as well as I do."

"Your choice. But it means that all I can do for you now is to medicate the pain and control the hormonal fluctuations. If you won't let me medicate the pain, there's nothing more I can do for you. Don't look to me for miracles."

"Please. Just get me through these next couple days. Please. I'm ready to let go once the children are safe. Just a couple more days." She made a choked noise, a stifled cry. Uncle Marsh looked at her sadly.

"All right," he said finally. "Then let me up your dosage just a bit. It might help take the edge off the pain and shouldn't have too much impact on your mental function."

She hesitated for a long moment. "All right, Number Two. Thanks."

"Don't thank me," he said angrily. His image vanished.

BREAK-IN

Daniel hated waiting.

They took Paint some McDonald's pseudo-space-food. Then, while Paint tried to find a way into the security software for Kaleidas, Daniel and Fox did a few more touristy things. They came back and Fox settled down to cruise the jello-net. Daniel unfaced, fed the complaining cat, and used Carli's bed to get some sleep. When he faced back into proxy, very early the next morning, Paint and Fox were asleep in the hotel room's lower bunk and the room was dark. So he cruised the *v*-net for a while.

A couple hours later he returned to find both men at the jello display.

"I'm back," he said.

Paint disconnected from the jelly. "Was just calling you. I'm in."

"Into the security systems, you mean?"

Paint nodded, grinning. Fox looked grave, but calm. Daniel's heart rate leapt.

"Then let's do it," he said.

They planned to pose as technicians scheduled to do some testing and repairs in the manufacturing area. Fox had stolen them some coveralls from Shasta's maintenance shop. They went over Kaleidas's layout (as best Daniel knew it, which wasn't well) and their search-and-rescue plan, one last time. Get into the secured areas, search till they found Carli—however long it took—then head for the nearest airlock, at which point they'd put everyone but Daniel into life bags and he'd tow them all along the outside of the habitat to Shasta and safety. Once Carli was free, the authorities would have to believe them, regardless of Patricia Taylor's influence.

They took Paint's comunit and Daniel's toolbox and headed out.

At the interhabitat elevators, Paint entered the phony access codes he'd inserted into the security software. After scanning their handprints—Daniel glanced at Paint, worried, but Paint gave him a wink;

Fox leaned over and whispered, "He's set it up to approve anything; don't worry"—the elevator syntellect let them aboard.

They rode the long way up the interhabitat shaft to the central node. At that point the other passengers debarked, and the syntellect gave them final clearance for transport to Kaleidas. Gravity turned upside down, and as the elevator descended, they swung around and climbed down the walls to the new floor. All like Daniel's earlier trip.

Except this time when they reached Kaleidas and the door opened, eight Marines were waiting there, with dart weapons trained on them.

"Put your hands in the air and don't make any sudden moves," the officer barked. They obeyed. Daniel and Fox glanced at Paint, who looked sheepish.

"Oops," he said.

CARLI

AN ASSORTMENT OF WILD GEESE

About the twentieth time Carli asked Byron to reshuffle the historical performance data, grouping them by yet a different set of criteria— while she turned a miniature scale model of the omni transceiver over, eyeing it—he threw his hands up and spun in his chair.

"Damn it, Carli. This isn't telling us anything. We only have a few hours left. I'm certain the problem's in the signal-translation coding— either the operating-conditions model, or assumptions we've made about the data sequencing, or . . . or something. *Not* in the physical design." He gestured irritably at the miniature MacLeod in her hands. "Why are you wasting your time with that?"

She gave him a sharp look. "And how many months have you been pursuing the translation angle?"

He didn't answer, only gazed at her sourly.

"It's a dead end, Byron. Look. Thirty-four omnis have been put in orbit since 2061." She pointed at the mishmash of data in the sensor field behind him. "Each has a somewhat different range. And all but three of them show a gradual drop in efficiency! Minute, but statistically significant. The coding is the same for all of them. The only way they could get that variation—and the decrease in efficiency—is by a design flaw. A flaw that responds slightly differently to the varying environmental conditions they are each under."

His jaw jutted. "In the first place, they are all in *exactly* the same environment: in orbit. Space is space. And a range of thirty-nine point eight to forty-one point two percent of the theoretical bandwidth is well within the bounds of reasonable variation."

"Oh, come on. All kinds of things could have been different about their environment. How they were placed. How they were transported. Aspects of their construction that were just slightly different. Their orbits are different: thirteen are in Earth orbit, one is around Mars, one around Jupiter, one around Mercury, and one aboard *Exodus*. Who knows what effect all those factors might have?"

"But we can't detect any of those differences!"

"Sure we can. At least some of them. There could be gravitational or magnetic effects. Electrical effects due to solar wind. If we define the differences, we can start to try to correlate performance with the different factors that might be affecting them."

He rolled his eyes. "The possibilities you listed all fluctuate with time, and the performance data haven't."

Carli sat back and looked him in the eyes. "After what you did to get me here, the least you can do is humor me."

"I've been examining this issue for a lot longer than you have, this time around, Carli, and I'm telling you, *you're on the wrong track.*"

"How can you be so sure?"

He sighed heavily. "I wanted you to assist me—not throw all my months of effort into the garbage can and go off on a wild tangent!"

So *that's* it, she thought. Professional jealousy. She only looked at him. He finally rolled his eyes.

"This is getting us nowhere. But all right. Fine." With another disgruntled sigh he turned back to the sensor field. "What sort criteria did you want again?"

GET SET . . .

Mother appeared in the middle of their simile, and hung inside the virtual replica of the habitat like a floating goddess. The crèche-born stopped what they were doing and turned to face her, and after a few seconds the automata froze, too.

"Are the charges set?" Mother asked.

Joe checked a personal readout. "The waldo team is just completing the task."

Pablo added, "The rest of us are doing one last simulation of the prelaunch evac."

She looked around at all the kids there. "Excellent. One moment." Her gaze turned inward and she murmured to herself. Then she said, "Jenna, Marsh, Byron, report."

Their disembodied voices sounded.

"Here."

"I hear you."

"Receiving."

"Good. We're all on-line. Now, listen up. Our launch window has opened. All charges are in place. It's time to do it. Everyone to your places. Prelaunch evac sequence will engage in fifteen minutes. Repeat, fifteen minutes, on my mark." She paused, and pointed a finger at the air. Fiery numbers appeared overhead: T-00:00:15:00.

"Mark," she said, and the numbers started counting down. She clapped her hands, smiling at them. "This is it. We're on our way. To your places."

Then she vanished.

We're going to pull it off despite you, Buddy, he thought, triumphant.

. . . Go!

Daniel saw Paint and Fox hustled through two other doors nearby as he was taken into a small room. A lieutenant came in a few minutes later with two enlisted men.

"You're in a shitload of trouble, Mac," the lieutenant said. "Who the hell are you and what are you doing, breaking into a secured facility?"

"My name's not Mac," he said. "And I'll tell everything I know, but only to the one in charge."

He had to repeat himself several times, in the face of escalating threats. Finally the lieutenant had his enlisted men try to rough Daniel up a bit, and Daniel responded by disengaging from the physical link; consequently, while one big bruiser tried to pin his arms and the other slugged him repeatedly in the gut, his proxy didn't budge a micrometer.

The lieutenant ordered them to lay off, and studied Daniel for a moment, eyes narrowed. Then he ordered his men out and followed, leaving Daniel there alone.

A bit later, Alan Rasmussen and a Marine officer in a uniform with a major's ensignia on the shoulder came in.

Rasmussen might be in on whatever Taylor was up to. But Daniel recalled a lot of animosity between Rasmussen and Taylor, during their briefing. So perhaps not.

I have to risk it, Daniel thought. He's my only chance.

"Mr. Rasmussen," he said. Rasmussen looked surprised, and exchanged a glance with the major.

"How did you know my name?"

"We've met recently. I'm Daniel Sornsen."

Rasmussen's eyes widened further.

"Ah," he said. Then, "You must know that cracking secured government systems and falsifying entry permits to a top secret research facility is a federal offense, Mr. Sornsen."

"Yes, sir. Of course I know that. But I have reason to believe that

Dr. Taylor killed Sam Krueger and kidnapped Carli D'Auber, and I believe that she is holding her here. On Kaleidas. I couldn't risk the chance she might learn we were coming, and try to stop us. Or harm Carli."

The major leaned forward and muttered something to Rasmussen, who nodded. The major stepped out. Rasmussen studied Daniel for a long moment. "Those are serious allegations."

"Yes, sir."

"Can you substantiate them?"

"All I can do is tell you what has happened over the past several days." And Daniel recounted everything that had happened. Rasmussen showed particular interest in his conversation with the senator, but let him finish his story without comment.

"You fled Austin. Why?"

"I . . ." Daniel hesitated. "I feel responsible for Carli. I was assigned to protect her."

Rasmussen made a noise, hand cupping chin. "Well, I have no love of Dr. Taylor, but the idea that she would resort to kidnapping and murder . . ." He shook his head with a frown. "Seems highly unlikely."

"At least check it out," Daniel said, leaning forward urgently. "Please. Carli's life may depend on it."

"Very well." Rasmussen stood. "I'll see what I can find out."

A muffled boom shook the floor. Sirens began to wail. The door to the corridor clicked as the lock disengaged, and a strong draft stirred the air. A calm female voice said, "Alert, alert. The hull has been breached. Decompression barriers descending. All personnel proceed to the nearest emergency station and don life-support equipment. Alert, alert. The hull has been breached. Decompression barriers descending. All personnel proceed to emergency stations . . ."

More muffled, distant booms went off. Rasmussen opened the door. The major was nowhere to be seen. The lieutenant who had tried to rough Daniel up snapped at the Marines gathering, "Get all personnel into life bags. Janus, Ordover, take the suits and mount a search-and-rescue. *Move your butts!*"

They saluted and ran off.

"Sir," the lieutenant said to Rasmussen, taking his arm, "this way."

Fear drew ugly lines on Rasmussen's face.

"Oh my God," he said, "oh my God, this is terrible," as the lieutenant hurried him away. Meanwhile, an enlisted man ushered Daniel into the hall. Big, bright, neon marquee arrows inside the walls scrolled around a corner. Paint and Fox were being hustled in that direction by two other Marines. Daniel and his "escort" fell in behind them, running. A steel wall descended behind them.

A few yards ahead was an emergency station. More muffled explosions sounded, making the floor tremble under their feet. Technicians, scientists, and support personnel, as well as Alan Rasmussen and several Marines, were climbing into bags and zipping them up. A couple Marines in space suits were locking their helmets on and fiddling with knobs and hoses. One man was panicking, screaming his lungs out. The scream was faint in the chill, thin air. A suited Marine grabbed him by the shoulder. Holding out a life bag, the Marine blared through a speaker in his suit, "Shut up and get in the bag!"

Instead, the man went at the Marine's life-suit hoses. The Marine slugged him in the gut and dropped a life bag over his head.

A new explosion went off, knocking everyone down as the wall ruptured inward. A howling wind blasted first away from, then toward, the hole, dragging with it everything not bolted down or hanging on. Someone's sealed life bag tore on the jagged edge of the hole as it tumbled out.

Daniel started after the life bag, stumbling, trying to keep his balance in the air blast. He might be able to help. At that instant he heard Paint yell. Paint had just stepped into a life bag velled to the wall and was zipping it up. Now, hair whipping around his face as if it were alive, he was screaming with all his might, *"Fox!"*

Daniel followed his horrified gaze—Fox was within a foot or so of the rupture, on its far side. He clung one-handed to a handhold, pulled almost completely off his feet by the wind. With his other arm he covered his head, shielding himself from objects flying past him and out the jagged hole.

The person in the punctured life bag was far gone by now, propelled by the initial blast of air. Daniel would never catch the bag, and Fox still had a chance.

It grew freezing as the air pressure plummeted. Though the wind was dying down, Fox had lost his grip and was sliding out the edge of the hole. He twisted his upper body, seeking something to grab, as his lower body was pulled out the opening. He just missed grabbing the hole's jagged edges.

"Exhale!" Daniel yelled, running for him. There was virtually no air left to carry his shout; he could barely hear himself. "Fox, *blow out your air!*"

Then Fox was gone.

Daniel grabbed an empty life bag. He spotted a fire extinguisher mounted on the wall, and snatched it free as he ran past. Building as much speed as his proxy's powerful legs could muster, he dove into space, tucking the bag between his legs.

Only a couple of seconds had passed since the explosion. Daniel had read that a human could survive up to thirty seconds in space before the blood boiled. Fox was moving into the station's shadow as he traveled in a straight line away from the rotating station, amid the last of the debris vomited out the hole by decompression. His eyes were squeezed shut and his face was a rictus of pain.

Daniel cranked his pain sense all the way down to sensory minimum—but the cold was still ferocious—and pulled the fire extinguisher's pin. Clutching the extinguisher under one arm, he curled as tightly as he could, to minimize both his uncontrollable shivering and tumbling. Setting the nozzle at his midsection, perpendicular to the course he wanted, he triggered the spray. Gently, gently, in a series of spurts. It pushed him in a wobbly, but pretty much straight, line. *Yes.*

He continued spraying CO_2, steadily checking and correcting his angle with respect to Fox. He couldn't aim right at Fox, or he would pass behind him; instead he had to make a wild-assed guess at where Fox would be when their trajectories crossed each other. This was harder than it seemed, because it was dependent on the amount of velocity the extinguisher would ultimately give him. In five or six seconds he figured he had enough momentum and let go of the extinguisher; the metal canister traveled alongside him as he unfolded himself.

His trajectory would now cross Fox's, just up ahead, and he was rapidly gaining. Daniel opened the life bag as he neared Fox.

He realized then that he had too much momentum—they were going to, just barely, miss each other. Daniel put the bag back between his knees and grabbed the extinguisher, which was still floating beside him. He brought it to his chest and threw it forward, *hard.*

The throw started him tumbling backward, heels over head, but it also slowed him . . . just enough. Fox stretched out as Daniel passed him, and grabbed the ankle cuff of his coveralls as Daniel's leg came arcing past. His angular momentum was translated to Fox; they were both tumbling now.

Daniel bent over and took hold of the bag by its outer handles; Fox climbed up him, seized the bag's inner handles, and folded himself in, swiftly and gracefully, as a muscle dancer would, while Daniel pulled the bag around Fox from the outside. Fox took one zipper, and Daniel the other; together, with some fumbling, they got him sealed in. Then Daniel pressed the strip of sealant fabric across the zipper. The reflective gold bag inflated, going spherical. Fox had triggered the air canister's release valve.

Clinging to the handles, Daniel peered through the tiny, clear plastic window. The bag's heating element and light had come on; Fox floated there, shivering violently; his chest rose and fell in great, heaving breaths. Daniel wasn't even sure he was conscious. His skin looked strange—purplish with white patches. Frostbite? Exploded capillaries? But still alive.

Fox might yet die; he'd certainly sustained serious injury. He had been in vacuum for a good twelve to fifteen seconds, Daniel estimated, and gas bubbles in the joints and internal organs—such as the heart or brain—or embolisms in the lungs, were all too likely . . .

Hurry, rescue team, Daniel thought, looking back toward the station. Find Fox's radio signal.

Then he stared in disbelief as gold bags started to tumble out of the several airlocks and the numerous ruptures in Kaleidas's hull. Glistening like a tossed handful of beads, they scattered into space around the habitat. Someone was chucking people off the secured side, he realized. Taylor and her crowd. It had to be. But why not just load them into the elevators?

The only reason he could come up with was that they must want to divert the attention and resources of Shasta by forcing a large-scale rescue effort. But divert them from what?

Daniel had a feeling that he was going to find out soon enough.

This was very bad news for Fox. Not only did it put more of a demand on the rescue teams, slowing recovery efforts; as one of the earliest ejectees, Fox was farthest out and would probably be among the last recovered.

We'll see about that, Daniel thought. He put his proxy on autopilot, sat up in the gel of Carli's squish, and used the omni line to call Shasta Station's hospital. It took several tries, but he got through to the emergency room. At his repeated insistence, the receptionist got one of the ER nurses for him.

"Sir, we have an emergency under way. I'm told your call is urgent?"

"Extremely," he said. Keep your story simple, Sornsen. "Please listen carefully. A man's life depends on it. I'm from the secured side of the orbital. I have a waldo and I've just used it to rescue a man who got sucked out a breach. He's in a life bag now, floating outside the habitat, but he was exposed to space for at least ten or fifteen seconds before I got to him and needs immediate attention. I know there are other life bags being tossed out, but this man's condition is critical—"

"I understand," she said. "We'll get a rescue sled right out to him." She reached below his line of sight. "Can you give me his approximate coordinates?"

Daniel couldn't plug back into his proxy and keep this line open at the same time. He tried to remember. "We were blown out a relatively low-gee level—less than point five, I'd say. From our trajectories I would guess that the breach would have been almost perpendicular to the habitat's plane of rotation."

"All right. Was it on the dock side or the sphere side of the rotational axis?"

"The sphere side. We're drifting toward the moon-side edge of the solar arrays, roughly. We aren't moving very fast."

"Got it. I'll send someone immediately. Is your waldo still with him? Is there any way you can send some kind of signal, when you see a rescue sled in the vicinity?"

"I'll see what I can do."

He signed off and returned to his proxy. The ferocious cold slammed against him and he started shivering again. Next chance I get, I'm writing some manual-override code for sensory inputs, he thought. Inside the life bag, Fox was curled in a little ball, still shivering. His eyes were glazed. Not in good shape.

Daniel looked around. There it was—a scooter with rotatable jets mounted on the ends of a long crossbar, on either side of the seat and steer stick. Curved sheets of metaceramic fanned out backward from the crossbar perhaps ten feet or so: shields that protected cargo from the jets' exhaust. The scooter was one of several that were harvesting life bags near the habitat, but this one had just veered off and was coming in their general direction. Behind the seat, he saw shortly, was a crane with a looped string holding three life bags, which trailed the scooter like metallic blowfish, or buoy balls on a fishing line.

Daniel waved an arm, as large a motion as he could make without losing hold of the bag. After a moment or two, the sled was on an intercept course with them. Their rescuer's space suit had a red emblem: snakes wrapped round a stick and the letters "EMT." Emergency medical technician.

Through the dark visor, he saw the EMT's eyes were very wide. It appeared to be a woman, Oriental, and she was staring curiously at Daniel. She matched velocities with Daniel and the bag. Then she pointed at Daniel and then the life bag, and made two parallel fists—meaning, presumably, *hang on tight*. Daniel gave her an OK sign.

Using a hook on a long pole, the EMT grappled the life bag by one of its handles. Clinging to her scooter with her legs, she levered them around and attached the bag to a big D-clamp tied to the rope that held the bags. Daniel caught a glimpse of one of the other occupants: the man stared at him with a stunned expression. Daniel gave him a friendly wave.

They headed for one of the docking slips along the latticework. As they approached, traveling in an arc in pursuit of the habitat's rotation, several small explosions, silent in space's vacuum, triggered in succession along the latticework a short distance away. A shock wave raced up the latticework only a dozen or so yards beneath their feet. Struts crumpled as if made of foil. Barely a second later, a big explosion blasted through the main connecting shaft, about a quarter of the way up from Kaleidas. Debris spewed outward.

Several things happened at once. An elevator fell partly out of the broken shaft, on the Shasta Station side. A piece of the broken latticework tumbled at them—Daniel shoved it away before it could strike the scooter or life bags. The blow struck his proxy's forearm; rubylike globules of red lubricant scattered. The end of the broken main shaft came descending on the scooter, gyrating wildly; the EMT veered sharply down and away, out of the way.

At the instant of the explosion, Kaleidas, carrying a short portion of the shaft, had started moving off in one direction, wobbling a little; Shasta Station, carrying the nulgy sphere, the central docking node, and the rest of the shaft, was now moving off in the opposite direction, wobbling, too—slowly, like a drunken top.

As the Shasta Station canister began to move away, the microgravity sphere, which had no momentum of its own, tried to stay in one place, while the lattice containing it tried to go with the rest of Shasta Station. Daniel saw as the EMT brought the scooter around that the sphere was tearing free from its containment lattice like a ball tearing through weak netting. The shredded sphere's lattice, along with the main latticework, then began to tear itself apart—snapping like a whip, then going still, then shaking violently, in a bizarre, unpredictable pattern—shedding long spears of metal and other shrapnel into the scooter's path. The EMT fired the jets again, dodging debris, heading for clear space.

Daniel craned his neck, looking back. Two shuttles—a U.S. military craft and a Lagrange Spaceways commercial craft—had been docked along the latticework, along with several smaller craft. The military shuttle and all of the smaller craft were hurled away from the habitat by the latticework's unstable harmonics. The commercial shuttle in the central node's main docking slip, however, remained socketed in the docking slip, and went off with the main habitat.

He saw that the EMT was steering them toward the microgravity sphere. It loomed before them, a planet in miniature: smooth, curved, and white. They orbited it till an emergency airlock appeared on the sphere's tiny horizon. The airlock lights blinked a welcome. Slowing the sled, the EMT signaled Daniel; he climbed forward. She handed him a line with a big clamp on it and pointed at the airlock. OK, he signaled, and launched himself. He caught a tethering loop below the airlock and secured the clamp to it while the EMT was attaching the string of life bags to the airlock tether.

Daniel opened the airlock and pulled himself inside, and, locking his legs around a bar set into the wall beside the door, reeled the life bags in. The technician came in with the fourth and last.

Just as she pulled herself in, in the distance Daniel saw the canister that had been Kaleidas, pointed at the moon. Shooting out its tail was a stream of fire. A rocket.

"I'll be fucked," he said, back in Carli's apt.

Then the EMT closed the airlock door and pushed a big red lever. The hiss of air filling the small chamber began. The fierce cold abated; with a sigh of deep relief, Daniel turned his sensory systems back up and looked through the plastic window at Fox. He was obviously in great pain: grimacing, sweating, still curled in a ball, shivering. Hold on, Daniel thought. The EMT fiddled with the radio at her chest, and her mouth was moving. Repressurization took a minute or two. Then green lights lit up around the inner door and a syntellect voice advised them that they could remove their life-support systems.

The EMT released her medkit, which floated next to her, and took off her helmet, which tumbled slowly toward the corner.

"Give me a hand," she said, floating over to unzip Fox's life bag. She had a trace of an accent, which Daniel couldn't place. Daniel helped her pull Fox out; he moaned.

"Easy," Daniel said. "Hang on."

The inner door opened, and the EMT kicked off and out to a small group of people floating there. "Do you have a hyperbaric chamber here? One big enough to put a person inside?"

"Yeah," one man in tech overalls said. "A few. We have a couple of high-pressure processing units and some test units. They're full of parts, but we can empty one out. I'll take you there."

"Good," the EMT said. "Empty them all out—we'll have other decompression cases coming in. In fact, get people started clearing out those rooms, and several others, entirely; we're going to be setting up triage, surgery, and patient-monitoring stations for at least a couple hundred people. You," she said to Daniel, "bring him," pointing at Fox. To the people gathering around, she gestured at the other life-bag occupants, who were struggling to get out of their own bags. "Help these folks out, and bring them along, too. I'll need to check them all out once I get this man's condition stabilized."

The man who'd offered to guide them pushed off through the tunnel dead ahead. Daniel pushed off, too, holding Fox under his arm and using the other arm to grab onto handholds and propel them around turns. Eventually they came to a room with two parallel curved walls opposite each other. The other four were straight walls that slanted a bit inward toward each other at one end. There was no floor or ceiling. At the larger end of the room was a big pressure chamber. People were pulling racks of data crystals out and sending them cruising across the nulgy space to others, who stashed them in cabinets. With Daniel's help, the EMT quickly stripped and examined Fox while the others were getting the pressure chamber ready.

"He's got severe frostbite and a good case of the bends," she told Daniel. "And some damage to the lungs, as well. We need to get him on oxygen and under at least thirty atmospheres right away." To Fox she said, "Can you understand me?"

His teeth were chattering. "Yes."

"Good. What's your name?" She dug around in her kit, pulled out a needle and empty test tube, and took some blood. Then, leaving the needle in, she replaced the original test tube with a big tube filled with clear liquid that looked as viscous as corn syrup; he twitched and winced. "Hold still, please."

"I'm Fox."

"Well, Fox . . ." She removed the needle and dabbed some Liquid Skin on the puncture. "I've just given you something that will increase the ability of your blood to reabsorb dissolved gases, and do some repair work on your damaged tissues. It takes a few hours to work. In the meantime, we've got a pressure chamber here we're going to put you in. I want you to relax as much as possible. We'll also be putting you on oxygen as soon as the gear shows up. It may be a while before you can come out. Do you understand?"

"Right," he said. "No big jig."

He sounded so weak. It worried Daniel.

"I'm right here with you," he said.

The EMT slapped some kind of transmitter in the crook of Fox's arm. "This will give us a continuous readout on your vital signs. Don't fiddle with it."

"Where's Paint?" Fox asked, as Daniel and the EMT towed him to the chamber.

Daniel shook his head. "I saw him getting into a life bag, right before you were pulled out the breach. He's not here yet, but I'm sure he's fine."

It was one of those reassuring, bullshit things you say to people when they're injured.

. . . GO! REDUX

Carli sat—or lay—semisupine, strapped into a specially designed, heavy-duty squish-couch on the ceiling of the crèche chamber, amid the banks of decorated, strapped-down crèches. Byron was just climbing into his own couch, after getting Carli buckled in. Marsh was also there, in a third couch, as were a few dozen uninhabited proxies, belted to upside-down slabs on the ceiling like rows of high-tech Frankenstein's monsters, or bizarre, human-shaped headstones next to sarcophagi crèches. Stacks of equipment were strapped or taped to the walls and floor.

I'm going to wake up any minute, she thought; Argyle will sit on my chest and demand to be fed. All this will go away.

Before them, also hanging upside down from tracks in the ceiling, was a big jelly. At seven feet high, it scraped the floor and must have been twelve feet across. In numerous cubes inside it, jello-avatars of Patricia Taylor, Jenna Steinberg, and several others were interacting. Their lips moved, and their eyes: tic-tic; many words streamed past Carli. They were all so very businesslike about it. It was as if they had done this a hundred times before.

Taylor said, "Marsh's team, report."

"Crèches and critical equipment secured in the safe area," Marsh replied, from his couch. "We're all strapped in, Number One. I'm prepared to lower decompression barriers and seal us in, on your signal."

"Good. Pablo's team, report."

"We've accounted for all non–Plastic Menagerie personnel in all areas, and are prepared to evacuate them on your signal, Mother. My own team is in place to begin evac at Levels Two through Twenty. Bombware has been downloaded to their main pursuit ships."

"Mara's team, report."

"We're in place to begin evac on Levels Twenty-one through Forty."

"Joe's team, report."

"The chemical rockets are ready; we're completing burn initialization sequence now. . . . There. Initialization complete. Ready to stabilize motion and begin main burn on your signal. Plasma jet is on standby to replace the chemical rocket once it's depleted."

"Jenna's team, report."

"We just completed a corrected mass-distribution analysis, for input to the burn calculation. The data are ready for transmittal to Joe on your signal, Number One." With a glance at Byron and Carli, she added, "The Trojan software was radioed to *Exodus* a little bit ago. Ready to implement Plan A—or Plan B—on your signal."

Byron started and frowned at Jenna's mention of Plan B. Taylor's avatar looked at Byron and Carli. "Jenna, transmit mass-distribution data to Joe's team."

"Standing by . . ." Joe said, and then, "Received. We're incorporating the new data into the burn simile."

"Byron's team, report."

Byron sighed and looked at Carli. "No progress yet on omni range expansion."

Taylor nodded. "Then we're go Plan B. On my signal, Jenna."

Jenna's avatar squinted; not quite a grimace, but close. "On your signal."

From Byron's devastated expression, Carli guessed: She'd lost her chance to save the astronauts. They were going to kill them instead.

"Byron said we had more time! You've given me less than a day!"

Taylor's avatar gave her a marble-eyed stare. "Why waste more precious hours and effort on a false hope? And why should I believe you'll help us, anyway, after your escape attempt?"

The scream came up from a place Carli didn't know existed. She threw herself against the straps. "You are evil. *Evil!*"

Taylor didn't bother to reply. "Obediah's team, report," she said.

"Decompression and separation charges set to blow on your signal."

"Very well, then. Any last comments, anyone? . . . None? All right, children. We're on our way." She paused. "Marsh, lower decompression barriers."

Marsh touched a button on a control device in his hand. "Decompression barriers descending. OK." He looked up. "We're sealed in."

"Obediah," Taylor said, "go decompression. Mara and Pablo, go evacs. All others, hold till my signal."

"Decompression, go," Obediah's avatar said.

Muffled explosions cascaded through the habitat's structure. Carli felt the air tremble; the gel of her couch quivered. She opened her eyes.

"Evacs in progress," Mara's and Pablo's avatars reported.

Views in the jelly showed chaos in the corridors and chambers: people running, screaming, holes blown in walls. Silently proxies moved through the evacuated areas, lugging life bags and tossing them out airlocks and orifices. Carli saw at least two or three people collapse or get blown out without life-support equipment. She closed her eyes again, sickened.

Mara and Pablo gave updates as they and their teams moved through the different levels. Perhaps fifteen minutes later, both reported that evacs were complete.

"Good." Taylor nodded. "Obediah, go separation."

"Brace yourselves. Separation, go."

It sounded like thunder: a rumbling that ended in an eardrum-shattering *BOOM!* Carli was thrown against her straps and then into her gel. Then gravity . . . just . . . went away. No, there was a very slight sense of motion, a wobbling rotation—just enough to make her dizzy. She clenched her jaw, nauseous.

Taylor said, "Joe, go burn."

"Brace yourselves again. Hull cuts, go."

Another set of explosions, smaller than the former but much closer, went off, throwing them toward the ceiling like a huge slap. Metal screamed. Joe's avatar was talking, but the words seemed like gibberish to Carli; she was so rattled by her fear, and by all the lurching and swirling about, which had worsened after the latest set of explosions, that she couldn't think.

"Status!" Taylor snapped.

Marsh checked readouts. "Seals are holding."

"Stabilization and targeting rocket in place," Joe said. "Gimballing . . . and firing."

There was a muted roar. The slight tumbling sense diminished, then reversed. In one of the cube panes, which showed a view from outside the habitat right next to the broken shaft, the Earth crept out of view, gradually, and then the moon crept into view, off to one side.

"Gimballing . . . reversing thrust again . . ."

Motion ceased.

"Stabilization and targeting burn complete," Joe reported.

"You miscalculated," Taylor said. Her avatar showed little enough expression, but she sounded angry. "We're not pointed at the moon."

"I undershot on purpose, Mother." His voice shook. "We're still rotating—just very slowly. I wanted to give myself time to prepare."

He was right; very, very gradually, the moon was still creeping toward the shaft.

"I should warn you, our trajectory could be off by as much as a few degrees," Jenna said. "Joe and I used the original as-builts to calculate mass distribution, but if major pieces of equipment were moved between then and now, we're screwed."

"She's right," Joe said.

Taylor replied, "Too late to worry about it now."

A long pause, till the shaft appeared ready to touch the moon.

"Chemical burn," he said, *"go!"*

Even as he spoke, a giant, invisible hand shoved Carli hard into the gel of her couch. Terror and helplessness drove her into an almost trancelike numbness. She watched her arms and lower torso and legs, as they slowly submerged into the translucent, trembling gel. It was maybe a gee of acceleration, at most, but after almost two days in only a fraction of Earth's gravity, it felt like a lot more. Even the model of the omni was partly submerged. She'd forgotten she was still holding it. God's blowtorch blasted underfoot: an inferno of impressive magnitude.

She stared at the model, which lay with her fingers curled around it, deep in clear, quivering, not-quite-solid cushioning.

"Oh, my God," she whispered, staring at the model. She thought about the erratic noise patterns in Byron's sensor field, as she watched the gel vibrate. Inspiration bloomed: a tiny, stubborn flower, through a crack in concrete. How obvious.

"I've got it!" she shouted at Byron. The rocket's noise overpowered her voice; he didn't hear. "I know what the problem with the omni is!"

He stared at her. The rocket had stopped burning while she was in midsentence; all the others heard her words.

Taylor's avatar stared at her. There was a jarring.

"Chemical rocket ejected," Joe said.

Taylor blinked. To Jenna: "Any sign of pursuit yet?"

"None."

"What are you talking about?" Byron demanded of Carli.

"Plasma jet descending," Joe continued. Amid mechanical sounds, a series of short, sharp shocks occurred.

"What's our velocity?"

"About six hundred meters per second. A good start."

Carli held up the model. "I'm talking about vibrations," she said. The noise level—clankings and metallic bumps—was growing; she raised her voice. "Vibrations in the particle-detector tub are interfering with its sensitivity."

"Unbolting flooring to put plasma jet in place. We'll need to remove the titanium sheeting, lower the plasma jet into place, and rebolt the flooring. It'll be a while before we can fire." More noises and jarring as he spoke.

"How much longer?" Taylor demanded.

"Twenty minutes, minimum," Joe said.

"We're still in range of their smaller craft. Hurry!"

"We are, Mother."

"But it's insulated against vibration!" Byron said. Carli frowned, trying to tune the others out.

"Don't you remember, Byron? Remember how we ran one of the circuitry conduits straight into the annulus surrounding the tub? We overlooked that."

"I don't remember that."

"Think, Byron. Picture the unit in your head. *We have harmonics in the detector gel.*"

Byron grew thoughtful. Taylor was studying them.

"I'm recalculating mass distribution," Jenna said, "based on our initial burn. We'll have corrections to you in a minute, Joe."

Byron said slowly, "I suppose harmonics are a possibility. But what can we do about it? We can't make design changes to a device seventy million miles away, in the time frame we have."

Carli turned to Taylor, intense. "If you have a shred of humanity left in you, please. Please. Give us a few hours more. I'm sure I'm right about this. Give us a chance to find a solution."

Jenna's avatar said, "Updated mass data on its way to you, Joe. Number One . . . let's give them the time. What harm is there?"

"New mass data received," Joe said. "Running plasma burn simile. Ready to implement once the jet is in place."

"I agree." It was Marsh. "Let them try."

Taylor's avatar was frowning. "Joe or Jenna, when do we reach lunar perigee?"

"About seventeen hours," Jenna replied.

"That's how long you have, then," Taylor told Carli. "Seventeen hours."

DANIEL

SHASTA REGROUPS

A while later, the Marine major who had been with Rasmussen during Daniel's questioning showed up in triage. Daniel had a sudden urge to hide. Instead he continued to keep an eye on Fox and monitor Fox's vital signs, as the EMT had assigned him to do. He did eavesdrop—although it was hard to hear; at least thirty casualties were now being cared for by Shasta Station medics, and the big room held a chorus of moans and people calling out vital signs and asking for first aid equipment.

"Who's in charge here?" the major asked the room at large. He entered the room and repeated the question more loudly when no one responded. Though obese, he navigated well in nulgy.

The chief physician from Shasta Station—a tall, lanky man, black, middle-aged, with spectacles and a lab coat—swam over and grabbed a handful of webbing. "I am."

The major held out his hand. The physician shook it, clinging to the personnel webbing with his other hand.

"Major Adam Maez, U.S. Marines. Head of the security detachment at Kaleidas."

"Elias Crosby, Shasta General's chief surgeon."

"I need Mayor Takamoto. I'm told she's here."

"Yes, she is." The physician gestured at an old woman floating near the pressure chamber. "She took a blow to the head and is unconscious."

Maez scowled. "Damn! We need access to the city's personnel rosters to complete our inventory."

A man strapped to a board floating nearby lifted a hand. "Excuse me! I know the password." They looked at the man. "I'm Mishiko's—the mayor's—chief of staff."

"Excellent." The major went over to him and they had a brief, whispered conversation. Then he pushed off.

"Major Maez," the physician said, "before you go—what is the status of rescue efforts? How many more casualties should we expect?"

The major stopped himself nearby using the webbing. "It's a little premature to say, Doctor. My men are still combing Shasta, and the scooter fleet is still collecting ejected personnel. But at last report, the most serious injuries have already been transferred here, and a majority of the civilian population has been accounted for. A small fleet of craft with medical transport personnel will be here in about eight or ten hours, to transport casualties back to Earth for treatment."

"Have conditions improved?"

"The habitat still isn't stable. The worst leaks are repaired, though, and the engineers report that no further air loss is likely. The biggest problem is the unstable harmonics the habitat has picked up. We're having a rocket flown in from Pinnacle City to help stabilize the habitat, and after that we can reassess conditions. A team of NASA engineers will also be arriving tomorrow to assist with repairs and stabilization."

"Thank God. How many people are still aboard her?"

"We estimate over forty-eight hundred. We're evacuating only those levels that are the most damaged. And the air-processing and heating systems are still functional, so a large-scale evacuation at this point won't be necessary."

"Thank you, Major. My wife insisted on staying behind to help with emergency repairs, and I was worried."

The physician turned back to his patient, and the major headed for the exit. Just as Daniel had thought he'd escaped trouble, Maez crooked a finger at him. "You, Sornsen. Come with me."

Daniel turned Fox's vital-sign monitor over to one of the medics and kicked off after the major.

"I take a dim view of people messing with my security systems," he said, as they hand-over-handed down a tube. "You should have brought your story to me, or to Alan Rasmussen, right away. We might not be in this situation if you hadn't decided to play cowboy."

That stung. Daniel replied, "With all due respect, sir, I didn't know what Dr. Taylor was about to do, and I didn't know who was in on it with her. She had the senator under her thumb. I couldn't afford to take the risk that she had other accomplices in positions of authority."

"Hmph." The major paused and looked at him. After a pause he said, "I've reviewed your personnel file, Sornsen. I know that you've been with KaleidoScope for over six years now. Your security clearance is top secret, and your performance ratings have always been excellent."

"Thank you, sir."

"Because of that, and because I need your special skills and knowledge, I'm going to include you in my planning sessions. But I'll be keeping a close eye on you. If you pull one cowboy stunt, or even *think* about it, I'm going to put your butt in the can and not let you out till the crows roost on the moon. Clear?"

"Clear as squish, sir."

"Good."

They had reached a large mess hall.

Hundreds of people were there, gathered into clusters, eating at dining tubules set into the netting: the uninjured and the walking—or rather, floating—wounded, who didn't need immediate attention. Marines were jetting through the room, talking to people and entering notes to kellies. The major led him into a smaller room down a side personnel tube. Another officer was there.

"Daniel Sornsen, this is Captain Broca, my second-in-command." They shook hands. Maez went on, "We're planning to mount a pursuit. In a few moments we'll be meeting with some local officials. First, I need to know everything you know about Taylor and her gang of thugs."

Daniel looked from one to the other of them. A major would have top secret clearance, at the least, especially if he headed up a security detachment guarding a secret research facility, and the captain almost certainly did, too. And in this kind of emergency, Daniel wasn't going to mince rules by demanding proof of clearance. "What do you know about Project KaleidoScope?"

"We haven't needed detailed information, hitherto, but we know the general picture," Major Maez said. "It's classified research to create waldos that look indistinguishable from humans, to be used in military and intelligence applications. Led by Patricia Taylor on Kaleidas and Samson Krueger in Austin, managed by a Board of Directors consisting of officers of a Waldos, Inc., affiliate, the DOEP, and the DOD, with oversight by a congressional subcommittee."

"We call them proxies," Daniel replied, gesturing at his own proxy body. "They're superstrong, can attain very high rates of speed, and have expanded sensory capabilities—particularly sight and sound. Their biggest advantage over flesh and blood is that they're invulnerable."

"Invulnerable to what?" Captain Broca asked.

Daniel shrugged. "Just about everything: heat, cold, vacuum, toxins, small arms weapons. Even moderate levels of radiation."

"A tough enemy to go up against."

"Mmm. How many of these machines do they have, and how many pilots?" Major Maez asked.

Daniel shook his head. "I'm unsure how many proxies they have. The limiting factor is the number of pilots, though. I've been told by Sam Krueger—or I guess by the impostor posing as him—that there are at least a couple dozen pilots."

"We outnumber them, then."

"But can we trust that information," Broca asked, "if it came from the impostor?"

The major pursed his lips. "True."

"They had no reason to lie to me," Daniel replied. "But I suppose it'd be wise to take it with a grain of salt. Umm, by the way, they're children, sir."

At this, Maez's eyebrows went up. "Children?"

"That's correct. I've been told the oldest of them is maybe fifteen or sixteen years old. Most are younger. As young as six or seven, I think."

"That's what was in those crèches." Broca looked disgusted. "They've got them beanlinked."

Maez sighed. "I guess frying them long-range with the X-ray cannon at Patriot Base is not an option."

"Well, and they have a hostage. Carli D'Auber."

Maez looked shocked. "The senator's daughter?"

Daniel nodded. "They may have others as well."

"Good point. Tell us more about these proxies. Do they have any special weaponry built in?"

"Not that I'm aware of, sir, but I was in software research and development, not hardware. I've heard rumors that some research was done a few years before I joined the project, with the aim of building disguised weaponry into the proxy body, but I don't know anything about it. It may have just been rumors. Since the Antarctic Conflict was officially resolved, I think the weapons research angle hasn't been as big a priority."

Maez nodded thoughtfully, eyeing Daniel. "What do you think their motives are, son? What are they trying to accomplish?"

Daniel shrugged. "I haven't got a clue, sir. But, as I told you before, I'm certain they're holding Carli D'Auber hostage, and I believe her father must know something about what's going on. He's chair of the congressional subcommittee that oversees the secret research."

The major didn't say anything for a minute. Then he inhaled.

"I think it's time for a word with my superiors. Captain, you and Sornsen round up the civilian authorities and find out what kind of supplies and support they can lend us for a rescue effort."

"Yes, sir."

Broca led him over to a dining tubule, where four people were velled to the personnel netting, sipping something from bags that looked like coffee, and talking in low voices. All four looked a bit frayed around the edges. Broca introduced them to Daniel: two members of the city council, the head of Shasta's cargo operations, and a vice president of Ciba-Geigy who was also director of operations at Penn Station—their name for the sphere.

"Penn Station?" Daniel repeated, eyebrows raised.

Kathy Crawford, the VP, smiled. "After the engineer who designed it. Honest."

"We plan to pursue," Broca told them. "Our military shuttle was damaged in the explosion, so we'll need to use the commercial shuttle, if it's navigable."

"We're told the Lagrange Spaceways shuttle is undamaged," Jason Falwell, one of the council members, said. "The shuttle's captain and copilot are still missing. But if you can supply a pilot, I'm sure Lagrange Spaceways will understand the need. We'll contact their community relations people right away."

"Good. We'll also need to come up with some makeshift tools to use in disabling the craft, once we catch up with it. I'd like to get my men on board right away, and have them make up a list of our needs. Who should I give my wish list to?"

The others exchanged looks. "Me, I suppose," Kathy Crawford said. "We've got plenty of machinery and equipment that might be useful."

George Odman, the head of cargo operations, said, "We've got some stuff you might be able to use, too. I'd like a copy of that list. We can also start fueling the shuttle right away."

"Excellent," Broca said. "Do that."

Odman spoke into his kelly.

"What is your launch window?" Falwell asked.

"And what's their destination?" Odman added, looking up from his kelly. "We can trim your fuel requirements down to the minimum to boost your acceleration."

"They're heading for the moon."

"The moon?" Crawford repeated, eyes widening. "Why?"

Broca shook his head, frowning. "We don't have a clue. Possibly to mount an attack on Einstein Station, but maybe to slingshot around it and pick up momentum. Which is why we need to launch quickly. They have a three-hour head start, but their acceleration is very slow. If we can get a craft outfitted and launched in the next four to five hours, we should be able to reach them before they reach the moon. After that, we can still intercept them at the moon . . . *if* they drop into lunar orbit instead of heading off to parts unknown. That's a big if, though. I'd rather catch them before that."

"Do you want some extra fuel, in case they go beyond the moon?"

Broca shook his head. "No. At this point we couldn't begin to guess how much fuel we'd need to pursue, if they don't drop into lunar orbit. I don't want to risk not catching them this side of the moon, by adding weight to the craft and slowing us down."

"Right," Odman said. "Just enough to get there and back, then."

"Make that one way plus five percent," Broca corrected him. "We'll refuel at Einstein Station or Patriot Base."

"Roger that."

"Let's get moving, then," Crawford said.

Broca headed off to gather some of his men for a strategy session. Daniel made his good-byes to the others and, after taking a bathroom break back at Carli's place, faced back in to help with rescue efforts. A new set of casualties came in—among them four McDonald's workers who had second- and third-degree burns, from being sloshed by a big, hot, floating grease globule freed from the deep-fry vats when the station's angular momentum had turned linear and gravity stopped. He helped with triage on them and, once that was done, checked on Fox again. The man still looked like hell, but didn't seem any worse, at any rate. And they had gotten him on oxygen, finally; green tubes entered his nose and a canister floated beside him. His breathing was easier now, Daniel noted.

"Where's Paint?" Fox asked.

"I'll see if I can locate him," Daniel said. "Don't worry if it takes a while—things are really disorganized."

Fox turned his worry-lined face to the wall. "Yeah, no jig."

Daniel went back to the mess and flagged down one of the Marines doing personnel inventories: a private, who took his name and personal stats, and then accessed the database.

"Paint," she said. "Paint. Nobody by that name here. Does he have a last name?"

"Hang on." Daniel called up the capture file he'd created, back when he'd had Carli under surveillance, but he hadn't recorded the information there. The name had something to do with paint or chemicals. DuPont. "Try DuPont."

"DuPont. Nope, not on the list. Sorry."

After this long, he should have turned up.

Daniel didn't want to go back to Fox with this latest tidbit and worry him, but if Daniel didn't show up, Fox would worry even more.

When Daniel told him Paint was still missing, Fox just nodded and thanked him, and then closed his eyes. The triage and medical-care areas seemed to have plenty of volunteers by now, so Daniel decided to put his proxy to good use and volunteered for repair work on the main habitat's exterior. Then he hunted down Captain Broca, to let him know where he'd be for the next several hours. Broca was in a meeting with a couple of lieutenants and a sergeant major.

"Ah, excellent. I was just about to send someone after you," Broca said when he saw Daniel. "Gentlemen, dismissed. Get busy."

The others kicked off and maneuvered past Daniel down the personnel tube.

"We're getting a crew and some weapons and armament assembled," he told Daniel. "We now have a plan for intercepting and disabling their craft. I'll be in charge of the pursuit and I want you along, to give us an idea of their capabilities. We'll be doing this seat-of-the-pants, and I want to minimize surprises."

"I was going to assist with the habitat repairs . . . but I suppose you're right," Daniel said. "I'm of more use to you."

"We're scrambling in two hours and"—Broca checked his kelly—"thirteen minutes. Get some rest, and meet us at Airlock Fifteen at twenty-one hundred fifty hours."

"Twenty-one fifty, check," Daniel said. "Airlock Fifteen."

He went to a quiet corner of the mess hall, velled onto the personnel webbing, put his proxy on autopilot, and unfaced.

Gravity took hold of him. A gentle rain spattered Carli's windows. The cat was asleep on the couch, on its back, paws and whiskers twitching. It was midafternoon.

Daniel was surprised; it seemed as if it should be midnight by now. He removed his beanie and climbed heavily out of the squish, massaging his itchy scalp, and stumbled into the bedroom. His real body ached with fatigue, and with pains and cramps ignored while he'd been faced in.

Twenty-one fifty hours. That meant 9:50 P.M., Shasta Station time, or 7:50 P.M., Mountain standard time. He set an alarm and lay down on Carli's bed to rest. After a while the cat came in and, purring, fell asleep across his lap. It was oddly comforting.

Maybe I'll get a cat, he thought drowsily. If I ever figure out what the hell I'm going to do with the rest of my life.

CLOSE CALL

Buddy had disappeared, Pablo was busy with his programming, and Dane had jumped monitors from one end of the station to the other, more times than she wanted to think about. She was getting bored.

For a while she watched the woman Aunt Carli, who was arguing desultorily with Uncle Byron. Then Dane cut loose from the face and drifted.

She found herself in a simile in which, now, he was a hairy-chested, mightily thewed male warrior, hacking at a horrible, scaled, three-headed monster with a sword. The sword, when it struck flesh, dripped phosphorescent green ichor and sang snatches of Wagner; the monster's heads darted at him, one after the other, looking for an opening; humid, foul breath from its gaping mouths spewed on him like a furnace blast, and its enormous teeth were yellow; when it leaped and twisted, dodging his terrible blows, the ground trembled under his feet, nearly knocking him down.

Someone behind him screamed and he turned his head—one of the heads had swooped down and snatched up another warrior. The distraction doomed him; the monster's mouth closed over his head; the simile faded in a wash of red and the sound of gurgling screams.

"Sorry, champ, you lose," a voice said. "Try again?"

"Yes," someone said. "Reload saved game *Buddy Number Eight*."

"Loading," the first voice replied; "please wait."

=Buddy?=

=Go away. I'm busy.=

The monster's head descended again, and the sword went up. Despondent, Dane cut loose.

In a darkened chamber not much larger than a closet, a stack of baby bodies was crammed. A cleaner waldo was dusting them. I wonder if they're operational, Dane thought. She hooked the cleaner waldo, and spent some time tinkering. While she worked, Pablo's thoughts trickled through to her.

"Don't worry," he was telling some people, in a private *v*-space. Mara, Joe, Obediah, and two others, Natasha and Ian, were there. They all used their bizarre-looking avatars; Dane knew who they were only because Pablo did. "We had the opportunity to do a few rounds of debugging. I feel confident that the bombware will work just fine. Pursuit is not a problem."

"I suppose it's not just that," Mara said. "It's Mother."

Pablo felt a stab of fear; Dane felt it even at her remove. "What about her?"

"Oh, come on. Everybody can see she's failing fast. What's going to happen to us if?"

She left the "if" hanging there as though it were the end of her sentence. No one spoke.

Dane happened to overhear, as she worked on the toddler proxy. Not if, she thought; when.

Pablo said, "Not if—when."

Then she felt his alarm.

=You're not Buddy. Who are you?=

Terrified, she remained silent. Meanwhile, the others were reacting.

"She's fine!" Joe blared. "You're making too much out of this. She's just tired."

"That's right," Pablo said, wearily. "I don't know what I was saying. She's just been working so hard for so long. That's all. She'll be fine once we reach *Exodus*. Don't worry."

Dane felt tears well up, back in the crèche. She realized that Pablo was remembering something Uncle Marsh had said—*it'll only get worse*—and abruptly he knew, too, what Dane had seen and heard: Mother-Not's last, private conversation with Uncle Marsh. For a single, terrifying instant, as that memory came to him, she saw him seeing her.

Better get out of here, she thought. While Pablo's attention was diverted by the others' protests, she whipped up to the face bar, selected a twin setting, and darted away, to continue her restless wandering.

CARLI

Carli was having a hard time concentrating on the problem at hand. Byron kept asking her questions, pointing at the diagrams and scrawls in the jelly and feeding her possibilities, and her responses kept tapering off, while she stared blindly at the schematics.

"Come on, Carli," Byron said finally. "Hang with me here. We only have twelve hours left."

They'd been going around and around like this for what seemed like forever. Every idea they'd come up with had been unworkable for one reason or another. She was more exhausted than she'd ever been in her life, and worse, she'd lost hope. With a gut-deep sigh, she pushed off from the counter by the chemical hood and dropped slowly, lotus style, toward the floor, arms huddled about her legs and chin on her knees. Byron's eyes were dark and his face grizzled and gaunt. She looked away from the desperation there.

Don't look at me like that. I have nothing left to give. She couldn't even summon the energy to say it.

Severe sleep deprivation on top of being kidnapped is bad for morale.

With a growl, he reached down and grabbed her arms, and tried to shake her, sending them both into a spin as she touched down on the floor. He released her and, righting himself by grabbing the hood, said, as she tumbled slowly backward, "I need you! Pull it together, damn it! Do you want the probe astronauts to die because you couldn't get your shit together?"

His words made her cringe. Not my fault, damn you! Not my fault. Carli bumped up against the wall and started floating toward the door. Come on, D'Auber, she thought. Maybe it's not your fault they're at risk, but you have a chance to save them, if you try.

"All right." Drawing a deep breath, she touched the floor with a toe as it came into view—below? above?—and kicked back toward Byron and the jelly. She tried to summon some reasonable semblance of organized thought. He caught her and helped her resettle on the counter next to the jelly.

"All right," she said again. "Let's run through the problem one more time."

"OK." He rubbed his face and then picked up the pointer. "One more time. We have vibrations in the receptor tub. We can't engineer a correction to the physical design, and we don't have time to program a big, complicated program that would model the noise mathematically and allow us to subtract it from the signal. Therefore, we need a quick-and-dirty way to subtract out the vibration."

The door opened while he spoke. They turned. There stood an angel: a boy-child not more than three, hand on the doorjamb, toes barely touching the floor, with curly, black hair with reddish undertones, dark skin, and huge, gorgeous, amber-brown eyes. He pushed off with a grace that belied his apparent age, straight for Carli, who braced herself with a drawer handle and caught the boy.

The child tried to hug Carli, but Carli held him at arm's length and gave Byron a look. The child-body was a proxy; the pilot could be anyone.

"One of the crèche children. That's one of the old tot models they used to use; I don't know where he found it. Whoever it is, he would have to be a good deal older than the body looks. Who are you, dear?" he asked the child.

The boy ignored him entirely. He was looking intently at Carli, struggling to get to her.

"Hold me," he demanded.

Disturbed, hesitant, Carli brought the child to her shoulder and patted him. The child snuggled in and rested against her, a perfect fit against her chest, and Carli just held him for a moment, rocking him. Then she held the child back.

"Who are you?"

The child shook his head. "I can't tell you."

"Why not?"

The child's face grew anxious. "I'm sorry I hurt you. Please don't be mad at me."

Carli shoved the child away with a suppressed scream. "Oh, my God—it's the one who tried to kill me."

Byron lifted a hand. "Easy—"

The child struck the wall, hard. Carli grimaced at the blow, but the child was, of course, unharmed; it was the shock of seeing a young child smack against the wall, and the completely demolished look on his face as he rebounded, that wrung Carli's heart. Without a word, the child rebounded yet again, off the ceiling, and kicked out the door.

"Wait—"

Carli kicked off, too, and pursued him into the hall, but he was already gone. Carli grabbed a handhold.

"What the fuck do you want from me?" she shouted. Her voice trailed away, and she buried her face in her hands. "Why don't you just leave me alone?"

ECHO-CHAMBER MIND

Pablo worried.

Part of it was simple logistics. He'd originally counted on Buddy to monitor for pursuit by Shasta Station—or other—craft while he, Pablo, handled the training for the takeover of *Exodus*. But Buddy was nowhere to be found. And the others, especially the younger ones, kept coming to Pablo, because Mother wasn't answering their calls. He spent a lot of time with them, singly and in small groups, trying to calm their fears and keep them going. The interruptions made it impossible to concentrate on the technical problems he faced. So—though in his heart he was relieved that Buddy was gone—he had way too much to do.

But part of it was this sense that he was haunted. Haunted by a lonely child who wandered around the fringes of his thoughts, longing for something he couldn't deliver.

DANIEL

TECHNICAL DIFFICULTIES BEYOND THEIR CONTROL

Daniel awoke after eight. He put some food out for the cat, who seemed at least mildly grateful, and then dragged himself groggily back to Carli's computer, set the beanie onto his jack, and woke up his proxy, back on Penn Station.

First he went to triage/urgent care. Fox had been removed from the pressure chamber and was sleeping in a nulgy hammock, in the makeshift patient unit across the personnel tube. He was still on oxygen, but he looked a little better. Daniel, after some internal debate, left a note for him rather than waking him. According to the medics, there was still no sign of Paint. Definitely not a good omen.

At the airlock, the Marines were gathering: ten enlisted men and women, a lieutenant, and Captain Broca. At precisely twenty-one hundred and fifty hours the first seven soldiers climbed into the airlock, lugging a bunch of duffels and pallets of tools, rope, and other equipment and supplies. The door closed on them while they were donning their life bags. A moment later the door opened again on an empty airlock.

Captain Broca slapped Daniel on the back. "Let's go."

They swam into the lock. While Daniel sealed the door, the others velled their bags to the walls and climbed in.

"Get the lock," Broca told Daniel, then zipped up his own bag. Bracing himself, Daniel minimized pain sensors, then canceled the normal pressure-down procedure by triggering the big red lever. The airlock opened, disgorging its air to space with an explosive whoosh.

A suited scooter driver was waiting outside. Like the EMT earlier, he stared, but Daniel nodded with a wave, as if it was completely normal for a human body to be tootling around in a vacuum in his shirtsleeves. KaleidoScope was finished; proxies would be all over the news in no time, and now that he'd been seen once already, Daniel didn't feel like wasting time with a life bag, when time was so precious.

Together they strung the bags onto a loop of nylon rope. Then Daniel grabbed hold and the driver accelerated away from Penn Station and the solar arrays, following the first scooter a dozen yards or so ahead, through the bits of debris that led like a trail of bread crumbs toward the distant speck that was Shasta Station.

They neared the station. Shasta, postseparation, looked like space debris. Shrapnel had scarred its surfaces and damaged some of its outer equipment; bits of latticework and cables wiggled and flopped around as it slowly tumbled; more junk trailed it like flies hounding an elephant's corpse. The Lagrange Spaceways shuttle clung tightly to the docking node, shy of the shaft's broken end. Behind and off to one side, Earth was mostly dark, except for a line of white and blue at the terminator.

They docked with the shuttle and entered through the open cargo bay. In the airlock, once it was pressurized, Daniel helped the enlisted men get out of their bags. They all climbed into the passenger compartment and buckled in, in the front two rows. Through the cockpit door, the pilot, copilot, and navigator were doing instrument checks. Bags of equipment and a dozen empty space suits were strapped to seats in the back few rows.

Broca and the lieutenant moved to the front. The lieutenant issued some orders Daniel didn't pay much attention to, since they had nothing to do with him, and then Broca spoke.

"The bad guys are within eight hours of reaching lunar perigee. They're accelerating steadily at one-hundredth gee and they've got a ten-hour head start on us, so we're going to have to make up some time. We'll be accelerating at two gees for the next hour, and will intercept them in, we hope, about seven to eight hours." He brought his hands together with a clap. "It's going to be close, boys and girls. Lieutenant Michaelson will be issuing further orders as we approach the intercept point. Stand by and avoid moving around till we finish the burn."

A murmur arose, then died away as the pilot gave them a countdown. The shuttle disengaged from the dock and moved away from poor, damaged Shasta, using the small maneuvering rockets. A moment later the main engine kicked in, pressing them into their couches.

Just before the engine's engagement Daniel muted his sensory inputs to avoid motion sickness, so the fact that something was wrong dawned on him only slowly, as the shouting differentiated itself from the engine's roar. He tuned back in.

Broca, nearby, was yelling, "What's the trajectory? *What's the trajectory?*"

The gees were a lot more than two; maybe four. All of the others were plastered to their seats, facial muscles distorted, mouths pulled into wide, ugly grins.

"I don't know!" the pilot yelled. He and the copilot were pinned in their seats, struggling to reach the controls.

Daniel looked at the Marines on either side of him. They stared back, eyes wide with terror, mouths grinning. Terror settled in his own gut. Then guilt; he alone had nothing to fear.

The pilot and copilot finally sat back, helplessly. The navigator yelled to Broca, "Sir, the navigational systems have been booby-trapped! We're heading into a much lower orbit! Unless the burn stops soon, we'll collide with Earth's atmosphere—if the engine doesn't blow first!"

"Eject fuel," Broca shouted back. The pilot turned back to the controls.

After a moment, she yelled, "No response!"

Daniel unbuckled himself and pulled himself up. Servos screamed in his shoulders, elbows, hips, and knees. "Permission to see what I can do, Captain!" he yelled.

"Permission granted!"

His proxy, in Earth's gravity, weighed about 320 pounds. In this acceleration, it weighed about 1,500 pounds. It took most the unit's strength to even move. He unbuckled himself and climbed with great effort into the cockpit, got the pilot's attention, and tapped his own ear. "Frequency?"

The pilot looked toward the navigator, who yelled, showing each number with his hands, "One four two point eight five megahertz!"

"Schematics?"

He had to repeat himself twice. The navigator gave him a helpless, minute shake of his head.

As he bumped down the now vertical aisle toward the airlock, Daniel called up his linkware, selected the communications software, and eye-clicked on the numeric icons to select the right radio frequency. Physical-stress warning lights were going wild in front of his eyes. Then he dropped into the airlock, crashed onto the bottom like a ton of metal ingots, strained upward to close the inner door, and crouched on the narrow strip of wall by the exit. His internal alarms subsided. The engine's roar was only slightly more muffled here.

Hanging on tight to a handhold, he threw a lever on the control panel between his feet, blowing the air out the lock. He weighed so much the sudden decompression barely made him sway. Sound ceased.

Muting the sudden pain from the cold, Daniel tucked himself over the edge, down into the cargo bay, and dangled from the door's edge there. The pistons and rods in his arms complained, silently, triggering a pain response and lights across his vision.

"Can you hear me?" he subvoked. "This is Sornsen. I'm in the cargo bay. Acknowledge."

He thought he heard a response, but wasn't sure—the roar could just as easily have come from radio noise as from a broadcast of the engine's firing—so he tinkered with his reception, cutting out all lower sound frequencies and augmenting the higher, and tried again.

"This is Sornsen. Acknowledge."

"Repeat, we copy," the pilot said. "Go ahead."

It was still hard to hear due to ambient noise at her end.

"I'm completely unfamiliar with shuttle technology," Daniel said. "I'll need you to talk me through this."

"Copy. Ship's unfamiliar to us, too, but we can make some good guesses. Need to cut off fuel to engines. In five minutes the orbit we end up with will slam us into atmosphere. Engine isn't made to burn at four gees for this long. It's heating up—could blow before end of burn."

"How soon?"

"Don't know. Three or four minutes."

Daniel called up a timer and set it at three minutes. "How do I get to the fuel pumps?"

A long pause. He thought he heard the pilot yelling to someone, perhaps the copilot or navigator. Then, "Look for access panel to fuel manifold room. Back of bay."

He twisted, looking around, and then down between his feet. The cargo bay was mostly empty; a few big fiberglass shipping containers were lashed to the shuttle's nonopening side, lower down. A huge crane lay folded nearby, its arm and claw retracted. On the other side of the door several maneuvering units were secured to the bulkhead.

The bay was maybe two hundred feet deep. Twenty stories straight down. He was half tempted to save time and just drop, but even in one gee that would be a long fall. Even if his proxy could take a four-gee, two-hundred-foot fall—which he doubted—he'd seriously damage the bulkhead on impact.

Along the nonopening bulkhead that ran along the length of the shuttle bay, about thirty feet away, was a personnel ladder that went all the way down. An access panel rimmed in high-visibility red lay below it, about ten feet from the ladder.

"I see it," he said. "Heading there now."

Two minutes fifty-five seconds left. He hand-over-handed, slipping and straining—with the engine's vibrations jerking him around like a pebble on a shaker table and his warning lights flashing—slowly across the handholds set into the crane's base, past the control booth to the ladder. Then he looked down again. Two minutes eight seconds left.

The fastest way down would be a controlled fall, using the ladder as a sort of "firehouse pole" to slow himself. About every fifteen to twenty feet were mountings that fastened the ladder to the bulkhead. In between them he could fall, and use friction against the ladder's poles to break himself before striking the mountings. He planted his hands and feet on the outside of the ladder, and just barely released his grip.

He dropped dizzyingly fast, and didn't react quickly enough as the first set of mounting clamps neared. The impact of the clamps against his palms nearly knocked him from the ladder. He managed to grab the rail with one hand, but the other slipped free—he smacked against the wall hard enough to dent it, and dangled one-handed until he could regain his grip. Then he dropped again, more careful this time to brake himself between the mountings.

Finally he struck bottom. His strain gauges declared permanent damage to his elbow, knee, and hand structures. One minute thirty-one seconds left. He crawled over to the access panel, leaving a trail of crimson smears. Friction had burned the artificial skin from his proxy's hands and exposed the inner tubing and infrastructure, but damage to the lubricant lines and muscle pistons could be ignored for now. The access panel lay on the floor, labeled "Pump Manifold Room—Authorized Personnel Only!" in big red letters, and had a security lock on it.

One minute nineteen seconds left. No time for subtlety. He braced himself and pulled with all his might. His strain lights, already blinking, began a frenzied, brightening staccato. "Cooling Failure Danger!" the linkware warned. Something gave and the door flew open, knocking him onto his butt hard enough to jar a few screws loose inside.

Daniel dropped into the manifold room and squatted on a large pipe a few feet below the opening. His internal overheating and structural-strain lights faded, slowly. Forty-eight seconds left.

"I'm inside the manifold room," he subvoked.

The room was unevenly lit. It was large, filled with equipment and piping. He straddled the pipe and bent down, hanging on tight in the shaking, and craned his head back and forth. At the bottom, amid a snarl of piping the size of sequoia trunks and valves so big a large man could stand inside them, he spotted the pumps: monstrous, odd-shaped structures with all kinds of multicolored pipes and conduits coming and going. Beyond them, on the bulkhead, he caught glimpses of bright infrared splotches. Even with his mostly deadened temperature sense, he could feel their heat against his proxy's skin.

"I see the pumps."

"Do you see power lines?" the pilot asked.

"Not sure. There are all kinds of conduits, but I don't know what's what."

"Look for pipe labels."

He crawled in further and looked around. Nearby were some labels. Electrical conduit was painted orange.

"Got it."

"Disable power to the pumps."

Twenty-nine seconds left, and the infrared blotches were growing bigger and brighter. More warning lights blinked across his vision. His cooling system was failing from the strain. Core temp was at 140 and climbing. System failure in two minutes. What the hell—the engine would probably blow them all to bits before that, and his antimatter core would simply atomize the debris.

"The valves are closer than the pumps. Are they fail-shut?"

"Affirmative. Standard practice."

"I'm going for them, then."

He climbed carefully down through the piping to the valve labeled "Oxidizer." The electrical conduit was a steel pipe about as thick as his wrist, painted orange. Seventeen seconds left. He grabbed the conduit and pulled. Fifteen seconds. It resisted—bent—broke. Eleven. He tore the wires loose. Nine. Blue fire spat out, jolting him. He flinched. Five. The linkware reported a visual sensor malfunction due to a short circuit, and color vision began winking in and out. Three.

Then the four gees of shaking, vibrating force dropped to zero, and over the radio, as he floated up, shouts of joy swelled to replace the roar of the engine. The angry infrared blotches that strobed against the bulkhead as his color vision came and went were already fading.

"You did it!" the pilot whooped. Daniel pushed off from the oxidizer valve, toward the fuel valve.

"I'll go ahead and stop the fuel flow," he said, "while I'm at it."

The main pump, running dry, blew—silently—flinging metal and metaceramic. Shrapnel sliced him nearly in two. With a scream, he unjacked and shot out of the squish. The cat started, and looked at him in alarm. He stared around, panting.

"God *damn* it!" he yelled. The words echoed oddly. His hands were clutching his completely intact midsection.

The proxy's antimatter pinch-bottle was in his lower torso. It would go any second—if it hadn't already. The Marines were dead.

There's still a chance. Move your butt, Sornsen. He leaped back into the squish and reset the beanie. The pilot was talking to him. He ignored her.

His proxy's pain sensors were screaming bloody murder, and red lubricant was floating in globs and drops all around, blocking vision. His right side was disabled, but his left arm and torso still functioned. He ignored the pain as best he could—it still hurt like hell—and pushed the lubricant globules out of his way. His pelvis and legs floated at an impossible angle, attached to the rest of him by a flap of skin. His artificial guts were hanging out. The linkware blared: "Antimatter Containment Failure Imminent! Evacuate all Personnel! Evacuate all Personnel!"

Looking down at half a body was too much for him. Back in Carli's squish, he tossed his cookies. Ignoring the wet and the stink, he forced himself to relax and sink back into the proxy. Then he spotted an access hatch to the shuttle's exterior maybe ten feet away. His proxy had some redundancies built in—battery power in case of reactor failure, and separate hydraulic systems for different parts of the body. But he couldn't last long with this much damage—if he didn't hurry, he was going to freeze up just like the pump had.

He grabbed the flap of skin, tore his lower half loose, and shoved it away, sending more hydraulic fluid flying. Then he pushed off against a pipe with his one good hand and shot across the room to the hatch. He smacked against the bulkhead and grabbed a handhold. There was no lock on the door's interior. He yanked it open. Space greeted him.

Daniel got a good grip on the doorjamb, aligned himself carefully, and shoved for all he was worth. Let it be enough, please, God. He tumbled away, spilling small parts and dribbling lubricant. He could even see the pinch-bottle dangling out. "CONTAINMENT FAILURE . . . EXPLOSION IMMINENT . . . CONTAINMENT FAILURE . . . EXPLOSION IMMINENT . . ."

"Hey, jocks. Do you copy?" he asked.

"We copy," the pilot said. "Are you all right? We registered an explosion back there—"

"My proxy—er, waldo—is about to blow," he subvoked, "and it's powered by antimatter."

"Shit!"

"It'll be a big boom, but I think you'll be OK. I'm outside the shuttle now, about a hundred feet from you and receding. The shock wave should be greatly diminished by the lack of air, and the unit will be vaporized, so shrapnel's not a significant concern. But you'd better brace yourselves."

"Roger." Daniel heard her relaying the message. Then, "We've recalculated our orbit and it looks like we'll skim Earth's atmosphere but not enter it. You saved our asses. Just barely."

Daniel grinned. He had a sudden urge to break into a rendition of "Benson, Arizona."

"So buy me a beer sometime," he said.

Then he looked moonward and sobered. Looks like you're on your own, Carli.

And there was light.

BYRON HAS A BRAINSTORM

"Oh shit." Byron suddenly slapped his forehead. "Shit, shit, shit. What a dumb mistake!"

"What are you talking about?" Carli asked, frowning muzzily.

He stabbed at the schematic. "We've been troubleshooting on our prototype! Current omnis are *multichannel*. All we have to do is send a signal to ourselves and we'll have it."

She shook her head. "Beg pardon?"

"Look, we've been acting as if we only have one channel to work with. But they accommodate several channels now! We send a known signal to ourselves, routed through *Exodus*'s omni. It goes out on one channel and comes back on another. By comparing signal-out to signal-in, we'll know exactly what the noise is at all times. We can set up a subroutine to subtract the vibrational noise automatically from our transmission signal on a third channel."

Carli's eyes went wide. It was so obvious, now that he pointed it out. She felt like an idiot.

"It should work," she said. "You're right."

It was hard to summon up much enthusiasm, though, over an insight that would allow these creeps to steal a spaceship.

Byron was beaming. He called up the comm menu on the jelly. "I'll get Patricia."

PABLO

THE LEAVE-TAKING

Again he tried to contact Mother with a report on the bombware's success in thwarting the pursuers, and again she didn't answer. Pablo made up his mind. It was time to talk to Uncle Marsh. Someone in authority needed to know what was going on.

He downloaded into his proxy in the crèche chamber and unstrapped himself from his launch slab. To his surprise, Uncle Marsh, Aunt Jenna, and Mother were floating beside her crèche, talking in low voices. They looked up when he came over. Uncle Marsh concealed something behind his back. Mother's face and body were so stiff . . . something was very wrong.

"I've been looking for you," he said. "The bombware worked exactly as planned. The Shasta pursuers are now jetting off in the wrong direction. We've analyzed our trajectory with respect to all civilian habitats, as well as Patriot Base and Einstein Station, and the possibility of interception is now minimal."

"Excellent," Mother said. "Anything else?"

He shook his head.

Uncle Marsh said gently, "We'd like some privacy, then, Pablo."

Pablo looked from one to the other. "What's going on?"

The three exchanged a look.

"It's all right," Mother said. "Pablo should know. He's old enough to understand.

"Come here." She held out a hand. Pablo, feeling dread, kicked forward and took it. She pulled him to her, and laid her hand on her crèche. He eyed it nervously.

"My flesh is very sick," she said. "It's suffering. I've tried to last as long as I could—"

"No." Pablo said it softly, shaking his head. Then something went wrong with his voice control—his voice rose in pitch and volume. "No, no, no. You're going to live forever, just like you promised. We all are."

"Pablo—"

PABLO   DANE   BUDDY

THE SHATTERING

He shrieked at the top of his volume. *"NO!* You promised! You can't go!"

"Pablo!" She grabbed his arms and gave him a hard shake. Her voice was low, but sharp. He stared at her.

Betrayal. Betrayal.

"Listen to me. I'm not like you kids. I started the drugs very late and my immune system fights them.

"I'm dying, Pablo. The treatments have given me thirty years I would never have had. But my flesh has cancer. I can't take the pain anymore. I've held on as long as I could. It's time for me to go."

She's leaving me! **The memory came back, as jagged and raw as if it had happened yesterday. She sat in the dark woman's lap.**

"You must promise to take good care of Pablito for me. He's always so sick. . . ."

And the dark woman wiped away tears, while Dane reached for dust motes in the stream of light that crossed her little hand.

The wild distress that emanated from Pablo disrupted his concentration so thoroughly, Buddy barely noticed when the Cyclops ran him through with its spear.

He canceled the game and tuned in.

What the *hell* was going on? Pablo was screaming, Dane was screaming; Buddy could barely think. He shut Dane out to better tune Pablo in.

"Do you know what cancer is?" Uncle Marsh asked. Pablo wanted to punch his patronizing, lying old face.

"Of course I do," he snapped. "I've seen it in loads of similes and broadcasts. Don't try to fool me. Flesh doesn't get cancer; bodies do."

Oh, my God. Pablo was right—she really *is* dying.

The realization stunned him.

Then joy bubbled up—fierce, acrid, sulfurous. He wanted to dance.

He sensed Buddy's return. The mental touch seared him, with its terrible rage. But he didn't have the strength to shut it out.

"But . . . but . . ." Uncle Marsh gave Mother a look. "It's that damn religion of theirs. Where do we start?"

Her face drawn and lips pulled down, Aunt Jenna stared at the walls, the floor, anywhere but Pablo's questioning gaze. Uncle Marsh, too, was evasive. But Mother was looking straight at him.

"Let me," she told Uncle Marsh.

Mother looked at him and made several starts. Finally she said, "I wish I didn't have to go, Pablo."

A long silence. "I never wanted children. All my long life I was happy with my choices. Then you came along." She smiled. "You, especially, Pablo. You were the son I never had.

"I still remember that first day, when your mother handed you over to my care. You cried for days, and for long afterward you let no one near you but me. I came to love you more deeply than I'd have believed was possible."

> *"No llores, Mamá,"* Dane had said, patting the dark woman's cheek with a thin little hand. *Don't cry.* The woman captured her hand and held it in a painfully tight grip.
>
> "He'll have excellent care, I promise you," the man said, holding out a piece of paper and a pen. "Just sign here."

He threw his shields aside, jubilant. Die, bitch! Die horribly!

Her pretense of grief was such a mockery, it made him want to spit in her face.

Lies, all lies. You never loved me. How could you love me and hurt me the way you did? All the insults, the criticism— shutting me in my crèche— I was just a little boy. I trusted you. My God, how you hurt me.

Bullshit. You don't know how to love.

Mother, no. You can't leave me. No.

She read his expression, and touched his face with a sigh. "You're too forgiving, Pablo. I wasn't." A pause. "I wasn't a good mother. Maybe it was a good thing I never had kids of my own. Just didn't have the patience for it." She turned away. "Let's get this over with," she said to Uncle Marsh, stiffly.

Uncle Marsh brought out the needle he had been hiding, and took hold of her IV pump.

"Wait." She grabbed Uncle Marsh's hand, stopping him, and lifted the crèche's lid. "One more thing."

Pablo screamed and tried to back away. Mother held on to him.

"It's all right," she said. "Don't be afraid."

Inside, floating in gel, was a shriveled, bald *thing* with tubes in it.

Pablo . . . Buddy felt despair. You poor, deluded fool.

That was the understatement of the millennium.

And Dane—but no. Not Dane. She was only a spectator. It was Pablito—tiny Pablito: frail, sick, and trusting—who realized as his mother signed the paper what was about to happen.

He clung to her, shrieking, while she tried to pry his arms loose and hand him over to the old white woman standing there.

His mother took an envelope from them while Pablito reached out for her, over the old woman's shoulder.

And she turned her beautiful face from him and walked briskly away, shoulders hunched as though she were caught in a hailstorm, ignoring his anguished screams.

The needle was filled with, what? Poison?
So you're jigging on us, old whore? Get us into a huge mess with people trying to kill us, and then slip away without telling anyone.
Figures.

He found Pablo's fear and revulsion contemptible.

=Oh shit—Buddy, help me!=

=Oh, go chill. It's just a lump of old flesh.=

Pablo watched, numb, as the thing's nail-less claw reached up and pulled off its respirator mask, then took hold of Pablo's hand and tried to pull him down.

But his own flesh crawled at the sight, too

It was wheezing and moaning in its nutrient gel, a flaccid hunk of dying flesh.

"¡Mamá! ¡No va—no va sin migo!"

Don't go. Don't go without me.

How could she have, and yet loved him?

He couldn't stand this—couldn't bear the sight, couldn't bear Buddy's terrible rage. With a mental scream he shrank away.

This was her? This pitiful creature was the raging, terrifyingly powerful woman who had made his life a living hell?

Love Trumps Rage Trumps Love

Buddy took prime as Pablo fled. The *thing* was tugging weakly at him. For an instant he resisted. It wanted to *kiss* him or something. Ugh. Its rheumy old eyes were peering up at him.

Then inspiration struck. He stopped resisting and bent down.

"Good-bye, Pablo," it croaked in his ear.

He wanted to put his hands around her neck and strangle her. "Mother . . ." he said. But the words that followed were someone else's. "I know how hard you tried. I love you."

Aghast, outraged, he stared inward. Pablo—it must have been. He'd tricked him. The fucker. Buddy's moment was stolen.

=I'll get you for that. I'll get you.=

The only answer was a deep, sorrowful wail that might have been Pablo, or might have been Dane. Or . . . someone else? He shook his head in confusion and sudden fear. Who else was there?

The creature's parchment kiss brushed Buddy's lips, ever so lightly. A satisfied look came onto its ancient, wrinkled face. He straightened, stiff with shock and disgust, lips tingling, as the creature nodded to Uncle Marsh and slipped its mask back on. Uncle Marsh stuck the syringe into the IV drip pump inlet and emptied it. Then Mother closed the lid to the crèche.

"You're in charge now," she told Buddy. "Protect the children."

He nodded stiffly. "We will."

"Jenna, Marsh," she said, "I depend on you to get them through these next few days, and safely away."

Aunt Jenna came forward and hugged her. Her voice sounded strained. "We'll make sure of it, Number One."

Then a look of shock grew on Mother's face. Aunt Jenna pushed away with a scared expression; Buddy and Uncle Marsh started as she screamed, arched her back, and began to thrash in midair.

"*It hurts!* Oh, God!" she cried. "Oh, God! Marsh—MAKE IT STOP!"

Then she froze, and her proxy eyes stared blindly.

"She's at peace," Uncle Marsh said. His face was as devoid of expression as a proxy on autopilot. He and Aunt Jenna tugged her over to the slab and strapped her down. They stood there looking at her, and her crèche, for a long time. Then Uncle Marsh laid a hand on Buddy's arm.

"Pablo, we need you to be strong. If you tell the others what happened just now, they'll panic."

Buddy was still looking at the crèche. Uncle Marsh's words barely penetrated.

She's really gone, he thought. A feeling swelled up, a huge, ungainly glob of several emotions all stirred together—swelled up and burst. He threw his head back, and laughed, and laughed, and laughed—in proxy and *in corpus*—uncontrollably, till his head felt as if it would explode and his diaphragm spasmed. Somehow, Aunt Jenna had gotten hold of him in a tight grip, and was saying, "It's all right. It's all right."

All right? It was a fucking *miracle!* Buddy doubled over, clutching his midsection. Finally, gradually, the peals of laughter faded. I'm free, he thought. Free.

He felt so sleepy.

He yawned, and laid his head on Aunt Jenna's shoulder.

AMNESIA STRIKES AGAIN

"—hear me?" Uncle Marsh was saying. "We have to keep quiet about this. Just till after we take *Exodus*. Jenna has prepared a simulacrum of her using your *virtu*-proxy technology, to get us through the transfer. Then we'll make a general announcement."

Pablo jerked up his head, which had been resting on Aunt Jenna's shoulder, and pulled away.

He'd had another blackout. His flesh ached from recent spasms; Buddy was gone again and Mother's crèche was closed. Her body was now strapped to the launch slab. She must have faced in again.

What had they been talking about before? He couldn't remember. When in doubt, stall for time.

"I won't say anything," he promised solemnly.

PLAN A, GO

A few moments later Byron turned back to Carli. "I can't get through. Let me try Jenna."

After several tries, Jenna's net avatar materialized in the jelly. Byron told her the news. The artificial face smiled.

"That's marvelous! Great work, both of you. I can program it, no problem; it's a simple concept. Just give me a while to get the signal set up and the subroutine written. By the time we reach lunar perigee, or maybe a little after, we should be go Plan A."

"Jenna, before you sign off—what's with Patricia? I'm getting worried. She's been out of touch since launch."

She hesitated. "I don't know. I think with her illness, all the stress—" Jenna shrugged. "She just hasn't been up for much. Probably saving her strength for the takeover."

"Right." Byron's frown cleared. He signed off and rubbed his hands together. "Hoo-*hooo!* We did it."

Carli rubbed her brow. Asshole. "I'd like to lie down somewhere for a while."

"Sure. Fine." He slapped her on the back. She wanted to slug him. "There's a row of suites one deck down. Take any of them."

DANIEL

HOMECOMING

He tried to get through to Shasta Station again, but this time even the omni lines were tied up. The news pages didn't tell him anything new. He gave it up for the night, slept long and hard, and woke up at about ten in the morning. While munching toast and sipping coffee—real coffee!—he mused over his proxy's dramatic ending, and how surprisingly unaffected he was over having been blown to smithereens.

Maybe I'm just numb, he thought. Maybe there'll be psychic hell to pay later. Or who knows? Maybe I got off lucky this time.

After breakfast he faced into the news nets and found the rosters of Shasta evacuees.

Fox had been one of the first to be medevacked; he had been brought back to White Sands and was being kept for observation in an Alamogordo hospital. His main injuries included frostbite and damage to the lungs; health status was listed as "stable and improving." And— Daniel broke into a big grin—Jackson Brennan DuPont, listed as having only minor injuries, was due to arrive at White Sands Skyport in two hours and fifteen minutes. If he hurried, they'd just make it.

Fox was overjoyed to see Daniel. He was in a ward with other evacuees, his limbs swathed in so much LiveSkin he looked like he had no fingers nor toes, and the rest of him all gelled up till he shone like an oiled beach freak. His black hair was tangled and he was covered with bruises and had red patches all over his face, chest, and upper thighs. In other words, he looked like hell. The doctors were reluctant to let him go, and made him sign a release to the effect that he was leaving against medical advice.

Then Daniel chauffeured him out to the Skyport.

They saw the shuttle landing, far away down the gypsum flats, as Daniel drove up to the curb. He talked an airport security guy into letting them leave the car (all it took was a glimpse of Fox and an offhand mention that Fox was a Shasta Station evacuee whose husband was on the next shuttle), and they headed for the airport security checkpoint

as fast as Fox could hobble. Daniel spotted a wheelchair down a side
corridor and had Fox climb in; from there they made better time.
Signs announced the arrival of Flight 882 from Shasta Station. Hundreds of well-wishers and media types were in the way.

"Excuse me!" Daniel said loudly, bumping the chair gently against
people's legs, earning glares. "Coming through."

They made it to the front just in time to see Paint come out of the
secured area, along with several others. A cheer went up, and the
crowd surged forward.

"Paint!" Fox yelled, waving with his LiveSkinned arm.

Paint looked around and spotted Fox, who had stood up. With a
gasp, Paint ran at Fox and grabbed him in a fierce hug. Tears squeezed
out of his eyes.

"Foxifox. I thought you were dead."

"Easy," Fox gasped.

"Sorry." With a contrite smile, Paint loosened his hold. He looked
Fox up and down and shook his head with a chuckle. "Is this a new
look for you?"

"Do you like it?"

"It beats the alternative, girlfriend."

A reporter waldo spotted them and came over. Shining a light on
them, it asked a couple of questions, which they answered briefly. Then
Daniel ushered Fox back into the wheelchair and they three left.

"Where were you?" Fox demanded as they made their way through
the concourse. " 'S sick-scared you were dead."

Paint shrugged. "Thought they might blame us for the explosion.
So I slipped away and hid. Searchers found me, though, finally. I
feigned confusion." He touched a bruise on his temple, smiling.
"Head injury."

He whistled, eyes widening, when he saw the collocar at the curb.
Daniel keyed the locks and held the back door open. A small crowd
had gathered; word had apparently spread that they were among the
survivors of the Shasta incident.

"You guys have been through enough. You deserve a little luxury.
I know Carli wouldn't mind."

Grinning, Paint helped Fox into the back, then climbed into the
spacious, camel-colored leather seat next to him. He opened the bar
door, got out some glasses and some tequila, salt, and lime, and poured
them both a drink.

Daniel faced into the controls and started the car. People were waving outside the windows. Daniel, Paint, and Fox waved back, and the car crept into the traffic.

Paint socked down a drink, then drew a deep breath and took Fox's wrapped hands, wearing a scared face.

"Marry me, Foxifox."

Fox pulled a hand loose and slugged him lightly on the arm. "We are married, dummy."

"No. I mean *married* married."

Fox wore a carefully neutral expression. "You mean renew our contract right away?"

Paint shook his head. "I mean till death do us part."

In the mirror, Daniel saw Fox's eyes go wide. Paint nodded at the unspoken question. "Don't want to lose you." Pause. "Ready to change my shoes, I guess."

A slow grin broke like sunrise on Fox's face, and he cupped Paint's chin in his hand.

"Yes," he said. "Oh, yes."

Smiling, Daniel closed and clouded the window between front and back as Paint and Fox came together in a deep, tender kiss.

He pulled onto the highway, the high-speed lane, back to Albuquerque. A twinge of envy got him.

Changed your shoes. Daniel frowned, thoughtfully, remembering Carli's words in the fog that night.

He thought about Morris some more, and about the others he had loved, who had been hurt or killed—struck down by illness or violence before their time.

Sure hurt, losing someone you loved. Sure made it easier to avoid hurting, if you didn't get too close to anyone. Be a hero, bury yourself in your work, keep people who want to know you at arm's length, and pursue the ones who aren't interested, just to keep yourself from noticing how lonely you are.

But he was tired of being a proxy-jock, of living in a superhero fantasy world and making up fantasy relationships to waste his time with. It was time for real life, for a change. A life with real people in it, like Fox and Paint had.

He thought about the whips he had killed. That night would join Morris's death and a few others in his portfolio of things to wake him screaming at night.

No, being a superhero was way overrated.

So. No more chimeras. No more antics, no avoiding the interested women and chasing the unavailable ones. Someone simple and loving, to travel with, to talk to, to make love to, to come home to every evening . . . It sounded wonderful. Someone who saw him for what he was and loved what she saw. A slow, thoughtful smile slipped onto his mouth as he considered it. And hell, why not? A cat. Maybe a dog, too. And a cockatiel. Yeah. He wondered if they still had cockatiels in South America.

CARLI

PHONE HOME

The communications linkware in one lab was functional. She stumbled across it shortly after they'd left lunar perigee.

She logged onto the comunit as a guest, not expecting any response—just in case somebody had screwed up—and called up the commware, and the jelly's menu display indicated that the omni linkware was active.

Somebody *had* screwed up. Carli stared at the display, mouth suddenly dry, heart racing.

They would be outside normal omni range by now. *Normal* omni range. But with the improved software, if in place—which it had to be for their hijacking to work—they could receive, and transmit, up to two and a half times farther: maybe fifteen thousand miles or so from the transmitter at Einstein Station.

She didn't know what their velocity and acceleration were, but it wouldn't be long till they were out of range. Whatever she did, she'd better hurry.

They'll detect the message as soon as I send it, she thought, almost certainly. I'd better prepare carefully. Record the message in advance. Was there a way to stop them—was there any bit of information she could send that would help a rescue effort?

Information would be good; opening a door to electronic invasion would be better. If their linkware was immobilized, they'd be trapped in their crèches, unable to further manipulate *Exodus*. But she didn't have enough computer experience to find any back doors into their linkware systems that outsiders might be able to use.

She recorded a message, floating before the comunit's camera.

"Dad, this is Carli. I'm transmitting from com number 46A-223-P990-147. I'm a prisoner of the people who blew up Shasta Station. There are thirty-one of them. Twenty-seven are the crèche kids; four are adults: Patricia Taylor, Marshall Sullivan, Byron Kowalski, and Jenna Sternberg. No other hostages but me.

"They plan to steal *Exodus*. We're accelerating at maximum thrust toward a planned rendezvous with the probe, at a point in a one-point-oh-five-oh-oh AU orbit. Since *Exodus* has much more powerful engines than ours, they intend for it to race up-system and then modify its trajectory to match ours. From that data you can get the approximate rendezvous point. I doubt anyone can intercept—our acceleration is already too great for us to be overtaken, and the rendezvous point is too far from Earth-space. But someone should check whether a scout or mining craft is in the vicinity and can get there in time. It'd be a miracle, but so is this open line. It's worth a check.

"Their takeover of the probe is entirely dependent on their linkware. Find a hacker—a *good* one—and call me back. We might be able to find a way into their systems and sabotage the linkware. This is your best chance. Hurry; we'll be out of range soon." Tears welled up in her eyes and her throat muscles tightened. "Tell Mom, Jo, and Paint, and everybody, that I love them. Keep me in your thoughts. If I don't make it back, I will all my worldly possessions to Jackson Brennan DuPont."

Then, wiping away tears, she encrypted the message as a super-compressed file. She picked the omni icon on the jelly display, chose her father's e-mail account as the recipient, identified the message as urgent, and transmitted it. Wringing her hands, she watched the confirmation bar fill with color. It only took a second or so for the linkware to confirm transmission. Successful!

She waited . . . and waited. Too damn long. They'd be out of range of Einstein Station's omni any moment.

Then—amazingly!—a call came. She picked up. It was her father, transmitting real-time. He gasped when he saw her.

"Carli. My God. It *is* you."

This man, whom she had spent much of her life idolizing, was just as responsible for what had been done to the crèche children as Taylor and her crew. She flinched inwardly from the thought.

"We don't have much time, Dad. Get a computer expert on this line right away."

"I've got someone here. The son of a colleague. We're ready to go."

Then Carli pressed fingers against her lips. She couldn't hold it back. "It was a terrible thing you did to these kids."

Ashes. Ashes. He gave her a stricken look and lowered his head. "You don't know how long I've wished I could undo it. . . ."

"You can set things right. Come clean."

He stared, and gasped. "My enemies would tear me apart. And what good would it do the kids now?"

"You owe it to the people who've put their trust in you, Dad. You know it's going to come out sometime, anyway."

A silence while he stared at her. Then he rubbed a thumb across his brow.

"Yeah," he said with a heavy sigh. "I suppose . . . maybe you're right."

She didn't want to sign off.

"We'd better get that hacker on-line." Her voice caught. "I love you."

"Love you, too, Coo," he said, hoarsely.

He kissed his fingers and reached out in response; she did likewise. They were both crying now. Her fingers touched the jelly's smooth, cool glass.

Then her father touched a button, and the view switched to a young man with waxed and sculpted, multilength, multicolored hair and a painted face. He gave her some instructions for how to set up her computer. When she confirmed the settings, he gave her a feral grin that reminded her a little of Paint. His teeth were filed to points and capped with gold.

"I'm going in," he said.

She reached out and cut the signal off. And a second signal came in, almost instantly. Her comunit answered on its own. Windows and menus lit up inside the jelly—icons and options flashed past that she'd never even known existed. Then musical notes sounded in rapid succession—he and the computer communicating in a tonal language.

The software started to complain of delays and time-outs. The signal was fading. She clutched the table's edge so hard her hands hurt. *Come on, come on,* she thought. *Move your ass.* Then the system froze up.

She sat back, chewing her lip. Had he managed to make it into the system? Had he done any damage? Or had it been a futile effort?

It hadn't been very long. It probably hadn't been enough time. But maybe, just maybe . . .

She bounced out of the lab and through the corridors, seeking Byron. Let's poke the anthill, she thought, and see if anything interesting scurries out.

FURTHER TECHNICAL DIFFICULTIES

They took Fox to St. Joe's, and Paint went with Fox to check him in. In the waiting area, meanwhile, Daniel accessed the jello-nets using his kelly, and checked on news of the space station, the Marines, Kaleidas, the project, or Krueger's murder.

Nothing new was posted on Krueger and the Austin project. Daniel's ID jello had been buried deep in a substory of a substory of the primary news item. Most international attention was on the disaster at Shasta Station.

The toll was twenty-two dead and 189 seriously injured, with over 600 minor injuries and one person still missing. A terrible toll . . . but it could have been worse. According to the several sources he found, Shasta was being stabilized and repaired in its new orbit. Kaleidas had just whipped around the moon and was heading for parts unknown in the outer solar system. None of the outer planets were in their path. One commentator speculated that they might be heading for the asteroid belt, intending to set up some sort of colony on one of the larger asteroids. There was no talk about Carli or the possibility of other hostages.

The Marines had been rescued without mishap, just a little while ago, after their brush with Earth's atmosphere. Captain Broca and his crew had refused to comment on what had happened, at least publicly, but apparently word was starting to spread through the nets about a manlike waldo that had been involved in rescue efforts at Shasta and on the Marine shuttle. One commentator speculated about a possible connection between the man-waldo and Waldos, Inc., which led the field in that area and had links with the Austin facility, where a prominent scientist had just been murdered. Waldos officials had denied any connection to or knowledge of a humanlike waldo.

It's starting, he thought. Just like D'Auber said. He checked on flights to Buenos Aires, and booked a seat on one, charging it to Carli's account. *Going to owe you quite a tab, Carli,* he thought. *But I'll pay you back someday. I promise. Please, God, let me have the chance to pay you back.*

Paint found him.

"They're done with the preliminaries."

"Right."

As he logged off, Daniel happened to note in the headlines that *Courier* had reached *Exodus* a while ago. They were preparing to depart for 47 Uma, but the probe was experiencing some sort of technical problems that were causing a delay in its departure. He frowned. He'd planned to bid Paint and Fox good-bye in the lobby and head for the airport; instead, he went with Paint and Fox to Fox's semiprivate room. The other bed was empty.

"I think we had better check this out," he said. While Paint put away Fox's clothes and Fox fluffed his pillows, Daniel switched the room's jelly on and tuned in the Space News channel.

The image in the jelly was a simulation of the *Exodus* and *Courier*, in solar orbit near Mercury. A scratchy voice that sounded as if it were coming through a tin can said, "*Beep!*—have gone inoperable. We're looking—*beep!*—a possible software malfunction."

Through the lowermost inch of the jello-tube, words scrolled: "Live Radio Broadcast . . . Captain Joseph H. Kraunz, Commanding Officer, Interstellar Probe *Exodus* . . . Live Radio Broadcast . . ."

A long pause later: "Problem appears to be corrupted data files, Mission Control. *Beep!* We have a big problem here. Everything's corrupted. *Beep!*—computer systems are totally messed up."

"*Exodus—beep!*—let's solve the communications problem and then we'll assist you in getting the rest of your computer sys—*beep!*—back on line."

Long pause. "Roger, Control. *Beep!*"

A moment later: "Retransmitting comm coding. *Beep!* Prepare to receive."

Long pause. "Copy that, Control. Receiving. Stand—*beep!*—by."

Then, "Damnedest thing. *Beep!* Try again." Another pause. "No go, Control. Something's really wrong. *Beep!* What do you mean, we're locked out of the system? Shit! What the hell—*beep!*—ing on?"

Several people walked on each other on the radio. Static was interspersed with people shouting. Daniel, Fox, and Paint stared at each other.

A commentator came on, netspecked and -gloved, looking alarmed.

"I don't know what's happening, Jim. All we know is something has gone seriously wrong. Mission Control reports it has lost radio contact with *Exodus*. Stand by for updates."

They continued to listen to the exchange. Within about twenty minutes, tracking telescopes reported that *Exodus* had undocked from Icarus and was accelerating away from the sun, back in Earth's general direction, at two gees. No one knew what had gone wrong, or precisely where they were headed.

Daniel buried his face in his hands, then lifted his head to look at Paint and Fox, and saw his own horrified realization reflected there.

CARLI

COURSE CORRECTION

She found Byron in the Face Lab, floating and bobbing, outfitted in a skinlink suit attached by several cords to a console at the wall. When she gripped his arm and shook it, calling him, he unfaced and removed his goggles. His expression was sour.

"Yes?"

"I want to talk to Taylor."

"Join the crowd. She's not talking to anyone."

"What's with you? I thought you had everything you wanted."

He frowned and didn't answer right away. Then he batted at the air with his hand. "Ah, they're just jerking me. Marsh is avoiding me, and he's evasive when I talk about starting the life-extension treatments."

Carli could care less about his life-extension problem, but she nodded noncommittally. "May I wear a suit?"

"Sure." He gestured at the row of dark, glossy, full-body suits hanging there. "Climb in. We have a great entertainment library."

She stripped down to her underwear and climbed into a suit.

"Oh, I meant to tell you," Byron said, as she pulled up the hood and adjusted the goggles. "Plan A was a success. They just wrapped things up a little while ago. It went very smoothly and all the astronauts are OK. *Exodus* is now on its way to meet us."

She stared at him in dismay. The programmer hadn't gotten into the system in time.

It had been a long shot, anyhow. She swallowed her disappointment and faced in.

The controls were pretty straightforward. She could choose from any number of similes and other options. Carli chose to search for other users. A scroll materialized in front of her, with a high-level schematic of Kaleidas's *virtu*-cosm and a list of who was where. She tried to track Taylor down, but when she pursued the links down to where Taylor was, the linkware refused her admittance. So Carli called Marsh.

Marsh answered the call in his sleep webbing. She'd obviously woken him.

"I'd like to talk to Dr. Taylor."

He sighed, heavily. "I'll let her know. But I've prescribed bed rest. Don't expect to hear from her before rendezvous."

"When is rendezvous?"

He hesitated. "I suppose it doesn't hurt for you to know. Three days from now, late evening. Around 10:30 P.M. Shasta time."

Then Carli peeked in on the crèche children. Several different similes were running. Mostly entertainment similes, though a couple were studying, and one kid, whose tag line was Pablo, was monitoring transmissions from Kaleidas.

Carli shuddered. He *said* he hadn't been the one who'd tried to slice 'n' dice her.

She floated his face, and spoke. "This is Carli. What's the status of the crew of *Exodus?*"

"Aunt Carli. You're faced in?"

"Using a skinlink."

"Ah. You're welcome to look for yourself."

The monitoring control menu suddenly became active. She chose visual/auditory, and watched views from *Exodus* cycle through. The crew was scattered throughout the ship; a handful sat in the mess, hunched over in the heavy gees, talking in low voices, with an occasional glance at the cameras; they knew—or at least guessed—they were being monitored. Another handful was on the bridge, engaged in some kind of data gathering and calculation—perhaps trying to figure out their trajectory and destination. The rest were either in their quarters or pursuing other tasks. Make-work, no doubt. To keep from going nuts. Rather like she was doing.

Everyone looked grim. Captain Kraunz was on the bridge; her old friends Greg and Lorraine Amos-Phelps were in the mess; Sid sat at a desk in her quarters, writing by hand in a journal. Carli felt tears well up. *I'm sorry. I'm so sorry for this.*

She wished for the zillionth time she'd found the open comm line even just moments sooner. Or that she hadn't spent those precious few seconds talking to her father.

BUDDY

SUPERHEROES R US

Buddy spent a while fuming. Mother, despite her death, had succeeded in her attempt to isolate them from the rest of humanity.

Well, but she really hadn't fully succeeded, yet. Until they were aboard *Exodus* and on their way to Ursa Major, he had a chance to stop them. Mother had convinced them they were monsters—pariahs, who'd be shunned by the rest of humanity. He knew they'd be welcomed as the heroes—no, superheroes—they really were.

He had time yet. Another few days to come up with a plan.

A BABY AT HEART

The flashback that Mother-Not's death triggered had illuminated areas hidden deep within. Dane explored that wilderness over the next day or so, and stumbled across a trail whose traces were almost completely covered over by undergrowth, erosion, tricks of illusion, evasion.

But Dane was patient. She was a born tracker. That was her single purpose: to seek. Not to destroy—that had been Buddy's influence—but to understand. To reunite. To heal.

So she didn't give up, didn't give in to the dodges and confusion, the false monsters, the darkness and sense of evil that lurked all around inside. Patient, dogged, she persevered, retraced steps, faced down demons that evaporated as she reached them. And at the very core she found Pablito.

He was buried very deep, trapped in darkness, in isolation. He was only two or so. Just a baby. He slept, and her mental touch—at first light, then more insistent—didn't rouse him.

He's our center, she realized. She could feel the strands that united her—and Buddy, and Pablo—to him. He's our father, and our child.

Unless he awakened, they would never be whole. They would always be in fragments—at odds with each other, in pain.

RETREAT FROM ANGUISH

Byron remained moody and quiet, ill disposed toward answering her questions, over the next three days. Marshall Sullivan was also laconic. And everyone else stayed in *v*-face. So Carli spent a lot of time alone, catching up on her sleep, crying sporadically in helpless frustration, and exploring the corridors.

On the second day she came across the closet with the infant and toddler proxies. They floated there, bound together with red electrical tape in a horrible parody of abuse, but unsecured to any surface. They were naked, with arms, legs, and heads protruding in a jumbled assortment: a mass, weightless grave of doll bodies. At the sight, she broke down and cried fresh tears.

Poor babies, she thought. They entombed you—imprisoned you in plastic—and hooked you up to tubes. They isolated you from real human contact and real sensation, and fed you their own, twisted version of reality. You've only ever seen the world through filters and funhouse mirrors. You never had a chance.

She wiped at her eyes. By now her face was sore and swollen from crying.

So many tears. It amazed her, how many tears she had inside. She ought to be all dried up: shriveled like a raisin, or a dead lizard, left out to desiccate in the desert sun. Instead, her eyes swelled endlessly forth with fluid, like fountains fed by some eternal underground spring, spilling over yet again, now, with big drops that fell out of her eyes and tumbled before her, sparkling like jewels.

She'd cried a lot of tears in her life. Tears not over the kind of mother Alison Almquist had been, but over the mother she *hadn't* been. Tears unto numbness and finally dull despair over Dennis's long, slow, hideous death. Tears of agony over the dreams that must die, when she'd left the space program for Jere and her communications research, and later, her outraged helplessness over OMNEX's snatching the MacLeod; her private, guilty anguish over Paint's imprisonment,

believing it had somehow been her fault. And then tears over losing
Jere. Despite his betrayal, oh, how she'd loved him.

Tears over the climbing death count, worldwide, from political
turmoil, famine, plagues, drought, flooding, storms; over the laying
waste of great expanses of the Earth that had once brimmed with animal and plant life.

A life could accumulate such pain and anger and grief. Such guilt
over things said and not said. So much regret.

Damn hope, anyway. Fuck that optimism and willingness to try
again that kept taking flight, phoenixlike, from her despair—that
opened her, again and again, to such pain.

And at that she realized that her aversion to the crèches was not entirely honest. On some level—like Byron—she wanted to follow the
crèche children into their virtual world, where life didn't take such a
toll: where death was temporary, and relationships—at least most of
them—were laid to waste only till you hit the reset button; where
mammals and reptiles and avians and a million species of jewel-like insects thrived, in forests and savannas of emerald, fuchsia, teal, and
honey gold; where songbirds still sang and frogs and toads—with the
proper number of limbs—still crouched on their lily pads, and Kodi-
aks caught salmon in glittering brooks; where coral reefs cast off their
bleached deadness, and burgeoned with weird and glorious sea life.

The real world lay in ruins about her. Why not retreat to a better
place?

She wanted to be quit of tears and pain.

She grew quieter, floating there amid the doll bodies, reflecting.
The world of pretend she'd lived in as a child, the string of fantasies she
had laid out for herself to escape her mother's craziness, those make-
believe universes that she'd found in books and twodeos and the nets,
and the fantasies she'd made up for herself and acted out with her
friends, the dreams she'd dreamed while tinkering with her junior scientist equipment: those had saved her life. Her sanity. And, as an adult,
the dreams for her future she'd thrown herself at like a star-crazed
groupie—the fantasies she'd had of success and fame—had sustained
her through those desperately lonely, self-doubting times.

All those pretend worlds—those dreams, the mental models she'd
borrowed or built—they'd given her respite, when reality was too
much for her. And often the games and stories and fantasies and ab-
stract thought had gifted her with some exciting insight that she could

take back home with her, an adventurer long away, finally returning home, pockets stuffed with intellectual or spiritual booty.

But the real world was always there, waiting for her. Home. Patient lover, waiting for her to get all the wanderlust, all the doubts and fear of commitment, out of her system. Marry me, it whispered, when she'd been away for too long. Stop hiding. Grab hold with both hands. You won't have me around forever.

Reality was an anchor. A promise—not of faerie glamour or glory and riches, not of heroic, galaxy-spanning adventure, or even a life without pain—but of other things. True and solid friendships. Deep love. Good sex, fine food and drink, satisfaction in a job well done. Day skies and night skies, and the sunsets and sunrises that spilled buckets of brilliant color across them, leaving her breathless and goose-pimply. Midday desert vistas, where impossibly distant tablelands danced like mirages, and dust devils—more tangible—whipped against her in a shower of pebbles. The fractal geometries of city skylines at twilight, their silhouettes laced with lights as small at this remove as Christmas tree lights, and the fractal complexities of human existence that must lie beyond all those millions of tiny windows. Huge, heaping storm clouds that boiled up, dark and powerful, against the mountainside and slammed their fists against the ground, and rumbled and roared and stabbed her furies and her wild joys out for her, and then departed swiftly, leaving the sun shining, and the world fresh, clean, wet, and rainbow-draped.

Knowing they were real mattered. They had been earned. They didn't shift or evaporate or twist on her, the way dreams could. They didn't lie, by obscuring or ignoring other realities. They weren't someone else's vision, being poured into her head. She and reality had a personal and intimate relationship; not always a good one—especially not right now—but it was *hers*, by God, with no intermediaries to interpret for her, to influence her thinking with their own opinions and prejudices.

The things she'd bought with her pain were priceless. They could never be duplicated in a programmer's simile. Pretend could reflect reality's sorrows and joys, but never create its own. She wouldn't trade an ounce of pain for the love she'd had for her brother, Paint, Jo, her parents, or even Jere; nor for the joy she'd had the first time she'd sent a MacLeod signal and the clocks had shown that no time had passed between transmission and receipt, and she'd known that she'd just created something that would change countless lives, for the better. She'd reached out, touched history, diverted its course.

All these things were real. That made them more hers than any dream.

Reality was exactly what the crèche children had been robbed of. An anchor to tie their flights of fancy to. They were modern-day Peter Pans, lost children, trapped in a house of mirrors: a world that comprised only abstraction, reflection, distortion, falsehood.

And in that realization she found . . . if not an anchor, then at least a little hunk of storm-tossed driftwood to cling to.

PLAN C

It was Uncle Marsh and Aunt Jenna who provided Buddy with the seed of an idea for his own plan—and the ammunition to carry it off. While Buddy was helping Uncle Marsh and Aunt Jenna pack up the medical supplies the day before rendezvous, Uncle Byron came into the lab.

"Marsh, I want a word with you."

His back to Uncle Byron, Uncle Marsh exchanged a look with Aunt Jenna, who rolled her eyes and bit her lip. Uncle Marsh turned, forcing a smile onto his face. "What can I do for you, Byron?"

"You know damned good and well what you can do for me. You can give me a straight answer and tell me when you're going to start me on the treatments. You've been dodging me for days now, and I'm getting tired of it."

Uncle Marsh cleared his throat. "Come on now, don't get paranoid. I haven't been dodging you. We've had a hell of a lot going on."

Uncle Byron rubbed at his face. "All right, all right. You're right. I'm just edgy." He paused. "So everything's still go on that front, then."

"Definitely. Everything's go. We'll beanlink you at the first opportunity, post-*Exodus*, and start the life-extension treatments."

"All right, then. That's all I needed to hear." Uncle Byron blew out a big breath of air and shoved off out the door. "I'll be counting on you, Marsh," he said from out in the hall, and went away. The door closed.

"When are you going to tell him?" Aunt Jenna asked softly, after he'd left. Uncle Marsh gave her a stern stare and looked around. Buddy drew back behind some bags. He activated a capture buffer, focused his vision on them through a crack, and cranked up his hearing.

"Where'd that crèche kid get to?" Marsh asked.

"I don't know. I think he ducked out earlier."

"You should be more careful what you say."

"Sorry."

"I'll have a talk with Byron after we secure *Exodus*," Uncle Marsh said. "I'll explain what really happened to Patricia, that I've concluded that there's a link, and I can't conscience giving him the treatments."

"He'll never forgive us for lying to him."

Uncle Marsh drew himself up with an indignant expression. "It wasn't a lie. I didn't know initially about the high failure rate, for subjects without congenitally disabled immune systems."

Aunt Jenna gave him an arch little smile. "Come on. You've been helping Patricia stave off cancer for years, with all those fancy gene treatments. You've known from the beginning this treatment would only really work for people with severe immune deficiencies."

He only glowered at her.

"Don't get all puffed up, Marsh. I'm only pointing out that you must have known that you wouldn't be able to treat Byron, even two years ago, and he'll figure that out."

Uncle Marsh looked at her. He rubbed his face. "What will we do?"

Aunt Jenna shrugged. "Send him back with the astronauts and D'Auber, I suppose."

"I suppose." Uncle Marsh sighed, and they continued packing.

Buddy used the "Save Certified" option to save the file. He could have modified their exchange and then save-certified it anyhow; he knew how to get around the constraints, and Uncle Byron would never have known. But he didn't have to. The real thing was damning enough.

Buddy encrypted and e-mailed the conversation to Uncle Byron with a note: "Don't show this to anyone else. Meet me in *v*-chamber 42 at 10:00 P.M."

Uncle Byron materialized right on time that night, after lights-down. His avatar's face was drawn in tight, angry lines.

"Which one are you," he asked, "and where did you get that recording? Is it some kind of joke?"

"It's no joke. It's real. They've lied to you and they've lied to us. We have to stop them."

"Why should I believe you? How do I know you didn't manufacture that sequence out of thin phosphors?"

"The sequence is real. Didn't you see the certification?"

Uncle Byron paused, eyeing him suspiciously, then grunted an acknowledgment.

"They had the conversation just after you left, earlier today. I was in the lab helping Uncle Marsh pack. After Uncle Marsh spoke to you, that's what happened. I'm telling the truth, and you can check for yourself."

"How?"

"Well . . . I can't do anything to prove their conversation was genuine, if you don't believe the save-certify stamp, but I can show you another way they're lying. Mother isn't just lying low; she's dead in her crèche. They're keeping her iced and running a simulacrum to help them get past rendezvous to exodus. You can check her crèche yourself."

Uncle Byron tossed his slick, avatar-silver head with a frown. "Oh, right. I'm supposed to open up and have a peek. 'Excuse the intrusion, Patricia; I thought you were dead.' "

"Don't worry, she won't have much to say."

The avatar made an exasperated noise and glared.

"All right, then—check her vitals. They have them on a loop. A very low-grade loop at that; they didn't need anything fancy, so they didn't bother. The casual observer wouldn't notice anything unusual, but if you analyze the output for a few minutes, you'll see all the patterns—heart, breathing, EEG, sympathetic nerve response, muscle stimulus—they all repeat, in the same sequence, every time."

Uncle Byron was silent for a time. "Patricia's dead."

"That's right. I witnessed it, just before lunar perigee."

"Murder?"

Buddy shook his head. "Assisted suicide. She was dying of cancer."

"I need to think this over."

"Take your time. You have till tomorrow night to decide if you're in or not."

"How will I contact you? I don't even know who you are!"

"*I'll* contact *you*."

TIME TO GO

On the third day, Byron and a proxy she didn't know came for Carli in her chambers. "Time to go," Byron said.

They climbed through the ladder tunnels to the bottom of Kaleidas. Inside a large antechamber, all the crèches were crowded around two big elevator doors. Marsh was there, checking them. They had been stripped of all their decorations, and looked more coffinlike than ever. They were strapped to fiberglass pallets in groups of three or four. Nearby were a few dozen large, lumpy duffel bags with handles.

Proxies, dozens of them, floated together, over to one side. From the way they had their backs and heads turned, they appeared to be avoiding the crèches. They're afraid of them, she realized with a start.

There were at least forty proxies: a lot more than the number of crèches. Patricia Taylor was there, too, in proxy; she kicked forward to Carli, Pablo, and Byron. Jenna, nearby, hovered at the enormous jelly that had been set up opposite the elevators, and was fiddling with the controls.

"Ms. D'Auber," Taylor said, with a nod, as if inventorying them, "Byron, Kali. We're all here. Let's get started. Switch over," she said to Jenna, who nodded.

A jello appeared, a schematic of *Exodus* and Kaleidas: bright, tiny icons, each labeled, spitting white flame. They were closing across a black expanse, trailing dotted lines. *Exodus* had earlier swooped in on a curve and passed Kaleidas, and was in Kaleidas's projected path now, slowing to match the slower craft's speed.

"Ten minutes to rendezvous point. Cutting Kaleidas engine," Joe's avatar said. The Kaleidas icon stopped spitting flame, and the dull vibration of the past three days ceased. The schematic then switched over to a close-up of the two crafts. "Initiating final matching sequence now."

It took several minutes for *Exodus* to close the gap and match velocities with them. Meanwhile Taylor said, "Give us visuals on the astronauts."

The view showed most of the *Exodus* crew on the bridge, watching Kaleidas close on their main viewer. They pointed at it and spoke to each other, staring. Two or three others were in the engine control room, messing with the controls. They all looked haggard and tense.

"Velocity-matching sequence complete."

"Go grappling," Taylor said.

"Grappling, go," Obediah replied.

A small missile shot out of Kaleidas's broken shaft, trailing a cable. In the jelly, the *Exodus* crew braced themselves, looking terrified, but the missile reversed itself and braked just shy of impact. It shot out a device with claws. The clawed device struck and grabbed a handhold at *Exodus*'s main airlock.

"Grappling complete."

"Patch me through," Taylor said. A little camera waldo lifted out of Jenna's hand and hovered before Taylor.

"Go ahead," Jenna said.

"Crew of *Exodus*," she said, "I am Patricia Taylor, chief scientist of Kaleidas, a secured research center."

Capt. Kraunz frowned. "Are you the one responsible for this insanity? Do you have any idea what the penalties—"

Taylor cut him off. "We are confiscating your craft. With the exception of your cargo-bay entry doors, all decompression barriers on your ship have been disabled. In sixty seconds all airlocks will be blown. You have until then to retreat to the cargo bay. To demonstrate that we are capable of doing this, I am now blowing your rearmost airlock."

"What the devil—?" Kraunz demanded.

At that instant another camera showed both the inner and outer doors of one airlock opening. Alarms went off on the bridge. A crew member shouted something Carli couldn't hear; Kraunz responded, sharply.

"Initiating countdown," Taylor said, "now."

In a corner of the jelly, a countdown timer appeared and started ticking. On *Exodus* the astronauts scrambled for handholds and dove through the corridors—trying to get to the cargo bay. In another view, debris was spewing out the open airlock.

"Time to migrate," Taylor said. "Let's go."

The proxies swarmed toward the pallets. Marsh was beside Carli now; he took her arm and gestured at an open, empty crèche, as Byron, with Jenna's help, climbed into another one and donned a mask. "Climb in."

She caught his gaze and held it, putting every ounce of contempt into the look that she could muster. After a moment Marsh dropped his gaze. Carli grabbed a handle on the inside of the crèche and pulled herself in. He put a mask with an aerogel seal on her face, then lowered the lid. She closed her eyes.

"Bastards," she whispered.

IT WAS THE BEST OF CASES; IT WAS THE WORST OF CASES

Everything was going beautifully—as smoothly as the best of his best-case scenarios.

Why, then, did he sense that something was terribly wrong?

Pablo shook off the foreboding as a bad case of the jitters. Once Uncle Byron, Uncle Marsh, and Aunt Carli were sealed into their crèches, the antechamber was decompressed and the elevator doors opened. Pablo and Mara went first; they shrouded the crèches, out of respect, then helped each other into their towing harnesses. Using the jet canisters strapped to their backs, they gingerly guided their pallet into the elevator shaft and secured the pallet to the grappling line.

Together they jetted down into space, towing their pallet. Against a swatch of stellar brilliance, the great, shadowed probe ship loomed: all curves and planes and smooth surfaces. It would never enter a planet's atmosphere, but at the speeds it was intended for, even in space its aerodynamics—"spatiodynamics"—would matter. It was immense—almost as large as Shasta Station, preseparation—and a good four fifths of it was its ring of interspersed, Brobdingnagian antimatter and plasma jets.

Pablo felt a twinge of loneliness. It should be Buddy helping him transport the pallet. The others who were twinning had their twins with them. The instant communication between the selves made control much easier. But Buddy was shunning him.

He wondered if the others had such difficulties with their other selves.

Using their canisters to propel themselves, he and Mara ferried the pallet across the gap toward the open airlock.

"All the astronauts are in the cargo bay," Obediah reported.

"Seal them in and cancel decompression sequence," Mother ordered, over the radio. "Recompress the ship while we transport. Let's move it—we want to give them as little time as possible to react."

Pablo looked over his shoulder. Behind them came more loaded pallets. He saw Buddy and his partner leaving the shaft with their pallet, and for an instant he was with Buddy looking at himself. But Buddy had put up a mental firewall so strong Pablo didn't have a clue what he was feeling.

So what's new? he thought. *I don't even know what I'm feeling.*

They loaded their pallet into the airlock and motioned the team that followed to do the same.

"Careful!" Pablo snapped, when Dalia and Ian bumped their pallet against his and Mara's.

They cycled the pallets through as quickly as they could. It took four cycles to transfer all the crèches. As they moved pallets into the corridor, other crèche-born ferried them away. The rest of the team came in the fifth, sixth, and seventh airlock cycles, bearing big bags of supplies. Mother came with the last group. As the others were clearing the corridor, she clapped her proxy's hands.

"Great work! We're on our way!"

His crèche-mates cheered. Pablo did, too, though he still felt unsettled and not like cheering. He avoided Buddy's gaze, though he sensed his twin's attention.

"Recompression complete," Aunt Jenna reported.

"All right. To your stations. You all know what to do. Secure the crèches and the other supplies, and prepare the ship for launch."

IT WAS UP TO HER

After the others had left down the elevator shafts, Dane came out of hiding, wearing the little-boy proxy, and followed the grappling line. From the end of Kaleidas's broken shaft, she-he watched as the last set of bags was being loaded into *Exodus*'s airlock.

Dane reached the airlock and closed her-his eyes, seeking Pablo or Buddy. Finally she found Pablo and peeked out through his eyes. He was among the last of those leaving the corridor inside the airlock. She-he waited a few seconds and then cycled through the airlock and into the probe ship.

Pablo and Buddy had severed all ties and were acting autonomously. Pablo was trying hard not to remember that Mother was dead. When he remembered, the dark, cold, pressurized mass of his horror and grief would explode outward against Buddy's blazing, vengeful joy. The collision could destroy them all. It was up to Dane to hold things together.

ASTRONAUTS UNDER GLASS

Mother led them all to a large processing area overlooking the cargo bay. About ten of his crèche-mates were there, along with Uncle Marsh and Aunt Jenna. Pablo looked down into the bay through a large window. The astronauts were down there.

Someone below spotted them and pointed—several of the astronauts shot up to where they were and floated on the far side, eyeing them. Three had crowbars or lengths of chain or large wrenches in their hands. Pablo noticed, then, the scratches in the window's thick metaglass surface. They'd been trying to break it.

Captain Kraunz pressed a button on a control console on his side of the window. His gaze was blazing-fierce. "You'll pay for this. I'll see to it personally."

Pablo expected Mother to make some retort. Instead, returning Kraunz's stare with a stony expression, she said merely, "Marsh, release Byron and Ms. D'Auber from their crèches. Frankie and Ian, you'll escort them down to the cargo entryway."

"Yes, Mother."

"Jenna, are you still tapped into the ship's systems?"

"Sure am, Number One."

"You have access to both *Exodus* and *Courier* controls, correct?"

"Yes."

"Good. On my signal, start a ten-second countdown and give us a verbal count. When it cycles to zero, seal *Courier*'s doors and decompress the cargo bay. Got that?"

"Got it, Number One."

"Good. Stand by, then."

She waited while Aunt Carli and Uncle Byron were removed from their crèches.

"What's going on here?" Byron demanded as they were escorted toward the door. "Let go of me!"

No one paid him any attention. A moment later, Frankie signaled that they were outside the cargo bay's entry portal. They studied the bay; none of the astronauts were near the opening.

"Open the door and put them inside," Mother ordered, "then close the door as quickly as possible and get back up here."

"Yes, Mother."

CARLI

Just outside a portal labeled "Cargo Bay," as the proxy escorting Carli reached for the hatch handle, both proxies froze in midmotion. Carli exchanged a look with Byron, who shook his head with a frown and a shrug. She pried her arm loose from her escort's grip, while Byron waved his hand in front of the other's face.

"Hello?" he said. No response. The proxies might as well have been made of wax.

"What's going on?" she asked.

"No idea."

They heard a noise and turned. Another proxy, done up as a young black male, was hovering nearby.

"I've deactivated them," he said. To Byron: "Are you in?"

"It's you," Byron said. "You sent me the film."

The other gave a single nod, with a chilling stare.

"Are you in?" he repeated.

Byron sighed, nodded. "I'm in."

The proxy looked at Carli. "This is a mutiny. We're going to free the astronauts. Are you in?"

What the hell—she had nothing to lose. Carli nodded. "I'm in. What's the plan?"

"They're about to blow the air from the cargo bay, to force the astronauts into *Courier*. We're going to let them loose in the ship, instead, and help them overpower Mother and her cadre."

"You're the one who tried to kill me, aren't you?" Carli demanded suddenly. The proxy gave her a long, hard look. It was answer enough.

"And you expect me to trust you?"

A shrug. "It was nothing personal."

"Fuck you!"

Byron took hold of her arm as she started at the proxy. "Look, you can fight about this later. We have to let them out *now*, or it'll be too late."

Carli glowered at the proxy. "All right. Do it."

Blow it Out Your Cargo Bay

"They're in position at the cargo-bay entry," Jebediah reported after a few moments.

Mother kicked over and pressed the talk button on the wall console.

"Captain Kraunz, in ten seconds the cargo-bay doors will be opened and all air evacuated. You and your crew have that long to board *Courier* before we seal *Courier*'s doors."

"Wait! Tell me what the hell you want with us!"

"I already told you, Captain. We want your ship. We don't intend you any harm. Do as we say and no one will be hurt. Jenna, initiate countdown."

"Ten," Jenna said.

With another curse, and a killing look, the captain barked, "All hands, board *Courier. All* hands. *Now.*"

"Nine."

Pablo pressed palms against the metaglass and watched. The astronauts scrambled for the shuttle. Four came out of hiding in cargo canisters or handling equipment—abandoning, apparently, a planned ambush.

"Eight."

Suddenly Pablo was looking out through Buddy's eyes, hearing with his ears. Reading his thoughts.

He was going to free the astronauts.

"Seven."

Pablo screamed, *"No!"* and shoved his way into Buddy's face.

CARLI

RESCUE ATTEMPT

Buddy kicked over and reached for the door handle. And froze.

"Let go!" he screamed suddenly, and grabbed the handle again, then threw himself backward, flailing, across the antechamber. "What are you doing? Are you insane? *You're* the insane one! Mama's boy! Traitor!"

"What the hell—?" Byron demanded. While the proxy caromed off the floor, and then the ceiling, yelling and fighting himself, Carli grabbed the cargo-bay door handle and slammed it open.

"Three," a woman's voice boomed. Across the bay, Captain Kraunz clung to a handhold at *Courier*'s airlock, shoving his people in.

"Cap'n Crunch!" Carli yelled. "This way!"

"Two."

Kraunz spotted her. His eyes widened.

"One."

"Too late!" he shouted back, waving his free arm. "Get back!"

"Zero. Cargo bay doors opening."

Courier's airlock door closed as the enormous cargo-bay doors slitted open. Alarms sounded. Wind swarmed past her, and she caught a glimpse of stars. Then the cargo-bay door slammed shut on its own.

Byron grabbed her arm. "We have to get out of here," he said. "They're going to be all over us."

As he finished, the room filled with crèche-born. They filled the air like a flock of birds, piling onto Carli and Byron, and onto the proxy who had tried to help them free the astronauts.

BUDDY

RENEGADE TWIN

His crèche-mates brought Aunt Carli, Uncle Byron, and Buddy back up to the processing area. Mother's proxy, Uncle Marsh, and Aunt Jenna were still there, as was Pablo. Through the window, the cargo bay was now completely open to space. *Courier* crouched in the huge bay, battened down next to the other shuttle, amid fiberglass and metal crates and tanks.

"What's the meaning of this?" Aunt Jenna asked.

"Frankie and Ian's faces were invaded and their bodies deactivated," Dalia reported. "It had to be one of us." She pointed a finger at Buddy. "Him."

Uncle Marsh floated over to Buddy and laid a hand on his arm. "Which one are you, son?"

Anger flared in Buddy. "I'm not your son. You're no different than *her.* All you care about is your stupid tests, sticking needles in us and probing and seeing what makes us twitch."

"Buddy," Pablo said, mournfully.

"And you! You're supposed to be our eldest—our leader. You let them walk all over us."

Aunt Jenna's eyes had narrowed during this exchange.

"That proxy is Pablo's spare," she said. She eyed Buddy, then Pablo. "Pablo . . . are you twinning? Are you the renegade?"

Pablo stared. "Of course not!"

"Took you long enough," Buddy said with a sneer. He turned to Pablo again. "She's dead, you know. Dead, dead, dead. You don't remember, do you?" He turned to the other crèche-born. A call must have gone out, because by now all of them were crowding into the room.

"When are you going to stop letting them lead you around by the nose? They don't care about us. All they care about are their tests and their drugs. They treat us like insects to be dissected."

Pablo was staring inward, blind. Buddy felt his turmoil, his terrible fear, felt him trying to push back down the memory of Mother's death.

"Look," he said, and darted over to the pallets of crèches. He knew which one was Mother's; he himself had transported it here. Everyone drew back with a collective, horrified sound.

Buddy hesitated. He didn't want to see what was in there, either. So he turned to Uncle Marsh.

"Tell them," he said. "Tell them the truth or I open the crèche."

Uncle Marsh stared at him. There was a long silence. Then Uncle Marsh released a long, slow breath.

He said heavily, "We were planning to tell you kids after the astronauts were launched. Mother Taylor prepared an announcement for you to hear. She wanted to share this moment with you, but she had cancer and couldn't last any longer. She died, peacefully, three days ago."

Peacefully, Buddy thought, remembering the last violence of her death. What a joke. The lies they tell to comfort themselves.

Shocked silence ensued.

Buddy forced the memory of her death past Pablo's barriers. He pointed at Mother's proxy, which was gazing at them with Mother's quizzical, rather supercilious expression.

"That is an impostor," he said. "A syntellect Aunt Jenna has created using *our* coding. Uncle Marsh, tell them why. Tell them why you and Aunt Jenna and Mother have conspired to exile us." Neither responded. His voice rose. "To save your own butts, that's why! Because you know you'll rot in prison for the rest of your lives, for what you've done.

"It's time," he said to his crèche-mates, "for a change of leadership. We should let the astronauts go on their journey to 47 Ursae Majoris, and we should go back home, back to Earth. Despite what they say"—he gestured at Uncle Marsh and Aunt Jenna—"we'll be welcomed with open arms.

"Think," he said, "just think what we can accomplish, what we can do for them! We can do things they can't even begin to imagine! We've been fed a diet of lies, all our lives. It's time for truth. Who's with me?"

No one spoke. Whispers started. Then Pablo arched his back and clutched his head.

"No-o-o-o!" he shrieked. *"¡Mamá! ¡No va—no va sin migo!"*

He curled into a tight ball. His anguish and betrayal beat Buddy back and pinned him against the wall.

This stinks, he thought. This isn't going as planned.

pablito

DON'T GO

Pablo pressed fists to his temples, trying to shut it out. But it was too late. Once released, like a growing fireball, the memory expanded—pursued him—outpaced him—wrapped itself about him in an embrace of searing pain, far worse than the worst nightmare he'd ever had.

The details were stark and fresh as raw, bleeding meat: how she looked in the creche, cold hard fingers digging into his arms, cold hard old eyes staring at him—disinfectants and plastic smells sickly-sweet in his sinuses, and her words—the memory of that final death spasm filled his mind in a corrosive wave—a poison, burning, killing.

In the toddler proxy, Dane paused at the portal to the room where Pablo, Buddy, and the rest floated.

Pablo was in trouble. Grief and rage exploded from him. She cringed as it engulfed her, and swept her into despair. The tiny wisp of awareness that was Pablito retreated deeper within, away from the turmoil.

¡Mamá!—no va-a-a...

Pablito was reliving it, and Dane with him: he strained and reached for his mother, screaming—but the strangers wouldn't let him go to her. Face turned away. Shoulders hunched. Brisk walk. Not even a single, furtive, backward glance.

Buddy sprawled against the handholds on the wall, beneath a buckling shield of anger, pummeled by Pablo's distress.

=You idiot! Stop dwelling on it! Let me handle it.=

But Pablo was treating him as if he didn't exist.

=Stop it!=he screamed.=Just *stop it*!=

He was no more able to stuff the memories back into their hidey-hole than Pablo was.

Abandonment.

He wanted to die, too. To follow her where she went.

It was his fault this had happened. He should have stopped her. He should have come through for her the way she'd needed.

And then rage: =It's all your fault, Buddy. This never would have happened if not for you.=

It was a stupid, ugly fight, but its familiarity was comforting. It gave the self-loathing someplace to go.

What vileness must he be, to deserve this abandonment?

=Don't go there,= she thought. =Stay with me. We need you.=

No response, only that pitiful wail. His memory was entangled in Pablo's, and the pain was just too intense.

Pablo was somehow Pablito's mirror-self—if she could get through to him, perhaps that would do it.

=Pablo, I'm Dane. Can you hear me? I'm here with you. I'm here to help.=

Soy malo . . . tengo toda la culpa.

=Pablo? Buddy?=

It was no use. They were too absorbed. If only I'd acted more quickly, she thought, none of this would have happened.

=Her dying is the best thing that ever happened to us.=

It came out unenthusiastic and tired, an overused mantra.

=I hope you do die,= Buddy sneered.

But he loved Pablo, the pathetic putz. Without him, Buddy would have nothing to live for.

I always go too far. Pablo would be happier if it weren't for me stirring things up all the time.

Troublemaker, he thought. Bad guy. This is all my fault.

But Pablo's scorn was too much for Buddy to bear.

=*My* fault? If you'd only listened while there was still time—=

=What a joke, coming from you. You *never* listen.=

Tiredly, = Oh, fuck you, Buddy. I'm so sick of your attitude.=

=Who are you talking to? Who's Dane?=

=I'm trying to *save* your ass! All of our asses! We can't go back. Don't you see that?=

Deep sadness filled him as he was left alone.

Why do we always end up here?

And he knew it didn't make sense, but he couldn't help wondering—Mother, why did you leave? How did we fail you?

Mamá, yo sea bien—yo prometo.

And Pablo and Buddy were off again, ignoring her, bickering, while Pablito wailed. The din was unbearable. She wanted to grab Pablito and shake him, shut him up.

=Stop crying! Stop blaming yourself! She's long gone. Get over it.= Then she winced at herself.

=I'm not talking to you, =she snapped at them.

This wasn't working. She couldn't hear herself think. She had to calm down. More yelling wouldn't help anyone.

She sealed them out, all three of them, and isolated herself. It was time to try a different tack.

¿Porqué, Mamá? ¿ Porqué?

=Pablo, you asshole, you don't know what you're talking about.=

=Keep out of this, Dane.

=You're being used, Pablo, and you're taking us down with you. . . .=

This was a waste of time. Pablo wasn't listening.

In disgust he threw up his barriers. No point in arguing with Pablo. It was the others he needed to convince.

"Hear me," he said to the rest, in-face. "Let me tell you why I'm right and Pablo is wrong."

DANE

PABLO!

Uncle Marsh was at Pablo's crèche, checking the readouts, trying to determine if his sudden paralysis was physiological. He was saying something to Aunt Jenna. It had only been a few seconds ago that she had entered the room.

But Uncle Marsh, Aunt Jenna, and the other adults—Aunt Carli and Uncle Byron—they, too, fell silent when Dane started moving toward Pablo again. She-he took hold of him, and looked at him but spoke to Pablito.

"=Look at me,=" she said and thought. "=*Look at me.*="

Her-his touch on Pablo's arms, her-his voice in his ears and his mind: they were enough. Pablo finally—for the first time—saw Dane. His eyes went very wide. She sought the words she needed.

"=Mother is gone,=" Dane said and thought, "=but I'm here.="

Pablito didn't hear, not really—but Pablo did. He was frowning.

"=You're part of me.="

She-he nodded.

"=Who are you? No, never mind. Just stay with me,=" he gasped, holding on to her-him, hand and mind.

"=I'm with you.="

She felt him strengthening, calming. Somewhere, Buddy was railing at the other crèche-born, and in the back of his mind, snarling at her for a traitor.

And she still had to get to Pablito somehow.

PABLO

As Planned

Pablo stood with a deep, steadying breath.

The tangled knot of anguish was still there, and the anger at Buddy.

Mother, he thought, I'll have to grieve you later.

Buddy was broadcasting to the others in-face.

"You're wrong, Buddy." Pablo spoke out loud *and* in-face, interrupting him, in a weird sort of stereo. It was hard to pull off, but it accomplished his goal: the dual effect jarred his crèche-mates back to their bodies. Buddy went silent, and they all blinked and stared at him. Pablo continued with ex-face voice alone. "They won't welcome us. We're not like them and they won't understand. *They're* the ones who'll treat us like insects."

He waved his arm at the splash of stars outside the cargo bay. All Mother's words came back to him—her private vision, which she'd shared with him in excited whispers, or in contrition, after rage and hurt.

She was right about this thing. She was right. And that calm certainty informed his words.

"Out there's where we belong. We're designed for space. Always faced in, long lives, that's us. Cramped quarters, no problem. Not them." He gestured at the astronauts in their shuttle. "They wouldn't be able to stand it. Not like us. We'll thrive out there. Back on Earth we'd be cripples. Freaks. Out there—a whole universe is waiting. That was Mother's dream for us. It's where we belong."

No one said anything.

"Well," he said, "you heard Buddy, and you heard me. Face in and vote."

THE BIG UGH, THE BIG HUG, AND THE BIG FAREWELL

Except for Jenna, all the proxies went motionless. It was creepy. Carli had the sudden sense, as earlier, that she was in a wax museum.

Jenna and Marsh exchanged looks. They seemed as weirded out as she.

"*That's* what they've been hiding from us," Jenna said.

"One thing they've been hiding, anyway." Marsh frowned and rubbed at his head. "Jenna . . . this is bad. This is really bad. It looks like Pablo has multiple personality disorder. Is it an artifact of the twinning process? How many of the others have it?"

Jenna shrugged. "Maybe it's twinning. Or maybe it was Patricia's excesses over the years. She *was* over-the-top a lot," she added, at Marsh's sharp glance. "It wasn't just the cancer."

He grimaced ruefully. "I should have intervened more."

"We both should have. It was hard to gainsay Patricia." Jenna sighed. "What do we do?"

Marsh shook his head with an exhaled breath. "No turning back. But we'll have access to plenty of diagnostic and treatment similes. We'll attempt to treat the condition once we're under way."

"Sure—*if* we can get them to cooperate. And keep their hands off our diagnostic and treatment tools."

They both looked scared.

"Looks like you've created something you can't control," Carli remarked. Maybe there was justice in the universe, after all.

An eye-blink later, the proxies reactivated. Pablo returned beaming. The proxy he had referred to as Buddy did not reactivate, though the little toddler proxy did. The toddler released Pablo's hand and kicked over to Carli. Surprised, she caught hold of him.

"The vote is for exodus," Pablo told Marsh.

"Did the twins get a vote?" Jenna muttered.

Marsh gave Jenna a warning glance and she bit her lip.

"I'm Dane," the toddler whispered. "A friend. I need . . . need help."

Carli lifted a finger to her lips. "Just a minute."

"Excellent," Marsh said. "Let's get Carli and Byron down to the cargo bay, then, get them all headed back to Earth, and be on our way."

Pablo pursed his lips and shook his head. "Uncle Marsh, we'll need that extra shuttle."

Carli gasped. The toddler tugged at her again.

"So do the astronauts," Marsh said, sharply.

"Not as much as we do. We're going back to Plan B."

"You can't!" Carli exclaimed.

"Damn right you can't," Jenna said. "I have the face controls."

"Look again," Pablo said, smugly.

Jenna's gaze turned inward. Then she swore. "Give me back the face, Pablo."

"Mother put me in charge. It's my decision."

"*Murderer!*" Carli shook fists. "How can you be so casual about killing?"

He gave her a casual shrug. "But it's just bodies."

She gaped at Pablo—and understanding dawned.

The toddler was still tugging at her, saying something about getting to Pablito. She released the toddler and kicked off to Pablo's crèche. All the crèche-born nearby shoved themselves away, or flailed helplessly without purchase, exclaiming in dismay, as she threw the crèche open.

There in a blob of gel lay a hairless, skeletal figure. Colostomy and catheter tubes punctured his abdomen; a beanjack crowned his bald pate; a clear mask with a flexible tube hooked to it covered most of his face. He had no fingernails, toenails, or body hair. His skin and features were Negroid. With his body so underdeveloped, his head was a good deal larger in proportion to it than that of a typical teenager.

The face, though, would suit an angel. His eyes were huge and dark in a child-man's face, and his lips were full and round and sweet. So vulnerable. So frail. The face was achingly beautiful and innocent. Nothing like those terrifying strong machine bodies. He blinked blearily at her through the mask, and his arms came up, reflexively, across his chest as she reached for him.

So vulnerable.

But her anger was too great.

She grabbed those matchstick arms, ignoring Marsh's sharp warning, and gave him a shake. "*This* is you. Not that muscle-bound *thing* you pilot around. *This* is what you're killing, if you space those people in there." She shook him again. "Look at me! Do you see me? Are my words reaching your ears? Can you feel my hands on you? *This* is your body. When it goes, you go." She flung an arm in the direction of *Courier. "It's the same for them.* Stop the killing!"

He stopped struggling, and croaked something.

"What?" she asked.

The toddler had come up beside her, looking somewhere between shocked and joyful. "He remembers. Pablito. Oh, no—don't go there again!"

Then both their faces crumpled into identical, anguished masks.

"Mamá . . ." the toddler and the pilot whispered together. Tears were flowing down the pilot's face. *"No va."*

Carli grimaced. "Shit."

I know that pain, she thought. She had a sudden intuition about the tears, and compassion shouldered revulsion and anger aside. Carli slipped her arms around the slippery, bony frame. After a pause, he hugged back, feebly, his nailless fingers scraping across her back.

He began to shudder and sob into his mask with such vehemence that Carli began to worry the fluids would choke him, or the convulsions dislodge his tubes. But gradually the sobs began to taper off. Marsh was there beside her.

"He's at risk of disease," Marsh said.

Carli released him and floated out of the way, while Marsh repositioned him in his blob of gel, which had started to work its way out of the crèche. He maneuvered the gel blob back into the crèche and closed the lid, and then checked the settings. Meanwhile, all the crèche-born proxies but Pablo and the little toddler had gone paraffinstill again, frozen floating bodies: mannequins suspended in midair, or clinging to handholds on the bulkheads.

Carli looked down at herself. She was covered with goo. Yuck. She tried to brush it off. The toddler was hiccuping, softly, in the aftermath of grief.

"Dane?" she asked. He blinked. Slowly he shook his head.

"Me llamo Pablito. My name . . . Pablito," he repeated, haltingly, in heavily accented English. He held his arms out to Carli, and when she took hold, clung to her.

He's the original, she realized, stroking his head. *The little boy whose mama left him in the hands of these strangers.* Carli didn't know why, but it was important that he was here.

"It's all right now," she said, holding him close. "You stay here with me."

He nodded and laid his head against her chest.

"Pablo?" she asked the adult proxy.

"Dane," the proxy said, slowly. "Pablo, he is . . . in-face." A look of fondness toward the toddler in Carli's arms, and a hesitation. "Pablito remembers touch. On our body. Our real body. He remembers Mamá. Nursing, tickling, holding." A long pause. "The astronauts—their bodies . . . the bodies . . ." The proxy struggled for words, face contorting. Carli waited. "The bodies *are* their flesh." He, or she—he-she?—sneaked a quick, inquisitive look at Carli. "Yes?"

Carli released an explosive breath. *"Yes."*

"I understand." The proxy got a remote look on his-her face, and said, "They're going to vote. I'll tell them."

More silence followed, while Carli and the other nonproxied adults eyed each other nervously, while the toddler proxy played with the zipper of her jumpsuit and babbled softly, and the gunk from the hug dried on her jumpsuit, neck, arms, and cheek, and started to itch.

"What's happening?" Byron demanded of Jenna, who also looked distracted.

"In-face powwow. Someone—calls herself Dane—just showed up." A pause. "Pablo is arguing that they can't afford loss of a shuttle and it's just bodies. Dane says . . . Hold on . . . she's hard to understand." Another pause. "Not a simile, real is different for us than them, she's killed flesh-bodies and she knows. It's different with us, it's wrong. It's not like for them. An ending that can't be undone, she says."

Then Jenna gave the rest of them a dismayed look. "She doesn't express herself very well, though. I can tell by their reactions they just don't get it. It's hard enough for *me* to understand, and I know what she's trying to get at."

"Can't we disable their crèche links?"

She shrugged helplessly. "I can't even reach the controls, Marsh. They're letting me watch, but that's it. Pablo is holding sway. He says they've all died before, what's the big deal? It's easy, it's quick, and we really need the shuttle. He's pushing hard for a vote."

Carli felt rage swell up inside. She wanted to scream. Maybe if I smash their crèche controls, she thought, and looked around desperately for something to break them with. The toddler squirmed in her tightening grip. She released him and kicked off toward the back of the room.

Pickings here weren't slim; they were nonexistent. There were cabinets, which appeared to be locked, and the pallets they'd brought over with them, which had supplies lashed to them, but nothing that readily announced itself to her as a useful weapon. And there wasn't even time to sort through the pallets, much less comb the ship. Where was a good bazooka when you needed one?

"Then we'll have to disconnect them from their crèches manually," Carli said.

"The hell you will," Jenna said. "It would kill them."

"So? You'd rather they murder the astronauts?" Carli demanded, and started for Pablo's crèche again. The Taylor doppelgänger—presumably at Jenna's command—intercepted Carli, and together they bumped into Jenna, who was coming at them from a different angle. Jenna gave them a shove. Together the doppelgänger and Carli floated to the nearest wall, and the Velcro patch on the doppelganger's back stuck there. Carli struggled, uselessly and silently, against the syntellect's grip. After a moment she gave it up. You're dead, she thought, staring into Patricia Taylor's impassive face, and I still can't get away from you.

Jenna's gaze had gone flat again.

"Wait! Another copy of Pablo is there—he's like an angry version of Pablo. Must be his twin. And it looks like Dane has gotten through to him. Sorta. He's frowning and talking about a man in a crèche whom they killed. Maybe, he says, for us, our bodies *are* our crèches." The smile on her face broadened. "Yes. Dane's excited and some of the others are wavering."

She was silent a moment, looking thoughtful.

"What's happening?" Byron demanded.

"Several people, talking at once. Just a second—shh!"

Then, with a frown, Jenna said, "Mara's pointing out that everybody knows the good guys don't kill the bad guys when they don't have to." She groaned. "Marsh—they don't get it. They're just treating this like another simile. . . . It's all just fantasy stuff."

"Whatever it takes to keep the astronauts alive," Marsh said, looking grim. "We'll work on the rest later."

Jenna listened. "Pablo is pissed! He's yelling at the dissenters that they're being incredibly stupid and making a big mistake. That we're tricking them."

Suddenly, looking scared, she said, "Oh, God. They're about to vote."

A second later, most of the crèche-born became animated again, all talking at once, starting up in midsentence, clearly continuing their in-face arguments. Pablo's face was a mask. Carli's stomach roiled, and bile spread over the base of her tongue.

Then Jenna broke into a surprised smile. "I've got control back!"

"Can you launch *Courier*?" Marsh asked.

She hesitated, gaze unfocused, then nodded. "Yes."

How close was the vote? Carli wondered. And who voted for what? She'd certainly never know.

"Thank you," Marsh said to the proxy children floating near him. "You've done the right thing." They ignored him, still caught up in their arguments—angry, excited, confused—using words and gestures Carli had never seen before, interspersed with dead spaces as those communicating ex-face cross-talked with those still in-face.

They may not have truly understood life and death, but the idea sure had them stirred up.

Jenna glanced Carli's way, and the syntellect's grip on her arms relaxed. Angrily Carli shoved the inert proxy away.

"Go ahead and repressurize the cargo bay, then," Marsh was saying to Jenna, "but keep the shuttle sealed up. We'll need to get Carli into *Courier* without letting the astronauts out." Then he turned. "Byron?"

"What?" Byron said it in a belligerent tone.

Marsh coughed. After a second he said, "Look, I'm sorry I lied to you about the life-extension treatments."

Byron's eyes glittered. "It's a little late for that."

"I suppose so. Well . . ." Marsh cleared his throat again. "You can go back with Carli and the astronauts, if you choose. But we want you with us, if you'll come. We could use your skills."

"And what choice do I have, I'd like to know?" Byron gestured at Carli. "I go with them, she'll tell the authorities about my involvement. I'll spend the rest of my life in prison!"

Jenna said, "Come with us, Byron. We need you." She paused. "You shared the dream, too. It wasn't just about living forever, was it?"

Byron hesitated, looking from one to the other of them. "Oh, all right," he said huffily. The other two laughed.

Camaraderie among thugs. You people make me ill, Carli thought, rubbing at the bruises on her arms that the Taylor doppelgänger had left.

*   *   *

They unpacked weapons from some duffel bags. Seeing them, Carli thought about Dane and the frailness of the boy-man in the crèche, and—grudgingly—decided she was relieved she hadn't known of their existence when the crèche-born were in-face, deciding the astronauts' fate. She would have used them—or tried to: it would have seemed the only alternative. And despite everything, the idea of killing these children was repugnant.

Then several of them—Jenna; someone in Pablo's proxy (there seemed to be any number of possibilities, and Carli didn't have a clue how to tell); the toddler proxy Dane had been wearing, still clinging to her (she presumed it was the one Dane had called Pablito, the original child); and a large escort of canister-jet-wearing, gun-wielding crèche-born—took Carli down into the cargo bay.

The armed crèche-born fanned out, bracing themselves and covering the airlock as Carli neared the shuttle. Pablo-or-Dane-or-whoever-the-hell-it-was jetted Carli—and Pablito, who hadn't loosened his grip on her—to the airlock.

"Good-bye," whoever-it-was said. "Thanks for helping me."

It must be Dane, Carli thought. Dane held out his-her arms, but Pablito clung to Carli and buried his face in her shoulder. Dane tried to pull him free. He fought Dane's grip.

"Come now. Time for her to go," Dane said.

"*¡No!*" he wailed, and buried his face in the crook of Carli's neck. "*¡No va!*"

Aw, shit, she thought. She looked back at *Courier*, and around at the crèche-born.

They were headed for infinity. Like it or not, they were the future of interstellar space travel. And they needed someone sane along. Someone who understood them, who would help moor them to reality. Marsh, Jenna, and Byron sure didn't fit the bill.

She'd have access to home, via the nets. It wouldn't be exile, not really. Besides. This way she just . . . might . . . live long enough to visit another solar system.

Carli rubbed at an itchy spot on her cheek. A dime-sized sheaf of *something* flaked off. It was just dried gel from the hug, but for an instant she wondered if she was shedding her old skin like a snake. I'm changing my shoes, she thought, remembering Daniel with a twinge of regret over what might have been.

She envisioned the phone call to her dad, and what he'd say. For a change it'd be her mother who would understand. And Paint, what would he think? And Jolynd and Carlotta. She wondered, too, what Daniel's reaction would be. A spasm of pain gripped her at the thought of never seeing her friends and family again. Never seeing Earth again, with her own eyes.

You play the cards you're dealt, she thought. She held Pablito snug against her hip, grabbing Dane's hand as he-she started to trigger the airlock switch.

"Forget that," Carli said. "I'm going with you."